"A striking and original writer, Laird Barron's sense of the wonderfully strange is fully developed. Often entertaining, always perception altering, Barron's short fiction defies easy classification. A first-rate stylist."
— Jeff VanderMeer, author of *Shriek: An Afterword* and *City of Saints and Madmen*

"Laird Barron is one of the best new writers of weird, unsettling fiction I've read in several years. I look forward to every new story by him, eagerly scouring the tables of contents in magazines and anthologies for his work. If you, dear reader, have not yet been lucky enough to come across his fiction elsewhere, I envy you the experience of opening up and reading this book. Prepare to squirm..."
— Ellen Datlow, co-editor of *The Year's Best Fantasy and Horror*

"Laird Barron is one of the most talented new writers around. Buy this book and read it and be creeped out — and enjoy every minute of it. I did."
— Gordon Van Gelder, Editor of *The Magazine of Fantasy & Science Fiction*

"Laird Barron concocts the most wonderful nightmares. And, as with writers like Joe Hill and Glen Hirshberg, you'll be willing to forgive him the sleepless nights. In fact, you'll find yourself impatiently waiting for more short stories by Barron as soon as you've come to the end of this batch."
— Kelly Link, author of *Magic for Beginners* and *Stranger Things Happen*

THE IMAGO SEQUENCE

Also By Laird Barron

Occultation and Other Stories
The Croning
The Beautiful Thing That Awaits Us All

THE IMAGO

SEQUENCE

AND OTHER STORIES

LAIRD BARRON

NIGHT SHADE BOOKS
NEW YORK

Acknowledgments:
I am deeply indebted to the editors and publishers who've brought out my work over the years: Ellen Datlow; Gordon Van Gelder; David G. Hartwell; Kathryn Cramer; Nick Mamatas; Sean Wallace; Andrew Fuller; Martin Sust; Paweł Ziemkiewicz; and John Betancourt. I'm tremendously honored to become part of the Night Shade Books authors' line -- thank you, Jason and Jeremy.

Thank you to Cory & Catska Ench and the Ench Gallery.

I wish to express profound gratitude to the following individuals for their support in writing and life: Professor Bradley Steiner, Ben Andrews, Chellemiko, C.E Chaffin, John Langan, and Jody Linn Rose.

Special thanks to my family: Barbara and Erin Baar; Jason & William Barron; Alison and Prakash Stirret; and Leah and Hun Ling Zhu.

Dedication:
For Erin

CONTENTS

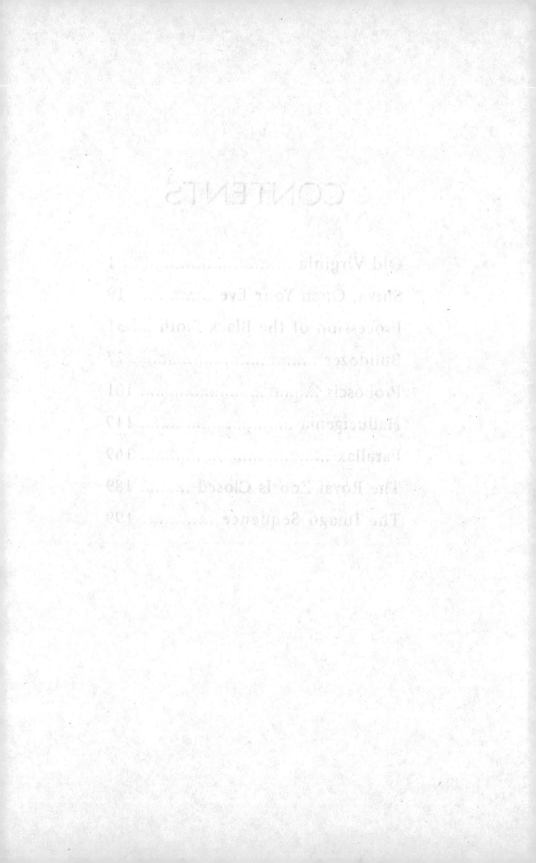

OLD VIRGINIA

On the third morning I noticed that somebody had disabled the truck. All four tires were flattened and the engine was smashed. Nice work.

I had gone outside the cabin to catch the sunrise and piss on some bushes. It was cold; the air tasted like metal. Deep, dark forest at our backs with a few notches for stars. A rutted track wound across a marshy field into more wilderness. All was silent except for the muffled hum of the diesel generator behind the wood shed.

"Well, here we go," I said. I fired up a Lucky Strike and congratulated my pessimistic nature. The Reds had found our happy little retreat in the woods. Or possibly, one of my boys was a mole. That would put a pretty bow on things.

The men were already spooked—Davis swore he had heard chuckling and whispering behind the steel door after curfew. He also heard one of the doctors gibbering in a foreign tongue. Nonsense, of course. Nonetheless, the troops were edgy, and now this.

"Garland? You there?" Hatcher called from the porch in a low voice. He made a tall, thin silhouette.

"Over here." I waited for him to join me by the truck. Hatcher was my immediate subordinate and the only member of the detail I'd personally worked with. He was tough, competent and a decade my junior—which made him twice as old as the other men. If somebody here was a Red, I hoped to God it wasn't him.

"Guess we're hoofing it," he said after a quick survey of the damage.

I passed him a cigarette. We smoked in contemplative silence. Eventually I said, "Who took last watch?"

"Richards. He didn't report any activity."

"Yeah." I stared into the forest and wondered if the enemy was lurking. What would be their next move, and how might I counter? A chill tightened the muscles in the small of my back, reminded me of how things had gone wrong during '53 in the steamy hills of Cuba. It had been six years, and in this business a man

1

didn't necessarily improve with age. I said, "How did they find us, Hatch?"

"Strauss may have a leak."

It went without saying whatever our military scientists were doing, the Reds would be doing bigger and better. Even so, intelligence regarding this program would carry a hefty price tag behind the Iron Curtain. Suddenly this little field trip didn't seem like a babysitting detail anymore.

Project TALLHAT was a Company job, but black ops. Dr. Herman Strauss had picked the team in secret and briefed us at his own home. Now here we were in the wilds of West Virginia standing watch over two of his personal staff while they conducted unspecified research on a senile crone. Doctors Porter and Riley called the shots. There was to be no communication with the outside world until they had gathered sufficient data. Upon return to Langley, Strauss would handle the debriefing. Absolutely no one else inside the Company was to be involved.

This wasn't my kind of operation, but I had seen the paperwork and recognized Strauss' authority. Why me? I suspected it was because Strauss had known me since the first big war. He also knew I was past it, ready for pasture. Maybe this was his way to make me feel important one last time. Gazing at the ruined truck and all it portended, I started thinking maybe good old Herman had picked me because I was expendable.

I stubbed out my cigarette and made some quick decisions. "When it gets light, we sweep the area. You take Robey and Neil and arc south; I'll go north with Dox and Richards. Davis will guard the cabin. We'll establish a quarter mile perimeter; search for tracks."

Hatcher nodded. He didn't state the obvious flaw—what if Davis was playing for the other team? He gestured at the forest. "How about an emergency extraction? We're twenty miles from the nearest traveled road. We could make it in a few hours. I saw some farms; one will have a phone—"

"Hatch, they destroyed the vehicle for a reason. Obviously they *want* us to walk. Who knows what nasty surprise is waiting down that road? For now we stay here, fortify. If worse comes to worst, we break and scatter. Maybe one of us will make it to HQ."

"How do we handle Porter and Riley?"

"This has become a security issue. Let's see what we find; then I'll break the news to the good doctors."

My involvement in Operation TALLHAT was innocent—if you can ever say that about Company business. I was lounging on an out-of-season New York beach when the telegram arrived. Strauss sent a car from Virginia. An itinerary; spending money. The works. I was intrigued; it had been several years since the last time I spoke with Herman.

Director Strauss said he needed my coolness under pressure, when we sat down to a four-star dinner at his legendary farmhouse in Langley. Said he needed an older man, a man with poise. Yeah, he poured it on all right.

Oh, the best had said it too – *Put his feet to the fire; he doesn't flinch. Garland, he's one cool sonofabitch.* Yes indeed, they had said it – thirty years ago. Before the horn rims got welded to my corrugated face and before the arthritis bent my fingers. Before my left ear went dead and my teeth fell out. Before the San Andreas Fault took root in my hands and gave them tremors. It was difficult to maintain deadly aloofness when I had to get up and drain my bladder every hour on the hour. Some war hero. Some Company legend.

"Look, Roger, I don't care about Cuba. It's ancient history, pal." Sitting across the table from Strauss at his farmhouse with a couple whiskey sours in my belly it had been too easy to believe my colossal blunders were forgiven. That the encroaching specter of age was an illusion fabricated by jealous detractors of which great men have plenty.

I had been a great man, once. Veteran of not one, but two World Wars. Decorated, lauded, feared. Strauss, earnest, blue-eyed Strauss, convinced me some greatness lingered. He leaned close and said, *"Roger, have you ever heard of MK-ULTRA?"*

And I forgot about Cuba.

The men dressed in hunting jackets to ward the chill, loaded shotguns for possible unfriendly contact, and scouted the environs until noon. Fruitless; the only tracks belonged to deer and rabbits. Most of the leaves had fallen in carpets of red and brown. It drizzled. Black branches dripped. The birds had nothing to say.

I observed Dox and Richards. Dox lumbered in plodding engineer boots, broad Slavic face blankly concentrated on the task I had given him. He was built like a tractor; too simple to work for the Company except as an enforcer, much less be a Russian saboteur. I liked him. Richards was blond and smooth, an Ivy League talent with precisely enough cynicism and latent sadism to please the forward thinking elements who sought to reshape the Company in the wake of President Eisenhower's imminent departure. Richards, I didn't trust or like.

There was a major housecleaning in the works. Men of Richards' caliber were preparing to sweep fossils such as myself into the dustbin of history.

It was perfectly logical after a morbid fashion. The trouble had started at the top with good old Ike suffering a stroke. Public reassurances to the contrary, the commander in chief was reduced to a shell of his former power. Those closest saw the cracks in the foundation and moved to protect his already tottering image. Company loyalists closed ranks, covering up evidence of the president's diminished faculties, his strange preoccupation with drawing caricatures of Dick Nixon. They stood by at his public appearances, ready to swoop in if he did anything too embarrassing. Not a happy allocation of human resources in the view of the younger members of the intelligence community.

That kind of duty didn't appeal to the Richardses of the world. They preferred to cut their losses and get back to slicing throats and cracking codes. Tangible objectives that would further the dominance of U.S. intelligence.

We kept walking and not finding anything until the cabin dwindled to a blot. The place had been built at the turn of the century; Strauss bought it for a song, I gathered. The isolation suited his nefarious plots. Clouds covered the treetops, yet I knew from the topographical maps there was a mountain not far off; a low, shaggy hump called Badger Hill. There would be collapsed mines and the moldered bones of abandoned camps, rusted hulks of machinery along the track, and dense woods. A world of brambles and deadfalls. No one came out this way anymore; hadn't in years.

We rendezvoused with Hatcher's party at the cabin. They hadn't discovered any clues either. Our clothes were soaked, our moods somber, although traces of excitement flickered among the young Turks—attack dogs sniffing for a fight.

None of them had been in a war. I'd checked. College instead of Korea for the lot. Even Dox had been spared by virtue of flat feet. They hadn't seen Soissons in 1915, Normandy in 1945, nor the jungles of Cuba in 1953. They hadn't seen the things I had seen. Their fear was the small kind, borne of uncertainty rather than dread. They stroked their shotguns and grinned with dumb innocence.

When the rest had been dispatched for posts around the cabin I broke for the latrine to empty my bowels. Close race. I sweated and trembled and required some minutes to compose myself. My knees were on fire, so I broke out a tin of analgesic balm and rubbed them, tasting the camphor on my tongue. I wiped beads of moisture from my glasses, swallowed a glycerin tablet and felt as near to one hundred percent as I would ever be.

Ten minutes later I summoned Doctor Porter for a conference on the back porch. It rained harder, shielding our words from Neil who stood post near an oak.

Porter was lizard-bald except for a copper circlet that trailed wires into his breast pocket. His white coat bore stains and smudges. His fingers were blue-tinged with chalk dust. He stank of antiseptic. We were not friends. He treated the detail as a collection of thugs best endured for the sake of his great scientific exploration.

I relayed the situation, which did not impress him much. "This is why Strauss wanted your services. Deal with the problem," he said.

"Yes, Doctor. I am in the process of doing that. However, I felt you might wish to know your research will become compromised if this activity escalates. We may need to extract."

"Whatever you think best, Captain Garland." He smiled a dry smile. "You'll inform me when the moment arrives?"

"Certainly."

"Then I'll continue my work, if you're finished." The way he lingered on the last syllable left no doubt that I was.

I persisted, perhaps from spite. "Makes me curious about what you fellows are up to. How's the experiment progressing? Getting anywhere?"

"Captain Garland, you shouldn't be asking me these questions." Porter's humorless smile was more reptilian than ever.

"Probably not. Unfortunately since recon proved inconclusive I don't know who wrecked our transport or what they plan next. More information regarding the project would be helpful."

"Surely Doctor Strauss told you everything he deemed prudent."

"Times change."

"TALLHAT is classified. You're purely a security blanket. You possess no special clearance."

I sighed, and lighted a cigarette. "I know some things. MK-ULTRA is an umbrella term for the Company's mind control experiments. You psych boys are playing with all kinds of neat stuff—LSD, hypnosis, photokinetics. Hell, we talked about using this crap against Batista. Maybe we did."

"Indeed. Castro was amazingly effective, wasn't he?" Porter's eyes glittered. "So what's your problem, Captain?"

"The problem is the KGB has pretty much the same programs. And better ones from the scuttlebutt I pick up at Langley."

"Oh, you of all people should beware of rumors. Loose lips had *you* buried in Cuba with the rest of your operatives. Yet here you are."

I understood Porter's game. He hoped to gig me with the kind of talk most folks were polite enough to whisper behind my back, make me lose control. I wasn't biting. "The way I figure it, the Reds don't need TALLHAT...unless you're cooking up something special. Something they're afraid of. Something they're aware of, at least tangentially, but lack full intelligence. And in that case, why pussyfoot around? They've got two convenient options—storm in and seize the data or wipe the place off the map."

Porter just kept smirking. "I am certain the Russians would kill to derail our project. However, don't you think it would be more efficacious for them to use subtlety? Implant a spy to gather pertinent details, steal documents. Kidnap a member of the research team and interrogate him; extort information from him with a scandal. Hiding in the woods and slicing tires seems a foolish waste of surprise."

I didn't like hearing him echo the bad thoughts I'd had while lingering in the outhouse. "Exactly, Doctor. The situation is even worse than I thought. We are being stalked by an unknown quantity."

"Stalked? How melodramatic. An isolated incident doesn't prove the hypothesis. Take more precautions if it makes you happy. And I'm confident you are quite happy; awfully boring to be a watchdog with nothing to bark at."

It was too much. That steely portion of my liver gained an edge, demanded satisfaction. I took off the gloves. "I want to see the woman."

"Whatever for?" Porter's complacent smirk vanished. His thin mouth drew down with suspicion.

"Because I do."

"Impossible!"

"Hardly. I command six heavily armed men. Any of them would be tickled to kick down the door and give me a tour of your facilities." It came out much harsher than I intended. My nerves were frayed and his superior demeanor had touched a darker kernel of my soul. "Doctor Porter, I read your file. That was my condition for accepting this assignment; Strauss agreed to give me dossiers on everyone. You and Riley slipped through the cracks after Caltech. I guess the school wasn't too pleased with some of your research or where you dug up the financing. Then that incident with the kids off campus. The ones who thought they were testing diet pills. You gave them, what was it? Oh yes—peyote! Pretty strange behavior for a pair of physicists, eh? It follows that Unorthodox Applications of Medicine and Technology would snap you up after the private sector turned its back. So excuse my paranoia."

"Ah, you do know a *few* things. But not the nature of TALLHAT? Odd."

"We shall rectify that momentarily."

Porter shrugged. "As you wish, Mr. Garland. I shall include your threats in my report."

For some reason his acquiescence didn't really satisfy me. True, I had turned on the charm that had earned me the title "Jolly Roger," yet he had caved far too easily. Damn it!

Porter escorted me inside. Hatcher saw the look on my face and started to rise from his chair by the window. I shook my head and he sank, fixing Porter with a dangerous glare.

The lab was sealed off by a thick steel door, like the kind they use on trains. Spartan, each wall padded as if a rubber room in an asylum. It reeked of chemicals. The windows were blocked with black plastic. Illumination seeped from a phosphorescent bar on the table. Two cots. Shelves, cabinets, a couple boxy machines with needles and tickertape spools. Between these machines an easel with indecipherable scrawls done in ink. I recognized some as calculus symbols. To the left, a poster bed, and on the bed a thickly wrapped figure propped by pillows. A mummy.

Doctor Riley drifted in, obstructing my view—he was an aquamarine phantom, eyes and mouth pools of shadow. As with Porter, a copper circlet winked on his brow. "Afternoon, Captain Garland. Pull up a rock." His accent was Midwestern nasal. He even wore cowboy boots under his grimy lab coat.

"Captain Garland wants to view the subject," Porter said.

"Fair enough!" Riley seemed pleased. He rubbed his hands, a pair of disembodied starfish in the weirding glow. "Don't fret, Porter. There's no harm in satisfying the captain's curiosity." With that, the lanky man stepped aside.

Approaching the figure on the bed, I was overcome with an abrupt sensation of vertigo. My hackles bunched. The light played tricks upon my senses, lending a fishbowl distortion to the old woman's sallow visage. They had secured her in a straitjacket; her head lolled drunkenly, dead eyes frozen, tongue drooling from slack lips. She was shaved bald, white stubble of a Christmas goose.

My belly quaked. "Where did you find her?" I whispered, as if she might hear me.

"What's the matter?" Doctor Riley asked.

"Where did you find her, goddamnit!"

The crone's head swiveled on that too-long neck and her milky gaze fastened upon my voice. And she grinned, toothless. Horrible.

Hatcher kept some scotch in the pantry. Doctor Riley poured—I didn't trust my own hands yet. He lighted cigarettes. We sat at the living room table, alone in the cabin, but for Porter and Subject X behind the metal door. Porter was so disgusted by my reaction he refused to speak with me. Hatcher had assembled the men in the yard; he was giving some sort of pep talk. Ever the soldier. I wished I'd had him in Cuba.

It rained and a stiff breeze rattled the eaves.

"Who is she to you?" Riley asked. His expression was shrewd.

I sucked my cigarette to the filter in a single drag, exhaled and gulped scotch. Held out my glass for another three fingers' worth. "You're too young to remember the first big war."

"I was a baby." Riley handed me another cigarette without being asked.

"Yeah? I was twenty-eight when the Germans marched into France. Graduated Rogers and Williams with full honors, was commissioned into the Army as an officer. They stuck me right into intelligence, sent me straight to the front." I chuckled bitterly. "This happened before Uncle Sam decided to make an 'official' presence. Know what I did? I helped organize the resistance, translated messages French intelligence intercepted. Mostly I ran from the advance. Spent a lot of time hiding out on farms when I was lucky, field ditches when I wasn't.

"There was this one family, I stayed with them for nine days in June. It rained, just like this. A large family—six adults, ten or eleven kids. I bunked in the wine cellar and it flooded. You'd see these huge bloody rats paddling if you clicked the torch. Long nine days." If I closed my eyes I knew I would be there again in the dark, among the chittering rats. Listening for armor on the muddy road, the tramp of boots.

"So, what happened?" Riley watched me. He probably guessed where this was headed.

"The family matriarch lived in a room with her son and daughter in-law. The old dame was blind and deaf; she'd lost her wits. They bandaged her hands so she couldn't scratch herself. She sucked broth out of this gnawed wooden bowl they kept just for her. Jesus Mary, I still hear her slobbering over that bowl. She used to lick her bowl and stare at me with those dead eyes."

"Subject X bears no relation to her, I assure you."

"I don't suppose she does. I looked at her more closely and saw I was mistaken. But for those few seconds...Riley, something's going on. Something much bigger than Strauss indicated. Level with me. What are you people searching for?"

"Captain, you realize my position. I've been sworn to silence. Strauss will cut off my balls if I talk to you about TALLHAT. Or we could all simply disappear."

"It's that important."

"It is." Riley's face became gentle. "I'm sorry. Doctor Strauss promised us ten days. One week from tomorrow we pack up our equipment and head back to civilization. Surely we can hold out."

The doctor reached across to refill my glass; I clamped his wrist. They said I was past it, but he couldn't break my grip. I said, "All right, boy. We'll play it your way for a while. If the shit gets any thicker though, I'm pulling the plug on this operation. You got me?"

He didn't say anything. Then he jerked free and disappeared behind the metal door. He returned with a plain brown folder, threw it on the table. His smile was almost triumphant. "Read these. It won't tell you everything. Still, it's plenty to chew on. Don't show Porter, okay?" He walked away without meeting my eye.

Dull wet afternoon wore into dirty evening. We got a pleasant fire going in the potbellied stove and dried our clothes. Roby had been a short order cook in college, so he fried hamburgers for dinner. After, Hatcher and the boys started a poker game and listened to the radio. The weather forecast called for more of the same, if not worse.

Perfect conditions for an attack. I lay on my bunk reading Riley's file. I got a doozy of a migraine. Eventually I gave up and filled in my evening log entry. The gears were turning.

I wondered about those copper circlets the doctors wore. Fifty-plus years of active service and I'd never seen anything quite like them. They reminded me of rumors surrounding the German experiments in Auschwitz. Mengele had been fond of bizarre contraptions. Maybe we'd read his mail and adopted some ideas.

Who is Subject X? I wrote this in the margin of my log. I thought back on what scraps Strauss fed me. I hadn't asked enough questions, that was for damned sure. You didn't quiz a man like Strauss. He was one of the Grand Old Men of the Company. He got what he wanted, when he wanted it. He'd been everywhere, had something on everyone. When he snapped his fingers, things happened. People that crossed him became scarce.

Strauss was my last supporter. Of course I let him lead me by the nose. For me, the gold watch was a death certificate. Looking like a meatier brother of Herr Mengele, Strauss had confided the precise amount to hook me. *"Ten days in the country. I've set up shop at my cabin near Badger Hill. A couple of my best men are on to some promising research. Important research—"*

"Are we talking about psychotropics? I've seen what can happen. I won't be around that again."

"No, no. We've moved past that. This is different. They will be monitoring a sub-

ject for naturally occurring brain activity. Abnormal activity, yes, but not induced by us."

"These doctors of yours, they're just recording results?"

"Exactly."

"Why all the trouble, Herman? You've got the facilities right here. Why send us to a shack in the middle of Timbuktu?"

"Ike is on his way out the door. Best friend a covert ops man ever had, too. The Powers Soon to Be will put an end to MK-ULTRA. Christ, the office is shredding documents around the clock. I've been given word to suspend all operations by the end of next month. Next month!"

"Nobody else knows about TALLHAT?"

"And nobody can—not unless we make a breakthrough. I wish I could come along, conduct the tests myself—"

"Not smart. People would talk if you dropped off the radar. What does this woman do that's so bloody important?"

"She's a remote viewer. A clairvoyant. She draws pictures, the researchers extrapolate."

"Whatever you're looking for—"

"It's momentous. So you see, Roger? I need you. I don't trust anyone else."

"Who is the subject?"

"Her name is Virginia."

I rolled over and regarded the metal door. She was in there, staring holes through steel.

"Hey, Cap! You want in? I'm getting my ass kicked over here!" Hatcher puffed on a Havana cigar and shook his head while Davis raked in another pot. There followed a chorus of crude imprecations for me to climb down and take my medicine.

I feigned good humor. "Not tonight, fellows. I didn't get my nap. You know how it is with us old folks."

They laughed. I shivered until sleep came. My dreams were bad.

I spent most of the fourth day perusing Riley's file. It made things about as clear as mud. All in all a cryptic collection of papers—just what I needed right then; more spooky erratum.

Numerous mimeographed letters and library documents comprised the file. The bulk of them were memos from Strauss to Porter. Additionally, some detailed medical examinations of Subject X. I didn't follow the jargon except to note that the terms "unclassified" and "of unknown origin" reappeared often. They made interesting copy, although they explained nothing to my layman's eyes.

Likewise the library papers seemed arcane. One such entry from *A Colonial History of Carolina and Her Settlements* went thusly:

The Lost Roanoke Colony vanished from the Raleigh Township on Roanoke Island between 1588 and 1589. Governor White returned from England after considerable delays to find the town abandoned. Except for untended cookfires that burned down a couple houses, there was no evidence of struggle, though Spaniards and natives had subsequently plundered the settlement. No bodies or bones were discovered. The sole clue as to the colonists' fate lay in a strange sequence of letters carved into a palisade—Croatoan. The word CRO had been similarly carved into a nearby tree. White surmised this indicated a flight to the Croatoan Island, called Hatteras by natives. Hurricanes prevented a search until the next colonization attempt two years later. Subsequent investigation yielded no answers, although scholars suggest local tribes assimilated the English settlers. No physical evidence exists to support this theory. It remains a mystery of some magnitude...

Tons more like that. It begged the question of why Strauss, brilliant, cruel-minded Strauss, would waste a molecular biologist, a physicist, a bona fide psychic, and significant monetary resources on moldy folklore.

I hadn't a notion and this worried me mightily.

That night I dreamt of mayhem. First I was at the gray farmhouse in Soissons, eating dinner with a nervous family. My French was inadequate. Fortunately one of the women knew English and we were able to converse. A loud slurping began to drown out conversation about German spies. At the head of the table sat Virginia, sipping from a broken skull. She winked. A baby cried.

Then it was Cuba and the debacle of advising Castro's guerillas for an important raid. My intelligence network had failed to account for a piece of government armor. The guerillas were shelled to bits by Batista's garrison and young Castro barely escaped with his life. Five of my finest men were ground up in the general slaughter. Two were captured and tortured. They died without talking. Lucky for me.

I heard them screaming inside a small cabin in the forest, but I couldn't find the door. Someone had written CROATOAN on the wall.

I bumped into Hatcher, hanging upside down from a tree branch. He wore an I LIKE IKE button. "Help me, Cap." He said.

A baby squalled. Virginia sat in a rocking chair on the porch, soothing the infant. The crone's eyes were holes in dough. She drew a nail across her throat.

I sat up in bed, throttling a shriek. I hadn't uttered a cry since being shot in World War I. It was pitchy in the cabin. People were fumbling around in the dark.

Hatcher shined a flashlight my direction. "The generator's tits-up." Nearby, the doctors were already bitching and cursing their misfortune.

We never did find out if it was sabotaged or not.

The fifth day was uneventful.

On the sixth morning my unhappy world raveled.

Things were hopping right out of the gate. Doctor Riley joined Hatcher and me for breakfast. A powerful stench accompanied him. His expression was unbalanced, his angular face white and shiny. He grabbed a plate of cold pancakes, began wolfing them. Lanky hair fell into his eyes. He grunted like a pig.

Hatcher eased his own chair back. I spoke softly to Riley, "Hey now, Doc. Roby can whip up more. No rush."

Riley looked at me sidelong. He croaked, "She made us take them off."

I opened my mouth. His circlet was gone. A pale stripe of flesh. "Riley, what are you talking about?" Even as I spoke, Hatcher stood quietly, drew his pistol, and glided for the lab.

"Stupid old bastards." Riley gobbled pancakes, chunks dropping from his lips. He giggled until tears squirted, rubbed the dimple in his forehead. "Those were shields, Pops. They produced a frequency that kept her from…doing things to us." He stopped eating again, cast sharp glances around the room. "Where are your little soldiers?"

"On patrol."

"Ha, ha. Better call them back, Pops."

"Why do you say that?"

"You'd just better."

Hatcher returned, grim. "Porter has taken Subject X."

I put on my glasses. I drew my revolver. "Doctor Riley, Mr. Hatcher is going to secure you. It's for your own safety. I must warn you, give him any static and I'll burn you down."

"That's right, Jolly Roger! You're an ace at blowing people away! What's the number up to, Captain? Since the first Big One? And we're counting children, okay?" Riley barked like a lunatic coyote until Hatcher cracked him on the temple with the butt of his gun. The doctor flopped, twitching.

I uncapped my glycerin and ate two.

Hatcher was all business. He talked in his clipped manner while he handcuffed Riley to a center beam post. "Looks like he broke out through the window. No signs of struggle."

"Documents?"

"Seems like everything's intact. Porter's clothes are on his cot. Found her straitjacket too."

Porter left his clothes? I liked this less and less.

Rain splattered the dark windows. "Let's gather everybody. Assemble a hunting party." I foresaw a disaster; it would be difficult to follow tracks in the storm. Porter might have allies. Best-case scenario had him and the subject long gone, swooped up by welcoming Commie arms and out of my sorry life forever. Instinct whispered that I was whistling Dixie if I fell for that scenario. *Now you're screwed, blued and tattooed, chum!* chortled my inner voice.

Hatcher grasped my shoulder. "Cap, you call it, we haul it. I can tell you, the boys are aching for a scrap. It won't hurt anybody's feelings to hunt the traitor to ground."

"Agreed. We'll split into two-man teams, comb the area. Take Porter alive if possible. I want to know who he's playing for."

"Sounds good. Someone has to cover the cabin."

He meant I should be the one to stay back. They had to move fast. I was the old man, the weak link; I'd slow everybody down, maybe get a team member killed.

I mustered what grace I possessed. "I'll do it. Come on; we better get moving." We called the men together and laid it on the table. Everybody appeared shocked that Porter had been able to pull off such a brazen escape.

I drew a quick plan and sent them trotting into the wind-blasted dawn. Hatcher wasn't eager to leave me alone, but there weren't sufficient bodies to spare. He promised to report back inside of three hours one way or the other.

And they were gone.

I locked the doors, pulled the shutters, peeking through the slats as it lightened into morning.

Riley began laughing again. Deeper this time, from his skinny chest. The rank odor oozing from him would have gagged a goat. "How about a cigarette, Cap?" His mouth squirmed. His face had slipped from white to gray. He appeared to have been bled. The symptoms were routine.

"They'll find your comrade," I said. A cigarette sounded like a fine idea, so I lighted one for myself and smoked it. I kept an eye on him and one on the yard. "Yeah, they'll nail him sooner or later. And when they do…" I let it dangle.

"God, Cap! The news is true. You are so washed up! They say you were sharp back in the day. Strauss didn't even break a sweat, keeping you in the dark, did he? Think about it—why do you suppose I gave you the files, huh? Because it didn't matter one tin shit. He told me to give you anything you asked for. Said it would make things more interesting."

"Tell me the news, Riley."

"Can't you guess the joke? Our sweet Virginia ain't what she seems, no sir."

"What is she, then?"

"She's a weapon, Cap. A nasty, nasty weapon. Strauss is ready to bet the farm this little filly can win the Cold War for Team U.S.A. But first we had to test her, see." He banged his greasy head against the post and laughed wildly. "Our hats were supposed to protect us from getting brain-buggered. Strauss went through hell—and a *heap* of volunteers—to configure them properly. They should've worked…I don't know why they stopped functioning correctly. Bum luck. Doesn't matter."

"Where did Porter take her?"

"Porter didn't take Virginia. She took him. She'll be back for you."

"Is Subject X really a clairvoyant?" My lips were dry. Too many blocks were clicking into place at once.

"She's clairvoyant. She's a lot of things. But Strauss tricked you—we aren't here to test her ability to locate needles in haystacks. You'd die puking if you saw…"

"Is there anyone else? Does Porter have allies waiting?"

"Porter? Porter's meat. It's *her* you better worry about."

"Fine. Does *she* have allies?

"No. She doesn't need help." Riley drifted. "Should've seen the faces on those poor people. Strauss keeps some photographs in a safe. Big stack. Big. It took so long to get the hats right. He hired some hardcases to clean up the mess. Jesus, Cap. I never would've believed there were worse characters than you."

"Strauss is careful," I said. "It must have taken years."

"About fifteen or so. Even the hardcases could only deal with so many corpses. And the farm; well, it's rather high profile. These three Company guys handled disposals. Three that I met, anyway. These fellows started getting nervous, started acting hinky. Strauss made her get rid of them. This was no piece of cake. Those sonofabitches wanted to live, let me tell you." He grew quiet and swallowed. "She managed, but it was awful, and Strauss decided she required field testing. She required more 'live' targets, is how he put it. Porter and me knew he meant Company men. Black ops guys nobody would miss. Men who were trained like the Reds and the Jerries are trained. Real killers."

"Men like me and my team," I said.

"Gold star!" He cackled, drumming the heels of his Stetsons against the planks. His hilarity coarsened into shrieks. Muscles stood in knots on his arms and neck. "Oh God! She rode us all night—oh Christ!" He became unintelligible. The post creaked with the strain of his thrashing.

I found the experience completely unnerving. Better to stare through the watery pane where trees took shape as light fell upon their shoulders. My bladder hurt; too fearful to step outside, I found a coffee can and relieved myself. My hands shook and I spilled a bit.

The man's spasms peaked and he calmed by degrees. I waited until he seemed lucid, said, "Let me help you, Riley. Tell me what Porter—what she—did. Are you poisoned?" There was a bad thought. Say Porter had slipped a touch of the pox into our water supply…I ceased that line of conjecture. Pronto.

"She rode us, Cap. Aren't you listening to ME?" He screeched the last, frothing. "I want to die now." His chin drooped and he mumbled incoherently.

I let him be. *How now, brown cow?* I had been so content sitting on that Coney Island beach watching seagulls rip at detritus and waiting for time to expire.

The whole situation had taken on an element of black comedy. Betrayed by that devil Strauss? Sure, he was Machiavelli with a hard-on. I'd seen him put the screws to better men than me. I'd helped him do the deed. Yeah, I was a rube, no doubt. Problem was, I still had not the first idea what had been done to us exactly. Riley was terrified of Virginia. Fair enough, she scared me too. I believed him when he said she could do things—she was possibly a savant, like the idiot math geniuses we locked in labs and sweated atom-smashing secrets from. The way her face had changed when I first saw her convinced me of this.

She's a weapon, a nasty, nasty weapon. I didn't know what that meant. I didn't care much, either. Something bad had happened to Riley. Whether Virginia had done it, whether Porter had done it, or if the goddamned KGB was cooking his brain with EM pulses, we were in the soup. How to escape the pot was my new priority.

I settled in with my shotgun to wait. And plan.

Nobody returned from the morning expedition.

Around 1700 hours I decided that I was screwed. The operation was compromised, its principal subject missing. The detail assigned to guard the principal was also missing and likely dead or captured.

What to do? I did what we intelligence professionals always did at moments like this. I started a fire in the stove and began burning documents. In forty-five minutes all paper records of Operation TALLHAT were coals. This included my personal log. Doctor Riley observed this without comment. He lapsed into semiconsciousness before I finished.

Unfortunately I decided to check him for wounds.

Don't know what possessed me. I was sort of like a kid poking a dead animal with a stick. I was *compelled*. Cautiously I lifted his shirt and found three holes in his back— one in the nape of his neck, two at the base of his spine. Each was the diameter of a walnut and oozed dark blood. They stank of rotten flesh, of gangrene.

She rode us all night, Cap!

Thank God for decades of military discipline—the machinery took over. If a soldier could regard the charred corpses of infant flame-thrower victims and maintain his sanity, a soldier could stomach a few lousy holes in a man's spine. I detached myself from this gruesome spectacle and the realization that this was the single most monumental balls-up of my career. What a way to go out!

I determined to make a break for the main road. A twenty-mile hike; more, since I dared not use the main track, but certainly within my range. At that point, I was certain I could sprint the distance if necessary. Yeah, best idea I'd had so far.

"Cap, help me." Hatcher's voice muffled by rain against the roof.

I limped to the window. The light had deteriorated. I made him out, standing a few yards away between some trees. His arms were spread as if in greeting—then I saw the rope.

"Cap! Help me!" His face was alabaster, glowing in the dusk.

I began a shout, but was interrupted by an ominous thump of displaced weight behind me. My heart sank.

"Yes, Cap. Help him," Virginia crooned.

I turned and beheld her. Her naked skull scraped the ceiling. A wizened child, grinning and drooling. She towered because she sat upon Dox's broad back, her yellow nails digging at his ears. His expression was flaccid as he bore down on me.

The shotgun jumped in my hands and made its terrible racket. Then Dox's fingers closed over my throat and night fell.

I did not dream of Cuba or the failed attack on Batista's garrison. Nor did I dream of walking through the black winter of Dresden surrounded by swirling flakes of ash. I didn't dream of Soissons with its muddy ditches and rats.

I dreamt of people marching single file across a field. Some dressed quaintly, others had forgotten their shoes. Many had forgotten to dress at all. Their faces were blank as snow. They stumbled. At least a hundred men, women and children. Marching without speaking. A great hole opened in the ground before them. It stank of carrion. One by one the people came to this hole, swayed, and toppled into the cavity. Nobody screamed.

I woke to see the cabin wall flickering in lamplight. Blurry, for my glasses were lost. Something was wrong with my legs; they were paralyzed. I suspected my back was broken. At least there was no pain.

The numbness seemed to encompass my senses as well—the fear was still present, but submerged and muzzled. Glacial calm stole over me.

"Doctor Riley was misled. Herman never intended this solely as a test." Virginia's voice quavered from somewhere close behind my shoulder.

Her shadow loomed on the wall. A wobbly silhouette that flowed unwholesomely. Floorboards squeaked as she shifted. The thought of rolling over brought sweat to my cheeks, so I lay there and watched her shadow in morbid fascination.

"It was also an offering. Mother is pleased. He will be rewarded with a pretty."

"My men," I said. It was difficult to talk, my throat was rusty and bruised.

"With Mother. Except the brute. You killed him. Mother won't take meat unless it's alive. Shame on you, Roger." She chuckled evilly. The sound withdrew slightly, and her shadow shrank. "Oh, your back isn't broken. You'll feel your legs presently. I didn't want you running off before we had a chance to talk."

I envisioned a line of men, Hatcher in the lead, marching through the woods and up a mountain. It rained heavily and they staggered in the mud. No one said anything. Automatons winding down. Ahead yawned a gap in a rocky slope. A dank cave mouth. One by one they went swallowed…

There came a new sound that disrupted my unpleasant daydream—sobbing. It was Riley; smothered as by a gag. I could tell from its frantic nature that Virginia crouched near him. She said to me, "I came back for you, Roger. As for this one, I thought he had provided to his limit…yet he squirms with vigor. Ah, the resilience of life!"

"Who are you?" I asked as several portions of her shadow elongated from the central axis, dipped as questing tendrils. Then, a dim, wet susurration. I thought of pitcher plants grown monstrous and shut my eyes tight.

Riley's noises became shrill.

"Don't be afraid, Roger." Virginia rasped, a bit short of breath. "Mother wants to meet you. Such a vital existence you have pursued! Not often does She entertain provender as seasoned as yourself. If you're lucky, the others will have sated Her. She will birth you as a new man. A man in Her image. You'll get old, yes. Being old is a wonderful thing, though. The older you become, the more things you taste. The more you taste, the more pleasure you experience. There is *so much* pleasure to be had."

"Bullshit! If it were such a keen deal, Herman would be cashing in! Not me!"

"Well, Herman is overly cautious. He has reservations about the process. I'll go back and work on him some more."

"Who are you? Who is your mother?" I said it too loudly, hoping to obscure the commotion Riley was making. The squelching. I babbled, "How did Strauss find you? Jesus!"

"You read the files—I asked the doctors. If you read the files you know where I was born and who I am. You know who Mother is—a colonist wrote Her name on the palisade, didn't he? A name given by white explorers to certain natives who worshipped Her. Idiots! The English are possibly the stupidest people that ever lived." She tittered. "I was the first Christian birth in the New World. I was special. The rest were meat. Poor mama, poor daddy. Poor everyone else. Mother is quite simple, actually. She has basic needs…She birthed me anew, made me better than crude flesh and now I help Her conduct the grand old game. She sent me to find Herman. Herman helps Her. I think you could help Her too."

"Where is your mother? Is she here?"

"Near. She moves around. We lived on the water for a while. The mountain is nicer, the shafts go so deep. She hates the light. All of Her kind are like that. The miners used to come and She talked with them. No more miners."

I wanted to say something, anything to block Riley's clotted screams. Shortly, his noises ceased. Tears seeped from my clenched eyelids. "D-did the copper circlets ever really work? Or was that part of the joke?" I didn't care about the answer.

Virginia was delighted. "Excellent! Well, they did. That's why I arranged to meet Strauss, to attach myself. He is a clever one! His little devices worked to interfere until we got here, so close to Mother's influence. I am merely a conduit of Her majestic power. She is unimaginable!"

"You mentioned a game…"

Virginia said, "Do you suppose men invented chess? I promise you, there are contests far livelier. I have been to the universities of the world, watching. You have visited the battlefields of the world, watching. Don't you think the time is coming?"

"For what?"

"When mankind will manage to blacken the sky with bombs and cool the earth so that Mother and Her brothers, Her sisters and children may emerge once more! Is there any other purpose? Oh, what splendid revelries there shall be on that day!"

What could I answer with?

Virginia didn't mind. She said, "The dinosaurs couldn't do it in a hundred million years. Nor the sharks in their oceans given three times that. The monkeys showed promise, but never realized their potential. Humans are the best pawns so far—the ones with a passion for fire and mystery. With subtle guidance they—you—can return this world to the paradise it was when the ice was thick and the sun dim. We need men like Adolph, and Herman, and their sweet sensibilities. Men who would bring the winter darkness so they might caper around bonfires. Men like you, dear Roger. Men like you." Virginia ended on a cackle.

Hiroshima bloomed upon my mind's canvas and I nearly cried aloud. And Auschwitz, and Verdun, and all the rest. Yes, the day was coming. "You've got the wrong man," I said in my bravest tone. "You don't know the first thing. I'm a bloody patriot."

"Mother appreciates that, dear Roger. Be good and don't move. I'll return in a moment. Must fetch you a coat. It's raining." Virginia's shadow slipped into the lab. There followed the clatter of upturned objects and breaking glass.

Her bothers, Her sisters and children. Pawns. Provender. My gorge tasted bitter. Herman helping creatures such as this bring about hell on Earth. For what? Power? The promise of immortality? Virginia's blasphemous longevity should've cured him of that desire.

Oh, Herman, you fool! On its heels arrived the notion that perhaps I would change my mind after a conversation with Mother. That one day soon I might sit across the table from Strauss and break bread in celebration of a new dawn.

I wept as I pulled my buck knife free, snicked the catch. Would that I possessed the courage to slit my own wrists! I attempted to do just that, but lacked the conviction to carry through. Seventy years of self-aggrandizement had robbed me of any will to self-destruction.

So, I began to carve a message into the planks instead. A warning. Although what could one say about events this bizarre? This hideous? I shook with crazed laughter and nearly broke the blade with my furious hacking.

I got as far as CRO before Virginia came and rode me into the woods to meet her mother.

SHIVA, OPEN YOUR EYE

The human condition can be summed up in a drop of blood. Show me a *teaspoon* of blood and I will reveal to thee the ineffable nature of the cosmos, naked and squirming. Squirming. Funny how the truth always seems to do that when you shine a light on it.

A man came to my door one afternoon, back when I lived on a rambling farm in Eastern Washington. He was sniffing around, poking into things best left…unpoked. A man with a flashlight, you might say. Of course, I knew who he was and what he was doing there long before he arrived with his hat in one hand and phony story in the other.

Claimed he was a state property assessor, did the big genial man. Indeed, he was a massive fellow—thick, blunt fingers clutching corroborative documents and lumpy from all the abuse he had subjected them to in the military; he draped an ill-tailored tweed jacket and insufferable slacks over his ponderous frame. This had the effect of making him look like a man that should have been on a beach with a sun visor and a metal detector. The man wore a big smile under his griseous beard. This smile frightened people, which is exactly why he used it most of the time, and also, because it frightened people, he spoke slowly, in a big, heavy voice that sounded as if it emerged from a cast-iron barrel. He smelled of cologne and 3-IN-ONE Oil.

I could have whispered to him that the cologne came from a fancy emerald-colored bottle his wife had purchased for him as a birthday present; that he carried the bottle in his travel bag and spritzed himself whenever he was on the road and in too great a hurry, or simply too hungover for a shower. He preferred scotch, did my strapping visitor. I could have mentioned several other notable items in this patent-leather travel bag—a roll of electrical tape, brass knuckles, voltmeter, police-issue handcuffs, a microrecorder, a pocket camera, disposable latex gloves, lockpicks, a carpet cutter, flashlight, an empty aspirin bottle, toothpaste, a half-roll of antacid tablets, hemorrhoid suppositories and a stained road map of Washington State. The bag was far away on the front seat of his rented sedan, which he had carefully parked up the winding dirt driveway under a sprawling locust tree. Wisely, he had decided to reconnoiter the area before knocking on the door. The oil smell emanated from a lubricated and expertly maintained thirty-eight-caliber revolver stowed in his left-hand jacket pocket. The pistol had not been fired in three-and-a-half years. The man did not normally carry a gun on the job, but in my case, he had opted for discretion. It occurred to him that I might be dangerous.

I could have told him all these things and that he was correct in his assumptions, but it did not amuse me to do so. Besides, despite his bulk he looked pretty fast and I was tired. Winter makes me lazy. It makes me torpid.

But—

Rap, rap! Against the peeling frame of the screen door. He did not strike the frame with anything approaching true force; nonetheless, he used a trifle more vigor than the occasion required. This was how he did things—whether conduct-ing a sensitive inquiry, bracing a recalcitrant witness, or ordering the prawns at La Steakhouse. He was a water buffalo floundering into the middle of a situation, seizing command and dominating by virtue of his presence.

I made him wait longer than was necessary—to the same degree as his assault on my door was designed to set the tone and mood—although not *too* long, because sometimes my anticipatory juices outwrestle my subtler nature. I was an old man and thus tended to move in a deliberate mode anyway. This saddened me; I was afraid he might not catch my little joke.

But—

I came to the door, blinking in the strong light as I regarded him through filtering mesh. Of course, I permitted a suitable quaver to surface when I asked after his business. That was when the big man smiled and rumbled a string of lies about being the land assessor and a few sundries that I never paid attention to, lost as I was in watching his mouth, his hands and the curious way his barrel chest lifted and fell under the crumpled suit.

He gave me a name, something unimaginative gleaned from a shoebox, or like so. The identity on his State of Washington Private Investigator's License read *Murphy Connell*. He had been an investigator for eleven years; self-employed, married with two children—a boy who played football at the University of Washington, and a girl that had transferred to Rhode Island to pursue a degree in graphic design—and owner of a Rottweiler named Heller. The identification was in his wallet, which filled an inner pocket of the bad coat, wedged in front of an ancient pack of Pall Malls. The big man had picked up the habit when he was stationed in the Philippines, but seldom smoked anymore. He kept them around because sure as a stud hound lifts its leg to piss, the minute he left home without a pack the craving would pounce on him hammer and tongs. He was not prone to self-analysis, this big man, yet it amused him after a wry sense that he had crushed an addiction only to be haunted by its vengeful ghost.

Yes, I remembered his call from earlier that morning. He was certainly welcome to ramble about the property and have a gander for Uncle Sam. I told him to come in and rest his feet while I fixed a pot of tea—unless he preferred a nip of the ole gin? No, tea would be lovely. *Lovely?* It delighted me in an arcane fashion that such a phrase would uproot from his tongue—sort of like a gravel truck dumping water lilies and butterflies. I boiled tea with these hands gnarled unto dead madroña, and I took my sweet time. Mr. Connell moved quietly, though that really didn't matter, *nothing* is hidden from these ears. I listened while he sifted through a few of the papers on the coffee table—*nothing of consequence there, my large one*—and efficiently riffled the books and *National Geographics* on the sagging shelf that I had meant to fix for a while. His eyes were quick, albeit in a different sense than most people understand the word. They were quick in the sense that a straight line is quick, no waste, no second-guessing, thorough and methodical. Once scrutinized and done. Quick.

I returned in several minutes with the tea steeping in twin mugs. He had tossed the dim living room and was wondering how to distract me for a go at the upstairs—or the cellar. I knew better than to make it blatantly simple; he was the suspicious type, and if his wind got up too soon…Well, that would diminish my chance to savor our time together. Christmas, this was Christmas, or rather, the approximation of that holiday, which fills children to the brim with stars and song. But Christmas is not truly the thing, is it now? That sublime void of giddy anticipation of the gaily colored packages contains the first, and dare I say, righteous spirit of Christmas. Shucking the presents of their skin is a separate pleasure altogether.

But—

Mr. Connell sat in the huge, stuffed lazy boy with springs poking him in the buttocks. It was the only chair in the room that I trusted to keep him off the floor and it cawed when he settled his bulk into its embrace. Let me say that our man was not an actor. Even after I sat him down and placed the mug in his fist, those accipitrine eyes darted and sliced from shadowed corner to mysterious nook, off-put by the cloying feel of the room—and why not? It was a touch creepy, what with the occasional creak of a timber, the low squeak of a settling foundation, the way everything was cast under a counterchange pattern of dark and light. I would have been nervous in his shoes; he was looking into murders most foul, after all. Pardon me, murder is a sensational word; television will be the ruin of my fleeting measure of proportion if the world keeps spinning a few more revolutions. *Disappearances* is what I should have said. Thirty of them. Thirty that good Mr. Connell knew of, at least. There were more, many more, but this is astray from the subject.

We looked at each other for a time. Me, smacking my lips over toothless gums and blowing on the tea—it was too damned hot, as usual! He, pretending to sip, but not really doing so on the off chance that I *was* the crazed maniac that he sought, and had poisoned it. A good idea, even though I had not done anything like that. Since he was pretending to accept my hospitality, I pretended to look at his forged documents, smacking and fumbling with some glasses that would have driven me blind if I wore them for any span of time, and muttered monosyllabic exclamations to indicate my confusion and ultimate verification of the presumed authenticity of his papers. One quick call to the Bureau of Land Management would have sent him fleeing as the charlatan I knew he was. I ignored the opportunity.

Mr. Connell was definitely not an actor. His small talk was clumsy, as if he couldn't decide the proper way to crack me. I feigned a hearing impairment and that was cruel, though amusing. Inside of ten minutes the mechanism of his logic had all save rejected the possibility of my involvement in those disappearances. No surprise there—he operated on intuition; *peripheral logic,* as his wife often called it. I failed the test of instinct. Half-blind, weak, pallid as a starfish grounded. Decrepit would not be completely unkind. I was failing him. Yet the room, the house, the brittle fold of plain beyond the window interrupted by a blot of ramshackle structure that was the barn, invoked his disquiet. It worried him, this trail of missing persons—vague pattern; they were hitchhikers, salesmen, several state troopers, missionaries, prostitutes, you name it. Both sexes, all ages and descriptions, with a single thread to bind them. They disappeared around my humble farm. The Federal Bureau of Investigation dropped by once, three years before the incident with Mr. Connell. I did not play with them. Winter had yet to make me torpid and weak. They left with nothing, suspecting nothing.

However, it was a close thing, that inconvenient visit. It convinced me the hour was nigh....

The tea grew cold. It was late in the year, so dying afternoon sunlight had a tendency to slant; trees were shorn of their glory, crooked branches casting crooked shadows. The breeze nipped and the fields were damp. I mentioned that he was going to ruin his shoes if he went tramping out there; he thanked me and said he'd be careful. I watched him stomp around, doing his terrible acting job, trying to convince me that he was checking the value of my property, or whatever the hell he said when I wasn't listening.

Speaking of shadows...I glanced at mine, spread out across the hood of the requisite '59 Chevrolet squatting between the barn and the house. Ah, a perfectly normal shadow, if a tad disfigured by the warp of light.

A majority of the things I might tell are secrets. Therefore, I shall not reveal them whole and glistening. Also, some things are kept from me, discomfiting as that particular truth may be. The vanished people; I know *what* occurred, but not *why.* To be brutally accurate, in several cases I cannot say that I *saw* what happened, however, my guesswork is as good as anyone's. There was a brief moment, back and back again in some murky prehistory of my refined consciousness, when I possessed the hubris to imagine a measure of self-determination in this progress through existence. The Rough Beast slouching toward Bethlehem of its own accord. If leashed, then by its own device, certainly. Foolish me.

Scientists claim that there is a scheme to the vicious Tree of Life, one thing eats another and excretes the matter another being requires to sustain its spark so that it might be eaten by another which excretes the matter required to sustain the spark—And like so. Lightning does not strike with random intent, oceans do not heave, and toss-axes do not ring in the tulgy wood or bells in church towers by accident. As a famous man once said, there are no accidents 'round here.

Jerk the strings and watch us dance. I could say more on that subject; indeed, I might fill a pocket book with that pearl of wisdom, but later is better.

Mr. Connell slouched in from the field—picking about for graves, by chance? —resembling the Rough Beast I mentioned earlier. He was flushed; irritation and residual alcohol poisoning in equal parts. I asked him how he was doing, and he grunted a perfunctory comment.

Could he possibly take a closer look at the barn? It would affect the overall property value and like that…I smiled and shrugged and offered to show him the way. Watch your step, I warned him, it wouldn't do for a government man to trip over some piece of equipment and end up suing the dirt from under my feet, ha, ha.

This made him nervous all over again and he sweated. Why? Two years before this visit, I could have said with accuracy. He would have been mine to read forward and back. By now, I was losing my strength. I was stuck in *his* boat, stranded with peripheral logic for sails. Mr. Connell sweated all the time, but this was different. Fear sweat is distinctive, any predator knows that. This pungent musk superseded the powerful cologne and stale odor of whiskey leaching from his pores.

To the barn. Cavernous. Gloom, dust, clathrose awnings of spent silk, scrabbling mice. Heavy textures of mold, of rust, decaying straw. I hobbled with the grace of a lame crow, yet Mr. Connell contrived to lag at my heel. Cold in the barn, thus his left hand delved into a pocket and lingered there. What was he thinking? Partially that I was too old, unless…unless an accomplice lurked in one of the places his methodical gaze was barred from. He thought of the house; upstairs, or the cellar. *Wrong on both counts.* Maybe his research was faulty—what if I actually possessed a living relative? Now would be a hell of a time to discover *that* mistake! Mr. Connell thought as an animal does—a deer hardly requires proof from its stippled ears, its soft eyes or quivering nose to justify the uneasiness of one often hunted. Animals understand that life is death. This is not a conscious fact, rather a fact imprinted upon every colliding cell. Mr. Connell thought like an animal, unfortunately; he was trapped in the electrochemical web of cognition, wherein curiosity leads into temptation, temptation leads into fear, and fear is considered an impulse to be mastered. He came into the barn against the muffled imprecations of his lizard brain. Curiosity did not kill the cat all by itself.

His relentless eyes adjusted by rapid degrees, fastening upon a mass of sea-green tarpaulin gone velvet in the subterranean illume. This sequestered mass reared above the exposed gulf of loft, nearly brushing the venerable center-beam, unexpressive in its obscured context, though immense and bounded by that gravid force to founding dirt. Mr. Connell's heartbeat accelerated, spurred by a trickling dose of primordial dread. Being a laconic and linear man, he asked me what was under that great tarp.

I showed my gums, grasping a corner of that shroud with a knotted hand. One twitch to part the enigmatic curtain and reveal my portrait of divinity. A sculpture of the magnificent shape of God. Oh, admittedly it was a shallow rendering of That Which Cannot Be Named; but art is not relative to perfection in any tangible sense. It is our coarse antennae trembling blindly as it traces the form of Origin, tastes the ephemeral glue welding us, yearning after the secret of ineluctable evolution, and wonders what this transformation will mean. In my mind, here was the best kind of art—the kind hoarded by rich and jealous collectors in their locked galleries; hidden from the eyes of the heathen masses, waiting to be shared with the ripe few.

Came the rustle of polyurethane sloughing from the Face of Creation; a metaphor to frame the abrupt molting bloom of my deep insides. There, a shadow twisted on the floor; my shadow, but not me any more than a butterfly is the chrysalis whence it emerges. Yet, I wanted to see the end of this!

Mr. Connell gaped upon the construct born of that yearning for truth slithering at the root of my intellect. He teetered as if swaying on the brink of a chasm. He beheld shuddering lines that a fleshly tongue is witless to describe, except perhaps in spurts of impression—prolongated, splayed at angles, an obliquangular mass of smeared and clotted material, glaucous clay dredged from an old and abiding coomb where earthly veins dangle and fell waters drip as the sculpture dripped, milky-lucent starshine in the cryptic barn, an intumescent hulk rent from the floss of a carnival mirror. To gaze fully on this idol was to feel the gray matter quake inside its case and reject what the moist perceptions thought to feed it.

I cannot explain, nor must an artist defend his work or elucidate in such a way the reeling audience can fathom, brutes that they are. Besides, I was not feeling quite myself when I molded it from the morass of mindless imperative. Like a nocturnal flower, I *Become*, after that the scope of human perception is reduced and bound in fluids nameless and profane. There are memories, but their clarity is the clarity of a love for the womb, warmth, and lightless drift; fragmented happiness soon absorbed in the shuffle of the churning world and forgotten.

Mr. Connell did not comment directly; speech was impossible. He uttered an inarticulate sound, yarding at the lump of cold metal in his pocket—his crucifix against the looming presence of evil. Note that I refrain from scoffing at the existence of evil. The word is a simple name for a complex idea, an idea far outstripping the feeble equipment of sapient life. It is nothing to laugh at. As for my investigator, I like to remember him that way—frozen in a rictus of anguish at wisdom gained too late. Imagine that instant as the poor insect falls into the pitcher plant. He was an Ice-Age hunter trapped in the gelid bosom of a glacier. It was final for him.

I reached out to touch his craggy visage—

My perceptions flickered, shuttering so swiftly that I could not discern precise details of what occurred to big Mr. Connell. Suffice to say what was done to him was…incomprehensible. And horrible, I suppose most people would think. Not that I could agree with their value judgment. I suffered the throes of blossoming. It tends to affect my reasoning. The ordeal exhausted me; yet another sign.

Mr. Connell vanished like the others before him, but he was the last. After that, I left the farm and traveled north. Winter was on the world. Time for summer things to sleep.

I only mention this anecdote because it's the same thing every time, in one variation or another. Come the villagers with their pitchforks and torches, only to find the castle empty, the nemesis gone back to the shadowlands. Lumbered off to the great cocoon of slumber and regeneration.

In dreams I swim as I did back when the oceans were warm and empty. There I am, floating inside a vast membrane, innocent of coherent thought, guided by impulses to movement, sustenance and copulation. Those are dim memories; easy to assume them to be the fabrications of loneliness or delusion. Until you recall these are human frailties. Interesting that I always return to the soup of origins, whether in dreams or substance. Every piece of terrestrial life emerged from that steaming gulf. The elder organisms yet dwell in those depths, some hiding in the fields of microbes, mindless as jellyfish; others lumbering and feeding on what hapless forms they capture. Once, according to the dreams, I was one of those latter things. Except, I am uncertain if that was ever my true spawning ground.

In fairness, I do not ponder the circumstance of my being as much as logic would presume. My physiology is to thank, perhaps. There come interludes—a month, a year, centuries or more—and I simply *am*, untroubled by the questions of purpose. I seek my pleasures, I revel in their comforts. The ocean is just the ocean, a cigar is just a cigar. That is the state of *Becoming*.

Bliss is ephemeral; true for anyone, or anything. The oceans have been decimated several times in the last billion years. Sterile water in a clay bowl. Life returned unbidden on each occasion. The world slumbers, twitches and transforms. From the jelly, lizards crawled around the fetid swamps eating one another and dying, and being replaced by something else. Again, again, again, until you reach the inevitable conclusion of sky-rises, nuclear submarines, orbiting satellites, and Homo sapiens formicating the earth. God swipes His Hand across Creation, it changes shape and thrives. A cycle, indeed a cycle, and not a pleasant one if you are cursed with a brain and the wonder of what the cosmic gloaming shall hold for you.

Then there is me. Like the old song, the more things change, the more I stay the same.

When the oceans perished, I slept and later flopped on golden shores, glaring up at strange constellations, but my contemplation was a drowsy process and bore no fruit. When the lizards perished, I went into the sea and slept, and later wore the flesh and fur of warm-blooded creatures. When ice chilled and continents drifted together with dire results, I went into the sea and slept through the cataclysm. Later, I wore the skins of animals and struck flint to make fire and glared up at the stars and named them in a language I don't have the trick of anymore. Men built their idols, and I joined them in their squalid celebrations, lulled by flames and roasting flesh; for I was one with them, even if the thoughts stirring in my mind seemed peculiar, and hearkened to the sediment of dark forms long neglected. I stabbed animals with a spear and mated when the need was pressing. I hated my enemies and loved my friends and wore the values of the tribe without the impetus of subterfuge. I was a man. And for great periods that is all I was. At night I regarded the flickering lights in the sky and when I dreamed, it occurred to me exactly what the truth was. For a while I evaded the consequences of my nature. Time is longer than a person made from blood and tissue could hope to imagine. Ask God; distractions are important.

But—

Memories, memories. Long ago in a cave on the side of a famous mountain in the Old World. Most men lived in huts and cabins or stone fortresses. Only wise men chose to inhabit caves, and I went to visit one of them. A monk revered for his sagacity and especially for his knowledge of the gods in their myriad incarnations. I stayed with the wizened holy man for a cycle of the pocked and pitted moon. We drank bitter tea; we smoked psychedelic plants and read from crumbling tomes scriven with quaint drawings of deities and demons. It was disappointing—I could not be any of these things, yet there was little doubt he and I were different as a fish is from a stone. The monk was the first of them to notice. I did not concern myself. In those days my power was irresistible; let me but wave my hand and so mote it be. If I desired a thought from a passing mind, I plucked it fresh as sweet fruit from a budding branch. If I fancied a soothing rain, the firmament would split and sunder. If I hungered, flesh would prostrate itself before me…unless I fancied a pursuit. Then it would bound and hide, or stand and bare teeth or rippling steel, or suffocate my patience with tears, oaths, pleas. But in the end, I had my flesh. That the monk guessed what I strove to submerge, as much from myself as the world at large, did not alarm me. It was the *questions* that pecked at my waking thoughts, crept into my slumberous phantasms. Annoying questions.

Stark recollection of a time predating the slow glide of aeons in the primeval brine. The images would alight unasked; I would glimpse the red truth of my condition. Purple dust and niveous spiral galaxy, a plain of hyaline rock broken by pyrgoidal clusters ringed in fire, temperatures sliding a groove betwixt boiling and freezing. The sweet huff of methane in my bellowing lungs, sunrise so blinding it would have seared the eyes from any living creature…and I knew there were memories layered behind and beyond, inaccessible to the human perception that I wore as a workman wears boots, gloves and warding mantle. To see these visions in their nakedness would boggle and baffle, or rive the sanity from my fragile intellect, surely as a hot breath douses a candle. Ah, but there were memories; a phantom chain endless as the coil of chemicals comprising the mortal genome, fused to the limits of calculation—

I try not to think too much. I try not to think too much about the buried things, anyhow. Better to consider the cycle that binds me in its thrall. For my deeds there is a season—spring, summer, autumn and winter. Each time I change it becomes clearer what precisely maintains its pattern. That I am a fragment of something much larger is obvious. The monk was the first to grasp it. There was a story he mentioned—how the priests prayed to their gods, good, and bad, to look upon men and bestow their munificent blessings. They even prayed to terrible Shiva the Destroyer, who slept in his celestial palace. They prayed because to slight Shiva in their supplication was to risk his not inconsiderable fury. Yet, the priests knew if Shiva opened his eye and gazed upon the world it would be destroyed.

But—

In the spring, I walk with the others of my kindred shell, nagged by fullness unsubstantiated.

In the summer, I see my shadow change, change and then I learn to blossom and suckle the pleasurable nectar from all I survey. Nail me to a cross, burn me in a fire. A legend will rise up from the ashes. Invent stories to frighten your children, sacrifice tender young virgins to placate my concupiscent urges. Revile me in your temples, call upon Almighty God to throw me down. No good, no good. How could He see you if not for me? How could He hear thy lament, or smell thy sadness? Or taste thee?

In the autumn, like a slow, heavy tide, purpose resurges, and I remember what the seasons portend. A wane of the power, a dwindling reserve of strength. Like a malign flower that flourishes in tropical heat, I wither before the advance of frost, and blacken and die, my seeds buried in the muck at the bottom of the ocean to survive the cruel winter.

I know what I am. I understand the purpose.

I left the farm and disappeared. One more name on the ominous list haunting law enforcement offices in seventeen states. I vanished myself to the Bering Coast—a simple feat for anyone who wants to try. An old man alone on a plane; no one cared. They never do.

There is an old native ghost town on a stretch of desolate beach. Quonset huts with windows shattered or boarded. Grains of snow slither in past open doors when the frigid wind gusts along, moaning through the abandoned FAA towers colored navy gray and rust. The federal government transplanted the villagers to new homes thirteen miles up the beach.

I don't see anyone when I leave the shack I have appropriated and climb the cliffs to regard the sea. The sea being rumpled, a dark, scaly hide marred by plates of thickening ice. Individual islets today, a solid sheet in a few weeks, extending to the horizon. Or forever. I watch the stars as twilight slips down from the sky, a painless veil pricked with beads and sparks. Unfriendly stars. Eventually I return to the shack. It takes me a very long time—I am an old, old man. My shuffle and panting breath are not part of the theater. The shack waits and I light a kerosene lamp and huddle by the Bunsen burner to thaw these antiquitous bones. I do not hunger much this late in the autumn of my cycle, and nobody is misfortunate enough to happen by, so I eschew sustenance another day.

The radio is old too. Scratchy voice from a station in Nome recites the national news—I pay a lot of attention to this when my time draws nigh, looking for a sign, a symbol of tribulations to come—the United Nations is bombing some impoverished country into submission, war criminals from Bosnia are apprehended in Peru. A satellite orbiting Mars has gone offline, but NASA is quick to reassure the investors that all is routine, in Ethiopia famine is tilling people under by the thousands, an explosion caused a plane to crash into the Atlantic, labor unions are threatening a crippling strike, a bizarre computer virus is hamstringing two major corporations and so on and on. The news is never good, and I am not sure if there is anything I wanted to hear.

I close my rheumy eyes and see a tinsel and sequined probe driving out, out beyond the cold chunk of Pluto. A stone tossed into a bottomless pool, trailing bubbles. I see cabalists hunched over their ciphers, Catholics on their knees before the effigy of Christ, biologists with scalpels and microscopes, astronomers with their mighty lenses pointed at the sky, atheists, and philosophers with fingers pointed at themselves. Military men stroke the cool bulk of their latest killing weapon and feel a touch closer to peace. I see men caressing the crystal and wire and silicon of the machines that tell them what to believe about the laws of physics, the number to slay chaos in its den. I see housewives scrambling to pick the kids up from soccer practice, a child on the porch gazing up, and up, to regard the same piece of sky glimmering in my window. He wonders what is up there, he wonders if there is a monster under his bed. No monsters there, instead they lurk at school, at church, in his uncle's squamous brain. Everyone is looking for the answer. They do not want to find the answer, trust me. Unfortunately, the answer will find them. Life—it's like one of those unpleasant nature documentaries. To be the cameraman instead of the subjects, eh?

Ah, my skin warns me that it is almost the season. I dreamed for a while, but I do not recall the content. The radio is dead; faint drone from the ancient speaker. The kerosene wick has burned to cinders. A flash from the emerald-colored bottle catches my eye; full of cologne. I seldom indulge in cosmetics; the color attracted me and I brought it here. I am a creature of habit. When my affectations of evolution decay, habit remains steadfast.

Dark outside on the wintry beach. Sunrise is well off and may not come again. The frozen pebbles crackle beneath my heels as I stagger toward the canvas of obsidian water, leaving strange and unsteady tracks on the skeletal shore. There is a sense of urgency building. Mine, or the Other's? I strip my clothes as I go and end up on the cusp of the sea, naked and shriveled. The stars are feral. They shudder—a ripple is spreading across the heavens and the stars are dancing wildly in its pulsating wake. A refulgence that should not be seen begins to seep from the widening fissure. Here is a grand and terrible happening to write of on the wall of a cave…God opening His Eye to behold the world and all its little works.

I have seen this before. Let others marvel in my place, if they dare. My work is done, now to sleep. When I mount from the occluded depths what will I behold? What will be my clay and how shall I be given to mold it? I slip into the welcoming flank of the sea and allow the current to tug my shell out and down into the abyssal night. It isn't really as cold as I feared. Thoughts are fleeting as the bubbles and the light. The shell begins to flake, to peel, to crumble, and soon I will wriggle free of this fragile vessel.

But—

One final kernel of wisdom gained through the abomination of time and service. A pearl to leave gleaming upon this empty shore; safely assured that no one shall come by to retrieve it and puzzle over the contradiction. Men are afraid of the devil, but there is no devil, just me and I do as I am bid. It is God that should turn their bowels to soup. Whatever God is, He, or It, created us for amusement. It's too obvious. Just as He created the prehistoric sharks, the dinosaurs, and the humble mechanism that is a crocodile. And Venus fly traps, and black widow spiders, and human beings. Just as He created a world where every organism survives by rending a weaker organism. Where procreation is an imperative, a leech's anesthetic against agony and death and disease that accompany the sticky congress of mating. A sticky world, because God dwells in a dark and humid place. A world of appetite, for God is ever hungry.

I know, because I am His Mouth.

PROCESSION OF THE BLACK SLOTH

"There are eighteen. One for every trespass."

Royce jolted and nearly upset his plastic cup of melted ice and vodka. They'd assigned him to a business-class window seat. The window was smooth and black. The rolled up blind rattled softly as the plane plowed ahead. He said, "Excuse me?"

"May I get that for you, sir?" A flight attendant leaned across a snoring man who'd fallen asleep with the overhead lamp on. The beam illuminated the sleeping man's slack face: Ted K., a computer monitor salesman from Cleveland. This was Ted's first trip to the Far East, could Royce imagine that? Fifty-seven years old come August and he'd never traveled outside the good old US of A. Thank God for adult education, huh? He'd talked animatedly at Royce for two hours, enthused about his prospects in the Asian market. He never got around to asking about Royce's business in Hong Kong before the Canadian Clubs did him in. Which was fine by Royce. He'd have only lied and claimed to be in marketing, anyway. Revealing to bored travel companions that your trade was a security consultant who specialized in countering industrial espionage tended to start conversations with no ending. *How did you get into that line, anyway? Well, I discovered I was a natural in the spy game while stalking my estranged college girlfriend....*

The attendant was small and as perfectly detailed as a doll. Her lipstick was very red against her face. Her hand brushed Royce's knuckles. Her red nails and lips and precisely bobbed hair complemented the two-piece uniform all the attendants wore. The girls were a matched collection, extras in a period piece. "Another, please," he said, slurring, his tongue heavy from unconsciousness and disorientation, more so than the effects of the liquor. Flight drugged him as reliably as the copious quantities of alcohol and Dramamine he indulged in to combat motion sickness.

"Sir?"

"May I have another of these?" He released the cup and smiled to allay her concerns. "Thank you, miss." She poured more vodka from the tiny bottles they always handed out on flights, and left. He turned in his chair and watched her push the service cart away. The gallery was dim as a nursery at night, its gloom interrupted by an occasional reading light, the emergency strips bracketing the aisle.

Royce finished his drink and shuffled papers from his carry-on briefcase, stared at them without really reading. In order to actually read he would've needed to find his glasses and no matter what style he'd tried, the effect was always unflattering. Anyway, his head ached and he already knew the report front to back. Thoroughness was his watchword. *Let that be my epitaph—He was thorough.* He unbuckled and gingerly squeezed past his comatose seatmate whose snoring hitched then resumed.

The fore restroom was occupied and two women waited for a turn. The older of the pair scowled at him with annoyance and suspicion. *I must look like hell. Or smell like it.* He decided to make the journey aft, chuckling about how uptight some people got when traveling. It had been a long, long flight. Almost everyone was asleep, and the few passengers who weren't didn't glance up from their laptops or their paperbacks, but persisted in these activities with glassy-eyed concentration. Most of the passengers were Americans, and wasn't it the modern way to fill every waking moment with some gesture to productivity, no matter how minor?

His own friends always vowed to avoid calling the office, or God help them, work on vacation, but they always did, to some degree, or worse, they eschewed the innocuous emails to the office and treated their tours like contests. The winner accomplished the most in the shortest period and the prize was bragging rights at some future cocktail party or barbeque where the participants compared notes and the victors counted coup on the losers. *Skin-diving, white-water rafting, wine-tasting, a fifteen-mile hike on a nature preserve, tango lessons and the opera by ten PM, and that was only on the day we landed. How about you, Mildred?* This obsessive-compulsive drive was a curiously American disease.

The rear facilities were vacant and he slipped inside and locked the door. He pissed, and as he zipped, the small fluorescent halo above the mirror sputtered and died. The cramped bathroom became black as a coffin. Royce hesitated, surprised and disoriented. He stepped back, feeling for the door handle which didn't seem to be in the right place. The light hummed and ticked and began to glow. Its elements ignited then failed in rapid succession and the ring pulsed within the surrounding blackness and swung like a pendulum. Its motion made him sick in the stomach. Between these staccato shutter clicks of light and dark, something happened in the tarnished mirror. He glimpsed a movement independent of his own obscured face, a momentary blur of alabaster like the belly of a large fish rolling on its back before it sank into abyssal night.

Certainly this entire sequence happened within the span of seconds. These seconds were elastic. They stretched to accommodate the flood of primeval darkness in his brain. His thoughts were jagged and fragmented; they swam against a tide. *I've got to be hammered. How many did I have? Those idiots should've cut me off. Wait-wait, how many did I have, really? What the hell was that?*

Normality was restored as the light brightened and illuminated the toilet in cold, sickly radiance. The shadows slipped back into their lairs. Royce blinked rapidly, weak from the adrenal rush. His face was green and gray in the mirror. He wiped away sweat with his sleeve and was in the act of passing his hands beneath the tap when he happened to glance down.

Holy Christ, somebody had an abortion in here! The plastic basin of a sink was splattered with black ooze; and not a little. He'd observed pro anglers fishing for sharks off the Barrier Reef, knew exactly what a bucket of chum looked like, and this was close, except for what might've been a hank of hair, maybe a whole scalp. He stepped back and almost tore the door off its hinges in his haste to escape.

"Whoa, Nelly!" Ted K. the salesman from Cleveland said as Royce collided with him. Royce gaped, at a loss as to where the man had come from so suddenly. Hadn't he left the guy dead drunk and sound asleep no more than two minutes ago? Ted K.'s doughy features were lumped in approximation of genial alarm as he clasped Royce's elbow to steady them before they stumbled over the stewardess who was only a few steps up the aisle giving someone a pillow.

"Hey, guy," Ted K. said, and his hands were all over Royce, which compounded his anxiety—he hated being touched unbidden, and especially by a stranger, a neurosis doubtless rooted in some childhood trauma. He'd even occasionally rebuked his lovers for putting their hands on him when he didn't expect it. The plump man smelled overripe as fruit fermenting in a dark, humid place. "Where's the fire?" his fellow passenger was saying, sounding concerned, yet half smiling. Maybe he was enjoying this.

"Sorry, sorry." Royce was repulsed by the man's marshmallow flesh against his, but he'd almost bowled the guy over hadn't he? Good lord, what if an air marshal popped out of his seat and slapped cuffs on him for making a scene aboard a plane? He suffered Ted K.'s groping and just repeated his apology until the stewardess turned around and asked if everything was all right. He pointed at the open restroom and assured her that in fact nothing was all right and she'd better have a look. The attendant's expression changed into the mask people in the service industry put on when confronted with the irrational and unpredictable passions of the public. Her mask said, *I've lost most of my English and must confer with my colleagues.*

Royce recognized that look and closed his mouth. He gave her a fake smile and gently extricated himself from Ted K. and returned to his seat without a backward glance, his heart thumping in his throat. Presently, the stewardess appeared at his side and asked if he wanted another drink. He laughed at the preposterous notion; the last possible thing on Earth he needed was another drop. On the heels of this, he realized he sounded borderline shrill, hysterical. He made conciliatory noises, thank you, but no thank you. As she began to retreat, he risked asking about the problem with the toilet. Her mechanical smile told him she thought *he* might be responsible for the mess. "Plumbing. No need to worry. All fixed. Okay?"

Plumbing. They jettison shit at cruising altitude, you know. It freezes into a block and plummets to earth. Or is that a myth? Blue ice? God, I remember something about blue ice. Strange to think of such an inane urban legend. *Was that a piece of skull I saw? A chunk of jawbone?* Royce started feeling cold and stopped thinking about the weird thing that had occurred in the bathroom. He preoccupied himself with football. He was a season ticket holder in Seattle despite the fact he seldom went, mostly passed his tickets to friends and associates. Nobody played football in Hong Kong. What did they play there? He had no idea whatsoever.

The plane was in its final descent when he realized Ted K. had never returned. Royce couldn't blame him, not after the whole incident. Regardless, the plane was filled to capacity and he briefly wondered where the guy had found another seat. Then the jet banked and the lights of the city were spread before him.

A large, impassive Chinese man in a black suit met him at the airport. Mr. Jen's face was crumpled and scarred as a piece of old, battered tin. He held a sign that read MR. HAWTHORNE. The man wasn't tall, but as he carried the luggage Royce stared at his impressively broad shoulders and thought someone could probably project a film on his back. Mr. Jen put Royce in the backseat of a new Lexus and drove him directly to the offices of Coltech Ltd.

The office was an austere marble plaza of interlinked cubicles lighted by cozy lamps with woven shades. The grand Coltech seal, a lion rampant before crossed lightning bolts, loomed over all. Scores of stolid, crisply dressed employees conducted business with quiet determination; even the clattering keyboards and buzzing phones seemed muted in that cathedral vault. After checking with security he eventually located the right receptionist and waited while she unlocked a cabinet.

"Fruit basket?" He said.

She ignored the remark, muttering to herself as she rummaged through various folders. "Ah, there we go. Here is your Octopus card, Mr. Hawthorne. And the keys to your apartment." The secretary appeared to be North American, although she wore her beehive hair and heavy eye shadow and a bright yellow space-age dress in the popular retro fashion of young, cosmopolitan Asian women. She handed him an envelope containing a plastic card and three keys on a ring. She seemed impressed with his expensive suit, the Sicilian darkness of his tan. Her eyes flickered slightly. "Unfortunately, the apartment won't be ready until Sunday. Mr. James extends his apologies. However, he took the liberty of reserving a room for you at the Hyatt."

"An Octopus card?" Royce said, bemused. He eyed the Möbius strip configured to form a sideways eight.

"'Eight place pass' from the Cantonese. A smart card, sir. For the train and the bus service. I buy cigarettes with mine." She covered her mouth when she laughed.

"Ah." He slipped card and keys into his jacket pocket.

"Mr. Jen will drive you to the hotel, if you're ready. Oh, you have a three o' clock tomorrow with Mr. James and Mr. Shea at the Demeter Lounge."

"I see. Where—"

"Mr. Jen will get you there," she said with a dismissive smile. "Welcome aboard, sir."

The home office laid out the scenario when they originally brought him in. Coltech, a subsidiary of his employers at BelCorp, manufactured various technologies, including nuclear hydraulics systems and satellite components. They'd recently lost three territorial overseas managers to another firm; a much bigger fish on the international scene, and the deserting managers took most of their staff with them. Rumors surfaced regarding industrial sabotage, the sale of trade data, and an alleged network of moles piping corporate secrets directly to Asian competitors. Coltech got panicky and pulled a bunch of key personnel from domestic projects and sent them to China and Taiwan in a frantic attempt to secure operations.

The company drafted Royce to investigate two minor production facilities in Hong Kong—these factories were among the few that hadn't relocated to Mainland China. Circuit boards and electronic actuators were assembled at one plant; hydraulic sleeves and rotary process valves at the other. His cover as a quality assurance consultant afforded him access to personnel files, factory records, and juicy trade documents.

Martin Reardon James and Miguel Shea, president and vice president of local operations respectively, explained the specifics in painful detail upon his arrival. Shea, in his role as major-domo did most of the talking during that introductory meeting in the luxurious confines of an upscale restaurant with a view down the western slopes and their towers of blue glass, all the way to the China Sea. He referred to the enterprise as a snipe hunt. "But, hell, whatever makes the boys in Georgia happy…"

Royce understood he'd be flying solo on this one. Atlanta had warned him about these two and they proved to be exactly what he'd envisioned. The officers—hefty, florid men—relished the perks of scotch, women and leisurely afternoons on the golf course to the exclusion of all else and were most interested in maintaining the status quo.

"Shrink is to be expected," Shea said, lighting a cigar and taking a few moments to get it properly smoldering. "No damned way we've got enough fingers to plug the holes in the dike. Pick your battles, kid. Have a drink. There'll always be something for someone to steal."

Royce waited long enough to be polite, then showed them a headshot of a blond, tan man in his thirties. "This is the individual I'm looking at."

"You're here to look at a bunch of people," Mr. James said. He was a thick, older man stuffed into a hand-tailored suit. His shrewd, bloody eyes were drowsy in an illusion of complacency, of boredom.

Royce knew a shark when he met one and felt sorry for the poor bastards with the misfortune to fall under the man's tender mercies. "I am. But this one…Atlanta likes him for some of your breaches. He may be the *architect*, in fact."

"Who's that?" Mr. James said. He took the photograph and stared at it.

"Brendan Coyne," Mr. Shea said. Despite his debauched good-old-boy shtick, Royce figured he was the kind of guy who knew everything about everyone in the immediate company. Probably the kind of guy to have names for the rats.

"What's his department?" Mr. James said. He downed a huge gulp of whiskey and looked at his watch.

"Consultant, communications."

"Oh, yeah? Any good?"

"He's good. What do you think? You hired him."

"I don't hire schmucks, do I?"

"No, indeed not," Mr. Shea said.

"Neither does Atlanta," Royce said with a dry smile. "As I said, I'll be looking at Coyne. Among other people."

"We hope you'll keep us informed of developments."

"I report to Atlanta. Orders."

Mr. Shea scowled and waited to see if Royce was resolved on that point. "I see. Maybe you could, uh, do us a courtesy now and again."

"Courtesy, Mr. Shea?" *Are you really thinking about bribing me?* A small part of Royce hoped they were shady enough to grease his palm for such harmless information. He considered himself a clean operator by industry standards; he pushed the boundaries without actually stepping over the line. A tiny bit of graft for harmless favors was simply a perk of the trade. He wasn't being paid to investigate Shea or James, although they could hardly feel secure about precisely what Atlanta knew regarding their laundry list of petty indiscretions on the company dime. Nervous executives with deep pockets had done much to pay off his college loans and his mother's tenure at the retirement home and potentially catastrophic hospital stay. Less nobly, such paranoid largess had also subsidized his vintage Mustang, a powerboat and a beachfront condo in Florida. "Absolutely, I'll pass along anything I'm able. We sure do appreciate your cooperation regarding this unpleasant matter."

"Anything we can do to help," Mr. Shea said. "But I gotta say, Hawthorne. It sure feels like Atlanta doesn't trust us."

"Do they trust anyone?" Royce said. The tension exhausted him. He ordered another vodka, knowing full well he was at the top of a long downhill slide.

Mr. James grunted at the photograph. "Isn't he pretty. I never liked pretty boys. Can't trust some asshole who spends that much time on his hair."

The next day, Shea took him into a wasteland of industrial ruins and gave him a tour of the only working factories within a mile. These were a pair of massive, rusting boxes connected by numerous catwalks, outbuildings and trailers. The vice president introduced Royce around and showed him his office, which was little more than a janitor's closet tucked into the heart of the structure where they manufactured the hydraulic sleeves. The hallways were slotted in a maze of grillwork and pipes with oversized spigots and valve switches painted in bright reds and yellows.

Royce couldn't have imagined a more monotonous, soul-killing assignment. Techs in hardhats, white coats and protective earphones rushed helter-skelter; workers were basically chained at the soldering tables and assembly lines. The laborers toiled sixteen-hour shifts in heat and noise, suffering these conditions for a menial wage; they received few breaks and were subjected to verbal and physical abuse from native overseers Royce knew would shock the hell out of working stiffs in Detroit. He had to admit, the Chinese were the perfect workforce. They slaved away as if the Devil himself were standing over their shoulders.

When not pretending to perform as a Coltech functionary, Royce was ensconced in the Lord Raleigh Arms, a housing project on the outskirts of the moribund industrial district. Lord Raleigh Arms, or the LRA as its inhabitants referred to it in casual conversation, was an exclusive compound reserved for employees of several affiliated companies; the executives, researchers and engineers who made things tick. The area proved quite pleasant, defying his expectations. Ministry officials desired a good face on things; they installed an arboretum and a couple parks to screen the quarter from defunct factories and warehouses and miles of tract slums.

The compound consisted of concrete and glass wings configured as a rectangle with a hollow center. There were guards at the gates, closed-circuit monitors, and regular patrols by the municipal police. Corporations paid for the private security forces. Terrorist threats weren't entirely uncommon, nor plain old kidnapping plots. Some employees had drawn indefinite postings and brought families—protection details were a basic necessity. The bulk of Royce's neighbors were Americans, Brits and Germans. He retained Mr. Jen to chauffeur him through seedier parts of the city; should he require special services, his company's hosts delegated a native to attend his needs.

His apartment was an economy model: a bedroom/living room combination, a pocket bath and closet-sized kitchen, all done in monochrome green and yellow. Fortunately, he traveled light, because the closets were tiny and there wasn't much room to hide anything particularly sensitive. This was why as a first order of business he purchased a small fire safe to secure hard-copy documents and other important items he couldn't encrypt on his computers.

Every piece of futuristic, plasticized furniture, every stainless steel appliance, radiated an aura of sterile, passionless utility. The terrace overlooked a quadrangle occupied by a swimming pool. The tile deck was decorated with plastic lawn chairs, folding tables, and umbrellas. Even during the rainy season, it attracted gobs of raucous kids. Come warmer weather, a score of elderly denizens slithered out of hiding like worms after a storm. Many of them wore dust masks common in China and Japan because the smog was so bloody awful. They congregated under the umbrellas and smoked generic cigarettes and bitched about the weather, the pollution and the kids.

Friendly residents warned that despite evidence of extensive remodeling, such cosmetics masked a host of problems. Plumbing leaked and power came and went at inopportune moments. At such times, the elevators were out of service, and the air conditioning offline. Then, the population of the Lord Raleigh Arms endured the blackness of sweltering apartments and listened to cockroaches scrabble in the hollow spaces behind freshly painted gypsum. Sirens bugled in the city where its towers formed the corner posts of a skein of nictitating lights.

He'd scarcely unpacked when he overheard complaints about noise, especially in regard to loud music practiced by an amateur flautist in a nearby block; then there was the indelicate matter of bag people creeping around late at night. One of his fellow American neighbors, an engineer he'd met in passing, heard a noise in the hall, an odd knock at the door. When he checked through the peephole, an eyeball blinked at him. "The freak's face must've been squashed up against the door!" The engineer was an excitable fellow given to padding bare-chested in striped pajama bottoms around the foyer and community annex. He said he realized the "freak" was a woman when she stepped back and ran away, giving him a better look at her. "Scurried, I mean. Like a cockroach hit with a light. Moved pretty fast, too. All this blasted security and we can't keep bums out! Next thing you know, we'll be getting stabbed in our beds, or rolled up in a carpet and carted off for ransom." For their part, the security personnel did immediately capture vagrants who slipped in on occasion, but denied the existence of any permanent interlopers.

Similar stories ran through the block. Elvira, as the English-speaking residents referred to the haunt, in reference to her black dress and bone-white face, seemed the most popular object of speculation. Elvira didn't haunt alone, in any case. One of the janitors confided "little friends" followed her around.

"Kids?" Royce said, thinking of the brats shrieking through the hallways, wild as the painted savages who populated Golding's dark vision.

The janitor, a sunburned elder statesman in blue paper work clothes, shook his head emphatically and motioned near his hip. "No, no. Little friends." He glanced nervously over his shoulder, then back at Royce. He smiled with the obsequious reflex of a career servant, and pushed his squeaking cartload of mops and brooms down the hallway of doors toward the distant elevators.

The sweep proceeded routinely and monotonously—the life of an investigator was unglamorous and fraught with glacial tedium. Prior to his insertion, he'd been provided a list of "at risk" technologies and the names of persons associated with them. It would've been impossible to monitor the scores of individuals who might be involved in nefarious activity. Instead, he relied on the installation of state-of-the-art security software designed to track anomalous activity on the company network. He received authorization to order a couple dozen wiretaps of private residences. He outsourced the data collection to local specialists and quickly acquired potential informants with connections to the black market. Occasionally, he arranged casual social meetings with subjects on the list and recorded all conversations via a microwire and relayed details of these transactions to his handlers back in the States. The bulk of his work was as involving as watching paint dry.

Royce felt restlessness more keenly than usual. This wasn't a run-down burgh in Soviet Russia, or a backwater in the South of Italy. This was Hong Kong in all its glitz and glory, a great, seething den of LED-brilliant iniquity; and him marking the hours like a two-bit private eye who'd been paid to keep tabs on a cheating spouse at the local Dew Drop Inn.

Many of Royce's colleagues frequented a posh cocktail lounge a few blocks from the compound. The bar was called the Rover in honor of its itinerant patrons; a smoky, dim place with poker lamps on chains over the lacquered chestnut tables, and curtained booths; the kind where three sides rise six feet and one could practically jam a small dinner party inside. The help were strictly locals; cute-as-buttons Cantonese girls who might be high school sophomores or thirty-year-old mothers of three. A burly ex-fire chief from the Bronx ran the show. Jodie Samuels was quite the character; gods, he looked uncomfortable in a suit and tie. Something of a taskmaster; he didn't have a choice about Asian servers, but he'd only hire white bartenders and chefs; forced HR to ship in personnel from England and America.

Racist management notwithstanding, the lounge ran like a top. They'd tucked an exclusive billiards room in the back; a gentlemen's club. Billiards weren't popular with the regular crowd and most of the power players belonged to swankier, more prestigious clubs in the hip, upscale districts; however it served as a convenient niche to entertain guests and relax after a stressful day at the office.

Royce wormed his way into Samuels' good books because he received an outrageous per diem and wasn't shy about spending it. Samuels probably could've scored a new Cadillac from the tips Royce left him. Before long, Royce got the nod to enjoy the accommodations. A small group of businessmen made the place their home away from home and he became chummy with many of them. They smoked cigars and drank a lot of XO and swapped more lies than he cared to remember. All this in order to maneuver close to his quarry, the irrepressible Brendan Coyne.

It wasn't difficult to make the connection: he spilled a drink on Coyne's shirt, bought him another round and insisted on picking up the cleaning tab. Soon they were comparing their exploits as Americans at large and marveling how they lived a stone's throw apart. After that, they socialized at the Rover three or four evenings a week. He methodically compiled a list of Coyne's business associates and social acquaintances, flagging several of these as potential conspirators. Coyne possessed peripheral ties to the Hong Kong underworld and a onetime convicted CEO of an extinct American corporation. In itself, these casual associations proved little; Royce personally knew and consorted with a baker's dozen crooked lawyers, accountants and corporate officers, most of whom functioned quite efficiently within their various organizations; a bit of skullduggery, like the graft Royce loved so well, went with the territory. Nonetheless, this compounded the difficulty of ferreting the truth about Coyne's extracurricular activities.

He knew plenty about his subject's personal life at this point: Coyne's father, a career Army lieutenant, dropped dead of a heart attack at a formal dinner a couple years back, and Coyne summoned his aged mother to Hong Kong rather than abandon her in Seattle among cold-hearted relatives. During their frequent interactions, Royce applauded his associate's loyalty while secretly speculating about his ulterior motives. Royce had been forced to put his own mother in a home and he doubted a would-be playboy like Coyne had an altruistic bone in his body.

Coyne and his mother lived in an apartment across the quadrangle. Coyne was a hard partier who'd broken up with a longtime boyfriend and developed a neurosis about staying in shape. He munched on trail mix and lifted weights at the gym every other day, basted himself in a tanning booth with regularity, and did laps in the pool at night; he invited Royce to join him. Royce laughed. All the chlorine in China wouldn't have persuaded him to stick so much as his toe in that water. "The sauna in the executive washroom suits me fine, thank you," Royce said.

Royce kept him under constant surveillance. He purchased a small, high-powered telescope from a shop that catered to private detectives and suspicious spouses; the proprietor dealt in hidden cameras, thumbnail recorders, lowlight scopes, and other apparatuses. During the day, he positioned a video camera on his terrace in a bamboo blind, lens oriented at Coyne's apartment. At night, he killed the lights and watched through his telescope while Coyne moved from room to room. On Tuesday and Friday when his mother was away at the community center playing bingo, Coyne slowly undressed, habitually lingering at a panel mirror in the bedroom. Other nights mother and son shared dinner before the dizzy blue screen of their television. He frequently made innocuous calls on the landline to his brother in Seattle, other colleagues overseas, a stock advisor in Taiwan; nothing damning; nothing remotely interesting, in fact. Coyne observed these rituals until his clockwork emergence for two dozen laps in the pool. The mechanical repetition of the affair caused Royce to ponder his own patterns, the automated nature of humans in general.

Other days, he followed Coyne around the city, making note of his itinerary, the people he visited. There wouldn't be any momentous revelation, no potboiler twist. Ultimately, success in these matters boiled down to the inexorable compilation of data.

After nearly a month of monitoring Coyne, lassitude eroded Royce's patience. It was an inevitable consequence of prolonged field investigations. Hypersensitivity, too much liquor and caffeine, cigarettes and lack of sleep coupled paranoia and mania to birth a form of high-functioning schizophrenia. Before Hong Kong, he'd kicked smoking and reserved his drinking for infrequent social occasions; both habits had returned with a vengeance. Such were the hazards of his occupation; alongside venereal disease from liaisons with barflies and unscrupulous prostitutes, and death or imprisonment at the hands of disgruntled foreign interests.

Sometimes, during the grind, he allowed himself to daydream about his erstwhile college plans to become an engineer, to marry the cute orthodontist in training, Jenny Hodge. Paranoia had always been a problem, though. *You never could buy the fact a babe like Jenny saw something in you, surely she was laughing behind your back, making time with the rugby stud in her dorm.* When she discovered his love of telephoto lenses and hidden microphones, his paranoid fantasies came home to roost. She sobbed during their melodramatic breakup scene, said she figured he'd lied about everything, when the truth was he'd only lied about half and the half was harmless, mostly. *Bye, bye, sweet Jenny, I loved thee well. Here I sit, fifteen years older and wiser in big bad Hong Kong trying to hang a guy by his testicles for corporate espionage. How much damage has he done? A hundred mil? Two hundred? Shit, I'm the poor man's James Bond. Eat your heart out, baby.*

As his mind wandered, he tended to focus on peripheral subjects: the elegant young lady in a single bedroom diagonally opposite his unit who'd moved in after the apartment waited empty as a cave; the previous family departed within a day of Royce's arrival after setting the place afire due to a stovetop mishap. Each evening she paraded in the choreographed flood of track lights, nude, but for a shiny waist chain and a bead necklace. Then the blond European couple, apparently engaged in a ceaseless war punctuated by broken windows and routine police visits. And finally, a squat, gray-haired woman named Mrs. Ward who trundled onto her balcony after dark and played shrill, discordant tunes on various woodwinds, she being the flautist so reviled in certain quarters of the LRA.

Royce learned she was a chief organizer of senior activities—the chairperson of bingo tournaments and the Saturday evening mixer in the Governor White ballroom. Something in her corpulent stature, the pagan timbre of her horrid musical pretensions, riveted him. She resembled almost completely an aunt on his mother's side, Carole Joyce, a dowager widow with a place just outside San Francisco. Mom and Dad pawned him and his brother on her one summer. He didn't remember much about that, except the house was gloomy and full of dusty furniture, and his aunt filled him with loathing. Carole Joyce had been a large woman as well, and vaguely unwholesome in her appetites. Her fetishes hadn't diminished with age. She enjoyed erotic art and favored French Renaissance gowns the better to display her ample cleavage; she wore black eye shadow and ghastly white pancake makeup that didn't blend where it ended under her jaw. Aunt Carole Joyce slept in her makeup, seldom scraped it off, preferring to add a new layer every morning. She was a dilettante spiritualist who'd managed some travel and vacillated between Buddhism, Taoism and more esoteric systems according to whim. Aunt Carole Joyce was particularly fascinated with punishment and doom and she'd told a wide-eyed Royce numerous hair-raising parables about wretched boys in foreign cultures going to the thousandfold hells in a hand basket where they were inevitably certain to suffer the most exquisite torments imaginable. *Be glad you're an American. We've got just the one hell.*

A bloated creature in her sixties, she prowled the boardwalks for handsome, tanned young men, solicited them with cash and gifts to come up and swamp the scummy pool and to hack at a halfacre garden, which had been overgrown for some thirty years. Royce was nine or ten and didn't know much, but he figured from their behavior Aunt Carole Joyce gave them the creeps too. She certainly went through a number of the strapping lads in the three months Royce spent in captivity. He never discovered whether his aunt tossed them aside, or if they cut and ran of their own accord.

Whenever Royce caught sight of Agatha Ward, he instantly revisited that summer with Aunt CJ and shuddered, but couldn't look away. Indeed, Royce cultivated a morbid preoccupation not only with Mrs. Ward, but the whole tribe of female elders. Mrs. Tuttle and Mrs. Fox, the inseparable canasta partners; Erma Yarbro, an emaciated wasp from Yonkers who made no secret her dislike of the Far East and its inhabitants; Mrs. Grant, who'd lost her legs to diabetes and trolled the quadrangle in a motorized wheelchair; and solemn Mrs. Cardin, an inveterate smoker with a button in her trachea. He fixated upon their poolside klatches, knitting parties and weekly luncheons at the community annex.

These women brought to mind so many seniors he'd known over the years, familiar in the interchangeable way of babies; they were the ghosts of teachers, librarians and neighbors who'd populated his childhood, although they didn't behave in the torpid, desultory manner of other seniors. Their movements seemed vigorous, their interactions lively. Occasionally, he caught a strange sign pass among them as they played at cards, or reclined poolside, soaking up infrequent sun; an occulted ripple of intention, a shibboleth that spoke of subterranean things; and some late nights, he spied their movements in the courtyard as they formed in disorganized groups and filed out of the compound. He felt like an anthropologist stealthily documenting the customs of an alien culture; scientist and voyeur in one pathological bundle.

He recorded hours of footage of Mrs. Coyne doddering about the courtyard, kibitzing with her friends. Occasionally, he paid one of the teen criminals loitering at the bus terminal three hundred Hong Kong dollars and a carton of cigarettes to follow the ladies on their weekly excursion to the shopping mall. He gave the kid a belt buckle cam and told him to stick tight and note if Mrs. Coyne talked to anyone besides her associates or the vendors. Royce studied these films in the bleakest hours of night, chain-smoking while lumpen, blue-haired women clumped on subways and tour buses, soundlessly jittered through boutiques and gift shops and food courts and traded gossip like a covey of magpies.

Chu, his agent in this intrigue, revolted after the fifth mission. They'd rendez-voused at night on a train platform. Rain hammered the shell of the station's slanted, plastic roof, poured from the lip of the overhang. Mist absorbed the fluorescent glare, the shuffle and scrape of commuters knotted in small groups, heads down and listless as cattle.

"I don't like them," Chu said. The boy was tall and whip-lean with black, spiked hair and a nondescript face. He wore a Houston Rockets warm-up suit and numerous cheap, death's head rings and was rumored to be affiliated with the Tong.

When Royce handed Chu his money and asked why he was quitting, Chu stuffed the bills into his jacket and lighted a cigarette. If Royce closed his eyes, the kid's voice would've conjured an image of any of the chess club nerds he'd known in high school. But Chu was way past all that; he slumped against a lamp post, shoulders hunched, his posture that of a razor half-folded. He looked a lot like an exchange student Royce tangled with his sophomore year. A real hardcase who brought the mean streets of Seoul with him. The Korean had worn rings, too.

"You want more money," Royce said.

"No. I'm done."

"You're done. Why are you done? Because you don't like them? The old women?"

Chu spat. His teeth weren't pretty. He sucked on his cigarette, almost panting. "Yeah."

It was suddenly so clear to Royce. "You're scared of them…you probably get sick to your stomach from old folks' smell. That stink of urine and sweat. The way they smack their lips and quaver when they talk. Yeah, very unpleasant, I'm sure. So much for revering your elders."

"C'mon, Whitey don't count."

"I thought you were tough, Chu."

Chu laughed, squeaky and hoarse. "Stupid Yankee." He flicked his cigarette over Royce's left shoulder into the surrounding darkness.

Royce didn't give him the satisfaction of flinching. "Then you must do what's best for you. I'll give the job to one of your associates. *They* look hungry."

"Not as hungry as you think, Yankee-doodle. Good luck with…everything." Chu raised his hood and slunk away, giggling. He was certainly correct regarding his friends—they uniformly ignored Royce's efforts to recruit them; none even acknowledged his halting attempts at Cantonese, and he soon abandoned the effort. In the days to come, Chu disappeared from his usual haunts; one of the shopkeepers thought he'd been arrested, or dragged off by rival gangsters. In either case, the disgruntled merchant didn't much care. He spat and professed joy at the hoodlum's absence; gods grant it be a lengthy one.

Later that week of Chu's defection, Royce staggered into the Rover after an evening of crashing from one strobe-lit dance hall to another in the wake of James, Shea and an entourage of yes-men, call girls and assorted hangers-on, all in the name of entertaining a visiting dignitary who owned a piece of the company, or wanted to buy one, it was difficult to recall.

He slid into an empty seat, nodded greetings to Gerald, the late-shift barkeep, and ordered a whiskey sour to match his mood. He'd downed the first and started on the second when he noticed the woman who resided in the unit across from his own standing near the end of the crowded bar. He'd gotten her name from one of the guys at work and switched into spy mode.

He ran her name through his formidable network and soon amassed a dossier. Shelley Jackson recently signed on as a cultural attaché for Coltech, her specialty being an interpreter of several Chinese dialects. The job dispatched her to points hither and yon on frequent diplomatic junkets; it was highly implausible he'd ever run into her at either of the factories, her sphere being of another cosmic order altogether. Her parents were well-off. She'd graduated from Western with honors and routinely traveled abroad since high school. She was single, although she apparently took frequent lovers—older, affluent men as a rule. Royce figured her for a pleasure seeker, a woman who thrilled in the proximity of power, rather than possessed of any agenda so mundane as gold digging or career advancement.

Tonight, she wore severe business attire—a gray skirt and white blouse—and chatted with an older fellow in a loose, silk shirt and suspenders; tall and lean with unruly black hair to the waist of his baggy, linen pants in a manner Royce identified as pure Eastern Euro-trash; a Balkan gangster prince at least a decade too old to dress as he did. Manny Poe, Manicevic Poe, something similar. An investment banker who occasionally frequented the billiards room. He put his mouth close to Shelley Jackson's ear and she laughed.

Shelley Jackson's dark hair was cropped in androgynous affectation, a style his old girlfriend Jenny had adopted near the end of their stormy run, and when she briefly glanced at him, Royce's cheeks warmed from the sensuous quality of her appraisal, the carnal thrill of his secret knowledge of how she glistened beneath her buttoned-down exterior. She returned her attention to the executive and didn't glance back again; not even to acknowledge the drink Royce had Gerald set before her.

He ordered a revolver of bourbon and tracked down Coyne in the billiards room. The man lay sprawled across a leather divan, his hair tousled, shirt unbuttoned to the breast, shoes propped on an ottoman. He smoked a Cohiba cigarette and watched two other men playing a game of baccarat. Royce didn't recognize either of them, they were in the fog that enveloped the world two feet beyond his center of gravity. He flopped across from Coyne and steadily gulped his stein of booze.

Coyne whistled softly. "Well, there's a sight. You look like a tiger what's gotten free of its pen."

They made small talk, reminiscing about college and their families back in the States, and as each spiraled deeper into drunkenness, Royce deftly steered the discussion to mother Mary and her social ring. Coyne expressed annoyance regarding his mother's newfound hobbies. "The damned busybody crones," he said.

"Who?"

"That's what Mom calls them. There's about a dozen of them—a tea party club without the tea. I asked her, 'Mom, isn't that a bit derogatory, referring to them as crones?' and she says, 'Oh no, that's what they call themselves.' I guess one of the ladies, Agatha, is a hard-line feminist. Agatha goes on about patriarchal oppression, ageism—especially prejudice against old women—and similar natter. She convinces her elderly chums to take back the so-called epithets, like hag and crone and treat them as tools of empowerment." Mary spent a majority of her time with the ladies, which should've been a relief for Coyne, considering how worried he'd been to locate companionship for her in this new, alien environment; yet as the months had worn on, some indefinable element of their communal bonding disquieted him.

"Bingo and knitting," Royce said with boozy assurance. "I doubt it's anything to get stirred up about."

"I dunno. They resent my *lifestyle* choices; Mrs. Grant—you know, that wretched woman with the wheelchair—says it's a rejection of the female as partner and mate. Mom stays out till all hours—I caught her sneaking into the apartment around dawn last week. She acts like a rebellious teenager."

"Second childhood. Sounds like Agatha's reliving the Women's Movement and bringing your mom along for the ride."

"Maybe. Those friends of hers… I found out Agatha hired on with a company as a clerical administrator so she could move into the Arms—"

"You spied on your poor mother's friend? You devious fellow."

"She flew halfway across the world to live in *this exact building*. What the hell is up with that?"

Royce said, "I've seen them go out at night. Very late. Kind of odd, I thought."

"Oh, yeah. That's the procession. Crazy bitches."

"The what?"

"The Procession of the Black Sloth." Coyne puffed on his cigarette and exhaled toward the lazily revolving blades of the ceiling fan. "Agatha's a religious nutter; thinks of her group in spiritual terms. Mom says the sisterhood originates here in the East. A sort of passive-aggressive protest against centuries of male dominance, which seems rational enough, all things considered. Rebellion against foot-binding and the like. There's a concentration of true believers in this area come to make obeisance to a guru who lives in one of the slum tenements."

"Black sloth? I don't get it. Why a black sloth?"

"Jeez, Hawthorne, you should ask them. I don't even remember if it's a sloth. It might be a black weasel or a marmot."

"Yeah, never mind. I probably don't want to know anything about a black weasel," Royce said.

Coyne swished the ice in his whiskey, concentrating on the glass with utter melancholy. "Anyway, Agatha's into these late-night strolls. Moon goddess nonsense, or some such effing crap. I'm not much for religion."

"Me neither. Sunday school hangovers lasted a lifetime."

"Soon as I escaped parochial, I burned my boy's suit and never looked back. Mom was raised Catholic, see; she goes to mass at the cathedral on Bonham. This hoodoo isn't like her."

Mama's boy. Royce filed that away, too. "Don't worry. My own dear mum went through a New Age period. She wanted to commune with Atlanteans." Which was a convenient lie to put Coyne at ease, to cement their bonding moment. His mother had been an Easter and Christmas Lutheran and that was the extent of her spirituality. She'd been more interested in the PTA and the little wine and cheese parties her friends held while pretending to have a weekly reading circle. His dad referred to it as her weekly "get loaded and gossip" circle. "Before you know it, it'll be back to bunt cakes and macramé. Just this morning I saw a bunch of them huddled outside playing canasta."

"Yeah, maybe. Say, c'mon over for lunch with us tomorrow. I'm barbecuing. You like ribs, don't you? Mrs. Ward and a couple of her cronies will be there. You can meet my mom, see what I mean."

"Uh—" Royce hurriedly considered possible excuses.

"For the love of Baby Jesus, I'm begging you," Coyne said. "You can't leave me alone with them."

Royce grudgingly agreed, although he actually welcomed the opportunity to chat with Mary Coyne and Mrs. Ward. Perhaps some unexpected providence would result.

He fixed an Irish coffee and sipped it while sitting in the gloom of his kitchen. The kitchen was spotless except for his dinner plate in the sink, a segmented trail of cigarette ashes on the table, and a mussed edition of the *I Ching* he'd accidentally kicked under a chair. Its pages were coming unglued and he'd left thumbprints on them, but couldn't call to mind anything of substance. The symbols were pretty and meaningless. He'd bought a dozen similar works when he first arrived in the city; just went to the biggest chain bookstore he could find and swept them into his basket along with tourist pamphlets, cookbooks and a couple regional histories in hardback. Eastern philosophy wasn't his bag; he did it because that's how it went wherever he stayed for any real duration. Being the perfect social chameleon demanded attention to the minute.

Presently, the familiar, discordant strains of Mrs. Ward's flute filtered through the wall and drew him into the clammy, dank air. When he stepped through the sliding glass door, the awful piping ceased mid-note, as if to accentuate a dramatic pause. He stood on the balcony and regarded the spectral façades of the Raleigh Arms. The pool glowed dully, a cradle of stagnant phosphorescence like mother of pearl embedded in black mud on the sea bottom. The water reflected upon the surrounding tile, the iron slats of the courtyard gate and the abutting concrete walls. Across the way, Coyne's apartment lay dark. However, a dim lamp flickered in the Jackson woman's window, and he waited a long time in the damp smog to catch a glimpse of her. The light snuffed abruptly. He lingered a moment, then went unsteadily inside.

He dozed in his chair, flicking through the five hundred channels advertised in his digital cable package. Old war movies and serials from America, big-game hunting and sports fishing, talk shows, the regular junk. He waded through the weird local stuff shot in low def at raves, and incomprehensible talent shows that were a cross between performance art and improv. Then there was the Asian horror cinema, which was gaining popularity abroad, but left Royce cold. He lingered on one bizarre scene: A man in office clothes shuffled into a vast cavern and approached what soon resolved as a mountain of knife blades. The man raised his hands, fingers bent into claws, and threw his head back and wailed, an Asian Charlton Heston. The man fell to his knees, still wailing, and crawled to the mountain of knives. On all fours, he began to climb.

Royce really, really hated horror, and the Eastern garbage wasn't any better than the kind they served in Hollywood. He surfed to a game show. Everyone was Asian: the audience, the announcer, the contestants, except for an American, a white guy in his fifties who wore a ten-gallon hat, a bolo tie and a well-cut suit. He was the spitting image of a guy who'd operated a salvage yard in Royce's home town. The contestants were taking turns answering questions highlighted on large board. When somebody got a question right, a rabidly grinning hostess in a polka-dot summer dress hopped in place and waved her tiny hands in abject joy. The words on the board were Chinese characters. Royce found he could get the gist through body language and deduction. It was surreal to watch the American cowboy's mouth move and hear Chinese come out. The man answered enough questions correctly and lights flashed, klaxons blared and parti-colored streamers billowed down in a storm. The grinning hostess scurried to the American and pinned gaudy ribbons to his breast while the host leaned on his podium and gabbled frenetically. The curtains slowly raised to reveal a shiny new jet ski.

Royce thought he'd cheerfully kill anybody who drove a pin through his twelve-hundred-dollar suit. The cowboy looked down at his breast, apparently sharing Royce's sentiment. The cowboy grabbed the hostess by her ponytail and jerked her toward him. He began punching her head. It was a farce, it couldn't be real, not with the way her arms and legs flew around like a crash dummy pitched through a windshield.

The TV image wavered and shrank and the people were folded into themselves. The lights in the apartment went out. The air conditioner whined to a stop and the room lay as dark and silent as a vacuum. He dopily marveled at the feeling of being cast adrift. Little by little, his eyes adjusted and signs of life penetrated the blackout: disjointed voices echoing from afar, the dim thump of bodies moving in the apartments above his own, the sullen orange glow of the city skyline.

A series of malformed thuds rattled glasses in a cupboard. He lay there, groggily staring into the gloom, trying to shake the lethargy of booze and bone-weariness, the quicksand gravity of his recliner. There came another sound, a low, raspy warble: a frog calling from the dark. The little beasts often hopped in from the surrounding parks, the encroaching marshland, and made their homes in the wet shadows along the pool until housekeeping came along with nets and buckets and carried them away. This vocalization was much deeper, more resonant and suggestive of inordinate size. However, as the sound repeated, its utterance was more a croak than the glottal wheeze and gasp of some other creature; almost a moan.

Thud. Someone struck his door with a fist. He reached over and tried the lamp, but the switch clicked, dead, so he fumbled through the apartment, flipping other useless light switches as he went. The air pressed him, dank and smothering as a foul, wet blanket.

Royce navigated the minefield of his apartment without breaking anything and staggered into the door and almost opened it before he sobered enough to remember where he was and who might be on the other side: corrupt government agents; terrorists; bandits; any of a dozen kinds of riffraff who might mean him bodily harm. He knocked a shade from a lamp, gripped it in his left hand. He located the peephole by touch and screwed his eye against the opening, not expecting to see much, if anything. A trickle of yellow light suffused the hall, its origin probably the threshold of some open apartment door. Someone wept, their faint moans emanating from a hidden source. The sobs were muffled.

He unlocked the door and stuck his head out. One of his neighbors, the German software designer, a couple doors down and across the way, had indeed set a paper lantern on the mat in the hall and Royce guessed the man probably stumbled off to wake the superintendent. The German was a can-do sort, the sort to burn the midnight oil. He'd been around since Hong Kong went back to the Chinese and was a veteran of these all too frequent LRA adventures.

Precisely at the outer ring of lamp light, a big lumpy sack slid and bumped along the floor, disappearing into the dark. Slippers rasped against tile and the sob sounded again, farther away, descending into the depths of the building. A man on another floor shouted foreign curses that echoed down through the grates and vents; these were answered in kind in a groundswell of slamming doors and broom handles rapped against pipes, grievances kindled by the humidity and heat, the ungodliness of the hour.

"Elvira?" Even as Royce invoked the name, chills raced along his arms; he clenched the muscles of his buttocks. He tiptoed a few steps down the hallway, compelled against his better judgment. The passage seemed to expand and contract with his pulse, as if he were being squeezed through an artery. He stooped to retrieve a wig where it had fallen upon the dingy floor. The wig was lush and black in his hands and smelled of rank cologne and cigarettes. The unwholesome intimacy of touching it sent thrills through his already weak stomach.

He went to bed and was asleep in moments despite, or perhaps in response to, the bizarre and somewhat shocking encounters of the evening.

Shelley Jackson, warm and slick and hungry as death, slipped under the covers. She kissed him and worked her hand beneath the waistband of his pajamas. She rolled atop him. Her eyes were lidless stones. Her throat bulged, impossibly bulbous, a pearly sac. She croaked softly and her frigid tongue unspooled into his mouth before she brought a bag down to cover his head. When the rough burlap closed over Royce's face, he inhaled to scream and Coyne, who replaced Shelley Jackson somehow, put a sticky finger against his lips, a shushing gesture that communicated a world of terror. They were mashed together, their breaths humid in the suffocating enclosure, the tightening ring. Coyne's face was also sticky; it seeped and ran like syrup from the broken skin of a peach.

Shh, Coyne whispered. *For God's sake.*

Royce clawed at the bag, woke thrashing and half-crazed with terror.

The next morning Royce noticed odd smudges on the outer panel of his apartment door; distorted imprints, as if someone had stamped his or her muddy face against the wood. One was near the top of the frame; two more below his knees. He grabbed a camera and snapped a few shots, such was his disquiet. After, he rang the front desk and a custodian soon arrived with a bucket and a sponge to wipe the unseemly marks away. It took the man over an hour of diligent scrubbing. The marks were stubborn.

Royce visited Shea and mentioned he'd enjoy meeting Ms. Jackson. Shea guffawed and said she wasn't exactly hard to get, but here was an invitation to a company soiree, all the same. Jackson would be there to smooth the way with the Chinese, who, like men anywhere, were amenable to a pretty face and a flash of cleavage.

Meanwhile, lunch with the Coynes proved a bizarre affair. Royce arrived a few minutes early with a bottle of wine and a bouquet of cheap flowers he'd picked up at the grocery. He said hello to Mary Coyne, who answered the door in a bulky sweater and fleece pants. "I'm frightfully chilled in this climate," she said, indicating her attire, and indeed her hands were cold in his. "Bad circulation. Since I was a girl I've had bad circulation. Just terrible. A condition, you see. My, aren't you handsome today."

Royce wore a polo shirt and cargo pants. He'd taken time to get his mustache trimmed at the salon and spent several minutes rehearsing sincerity before the mirror. In his experience, elderly women were readily disarmed by young men who dressed and smelled nice. Polite, well-groomed lads were considered trustworthy. He also wore the wig he'd taken from the hall and was mystified by his compulsion to do so. His own hair was dark, and, yes, thinning a bit at the crown, yet not unattractive considering he kept in decent shape with light calisthenics, a few laps here and there on the treadmill at the gym.

God, it's started. Cuckoo time. Yeah, yeah—it's happened before. You really go bugshit on these missions, man. That job on the oil refinery. You wore the Slav's corduroy jacket for a month. And that one guy, the dude from Arkansas, you swiped his cowboy boots and the buckle with the razorback. Why do you do shit like that? It's the chameleon trip, isn't it? How did you score their personal belongs, by the way? They ran out on their jobs, just lit out without a goodbye or screw you. Funny how that works…Where do suppose this wig comes from? I'm sure it'll be a surprise.

It was hardly just the wig. Only last week he'd come across an expensive wristwatch and a class ring inside his safe and had no idea how they got there. When he worked out these items had belonged to Ted K., the boring guy who'd shared his flight into Hong Kong, he felt ill again, just like he'd been sick the previous night. He managed to resist the urge to wear the ring and the watch, and tossed them into a Dumpster instead. He considered, and not for the first time, it might be wise to visit a therapist and discuss whatever subconscious demons were eating him. The main reason he didn't was primarily because he already knew what the doctor would say—a man could hardly expect to live a double life without facing a few consequences.

Mary accepted the flowers, exclaiming it wasn't necessary. "We're only having lunch, for goodness sake!" She rushed into the kitchen to pare the stems and get them into a vase, calling out that Brendan was on the deck. Royce followed the odor of charcoal and sizzling beef to the terrace where Coyne turned fat slabs of beef on the grill with a big prong.

Coyne handed him a beer from the ice chest and waved at a patio chair. He squinted at Royce, and frowned. "Is that a wig?" And when Royce neither confirmed nor denied this, he frowned again and let the subject drop, although he shot odd glances for the remainder of the afternoon, his expression a mixture of petulance and fascination.

They sat and drank beer and smoked cigarettes and made small talk about the weather and work, until the rest of the lunch party arrived. Mrs. Ward slouched into the apartment in a red and gold mandarin gown that clung and cleaved to her bulging thighs, the rounded curve of her belly. Her rose-lipped mouth grimaced and gaped, and slightly crossed eyes twitched with astigmatism.

Royce carefully shook her fleshy hand and tried not to stare at the wattles of her neck or the wen on her chin.

"Mm-hrmm, my you *are* certainly a handsome one," Mrs. Ward said, and her voice slid forth, gravelly and low, descending to a murmur at the end of the sentence. She licked her lips and grinned with half her mouth, lending her the aspect of someone who'd suffered a minor stroke. "Lila, isn't he a handsome boy? A bit long in the tooth for a boy, but you take my meaning."

"Why, my stars, yes." Lila Tuttle emerged from Mrs. Ward's shadow, a moon orbiting its planet; frail and wrinkled and bent as a twig, she smiled ceaselessly and with vacuous conviction. She wore a shawl wrapped around her head and clutched an ancient handbag to her bony breast. "Lovely to meet you, Mr. Hawthorne. Lovely, lovely indeed." She pecked a lock of his hair with a long, hooked nail the color of a chicken's foot, and tittered.

The merry group retired to the kitchenette for plates of ribs and steins of Sapporo beer Coyne had imported from Japan. None of the elderly women was particularly fastidious in regards to tucking into the meal. Mrs. Ward gnawed at the bones with an almost sexual intensity that called to mind the hoary old painting of *Saturn* chewing his hapless children to bits. Mrs. Tuttle and Mrs. Coyne followed suit. This concordance of slurping and smacking in lieu of conversation turned his stomach.

"What are you reading today, Mrs. Coyne?" Royce said by way of distraction from the unsavory relish of the diners. He noted the Coynes kept many books on hand; dozens of paperbacks and magazines were scattered about the apartment; romances and travelogues on the main, and older, clothbound tomes stacked on a floor-to-ceiling rack in the living room beside the television. He recognized the faux mahogany shelf as the exact model he himself had purchased from an upscale department store.

Mrs. Coyne and Mrs. Tuttle twittered and tee-heed over some romantic clap-trap they'd been perusing. Then, Mrs. Ward said, "I'm enjoying *Journey to the West*. Have you ever read that one, Mr. Hawthorne?"

"It sounds familiar."

"Mrmm-hmm, a classic, I daresay. My father was something of a bibliophile. He worked for the great museums in England and Germany. They sent him to the four corners after antique manuscripts. A few he kept for his library at home, and some of these he read aloud to me when I was a child. His copy of *Journey to the West* is exceedingly rare, perhaps an original. Father related it to me in Mandarin, no less."

Coyne snorted and Royce could tell the man was more than a touch drunk from all the Sapporo he'd been downing. "I find that difficult to swallow, Mrs. Ward. An extant copy of *Journey to the West* would fetch a fortune on the collectors' market. Surely you'd have cashed in by now."

"You speak Mandarin?" Royce said quickly. "And what else, I wonder."

Mrs. Ward shrugged and smiled into her napkin. "I dabble here and there; enough to get by in the country if I'm ever stranded on the mainland. Are you married, Mr. Hawthorne?"

"Divorced. The traveling life doesn't agree with everyone." Actually, Royce had lived with Jenny, the future orthodontist, for several years, but he'd never actually gone so far as marriage. He was interested to see her reaction. That, and when it came to his personal history, he was a habitual liar. "Why do you ask?"

"No reason, really. And children? You don't seem the type, but then who knows?"

"I hate children."

"Do tell. Don't we all, eh?" Mrs. Ward licked a bone; her tongue lolled overlong and came to a point. She probed and teased forth the marrow. Her face seemed a feeble mask slipped over the crude geometry of some atavistic visage. Her inflection remained neutral. "Not much call for children in this modern world, I suppose. Nor marriage. The need for fecundity has passed into twilight, yea."

"I have three daughters," Mrs. Tuttle said. She counted her crooked fingers: "and eight, wait, nine grandchildren. Angels, they are. Mary?"

"Only Brendan. He was quite enough, I assure you." Mrs. Coyne crinkled her cheeks to soften the barb. Royce thought he glimpsed a darker current beneath kindly seams and tender wrinkles, a flex of the iris like a shard of ice heeling over into the depths. It was not difficult to envision the source of her jovial bitterness; perhaps a deep, ragged cesarean scar, a white fissure ripped along the once-tanned axis of her bathing beauty abdomen. Baby Brendan would've consumed her best years; frightened away the pretty men, repaid her maternal generosity with shriveled breasts whence his greedy mouth had sucked dry all semblance of taut youth.

"Is that why you've journeyed to the East, Mrs. Ward? To free your sisters from the yoke of institutional patriarchy?" Royce said, averting his gaze from Mary Coyne's flaccid chest. He shuddered at the unbidden image of infant Brendan feasting there; a fat, red leech.

"Watch yourself, dear Brendan. This one's a tricky devil." Mrs. Ward patted Coyne's arm, although the man was so deep into his cups Royce doubted he understood the implicit warning.

Can she know? How in the hell could she? Royce gulped beer to cover his discomfort and confusion. "I'm hardly a devil, Mrs. Ward. A humble cog in the great machine and no more."

"We know our hell-dwellers, and you are certainly one. Girls?"

"Oh, yes," Mrs. Tuttle said and Mrs. Coyne echoed the sentiment. "A handsome white devil!"

"Don't worry, dear," Mrs. Ward said. "Nothing personal—all white men are devils here. Especially the British and the Canadians. You aren't a Canuck, thank heavens."

"Yeah, thank God for something," Royce said, relaxing slightly.

Lunch petered out after that. Coyne brooded and the old women nattered about cards, shopping and whose kids were doing what. Royce excused himself. Mrs. Ward took his elbow at the door. She said, "You should do more than window shop."

"Excuse me?" Royce said.

"Miss Jackson. The girl in 333. She's very charming. You should take a chance. I think the two of you have common interests. She's a bird watcher."

"I don't understand what you mean, Mrs. Ward." Royce kept smiling, kept playing it cool. *What the hell is your game, lady?*

"Don't you?" A shadow crossed her face. Her eyes congealed in their sockets. "Try to join us at one of our weeklies. Miss Jackson has promised to come make the acquaintance of my circle."

"Oh, um, sure. I'll have to drop by, then."

"Yes. Please do that." She released his arm and extended him a motherly pat on the cheek. Her thick, sharp thumbnail pressed lightly into the flesh under the hinge of his jaw and Royce's head swam with the childhood memory of a butcher shop, and the butcher in his ruddy apron sizing up the raw red meat, slapping it with his left hand, bringing the cleaver with the right, and whistling a wry, cheerless tune while customers waited in a line, batting the occasional circling fly with their newspapers, their parasols or panama hats.

Royce said goodbye, and as he escaped into the hall, Mrs. Ward leaned out and said, "Safe travels. Oh, and Mr. Hawthorne, do be careful about answering your door at night, hmm? In this place, you never know who might come calling." She shut the door on his answer.

He'd been combing his stacks of video and photographic material in a mindless evening ritual held over from one of his first cases, when he turned up a cartridge labeled CHU/6. Chu's series of surveillance tapes ended at number five. Royce scratched his head and ran the feed through his television so he could relax in his armchair with the lights turned down.

Right away, he decided he'd definitely made some odd labeling error.

This wasn't a surveillance tape, but rather a homemade documentary. The documentary was filmed on a handheld and the picture shook as the camera operator walked. An old, old heavyset Chinese woman in a nurse's pinafore was giving the unseen narrator a tour of what seemed to be an abandoned sanitarium. She carried a flashlight and swept its watery beam over ceilings that leaked plaster and stringers of wiring. Piles of debris littered the corridor. The corridor was notched by small white iron doors. She stopped at each door, pointed and muttered into the camera. Dubbing was poor and her mouth and the sound from her mouth moved at different speeds.

"Di Yu," the nurse said in a hoarse monotone. "Di Yu. Di Yu."

When the camera zoomed in on her pointing finger, one could resolve metal placards with lettering. 2: CHAMBER OF GRINDING, said one. 8: CHAMBER OF MOUNTAIN OF KNIVES, said another. "Di Yu. Di Yu," the nurse said. Her face was white and soft as dough, except for her eyes and mouth, which were black. "Di Yu. Di Yu." She came to a larger door set into a slab of masonry. The door was barred and heavily corroded by rust. Its placard read: BLACK SLOTH HELL.

"Aunt CJ." Royce was certain. That was his dearly departed Aunt Carole Joyce under the chalky paint. No, no, that wasn't right. It was Mrs. Ward, how could he have missed the malice in her eyes, her awkward gait?

A jumble of misaligned frames heralded a scene change, which slowly resolved as the interior of a room. Darkness prevailed except for a glass cube spotlighted against a black backdrop. The cube was a museum display on the order Royce recognized from childhood visits to the Met, the kind of massive box intended to house dinosaur exhibits. Shadow-figures assembled at the base of the display, dwarfed by its immensity, the sheer girth of the specimen preserved within. He'd seen the animal on a grade school field trip, had seen it since in a dozen evil dreams, this father of cold sweats and night terrors. The thing reared in excess of twenty-feet high; it might've snapped the back of an elephant, torn the tops from trees. Its pelt was oily and black. Its claws were also black and hooked like daggers. The metal tag on the exhibit said: *Megatherium. S. America, ca Pleistocene epoch.*

There was a difference from Royce's personal beast, however. This relic, this patent fabrication, a paleontologist's reconstruction with its artificial fur and sawdust stuffing, was a hybrid of the museum curiosity he'd seen in the tour group with all the other bored sixth graders. Vaguely toadlike, somehow obscene; its shape altered for the worse as shadows moved across its monstrous bulk.

The camera swooped in tight. Dozens of naked men and women pressed against the base, hands splayed and grasping. Their skins sagged and drooped from the relentless gravity of age. More ancients shuffled and crawled from the outer darkness to prostrate themselves before the idol, and in their eagerness to worship, they pressed the first rank and crushed them until blood shot against the glass. The petitioners moaned and their cries echoed the bestial croaks he'd heard in the night outside his door.

Mrs. Ward stood among the mewling throng, her white face and white pinafore shining. "Di Yu. Di Yu." The camera zoomed tighter, tighter, focused upon her mouth, and the tape ended.

Royce's skull felt like an anvil. He rose to make for the bathroom and almost tripped over a body. Before he could yell, lights came up, revealing the bald furnishings of a decrepit theater. The projector was still shuttering, splashing arcane symbols on the screen. A half-dozen filmgoers ignored him as they retrieved jackets and hats and squelched along the seedy aisles toward the exits.

He rushed to the lobby and accosted the girl sweeping popcorn from the carpet. She recoiled from his urgent demands for information. What theater was this? When had he arrived? Who'd brought him here? She spoke no English. Her manager didn't know much English either, was only able to relate the name of the theater—The Monsoon Gallery, which specialized in independent and art films. The man wrung his hands and implored Royce to leave in peace. There was no record of a ticket transaction; perhaps he'd been drinking and stumbled in through the side door, yes? Many fine bars were located nearby, much action!

The manager's bewilderment and distress seemed genuine.

Royce gave up haranguing him and wandered into the street. It was nearly eleven PM. According to his watch, he'd misplaced about four hours. He caught a taxi and rode the twenty-odd blocks back to the compound. Unsurprisingly, the security at the gate had no record of his leaving the LRA that evening.

He locked himself in the apartment and searched for the tape. Two hours of ransacking his desk and file cabinets, the dozen or so cardboard boxes jammed in a closet, proved fruitless. In the end, he slumped at the kitchen table and covered his face with his hands. Television laughter came through the vents.

Ming Cho, chief liaison to a mainland conglomerate that contracted Coltech to manufacture jet navigational computers, had invited a bunch of management types to dinner at a Mandarin restaurant. They arrived late because of traffic. Tardiness was a major faux pas in China; fortunately, Ming proved extremely acclimated to Westerners' legendary indiscretions and he cut them some slack. He and his cadre of flunkies arranged an elaborate banquet: music, pretty dancing girls, karaoke.

Marty James climbed on the stage at one point, his three-hundred-dollar haircut mussed from the attentions of the party girls, his tie loosened so it drooped low across his considerable belly, and led the restaurant in a rousing chorus of "Camp Town Races" until he almost pitched head over heels into the front row of diners; Cho and Liu Zhu came to the rescue and dragged him back to the table, the trio red-faced and nearly bawling from exertion and hilarity. Zhu kept refilling his glass, any glass within reach, with rice wine, shouting, "Gombay! Gombay!" the Chinese equivalent of "Bottoms up!" The Americans who responded were dropping like flies. Royce managed a few half-shouted pleasantries with the lovely and alluring Ms. Jackson. Her handshake was warmer than her eyes or her impersonal smile. She'd arrived in a white dress cut down the center and slashed up the flanks and the men seemed to have trouble keeping their mouths shut.

There was an exception, however. About two-thirds of the way through the meal Royce noticed Bill Zander—Billy Zed, the resident Brits called him—staring at the crowd. They'd pulled two tables together and barely had enough room for the whole party. Bill was down at the end. Royce couldn't ask him who he was looking at without shouting. He ignored Bill for a while, but then the junior production manager made an awful expression. It reminded Royce of candid photos taken at amusement parks of people on the rides, some of which were classic studies in human terror and vulnerability.

Such was Bill's expression. His face sagged and his mouth did the same. For a second Royce thought Bill would begin to shriek right there in that packed restaurant.

Oh, God, how much has that silly s.o.b. had to drink? Royce craned his neck to see what the hell was going on. It seemed as if Bill was staring at a table full of Germans. Nothing odd about those people, except they were drunk and noisy, probably competing with the Coltech crowd. Gradually, he concluded Bill wasn't looking at the other table; he'd focused on a copse of rubber plants: big specimens in ornamental clay pots. The restaurant could've doubled as rainforest on a movie stage; yards of exotic plants, bamboo and hanging vines. Groupers and lobsters drifted in dim aquariums—one picked out one's own dinner and a guy with a net on a pole scooped it up and hustled it into the kitchen. He didn't spot anything particularly unusual and Bill eventually settled down, although he drank enough of the house whiskey to put an Irishman in a coma.

When the party finally staggered outside to load into cabs, he caught Bill's arm and asked if he felt all right. The man was so boozy, he'd gone cross-eyed. Bill clutched Royce's coat and pulled him close and whispered he'd seen something in the rubber plants. He slobbered gibberish on Royce's collar, whimpering about children, terrible little beasts. Bill's expression raised the hairs on the back of Royce's arms.

Shea privately informed him Bill had partaken earlier of some particularly potent Thai grass they'd gotten from a Cambodian in the Mount Victoria region. Allegedly, the stuff carried an LSD-class wallop with a plethora of nasty side effects—including total, all-consuming paranoia. Bill became incomprehensible and started singing pieces of the Chinese pop song he'd mangled during his turn at karaoke. Royce and Shea carried him to the curb. He puked all over his pants and they packed him into the cab. His luckless compatriots protested mightily and tried to pitch him back into the street. They might've succeeded, except Royce and Shea pressed their bodies against the door until the taxi rolled away into the bright scrum of traffic.

Royce offered to share a ride with Shelley Jackson. She raised a brow at the spittle on his collar and declined, joining forces with Shea, James and Cho as they went club-hopping in a company limousine.

Everybody forgot about him standing in the rain before the restaurant exit. There were no more taxis. He stuck his hands in his pockets and let the sidewalk crowd sweep him in the direction of home away from home.

Midnight found Royce and Coyne, a disconsolate pair, lounging poolside. Balmy drizzle cut through the smog, plastered their hair, their clothes, glittered in puddles in the dips of the tiles. Neither of them were particularly sober; however, as Coyne pointed out early on, he wasn't nearly as drunk as he'd have preferred. He'd returned from a black tie affair thrown by some Texas tycoon. The fellow who invited him, a foxy corporate lawyer, disappeared on the arm of some other guy. Aggrieved by this unceremonious treatment, Coyne did his best to decimate the open bar. After a couple loud arguments with better-dressed, better-connected guests, he got tossed into the street by a squad of bull-necked security people and ended up walking two miles back to the safety of the LRA. An ill-advised shortcut through the park resulted in his tripping over a bush and sliding on his ass down a small hill.

He sat with his head lowered, his white shirt splashed with mud, dinner jacket a sodden lump between his feet. He'd removed his shoes and socks and dipped his feet to the pants cuff into the pool water.

Water rolled in its shallow basin, scuffed by the rain and an occasional gust, and slopped over the rim onto the deck. Shelley Jackson's light blinked on and silhouettes moved against the drapes. He cursed, and wondered wherefrom this irrational jealousy.

"Behold!" Coyne said with a sarcastic flourish.

Figures emerged from the building, pale and wan and silent as ghosts. He recognized them: Mrs. Degive from 129, tall and hollow-eyed, her nightgown hung drenched as if she'd crawled from a shipwreck onto some night shore; Mrs. Yarbro and Mrs. Tuttle shuffling together like recently separated Siamese twins; and Mrs. Cardin, tapping with her cane, free hand to the hole in her throat. They gravitated toward the pool, shambling with empty determination (except for poor, crippled Mrs. Grant; she humped along the ground like a centipede): the women bore the witless expressions of sleepwalkers, their spectral forms lighted by undulating reflections from the shallows.

Agatha Ward coalesced near the dense shadows in the courtyard entrance and winded a brief, decadent trill on her panpipe. Her face was dark and convulsed; the face of a medieval goodwife transfixed in agonizing labor. At her side hunched a lean, pale youth, nude but for a pair of goggles on a strap around his neck, and a pair of immodestly snug swim trunks. He stood, eyes to the ground, awkwardly bowed at elbows and knees. His ankles and wrists were apparently bound. His head was shaved and it shone in the eerie light.

Agatha bared her teeth, glared blindly. She opened a service door inset between the entry arch and a shrub, and the women filed through into darkness. She went last, leading the youth by his wrist; the boy half hopped, half staggered. The door shut behind them, its edges vanishing neatly as the edges of a spider's trap.

"Oh my God." Royce blinked water from his lashes. "I've seen them down here a few times, but I never got a good look at…Was that the—what did you call it?"

"Yeah," Coyne said. "What've I been saying? The old broads are effing creepy."

"Who the hell was the kid with them?"

"I dunno about the kid. One of those kinky buggers from a sex club, I bet. The witches are gonna use him in a fertility rite. 'Course their snatches likely got cobwebs growing in 'em, so a lotta good it'll do."

"You're kidding. You mean they fuck him?"

"Who knows? Why not? This is the East, my friend. Freaky shit all around us, all the time."

Royce tasted acid. He found a cigarette and spent a few long moments lighting it in the rain. His hand shook. "My brother was a swimmer. Good body, like that kid."

"Yeah?"

"Yeah. Search and rescue diver for the Coast Guard." Royce nodded and dragged on his cigarette until the smoke scorched his lungs and he came up gasping. "He died. Good looking kid. Left a lot of girls crying." They sat like that for a while. Finally, Royce said, "God, that's too weird for me. Where'd they go?"

"Huh? Inside."

"I know they went inside. I thought they usually went out, into the community."

"What, you think the bus to the casino runs this late? Ask the schmucks at the gate if you wanna know." Coyne chuckled bitterly and splashed his foot. "Who cares, man? Who gives a shit, anyway? Aren't you sick of this place yet? A party every night. Rich slants with bad skin and worse teeth holding court. Buncha effing hyenas. Give a brother a drag?"

Royce handed him the cigarette. He immediately thought of long-lost Chu and the honking brays of laughter; of the mainland business partners who'd attended the dinner, the slyly insouciant glances they'd shot Shea and James, these latter worthies grown sleek and sanguine with food and wine, and complacency; wild pigs softened from their more vicious natures. "Hyenas and boars," he said. "And not a lion in sight."

Soon it grew cool and they were out of cigarettes. Each mumbled his farewells and tottered off to bed. Royce lay on his back, still dressed in his soaked clothes and shivering from a chill. In the twilight divide between waking and dreaming, he replayed the bizarre tableaux at the pool a hundred times. The boy looked over his shoulder and Royce met his brother's eyes, his frightened cow eyes...

The next Saturday mixer got started earlier than usual. Royce straggled in from a meeting with his local support crew and saw a crowd gathered near the entrance to the ballroom and community annex. He slipped through to his apartment and laid out some casual evening wear and then took a quick shower, contemplating the merits of making an appearance downstairs.

An email message from an unknown sender blinked in the inbox when he climbed from the shower; it had been piped through a secondary account known only to his handlers in Atlanta. He opened the message with a laptop reserved for correspondence that might compromise the sensitive documents on his primary computer. Encryptions were made to be broken; such was the axiom of a journeyman intelligence officer he'd interned under after college. Royce kept four computers on the premises, each with a specific backup or decoy function, each protected with the latest and greatest high-tech ciphers the lab boys could devise. Their hard drives could be wiped at the press of a key.

The message itself was blank with an attached video file. The label said: M.POE.; D. ANDREWS; J. STEVENS. CHAMBER OF MAGGOTS. His heart began to speed up. Royce clicked it, watched the video begin to load. He lighted a cigarette and went to the terrace. It was a calm evening. People continued to gather around buffet tables set up in the quadrangle. Electric light poured through the open doors of the community annex. Orchestra music from the ballroom and bits of conversation drifted past him, carried toward a surge of stars that blazed through breaks in the omnipresent smog. The Saturday mixer was generally a muted affair, an attraction for the geriatric set and a few young lonely singles. Agatha Ward had secured a sextet from the philharmonic and it had drawn this lively crowd of suits and dresses, among these an amazing number of couples who hadn't yet achieved the half-century mark.

He crushed out his cigarette, returned to the computer, sat patiently until the video loaded and a slightly unfocused image flickered on the monitor: black and white, interrupted by wavery lines and occasional fuzz; probably shot by a security camera.

A garbled voice intoned, "*Those who perform crooked deeds and malpractice are thus served.*"

The location appeared to be a large, drab room; a storage area, perhaps. It possessed concrete walls and floor, a dangling bulb swollen with feeble light. The bulb swung gently, casting shadows at weird angles. A trio of figures stood in a loose triangle near the center of the room; Royce couldn't discern their genders because of the bad lighting and the individuals' voluminous garb. They wore heavy robes or dresses; their faces were obscured by cowls.

What the hell is this? He didn't like it for several reasons, not the least of which being the anonymity of the sender. This, and the footage with its isolated stage and motionless actors, the enigmatic intention of whoever lurked behind the camera, evoked a sense of creeping dread. Several minutes passed and the image remained static. Royce glanced at his watch, considered calling it quits and catching the tail end of the party. Agatha Ward had left an invitation suggesting Shelley Jackson would be in attendance. The prospect appealed to him despite the utter lack of encouragement Jackson had shown him thus far. He couldn't bear the idea of being alone with this eerie video. It reminded him too much of the last bizarre film he'd stumbled across, the one that precipitated, or was a product of, a delusional episode. He reached for the escape key.

The picture stuttered, shifted to a different camera angle, this one slightly off center and much closer to the figures. From this new, extreme perspective, he perceived minute twitches of hands and limbs, the abrupt shudder of a torso. Small chunks of something dislodged and fell. Straining to comprehend the bizarre nature of the image, a very bad thought occurred to him. He located his seldom used bifocals, unfolded them and slid them over his nose.

He trembled to realize from a telltale sliver of reflected light the figures were suspended from the ceiling by slender wires that terminated at their necks. He couldn't detect how these wires were attached.

A hangman's noose? A fishing hook in the spine? A film school prank? Their robes, their cowls, gray-white through the cheap lens, were not cloth at all, but rather colloidal masses of rice slathered to naked flesh. The rice squirmed upon them like a living, bloated thing. More gray-white pudding spread around the feet of the triad, flowing up from drains in the concrete floor. The closest figure raised an emaciated arm in a weak, swiping gesture at its face, and a charcoal-dark eye yawed wildly. The video ended.

M. Poe. Manichev Poe, the Balkan investment banker he'd seen at the Rover with Shelley Jackson. Manichev Poe of the open-collared shirts and long, black hair. He'd never heard of Andrews or Stevens. Doubtless they'd committed the sin of crooked deeds as well.

Royce swallowed hard and wondered briefly if he was going to be sick. He chewed on his knuckle. Once the fogs partially receded, he initiated the protocol to wipe the hard drive. Then he lifted the computer and carried it into the bathroom and smashed it repeatedly in the tub until only bits of circuit board and snags of wire remained.

The phone beeped for God knew how long before he shrugged off his daze and picked up. The line was dead by then and the display logged the caller as anonymous. He decided to fix a drink, but the scotch was gone and the last beer too; even the mini bottles of Christian Brothers he kept in the pantry, with the oatmeal, flour, and mouse traps.

Royce walked downstairs without recollection of forming the intent to leave his apartment. Full dark had come and the sodium lamps kicked on, masking the faces of the guests in shades of red and amber. He scooped several glasses of champagne from an unattended platter, retired to one of the small tables, and drank rapidly and with little pleasure.

Agatha Ward waded toward him, Shelley Jackson in tow. "Mr. Hawthorne! I presume you remember Miss Jackson. I'm thrilled you decided to join us."

"Everybody was having such a swell time, I couldn't resist." He rose unsteadily and nodded at Shelley Jackson. "A pleasure to see you again."

Shelley Jackson was dressed in a mohair sweater. She radiated ennui. "I'm sure. Well, Agatha, thanks for the party. I've an early flight to Beijing—"

"Why don't you dears visit a moment while I attend to some crashingly dull social niceties?" Mrs. Ward smiled with implicit cruelty at the younger woman, ducked and bobbed in pantomime, and retreated.

"Damn it," Shelley Jackson said. She snapped her fingers at a melancholy waiter in a tuxedo jacket and bade him fetch her a double bourbon, neat. She downed it without a wince, eyed Royce hatefully, and demanded the bottle. She said to Royce, "Where'd we meet, anyway?"

"At that Mandarin place, the other night—"

"Yeah, right. The guy threw up on you." She chuckled, low and nasty. "Nice. I've seen you around, haven't I?"

"I live right up there." He pointed, but she didn't follow his gesture, concentrated on her bottle. The champagne was hitting him hard now; his cheeks were numb and he had to carefully enunciate. He plunged recklessly ahead and killed another glass, pouring it down his throat to stifle the sense of misery and helplessness.

"*Love* your hair," she said.

"Thanks," Royce said. They stood shoulder to shoulder; close enough he smelled her bath oils, the sweet exhaust of gin on her breath. "Cigarette?"

"No. They ruin your teeth."

He lighted one for himself, suppressed the urge to fidget with his lighter. After the silence between them dragged out, he said, "A mushroom walks into a bar—"

"Oh, shit."

"A mushroom walks into a bar. Sees this gorgeous woman sitting by herself. So he buys her a drink and asks if she'd like to dance. The woman looks him up and down and finally says no thanks. And this mushroom is pretty deflated, so he asks why not. The woman says it's nothing personal, 'I don't dance with mushrooms.' And he says, 'Oh, c'mon, I'm a real fungi!'"

She delicately wiped her mouth on the sleeve of her sweater. "Can you?"

"Dance? Sure. I learned to tango at charm school."

"I meant in your condition. You're pretty shit-faced. Besides, the band's calling it a night."

She was correct; the sextet began to break down their instruments and pack them toward the gatehouse. Royce sighed. "Maybe next time. The Rover has live music on weekends. If you like jazz hits rendered by girls whose English consists of "hello, mister" and most of the words to most of the songs—"

"Here's a better idea: Why don't we nip off to your place and have a nightcap."

"I'm out of stock" he said, trying for a light touch.

"Or better yet, let's skip all the bullshit. I'll get down on my knees and suck your cock. Does that work for you?" She tilted her head to meet his eyes. Her face was smooth and white and luminous.

Royce floundered for an appropriate response; between the horror show of a video, the half-magnum of pink champagne, and the surrealistic conversation, it took several seconds to deduce she'd been toying with him. Heat rushed through his skull and he overcame the nearly overwhelming urge to crack her across the face, to grab her shoulders and shake her until she rattled. His gorge rose; he forced his fingers to unclench. He said, "I suppose you're good with your mouth. James and Shea know talent when they see it, right?"

She chuckled and flipped the bottle underhand. It splashed in the pool. "Nighty-night, sweet prince. Go sleep it off, hey? You stink like a rat."

Rat? There was a provocative choice of words. Shelley Jackson and Agatha Ward must've compared notes. Maybe they knew something, maybe he'd slipped along the line; his work was art, not a perfect science, and he was far from flawless — especially of late. He was up to his neck in mistakes. For the first time in an age, he wanted to go home, whatever that meant. He could take a vacation, look up some of his college buddies, an old girlfriend or two with whom he hadn't managed to burn every bridge.

"Screw you, bitch. You look like a boy, anyway." Shelley Jackson was too far away to hear, but the morose waiter gave him a pitying look as he came to retrieve the empties. The man used one of the deck chairs to snag the bottle floating in the pool.

Agatha Ward stood near doors to the ballroom in a tight circle, which included the building superintendent, an elegant gentleman named Bertram Harris; Mrs. Tuttle; and several geezers Royce vaguely recognized from around the complex. Mrs. Ward waved to him as he listed for the elevator. Her body rippled and became transparent, revealing her skeleton suspended in its jelly. The bones were too long, too sinuous for a woman of such enormous girth; her spine recoiled like a chain of knives as her skull swiveled to track him. The mirage fanned outward and the crowd was abruptly transfigured into a mobile of skeletal X-rays. For an instant the flesh of his own hand gave way to showcase his finger bones, the metacarpal with its scar and the pins from a long-ago biking mishap in the Pyrenees, the slender tube of forearm—

Royce collapsed into the lift. When the doors parted, he'd gone completely rubbery and had to slide along the wall to his door. *Too much champagne.* Or something more sinister. He'd heard the cautionary tales about Mickeys in the wine, the date rape drugs kidnapers preferred. Worst case scenario, in a few hours Atlanta would receive a call from a disembodied voice demanding X amount for Royce's safe return. Maybe they'd send Atlanta a finger or an ear first, just to set the ground rules. If he worked for the Germans, or the French, or the Italians, there'd be no question about whether they'd cough up the ransom. American companies were more unpredictable. Next time, he'd definitely go with the Italians, just to be on the safe side.

Too much champagne, I'm fine, everything is fine. Full speed ahead, Royce, old bean. Kick the door shut. There's a boy.

Finally, he made it to the bed and sprawled on his back. He pawed at the phone in his pants pocket, unaware of who he might call at this late hour, who might gallop to his rescue, if not the police, and he knew from a thousand dirty deals the police were never to be trusted, but all feeling leaked from his fingers and a few moments later he fell unconscious.

Somewhere in the void of night Shelley Jackson crept into his bed. He jerked awake and shoved her to the floor in a moment of stark terror, his brain confused as to whether this was another nightmare, a hallucination fueled by his earlier kamikaze excesses. Shelley Jackson laughed crazily. A tendril of blood leaked from her nostril. The blue and red running lights of a low-flying helicopter traveled across the room, briefly illuminating the wildness of her expression, her feral, inhuman beauty.

Royce froze in a half-crouch upon the edge of the bed, now very much convinced this was the real deal for once, not a fever dream. A hundred thoughts crashed into each other, among them, *How the hell did she get in here?* He didn't have much of a chance to analyze the situation. As the light from the chopper dwindled, Shelley Jackson was blurred in the shadows and she sprang upon him, knocked him supine, twisting in his arms, wiry and ferocious. She ravished him with sloppy kisses and nipped his lips, his tongue. She tasted of liquor and blood and darkness. Her skin was damp and hot against his. Her hair was matted and tangled and smelled of animal sweat. She tore his clothes away and licked his chest and belly. As her frantic mouth sealed his cock and her tongue began to circle in tight, efficient strokes, he wondered whose bed she'd recently crawled from before tumbling into his. He came then and the thought was obliterated as he turned inside out.

Later, she straddled him, her sleek, powerful thighs locked against his hips, and rocked slowly, muscles shuddering, her teeth gleaming in the dark as she panted. Royce lay flattened and nearly lifeless from absolute exhaustion, yet his cock profoundly engorged as she took him in until his balls were tight against her ass. She groaned in Cantonese. Her palms ground into his chest and he winced, thinking dimly of the bruises sure to come. His gasp was cut short as she leaned down and clamped her hand over his mouth and nose and shut off his air. He bucked in pseudo orgasms, his hands prying at her wrist and forearm. No way could she maintain her grip; he thought this as fire turned his lungs to ash and black tracers shot through his brain.

Above the thunder in his ears a raucous, eager croaking resounded from the darkness and grew close. Half-formed shapes gathered around the bed, witness to his pathetic struggles. He glimpsed lank hair fanned across elongated breasts, and round paunches rugose as elephant hides. Withered lips fastened to his nipples, the span of his inner thigh. Mouths, toothless as hagfish, slobbered on him. He was dimly mortified and repulsed as his erection intensified and he came again so powerfully he thought his back might break.

He went deaf and blind and spun in clockwise revolutions, faster and faster until he was plunged down the drain into insoluble night.

"Black Weasel."

"Huh?" Royce's eyes were glued shut. Dull, cold light pressed against his lids. His mouth was dry and chapped. He'd curled into the fetal position; his entire body felt like it had been beaten with a club.

Shelley Jackson said, "I don't think it's black sloth. I think it's black weasel hell. A Buddhist punishment."

He covered his face with his arm. "Oh, boy. What?"

"You were raving."

"Oh," he said, and stuck his aching head under a pillow.

Shelley Jackson wouldn't let up. She said, "What's the worst predicament you've ever been in? Me, I got lost in Bangkok; drunk, drunk, drunk, don't you know; separated from my friends who actually knew their way around the goddamned rat warren. Some guys started following me, chased me into a really slummy part of town. The whole city is slummy, but this took the cake. Very spooky."

"But you made it." He licked his blistered lips, tried to clear the rust from his throat. The previous evening was becoming as distant and mysterious as the depths of the oubliette he'd once seen at a tourist castle in the Loire Valley. He had to piss in the worst way, yet his cock was so sore he dreaded the slightest movement. "You escaped their clutches."

"Did I?" Shelley Jackson's voice was scratchy. She snuggled her warm, solid weight against him, one leg flopped across his own. "All's well that ends well. I could be living in a bamboo box giving head to faceless sonsofbitches who pay for that sort of thing. I'm a lucky girl, then."

"White slavery isn't the trend. They probably wanted your kidneys."

"Not these sorry bastards, they don't. You weren't kidding when you said you were dry. I looked everywhere and nada. I need a drink."

Metal snicked and cigarette smoke coiled into Royce's nose. He moaned and held out his hand until she stuck the cigarette into his mouth for a long drag. He coughed hard enough his guts churned, but the nicotine rush began to do its magic straight away. Eventually he said, "I thought you didn't smoke." When no answer was forthcoming, he continued, "I'll tell you what I need. Coffee."

"Me too. Get up and make some."

They had coffee on the terrace; she in a set of his boxers and a white dress shirt; he wrapped in a towel. It was raining again. Gray clouds erased the city beyond the walls of the compound.

"How come you trashed your TV?"

Royce had to think on that. His TV? It came back to him then, how he'd been trying to find the news, but every channel was filled with either black static, or the repeating image of a chamber filled with dozens of screaming people. The latter was filmed at some distance so the actors were indistinct miniatures. The people screamed because they were strapped to tables, or slung from poles, or trapped inside small baskets. Torturers were quartering them with winches and chains, stabbing them with barbed prongs, or slowly sawing them to pieces. And childlike figures cowered beneath the killing tables in the lakes of gore, bloated bellies like famine victims, and unnaturally slender necks—cranes' necks—and alabaster faces that shone with pure, ravenous horror. Channel after channel of this, and somewhere in the confusion the remote died and the images ran together, faster and faster, and the sounds—! He'd flown into a vicious rage and speared the monitor with one of the fancy plastic kitchen chairs. When was this? A week ago? Two? The little details kept slipping his mind.

Royce said, "Something on the news pissed me off."

"You crazy, Hawthorne? That's it, I bet." She eyed him over her cigarette. "And what the fuck is up with the wig? Ashamed of the ol' bald spot? Overkill."

"Guess I'm a diva at heart."

"Yeah, okay. So. What's yours?"

"My what?"

"Predicament. The worst fix you've ever been in."

"Most people would ask what's the worst thing you've ever done, or what's the worst thing that's ever happened to you…"

"Yeah, but I didn't. Pay attention, fool."

"I got locked in a trunk. Russian mobsters. A bunch of amateur slobs. They were just trying to scare me off a job at a munitions factory, but damn." Royce enjoyed the lie because it came so naturally and was so close to the ugly truth of his profession. He *had* worked at a Russian factory, and if they'd ever caught him spying he imagined they'd have done something drastic, probably far worse than scare him. Yet, even as the lie rolled from his tongue, the brutal peasant faces of his imaginary captors, the suffocating darkness of the trunk, his terror and panic and despair were solid as memories ever got. A black gulf opened in his mind's eye and he shivered and looked away.

"Holy crap. Did it work? They scare you off the job?"

"Hell yes." Royce dragged on the cigarette and blew a rolling cloud of smoke. "Hell, yes."

"That's good stuff, Hawthorne. I ain't ever met anybody who'd been kidnapped by Russkies. You spies live on the edge, doncha?"

There it was, game over. He wondered how it'd happened and discarded the thought. It didn't matter, did it? He turned his face to stone, ticking off the possibilities, the likely outcomes, the avenues of escape. "Excuse me?"

"Lighten up, boy. You've got telescopes and cameras up the wazoo…Either you're a perv, which I bet is incidental, or you're keeping tabs on somebody here at the LRA. Besides, I've done a little checking on you; you got a lot of free time for a QA."

"I'm a hobbyist," he said, his heart beating double time. "Majored in film back in the day. Been thinking of shooting a documentary about voyeurism."

"Bullshit. But it's okay if you've got secrets. It's sexy in a creepy way."

"Wow, thanks."

"No problem, eagle eyes. So, since you mentioned it, what's the worst thing you've ever done. And I don't mean spying on broads in their undies. I mean the worst."

"Be prepared for disappointment. I've lived a blameless, pedestrian life. Besides getting stuffed in the trunk, of course."

"Now you're boring me," she said. She stubbed her cigarette and hugged her knees as the wind came up and rattled the loose bars in the rail. "Wanna know why I decided to come over here? Wanna know what changed my mind?"

Royce shook his head. "Don't jinx it."

"But c'mon—be honest. Isn't all this a bit much? Isn't it kind of unreal? That's what I said when I woke up and saw you half-dead next to me. I said, 'Shell, what kind of freaky shit were you drinking last night, girl?' Admit it. You thought the same thing, except yours was probably more like, 'Fuck yeah! I'm the stallion!'

Right?"

His mind filled with pink and black clouds. He said, "I better get dressed. Big day at the factory."

After Royce didn't see Shelley Jackson for a couple days he checked with his sources and discovered she'd gone to Beijing with James for a multinational trade conference and tour of manufacturing provinces, which meant a week or so of morning confabs and afternoons and evenings of drunken debauchery; fully comped, naturally.

Royce broke into her apartment in the middle of the afternoon when activity in the compound was at its ebb. He told himself the trespass wasn't premeditated—he'd come home from work early and paced around the kitchen with caged nervousness, his head throbbing from squinting through the telescope at the same humdrum activity that was a mirror of the past several months. That didn't wash, though; he'd lifted her keys while she snoozed after their second evening of anguished screwing and made copies with a key-mold he stashed in a locked drawer. On the other hand, he'd barely made the conscious decision to do the deed when he found himself before the door as if in a dream or nightmare wherein the sequence of events conforms to the need of the story. The scenes just merged.

You've gone round the bend, pal o' mine. For Chrissake, just walk away. This isn't the silly shit you pulled in college when you were young and dumb and a little obsessive-compulsive behavior was a forgivable side effect of hormones and a lack of judgment. What the fuck do you think you're doing?

The proceedings continued to unravel with the dreamlike quality. He couldn't shake the stupor that descended upon him, that rendered him a helpless observer to his moving hands.

In this dream that was not a dream, Royce peeled yellow caution tape from the threshold; the tape had gone waxy and brittle with age. How could her unit be sealed when he saw her moving around in there so many nights over the recent months? He hesitated to turn the knob, nearly paralyzed by the utter certainty he'd be sorry in the end for this ill-conceived intrusion. *Maybe Jenny was right—you're nothing more than a stalker, justify it anyway you want.* His hands followed their own agenda and pushed open the door. *You'll regret it. Wait and see! Your dick gets you in trouble every time.* But it was too late, he'd ignored the appeals of his better angels and set the machinery in motion. He'd succumbed to curiosity, jealousy and let the dream be his insulation from blame.

It was worse than he'd imagined. Shelley Jackson's unit reeked of carpet vinyl burned to slag, and a richer, headier undercurrent of cooked blood. The apartment was a series of connected boxes, each charred and ruined. A futile cascade of the sprinkler system had burst plumbing and devastated the enclosure beyond even the scope of the fire. Bits of plaster and melted wiring dangled from the ruptured ceilings; water dripped from exposed pipes. He gaped dumbfounded at a half-dozen sides of beef suspended by thick ropes. The slaughtered meat was wrapped in translucent plastic that mitigated the rank decay, muffled the buzz and whine of flies at work. Blood had dripped until it formed a small lake of black pudding. A partially skinned cow head remained attached to one carcass, a grotesquerie of flattened muzzle and bulging eye. Royce tapped the bovine eyeball through its plastic shroud, found it to be as unyielding as a knot of hard leather.

I was in a slaughterhouse once. When was that? Was I really? Oh, yes. You were thirteen, remember? Cousin Tobe's farm; he showed you the old barn where they killed the cows. Tobe's family hadn't used it, not in years. Didn't matter, you held the hammer, saw the chains and the hooks, you practically heard those cow ghosts bawling as they were strung up. What an imagination you've got there, son.

Royce fumbled for the tiny camera he'd dropped into his pocket and clicked an entire memory card of photographic evidence. He poked about the room, snapping his shots and wondering at the absurdity of it all. The dreamlike flow of continuity compelled him to open a cabinet wherein he found a metal box with the paint stripped from intense heat. Inside were a number of half-melted identification cards and blackened passports, each bearing Shelly Jackson's face, but with radically different names and hairstyles. The pictures and passports went into his jacket after a bit.

Someone grunted in another room, followed by a drawn out ripping sound and he almost jumped from his skin. Slivers and shards of imploded light bulbs gleamed amid the crystallized lumps of linoleum, the heaps of scorched furniture. The floor creaked uneasily beneath his cautious tread. The curtains of plastic broke the fading light into fragments and did nothing to illuminate the dim corners, the gaping holes in sheetrock that burrowed into deeper darkness.

He peeked around the doorjamb into the shelled remnants of the bedroom, driven by the sickly fascination of a child spying for the first time upon his parents coupling. The bed was destroyed except for its brass frame. Mrs. Ward squatted inside the frame. She was naked as a fish. Her blubber seemed magnified in the bluish-tinted light, a crippling excess. Yet beneath this excess were sheets of muscle that belied terrible strength and contributed to the overall impression of unnaturalness and perversion. A grimy burlap sack rested at her feet. It was easily the length of a sleeping bag, only wider, and if Saint Nick had butchered reindeer this was exactly the kind of bag he'd carry.

Mrs. Tuttle, Mrs. Yarbro and Mrs. Coyne sat around her in lotus fashion, and they too were naked. They gleamed like ivory totems and in contrast to the inimitable Mrs. Ward, each seemed absolutely cadaverous with sunken chests and exposed ribs, the skeletal grimaces of cancer patients on the last leg of the journey. The women feasted on the leathery remains of a haunch of cow. Their hollow faces were caked in old blood. Gnawed bones lay heaped all about the room. Mrs. Tuttle gouged a hunk of meat free with long and tapered fingers and tenderly fed Mrs. Ward. Mrs. Yarbro and Mrs. Coyne rocked wildly and uttered joyful croaks that were far removed from humanity.

Royce swayed in place as the world splintered beneath his feet. As one, the four women raised their bloody faces to regard him and he thought of primates, of the hominids in their caves, an awful feast spread across rocks and dirt. Mrs. Ward's mouth yawned in evident pleasure at his appearance. She made a glottal exclamation and raised her hand to point. Mrs. Coyne, Tuttle and Yarbro cackled and scattered. Mrs. Coyne hesitated in the wreckage of the wall of the bathroom to titter at Royce. She leaped straight up into a crack in the ceiling and vanished.

Mrs. Ward patted the filthy, lumpy sack without looking away from him. "Some of your friends are waiting." She levered herself into a crouch, oriented as if to spring. Her neck swelled.

Pitch flowed across the windows, like heavy satin curtains dropping on an opera stage, and all light was extinguished. Royce fell sideways, capsized in the blackness and struck his hip and shoulder on the door jamb, drove a jag of glass into his calf. He threw his hands before his face in an instinctive gesture and the darkness peeled from the windows, revealed the burned room. Mrs. Ward was gone. He was alone, kneeling amid the ashes, an unwilling supplicant.

His perception of the known world, which had taken a number of blows lately, slid a little further into terra incognita. He approached the day manager and asked how the LRA could let a burned out unit to someone. The guy looked at him quizzically and said the appropriate repairs had been affected and approved by the building authorities, but if the kind sir was concerned regarding the issue he might broach the matter with Superintendent Harris. Royce was left with soot smudges on his fingers, the acrid cloy of cinders in his hair and a deepening sense of dislocation. He fled to the Rover, hungry for the presence of familiar surroundings, the comfort of a crowd. He drank himself senseless and someone called Coyne who came and dragged him home.

Royce emerged from his coma the following afternoon. His skull was filled with the familiar pink and black cloud and he told himself his visit to Shelley Jackson's apartment had been a dream, the worst kind. Deciding it had been a dream instantly made him feel one hundred percent better. He thought about going back over, just to verify that the universe was whole and sane. Instead he poured himself a tall glass of XO and watched his neighbors walk around the quadrangle, flitter like shadows behind the windows of their apartments.

Mr. Shea flagged down Royce as he left the office on a Friday evening and invited him to a private get-together he was throwing the next afternoon. The occasion was informal; there'd be free food and liquor. "We'll probably bore the shit out of you. You look mopey, is all," Mr. Shea said. "I hope you aren't letting some broad get you down."

Royce laughed, but there was no question he'd been mooning like a lovesick teenager. His productivity at the cover job was taking a hit; on the spy front he'd all but abandoned his mission, preferring to vegetate on his couch waiting for the girl to return. Two weeks and no sign of Shelley Jackson. It was like the old line: she doesn't call, she doesn't write, oy…

In fairness, she might've called once, at about four AM. The connection was full of static and her voice sounded like it was coming through crumpling paper. *I fucked you because you look exactly like a guy I knew in college. I worked in a hospice and this younger dude was dying of cancer or something, he was mostly gone. A sack of bones; smelled like he was rotting. Couldn't talk much, in and out of reality, but really nice. His mom left some photos on the dresser. Him and his family. Him playing catch with a dog. Him and his girlfriend at the prom. He'd been a handsome guy. I couldn't get over how much his girlfriend and I looked alike, either; we could've been sisters. It was weird. At least I thought so until I met you and it sank in who you reminded me of—crap, that's pretty twisted, I know. Anyway, I'll show you the prom picture when I get back. Yeah, yeah, I stole it when the kid died. Dunno why. Nobody ever said anything. Later!*

Royce had shouted into the phone, tried to interrupt her rambling monologue. She couldn't hear him and just kept talking about this dying kid and his high school sweetheart and then static swept her voice away. He couldn't be certain what was real. There was no record of the call on his line and in the light of day the conversation seemed increasingly implausible. *She's on vacation. Traveling, I dunno where*, according to an increasingly bellicose Mr. James when hectored on the matter. Royce, clinging to some tiny shred of pride, swallowed his frustration and obsessed in private. He couldn't fathom his overwhelming compulsion to rut with her, a need so singularly powerful stray memories of her breasts as they gleamed with perspiration, the wicked O of her mouth as she teased the head of his cock, caused him to stiffen at the most awkward moments at work. He made certain to carry a clipboard at all times for strategic positioning. Good God, it was life at fourteen all over again.

Mr. Shea said, "Be there, two PM. Bring that Coyne fellow. You haven't given up on him, have you? Good, bring him along. Maybe he'll loosen up a bit."

Royce reluctantly agreed to the daytrip, despite the fact he'd have been happy to spend the weekend as a shut-in. He arranged for Mr. Jen to swing by the LRA and squire Coyne and himself to the rendezvous—a seaside resort at the edge of the New Territories. It proved to be a gloomy ride. Coyne, who at the outset seemed overjoyed by the opportunity to schmooze with the fat cats, became absorbed with his handheld computer and cell phone. Mr. Jen drove in stoic silence for the entire forty-minute ride. He didn't even utter a word when a flatbed truck loaded with lumber cut them off on a sharp curve, forcing him to pump the breaks and twist the wheel hard to slide their vehicle between two cars in the slow lane. Royce clung to his armrest, wondering how the driver could wedge them in the crease so tightly without trading paint. Coyne retrieved his phone from the floorboard and laughed at Royce and patted his leg before resuming conversation with whomever was on the other end.

Mr. Jen's eyes were flat and black in the rearview mirror.

Once they passed the city outskirts and climbed through densely wooded hills, traffic thinned. They shared the winding highway with tractor trailers, buses and a very few private vehicles. Eventually the road descended and paralleled the water. The mountains rose green and mysterious on the right. Mangroves spread across the wetlands far out to the distant tidal flats.

The resort wasn't much—a batch of outdated brown and white buildings atop a low bluff overlooking a rough beach. It appeared to be the off season, not that Royce could be certain; he seldom surfaced from the microcosm of his secret world to mark the seasons, the holidays, or nearly anything related to real life. Placid tourists in garish flower-print shirts wandered the grounds in singles and pairs. There was a collection of architecturally uninspired fountains, rock gardens and topiary quartered by gravel paths. A lone souvenir shop remained open. Most of the other windows were dark.

Mr. Jen parked alongside a nondescript sedan near the hub. The hub was the largest of the buildings, a former western-style house remodeled as a hotel. Its cantilever roofs were covered in moss, its many terraces dripped red and green and blotches of yellow and violet. The big man silently escorted Royce and Coyne into the foyer. The concierge was young and thin and supremely diffident. Upon their arrival, the man exchanged words with Jen in a dialect peculiar to Royce's ear. The concierge barked over his shoulder and clapped impatiently. A pale girl in the brown and white resort uniform emerged from a back room. She bowed and beckoned. She led them through an arch flanked by bronzes of regal mandarins and down a hall into a kind of ovular lounge encircled by bay windows. A rain squall tapped the skylights.

Twenty or so men congregated in small groups about the lounge, smoking and sipping expensive liquor and chatting in a loud, bluff manner that suggested most of them were well into the sauce. Royce recognized a few from the central office, a couple more from the management at the factories. The rest were strangers. He got the impression from snippets of conversation a lot of them had flown in from parts unknown and were taking a pit stop to enjoy the hospitality of their fellow overseers. The guests were uniformly white and male; it was the unwritten code these types of parties were part of the grand old gentleman's tradition. Women and minorities might be invited as curiosities, but such was rare. His collar felt tight and he'd started sweating. He always forgot how sick he was of these affairs until the latest one rolled around.

Mr. James and Mr. Shea waited, drinks in hand at the wet bar. An ornate floor lamp glowed ruddily several feet away near a coffee table loaded with sandwiches, the kind sliced into neat triangles transfixed by a toothpick, and gourmet crackers and a tea service. Large pieces of mismatched furniture had been cast about the room, legacy of the vision of multiple designers, each making additions without heed for style or continuity. It hurt Royce's eyes. He put on a jovial smile and shook hands and accepted a generous scotch dealt by a dour bartender who might've been the elder brother of the concierge.

Mr. Shea grinned affably at Royce. "Glad you made the scene, old man. I wasn't sure I could snap you out of your little funk."

Mr. James said, "It's damned silly to pine over a broad! Who needs them, says I, three divorces later. We're like four amigos; us against the world, eh?" His broad, heavy face was red as brick from drinking. He behaved as a man who'd become so accustomed to perpetual intoxication he'd developed immunity to its lesser effects, a snake handler's tolerance for venom.

"We're like pigs in a blanket," Mr. Shea said. "We're positively cozy. Hit me again, Wang." He traded his empty to the bartender for a fresh glass. "Except for that fellow. Who's he?" He pointed to Mr. Jen. Mr. Jen stood implacably near the door. "I don't like him, I fear."

"That's Mr. Jen. He's my driver," Royce said.

"Ease up on the booze, man," Mr. James said. "He's Hawthorne's driver. Personnel gives all our main men drivers."

"They do? What a cash sink. You're practically stealing our money then, aren't you, Hawthorne?"

"Shut it, Miguel. You want these guys to drive themselves?"

"Go on, Mr. Jen. Shoo, shoo!" Mr. Shea flapped his hand until Mr. Jen wheeled and silently stepped out of the room. "All right. I feel much better. Oh, Wang, you get lost too, yeah? Just leave the bottle handy, will you?"

The bartender grimaced and flung his apron on the counter. He gave them a wondering look and stomped after Mr. Jen.

"Hungry? Let's eat!" Mr. Shea went for the sandwiches and Mr. James magnanimously waived Coyne and Royce to the table ahead of himself. "Bloody excellent, I must say. Bloody excellent," Mr. Shea said before he wiped his fingers on one of the fancy cloth napkins.

"It's great," Coyne said. His head was on a swivel, taking in the sights and sounds. He seemed in his element.

"Hip-hip-hooray," Mr. James intoned. He laughed at his own impression and ate another sandwich. "Miguel, we need to hire the bugger who catered this. These bloody things are bloody divine!"

Royce watched Coyne from the corner of his eye. His own stomach was tied in knots. None of the other guests, the blowhard captains of industry, intruded upon them. It was like an invisible barrier had sprung up. The executives continued to drink and exchange their coarse inanities, dutifully blind. He also noticed two hard-looking men in pea coats had melted into the room, casually situated between everyone and the door to the foyer. They waited patiently, a pair of hunting dogs on the leash. His picture of Mr. James and Mr. Shea underwent an unwelcome sea change in that instant. He took another drink. The crumbling façade was a palpable thing.

Why are we here? In his guts, he knew the answer. Mr. James and Mr. Shea managed to get the goods on Coyne and intended to announce the truth. Coyne would be apprehended and Royce informed his services were no longer required, and so on. His performance had been so sloppy, so inarguably negligent, he stood to receive a reprimand from Atlanta when they finally discovered the facts of this debacle. *You'll never work in this town again!* If this had been that insane game show with the lunatic cowboy, all the bells and lights and streamers would've announced his most telling deduction. *So what's the prize?*

"Grab your drinks, boys. I'll give you the tour. You've got to see the cavaedium…" Mr. James heaved to his feet and beckoned them as he headed for one of the side passages.

"Oh, goodie!" Coyne said with only a modicum of sarcasm, which Royce had learned was a benign affectation intended to impress superiors and potential lovers.

Mr. Shea half covered his mouth and said to Royce *sotto voce*, "Don't act too impressed. It's just an atrium and it's roughly as shitty as the rest of this place."

Royce lighted a cigarette, unsure whether to be depressed or relieved that this assignment was about to enter the books in the loss column. He handed the cigarette to Coyne and lighted another for himself, then rose to follow Mr. James and Mr. Shea. The group meandered through a series of dim, unrefined corridors decorated with ubiquitous potted ferns and bland still-life prints and lifeless seascapes. Anonymous doors shut off what Royce guessed to be dark, empty spaces.

The atrium was mundane as Mr. Shea promised. Rain sizzled on cracked and worn tiles of the concave floor and collected in a puddle. Gnats hummed in Royce's ears, bit his neck. He tried to stay dry by standing in the shadows of the marble columns.

Mr. James said to Coyne, "This land was once owned by a Canadian whose family did quite well in textiles. A Japanese consortium acquired the facilities in, what was it? Ninety-five, ninety-six—?"

"Ninety-six," Mr. Shea said. "The Yakuza bought the deed. God knows what went on in the back rooms, eh?" He made slicing motions with his hand.

"It was not the fucking Yakuza," Mr. James said. "The Yakuza operate in Japan, anyway. It was a group of Japs from Okinawa."

"This looks like a nice place for second tier entertaining," Coyne said.

"Exactly!" Mr. James jabbed with his cigar. "One of our clients gets rowdy, it cleans up easy enough—"

"And nobody stays in the hotel in the winter, so you could scream your lungs out if you wanted," Mr. Shea said.

Mr. James led them past the atrium and along a covered walk. The walk let into a garden. The garden contained a sand pit and shrubbery, a Koi pond and some marble benches. Wood slats bobbed in the pond and Royce thought it must be a fish trap for the Koi. Bamboo closed off three sides of the area, and beyond that were dim contours of a wall. The group halted at the edge of the garden under an eave.

"Hawthorne, I want to commend you," Mr. James said. "I'd been under the impression you were squandering our time and money on this snipe hunt of yours—"

"Yeah, we thought you came for the whores and the liquor and free rent!" Mr. Shea said, and laughed. "Sorry, pal. Don't hold it against us, we get freeloaders and bums galore in this biz. I'm sure you understand."

Royce wasn't certain he understood anything. He glanced at Coyne, couldn't gauge the man's reaction. "Right," he said.

"But look, Hawthorne. Pointing us to the woman…that was brilliant. And subtle," Mr. Shea said.

"Almost *too* subtle," Mr. James said.

"Yes, almost too subtle," Mr. Shea said. "You could've been a bit more direct. Nonetheless, who are we to question the methods of a consummate professional such as yourself?"

"Quite right." Mr. James tossed his empty glass into the bushes.

Coyne looked from face to face. His was the expression of a man who'd missed the punch line of a joke. "Royce, what's this he's saying?"

"Don't worry about it," Royce said. His smile was a blank as he tried to get a handle on what the hell was happening here. He automatically stepped slightly away from Mr. James and Mr. Shea and tried to locate the goons lurking somewhere behind them.

"What's that?" Coyne stepped into the garden and focused on the pond. Slapping and snorting came from the water and the pieces of wood wobbled side to side.

"You are one smooth operator," Mr. Shea said to Royce. "We haven't figured out how the CIA let her sneak off the reservation—"

"Oh, but we will," Mr. James said. "And we're going to see who's been feeding her information." He glanced meaningfully at Coyne's back. Coyne had walked to the pond and was standing at the edge, staring into the water. "She's just the mule. We still need the traitor who ripped us off in the first place."

"Look at this bullshit." Mr. Shea passed Royce a handful of government-issue identification cards. The cards were partially melted, their lettering and photographic portraits distorted by bubbling and scorch marks. Royce instantly knew them. "The broad's like Lon Chaney. She's got a name and look for every occasion. CIA cut her loose six years ago and she's been freelancing ever since, near as we can figure. She went to the dark side."

"One of our people in Taiwan was able to put the finger on her, too. Treacherous bitch." Mr. James' bloody eyes seemed to distend with the force of his anger.

Royce pretended to study the pictures on the cards and tried to compute, to wrestle the implications. He felt strangely weightless after only the one drink. The pink and black fog seeped into his thoughts. It was never far away these days.

They were in a little metal box nearly ruined by fire. Where did I put the box? In the safe. Are you sure? Yeah, I'm sure. For the life of him, for the sake of his sanity, he couldn't dredge up any recollection of handing the evidence, such as it was, over to Mr. Shea or Mr. James. *Get a grip, Hawthorne—you think you've got a split personality? You think your evil twin dropped the dime on her and left you in the dark? You aren't the Manchurian Candidate. They broke into your place and heisted the box. There's your answer to the mystery. When's the last time you even checked?* But he'd checked last night, hadn't he? He'd awakened from tossing and dreaming of Shelley Jackson's supple body opening for him, and retrieved the sooty box from his safe and spread all her pieces of false ID on his bed. How long had he feverishly arranged and rearranged those cards, trying to assemble the puzzle? Nobody had stolen into his room. Nothing so simple was at play here. *Is this how it feels to go off the deep end? Ah, come off it—you've been total whack for a while.*

Coyne screamed and startled everyone. He lurched from the pool, cast a terrified look at Royce and ran headlong into the bushes. Saplings whapped and shook with his passage. He clambered over the wall and was gone.

"Where does he think he's going?" Mr. James said to Mr. Shea.

Mr. Shea shrugged and sipped his drink. "Boy's got a guilty conscience."

The cards dropped from Royce's fingers. He walked along the path to the Koi pond and its ominous splashing; the commotion of too many fish in a confined space. There were no Koi in the shallow pond, but instead a rectangular cage of woven bamboo. A body trapped in the coffin-shaped cage was completely submerged except for an oval of mouth and nose. The splashes were caused by the person struggling to arch his or her back in order to keep breathing. The person's skin was withered and gray and beginning to slough, rendering their features unrecognizable.

"She'll tell all," Mr. Shea called with raucous good humor.

Royce wanted to sit. He tried to speak, to formulate a question, a protest, anything. Bubbles foamed over the person's face as they gasped and thrashed.

"You should lie down," Mr. Shea said in his ear.

"Rest a while. You're nearly finished," Mr. James said in his other ear.

How can anybody move so fast? Royce began to turn and then they pulled a hood over his eyes.

Rain clouds rolled back as daylight ebbed. Royce didn't know how long he'd been staring out the window at the panoptic expanse of twilit countryside. The car purred, leaving the ocean and the mangrove thickets below, following the road into the foothills, returning to the distant city. Highway lights flickered to life.

Mr. Jen drove. His black suit and sallow flesh were grainy-blue with shadow. He watched Royce in the rearview mirror more than he appeared to watch the road.

"You in on it?" Royce said, resting his cheek against the window. The ocean slid away while the subtropical forest closed, its green wall holding back a great darkness. "You in it, Jen? You in on it?" He didn't really care if Mr. Jen was in on the vast conspiracy against the sanity of one Royce Hawthorne.

Mr. Jen stared at Royce. He didn't glance from the mirror even as the car tracked around a sharp corner and a truck rushed past them in the opposite lane with a horn blare and the clang of a trailer jouncing on pavement.

Royce laughed and hunted in his pockets until he recovered his cigarettes. He lighted the last one. "Yeah, you're in on it, all right."

Chu said, "Stupid Yankee." He'd come from nowhere to share the backseat. "Do you have any idea how long it lasts?" He cuffed Royce. "Do you have any idea?"

"No," Royce said, shrinking away.

"Idiot. Fool. That's why they call it the Drink of Forgetfulness. Still, the wheel goes round and round, my Yankee friend. Forgetfulness wears thin and atonement must follow. They've a chamber for every trespass, you see."

"Eighteen," Royce said. "Eighteen."

"I was in the Chamber of Wind and Thunder for seven lifetimes. And now I'm here and I can't say which is worse—the injury or the insult."

"I'm dead." There was the answer, elegant in its simplicity. Royce drew on his cigarette and nodded in morbid celebration. "Or I'm comatose in a country hospital and this is a hallucination. You aren't even real, Chu."

Chu cackled and the fine bones of his face lent him an aspect of profound cruelty. There was a stiletto in his hand like magic and he stabbed Royce in the arm. "Do you feel dead, you fucking moron?" He said to Royce's cry of anguish. "Don't you get it? Everybody lives in hell."

Royce clutched his arm, knew even as the blood seeped into the crook of his elbow, the wound was minor, which helped, although not much. Chu seemed happy enough with the result. He made the knife disappear and looked away, out the window into the forest.

Just ahead, a steep grade carried the road into the mouth of a tunnel. The car zoomed in and the world went black. The only illumination was the red glow from Royce's cigarette where it warmed the window glass. The car stopped without braking, without any sense of deceleration whatsoever, and hung in weightless space.

And he was in his apartment, seated before the destroyed TV with the blue light of evening coming through the window, soft as a cloud. The power was down and it would be dark soon.

He finished his cigarette, took his sweet time, and when it was done he went into the silent hall and walked down the stairs and crossed the quadrangle. A group of kids ran in circles at the opposite end, shrieking and laughing and rehearsing their eventual death scenes. The pool man leaned over the water, fishing for leaves and dung with his net. He watched Royce go. There were more children in the far stairwell; they hid in the corners and the space beneath the stairs and their overlarge heads wagged on straw necks and they clutched bellies swollen with hunger. He knew the ravenous ghosts had no business with him and ignored the croaks and groans, the restless snick of claws on cement, the strangled click of saliva in constricted throats.

Coyne's door was open.

"Hello, Aunt CJ," Royce said, standing at the threshold. He dug his fingers into the frame, half-expecting the world to tilt and drop him into an abyss of starry sky.

"Is that who you see when you gaze upon me?" Mrs. Ward said. "How tragically ordinary." She swung her bone-white face back to Coyne's body, which lay supine and still, and continued to roll him into a ball and stuff him into her filthy burlap sack. Coyne seemed rubbery, deflated, little more than a sack himself. But his mouth worked soundlessly, his eyes were wet and it was possible he saw Royce there in the doorway.

"Who are you?" Royce said, so quietly it was almost a thought.

"I'm your Aunt Carole Joyce, dear."

"The hell you say."

She wheezed and shoved the top of Coyne's head until he disappeared completely into the sack. She bound the neck of the sack in barbed wire and grinned up at Royce, licking her bloody fingers. Darkness filled the room and her white face seemed to float. "We're caretakers. Who are *you*, love?"

He wiped tears from his cheeks, unable to meet her gaze. Her cold hand caressed his shoulder, guided him into the hall. The white iron doors were there: the Chamber of Pounding; the Chamber of Fire; the Chamber of Blood; and the rest. When they came to *his* door he saw what the doorplate said, the judgment rendered of him, and hung his head. Mr. Jen stepped out of a recess in the wall and held the door. His eyes glittered like the carapace of a beetle.

Mrs. Ward squeezed Royce's shoulder. "There are far worse. The Chamber of Black Sloth, for one. Have courage. Everyone comes to this house."

Royce saw flashes of the beast in its cube, the man climbing the mountain of knives, the sawing and the blood, a mob of children with thin necks and fat bellies crawling along the shore of bubbling lakes of tar, and wept.

His chamber was circular and windowless. Tiers of benches ascended in the architectural style of an amphitheater. A large projection screen was centered upon the far wall. Mrs. Ward helped him to his seat of honor and her hand fell from his shoulder as she rejoined the rising darkness. The last of the light drained away and it grew cold.

Whispers and small rustlings circulated as the screen glowed faintly and reflected the patina of a scarred lens. Numbers reversed toward the beginning. So many numbers, so many beginnings, his heart became wooden in his chest.

From nearby, Shelley Jackson said, "These are your lives, Royce Hawthorne."

Royce tried to smile through tears, but it cracked to pieces and he shook as grief and sorrow claimed him. The images on the screen blurred, became incomprehensible, and that was a small blessing. "I understand now," he said. He inhaled and pushed his thumbs deep into the corners of his eyes, and pulled.

BULLDOZER

—Then He bites off my shooting hand.

Christ on a pony, here's a new dimension of pain.

The universe flares white. A storm of dandelion seeds, a cyclone of fire. That's the Coliseum on its feet, a full-blown German orchestra, a cannon blast inside my skull, the top of my skull coming off.

I better suck it up or I'm done for.

I'm a Pinkerton man. That means something. I've got the gun, a cold blue Colt and a card with my name engraved beneath the unblinking eye. I'm the genuine article. I'm a dead shot, a deadeye Dick. I was on the mark in Baltimore when assassins went for Honest Abe. I skinned my iron and plugged them varmints. Abe should've treated me to the theater. Might still be here. Might be in a rocker scribbling how the South was won.

Can't squeeze no trigger now can I? I can squirt my initials on the ceiling.

I'm a Pinkerton I'm a Pinkerton a goddamned Pinkerton.

That's right you sorry sonofabitch you chew on that you swallow like a python and I'll keep on chanting it while I paint these walls.

Belphegor ain't my FatherMother Father thou art in Heaven Jesus loves me. Jesus Christ.

My balls clank when I walk.

I'm walking to the window.

Well I'm crawling.

If I make it to the window I'll smash the glass and do a stiff drop.

I've got to hustle the shades are dropping from left to right.

Earth on its axis tilting to the black black black iris rolling back inside a socket.

I'm glad the girl hopped the last train. Hope she's in Frisco selling it for more money than she's ever seen here in the sticks.

I taste hard Irish whiskey sweet inside her navel. She's whip smart she's got gams to run she's got blue eyes like the barrel of the gun on the floor under the dresser I can't believe how much blood can spurt from a stump I can't believe it's come to this I hear Him coming heavy on the floorboards buckling He's had a bite He wants more meat.

Pick up the iron southpaw Pinkerton pick it up and point like a man with grit in his liver not a drunk seeing double.

Hallelujah.

Who's laughing now you slack-jawed motherfucker I told you I'm a dead shot now you know now that it's too late.

Let me just say kapow-kapow.

I rest my case, ladies and gennulmen of the jury. I'm

2.

"A Pinkerton man. Well, shit my drawers." The engineer, a greasy brute in striped coveralls, gave me the once-over. Then he spat a stream of chaw and bent his back to feeding the furnace. Never heard of my man Rueben Hicks, so he said. He didn't utter another word until the narrow gauge spur rolled up to the wretched outskirts of Purdon.

Ugly as rot in a molar, here we were after miles of pasture and hill stitched with barbwire.

Rude frame boxes squatted in the stinking alkaline mud beside the river. Rain pounded like God's own darning needles, stood in orange puddles along the banks, pooled in ruts beneath the awnings. Dull lamplight warmed coke-rimed windows. Shadows fluttered, moths against glass. Already, above the hiss and drum of the rain came faint screams, shouts, piano music.

Just another wild and wooly California mining town that sprang from the ground fast and would fall to ruin faster when the gold played out. Three decades was as the day of a mayfly in the scope of the great dim geography of an ancient continent freshly opened to white men.

Industry crowded in on the main street: Bank. Hotel. Whorehouse. Feed & Tack. Dry Goods. Sawbones. Sheriff's Office. A whole bunch of barrelhouses. Light of the Lord Baptist Temple up the lane and yonder. Purdon Cemetery. A-frame houses, cottages, shanties galore. Lanky men in flannels. Scrawny sows with litters of squalling brats. A rat warren.

The bruised mist held back a wilderness of pines and crooked hills. End of the world for all intents and purposes.

I stood on the leaking platform and decided this was a raw deal. I didn't care if the circus strongman was behind one of the piss-burned saloon façades, swilling whiskey, feeling up the thigh of a horse-toothed showgirl. I'd temporarily lost my hard-on for his scalp with the first rancid-sweet whiff of gunsmoke and open sewage. Suddenly, I'd had a bellyful.

Nothing for it but to do it. I slung my rifle, picked up my bags and began the slog.

3.

I signed *Jonah Koenig* on the ledger at the Riverfront Hotel, a rambling colonial monolith with oil paintings of Andrew Jackson, Ulysses S. Grant and the newly anointed Grover Cleveland hanging large as doom in the lobby. This wasn't the first time I'd used my real name on a job since the affair in Schuylkill, just the first time it felt natural. A sense of finality had settled into my bones.

Hicks surely knew I was closing in. Frankly, I didn't much care after eleven months of eating coal dust from Boston to San Francisco. I cared about securing a whiskey, a bath and a lay. Not in any particular order.

The clerk, a veteran of the trade, understood perfectly. He set me up on the third floor in a room with a liquor cabinet, a poster bed and a view of the mountains. The presidential suite. Some kid drew a washtub of lukewarm water and took my travel clothes to get cleaned. Shortly, a winsome, blue-eyed girl in a low-cut dress arrived without knocking. She unlocked a bottle of bourbon, two glasses and offered to scrub my back.

She told me to call her Violet and didn't seem fazed that I was buck-naked or that I'd almost blown her head off. I grinned and hung gun and belt on the back of a chair. Tomorrow was more than soon enough to brace the sheriff.

Violet sidled over, got a handle on the situation without preamble. She had enough sense not to mention the brand on my left shoulder, the old needle tracks or the field of puckered scars uncoiling on my back.

We got so busy I completely forgot to ask if she'd ever happened to screw a dear chum of mine as went by Rueben Hicks. Or Tom Mullen, or Ezra Slade. Later I was half-seas over and when I awoke, she was gone.

I noticed a crack in the plaster. A bleeding fault line.

4.

"Business or pleasure, Mr. Koenig?" Sheriff Murtaugh was a stout Irishman of my generation who'd lost most of his brogue and all of his hair. His right leg was propped on the filthy desk, foot encased in bandages gone the shade of rotten fruit. It reeked of gangrene. "Chink stabbed it with a pickaxe, can y'beat that? Be gone to hell before I let Doc Campion have a peek—he'll want to chop the fucker at the ankle." He'd laughed, polishing his tarnished lawman's star with his sleeve. Supposedly there was a camp full of Chinese nearby; the ones who'd stayed on and fallen into mining after the railroad pushed west. Bad sorts, according to the sheriff and his perforated foot.

We sat in his cramped office, sharing evil coffee from a pot that had probably been bubbling on the stove for several days. At the end of the room was the lockup, dingy as a Roman catacomb and vacant but for a deputy named Levi sleeping off a bender in an open cell.

I showed Murtaugh a creased photograph of Hicks taken during a P. T. Barnum extravaganza in Philadelphia. Hicks was lifting a grand piano on his back while ladies in tights applauded before a pyramid of elephants. "Recognize this fellow? I got a lead off a wanted poster in Frisco. Miner thought he'd seen him in town. Wasn't positive." The miner was a nice break—the trail was nearly three months cold and I'd combed every two-bit backwater within six hundred miles before the man and I bumped into each other at the Gold Digger Saloon and started swapping tales.

"Who wants to know?"

"The Man himself."

"Barnum? Really?"

"Oh, yes indeed." I began rolling a cigarette.

Murtaugh whistled through mismatched teeth. "Holy shit, that's Iron Man Hicks. Yuh, I seen him around. Came in 'bout June. Calls hisself Mullen, says he's from Philly. Gotta admit he looks different from his pictures. Don't stack up to much in person. So what's he done to bring a Pinkerton to the ass-end o' the mule?"

I struck a match on the desk, took a few moments to get the cigarette smoldering nicely. There was a trace of hash mixed with the tobacco. Ah, that was better. "Year and half back, some murders along the East Coast were connected to the presence of the circus. Ritual slayings—pentagrams, black candles, possible cannibalism. Nasty stuff. The investigation pointed to the strongman. Cops hauled him in, nothing stuck. Barnum doesn't take chances; fires the old boy and has him committed. Cedar Grove may not be pleasant, but it beats getting lynched, right? Iron Man didn't think so. He repaid his boss by ripping off some trinkets Barnum collected and skipping town."

"Real important cultural artifacts, I bet," Murtaugh said.

"Each to his own. Most of the junk turned up with local pawn dealers, antiquarians' shelves, spooky shops and you get the idea. We recovered everything except the original translation of the *Dictionnaire Infernal* by a dead Frenchman, Collin de Plancy."

"What's that?"

"A book about demons and devils. Something to talk about at church."

"The hell y'say. Lord have mercy. Well, I ain't seen Mullen, uh, Hicks, in weeks, though y'might want to check with the Honeybee Ranch. And Trosper over to the Longrifle. Be advised—Trosper hates lawmen. Did a stretch in the pokey, I reckon. *We* got us an understandin', o' course."

"Good thing I'm not really a lawman, isn't it?"

"What's the guy's story?" Murtaugh stared at the photo, shifting it in his blunt hands.

I said, "Hicks was born in Plymouth. His father was a minister, did missionary work here in California—tried to save the Gold Rush crowd. Guess the minister beat him something fierce. Kid runs off and joins the circus. Turns out he's a freak of nature and a natural showman. P. T. squires him to every city in the Union. One day, Iron Man Hicks decides to start cutting the throats of rag pickers and whores. At least, that's my theory. According to the docs at Cedar Grove, there's medical problems—might be consumption or syph or something completely foreign. Because of this disease maybe he hears voices, wants to be America's Jack the Ripper. Thinks God has a plan for him. Who knows for sure? He's got a stash of dubious bedside material on the order of the crap he stole from Barnum, which was confiscated; he'd filled the margins with notes the agency eggs still haven't deciphered. Somebody introduced him to the lovely hobby of demonology—probably his own dear dad. I can't check that because Hicks senior died in '67 and all his possessions were auctioned. Anyway, Junior gets slapped into a cozy asylum with the help of Barnum's legal team. Hicks escapes and, well, I've told you the rest."

"Jesus H., what a charmin' tale."

We drank our coffee, listened to rain thud on tin. Eventually Murtaugh got around to what had probably been ticking in his brain the minute he recognized my name. "You're the fellow who did for the Molly Maguires."

"Afraid so."

He smirked. "Yeah, I thought it was you. Dirty business that, eh?"

"Nothing pretty about it, Sheriff." Sixteen years and the legend kept growing, a cattle carcass bloating in the sun.

"I expect not. We don't get the paper up here, 'cept when the mail train comes in. I do recall mention that some folks are thinkin' yer Mollies weren't really the bad guys. Maybe the railroad lads had a hand in them killin's."

"That's true. It's also true that sometimes a horsethief gets hanged for another scoundrel's misdeed. The books get balanced either way, don't they? Everybody in Schuylkill got what they wanted."

Murtaugh said, "Might put that theory to the twenty sods as got hung up to dry."

I sucked on my cigarette, studied the ash drifting toward my knees. "Sheriff, did you ever talk to Hicks?"

"Bumped into him at one of the saloons durin' a faro game. Said howdy. No occasion for a philosophical debate."

"Anything he do or say seem odd?" I proffered my smoke.

"Sure. He smelled right foul and he wasn't winnin' any blue ribbons on account o' his handsome looks. He had fits—somethin' to do with his nerves, accordin' to Doc Campion." Murtaugh extended his hand and accepted the cigarette. He dragged, made an appreciative expression and closed his eyes. "I dunno, I myself ain't ever seen Hicks foamin' at the mouth. Others did, I allow."

"And that's it?"

"Y'mean, did the lad strike me as a thief and a murderer? I'm bound to say no more'n the rest o' the cowpunchers and prospectors that drift here. I allow most of 'em would plug you for a sawbuck...or a smoke." He grinned, rubbed ashes from his fingers. "Y'mentioned nothing stuck to our lad. Has that changed?"

"The evidence is pending."

"Think he did it?"

"I think he's doing it now."

"But you can't prove it."

"Nope."

"So, officially you're here to collect P. T.'s long lost valuables. I imagine Hicks is mighty attached to that book by now. Probbly won't part with it without a fight."

"Probably not."

"Billy Cullins might be fittin' him for a pine box, I suppose."

I pulled out a roll of wrinkled bills, subtracted a significant number and tossed them on the desk. Plenty more where that came from, hidden under a floorboard at the hotel. I always travel flush. "The agency's contribution to the Purdon widows and orphans fund."

"Much obliged, Mr. K. Whole lotta widows and orphans in these parts."

"More every day," I said.

5.

BELPHEGOR IS YOUR FATHERMOTHER. *This carmine missive scrawled in a New Orleans hotel room. In the unmade bed, a phallus sculpted from human excrement. Flies crawled upon the sheets, buzzing and sluggish.*

In Lubbock, a partially burned letter—"O FatherMother, may the blood of the-(indecipherable)-erate urchin be pleasing in thy throat. I am of the tradition."

Come Albuquerque, the deterioration had accelerated. Hicks did not bother to destroy this particular letter, rather scattered its befouled pages on the floor among vermiculate designs scriven in blood—"worms, godawful! i am changed! Blessed the sacrament of decay! Glut Obloodyhole O bloodymaggots Obloodybowels O Lordof shite! Fearthegash! iamcomeiamcome"

Finally, Bakersfield in script writ large upon a flophouse wall—

EATEATEATEATEAT! *Found wedged under a mattress, the severed hand and arm of an unidentified person. Doubtless a young female. The authorities figured these remains belonged to a prostitute. Unfortunately, a few of them were always missing.*

The locket in the delicate fist was inscribed, For my little girl. *I recalled the bulls that stripped the room laughing when they read that. I also recalled busting one guy's jaw later that evening after we all got a snoot-full at the watering hole. I think it was a dispute over poker.*

6.

Trosper didn't enjoy seeing me at the bar. He knew what I was and what it meant from a mile off. First words out of his egg-sucker's mouth, "Lookit here, mister, I don't want no bullshit from you. You're buyin' or you're walkin'. Or Jake might have somethin' else for you."

I couldn't restrain my smile. The banty roosters always got me. "Easy, friend. Gimme two fingers of coffin varnish. Hell, make it a round for the house."

The Longrifle was a murky barn devoid of all pretense to grandeur. This was the trough of the hard-working, harder drinking peasantry. It was presently dead as three o'clock. Only me, Trosper and a wiry cowboy with a crimped, sullen face who nursed a beer down the line. Jake, I presumed.

Trosper made quick work of getting the whiskey into our glasses. He corked the bottle and left it in front of me.

I swallowed fast, smacked the glass onto the counter. "Ugh. I think my left eye just went blind."

"Give the Chinaman a music lesson or shove off, pig. You ain't got no jurydiction here."

"Happy to oblige." I did the honors. Flames crackled in my belly, spread to my chest and face. Big grandad clock behind the bar ticked too loudly.

Good old Jake had tipped back his hat and shifted in his chair to affright me with what I'm sure was his darkest glare. Bastard had a profile sharp as a hatchet. A regulator, a bullyboy. He was heeled with a fair-sized peashooter in a shoulder rig.

I belted another swig to fix my nerves, banged the glass hard enough to raise dust. Motes drifted lazily, planetoids orbiting streams of light from the rain-blurred panes. I said to Trosper, "I hear tell you're chummy with a bad man goes by Tom Mullen."

Jake said, soft and deadly, "He told you to drink or get on shank's mare." Goddamned if the cowboy didn't possess the meanest drawl I'd heard since ever. First mistake was resting a rawboned hand on the butt of his pistola. Second mistake was not skinning said iron.

So I shot him twice. Once in the belly, through the buckle; once near the collar of his vest. Jake fell off his stool and squirmed in the sawdust. His hat tumbled away. He had a thick mane of blond hair with a perfect pink circle at the crown. That's what you got for wearing cowboy hats all the fucking time.

Making conversation with Trosper, who was currently frozen into a homely statue, I said, "Don't twitch or I'll nail your pecker to the floor." I walked over to Jake. The cowpoke was game; by then he almost had his gun free with the off hand. I stamped on his wrist until it cracked. He hissed. I smashed in his front teeth with a couple swipes from the heel of my boot. That settled him down.

I resumed my seat, poured another drink. "Hey, what's the matter? You haven't seen a man get plugged before? What kind of gin mill you running?" My glance swung to the dim ceiling and its mosaic of bullet holes and grease stains. "Oh, they usually shoot the hell out of your property, not each other. Tough luck the assholes got it all backwards. Come on, Trosper. Take a snort. This hooch you sling the shit-kickers kinda grows on a fellow."

Trosper was gray as his apron and sweating. His hands jerked. "H-he, uh, he's got a lotta friends, mister."

"I have lots of bullets. Drink, amigo." After he'd gulped his medicine I said, "All right. Where were we? Oh, yes. Mr. Mullen. I'm interested in meeting him. Any notions?"

"Used to come in here every couple weeks; whenever he had dust in his poke. Drank. Played cards with some of the boys from the Bar-H. Humped the girls pretty regular over to the Honeybee."

"Uh, huh. A particular girl?"

"No. He din't have no sweetheart."

"When's the last time you saw him?"

Trosper thought about that. "Dunno. Been a spell. Christ, is Jake dead? He ain't movin'."

"I'll be damned. He isn't. Pay attention. Mullen's gone a-prospecting you say?"

"Wha-yeah. Mister, I dunno. He came in with dust is all I'm sayin'." Trosper's eyes were glassy. "I dunno shit, mister. Could be he moved on. I ain't his keeper."

"The sheriff mentioned Hicks had a condition."

"He's got the Saint Vitus dance. You know, he trembles like a drunk ain't had his eye-opener. Saw him fall down once; twitched and scratched at his face somethin' awful. When it was over, he just grinned real pasty like, and made a joke about it."

I got the names and descriptions of the Bar-H riders, not that I'd likely interview them. As I turned to leave, I said, "Okay, Trosper. I'll be around, maybe stop in for a visit, see if your memory clears up. Here's a twenty. That should cover a box."

7.

I was riding a terrific buzz, equal parts whiskey and adrenaline, when I flopped on a plush divan in the parlor of the Honeybee Ranch. A not-too-uncomely lady-of-the-house pried off my muddy boots and rubbed oil on my feet. The Madame, a frigate in purple who styled herself as Octavia Plantagenet, provided me a Cuban cigar from a velvet humidor. She expertly lopped the tip with a fancy silver-chased cutter and got it burning, quirking suggestively as she worked the barrel between her fat red lips. The roses painted on her cheeks swelled like bellows.

The Honeybee swam in the exhaust of chortling hookahs and joints of Kentucky bluegrass. A swarthy fellow plucked his sitar in accompany to the pianist, cementing the union of Old World decadence and frontier excess. Here was a refined wilderness of thick Persian carpet and cool brass; no plywood, but polished mahogany; no cheap glass, but exquisite crystal. The girls wore elaborate gowns and mink-slick hair piled high, batted glitzy lashes over eyes twinkly as gemstones. Rouge, perfume, sequins and charms, the whole swarming mess an intoxicating collaboration of artifice and lust.

Madame Octavia recalled Hicks. "Tommy Mullen? Sorry-lookin' fella, what with the nerve disorder. Paid his tab. Not too rough on the merchandise, if he did have breath to gag a maggot. Only Lydia and Connie could stomach that, but he didn't complain. Lord, he hasn't been by in a coon's age. I think he headed back east."

I inquired after Violet and was told she'd be available later. Perhaps another girl? I said I'd wait and accepted four-fingers of cognac in King George's own snifter. The brandy was smooth and I didn't notice the wallop it packed until maroon lampshades magnified the crowd of genteel gamblers, businessmen and blue-collar stiffs on their best behavior, distorted them in kaleidoscopic fashion. Tinkling notes from Brahms reverberated in my brain long after the short, thick Austrian player in the silk vest retired for a nip at the bar.

Fame preceded me. Seemed everybody who could decipher news print had read about my exploits in Pennsylvania. They knew all there was to know about how I infiltrated the Workers Benevolent Association and sent a score of murderous union extremists to the gallows with my testimony. Depending upon one's social inclinations, I was a champion of commerce and justice, or a no-good, yellow-bellied skunk. It was easy to tell who was who from the assorted smiles and sneers. The fact I'd recently ventilated a drover at the Longrifle was also a neat conversation starter.

Octavia encouraged a muddled procession of counterfeit gentry to ogle the infamous Pinkerton, a bulldozer of the first water from the Old States. Deduction was for the highbrows in top hats and great coats; I performed my detecting with a boot and a six-gun. I'd bust your brother's head or bribe your mother if that's what it took to hunt you to ground and collect my iron men. Rumor had it I'd strong arm the pope himself. Not much of a stretch as I never was impressed with that brand of idolatry.

Introductions came in waves—Taylor Hackett, bespectacled owner of the Bar-H cattle ranch; Norton Smythe, his stuffed-suit counterpart in the realm of gold mining; Ned Cates, Bob Tunny and Harry Edwards, esteemed investors of the Smythe & Ruth Mining Company, each beaming and guffawing, too many teeth bared. An Eastern Triad. I asked them if they ate of The Master's sacrifice, but nobody appeared to understand and I relented while their waxy grins were yet in place. Blowsy as a poleaxed mule, I hadn't truly allowed for the possibility of my quarry snuggled in the fold of a nasty little cult. Hicks was a loner. I hoped.

After the contents of the snifter evaporated and got replenished like an iniquitous cousin to the Horn of Plenty, the lower caste made its rounds in the persons of Philmore Kavanaugh, journalist for some small town rag that recently folded and sent him penniless to the ends of creation; Dalton Beaumont, chief deputy and unloved cousin of Sheriff Murtaugh; John Brown, a wrinkled alderman who enjoyed having his toes sucked and daubed mother of pearl right there before God and everyone; Michael Piers, the formerly acclaimed French poet, now sunk into obscurity and bound for an early grave judging from the violence of his cough and the bloody spackle on his embroidered handkerchief. And others and others and others. I gave up on even trying to focus and concentrated on swilling without spilling.

There wasn't any sort of conversation, precisely. More the noise of an aroused hive. I waded through streams and tributaries from the great lake of communal thrum—

"—let some daylight into poor Jake. There'll be the devil to pay, mark me!"

"Langston gone to seed in Chinatown. A bloody shame—"

"First Holmes, now Stevenson. Wretched, wretched—"

"—the Ancient Order of Hibernia gets you your goddamned Molly Maguires and that's a fact. Shoulda hung a few more o' them Yankee bastards if you ask me—"

"—Welsh thick as ticks, doped out of their faculties on coolie mud. They've still got the savage in them. Worse than the red plague—"

"Two years, Ned. Oh, all right. Three years. The railroad gobbles up its share and I get the pieces with promising glint. California is weighed and measured, my friend. We'll run the independent operations into the dirt. Moonlighters don't have a prayer—"

"—Barnum, for gawd's sake! Anybody tell him—"

"I hate the circus. Stinks to high heaven. I hate those damned clowns too—"

"No. Langston's dead—"

"—poked her for fun. Dry hump and the bitch took my folding—"

"—Mullen? Hicks? Dunno an don' care. Long gone, long gone—"

"The hell, you say! He's bangin' the gong at the Forty-Mile Camp, last I heard—"

"—the Professor's on the hip? I thought he sailed across the pond—"

"My dear, sweet woman-child. As quoth The Bard:

Age cannot wither her, nor custom stale
Her infinite variety;

"It wasn't enough the cunt sacked me. 'E bloody spit in my face, the bloody wanker—"

"—stones to *kill* a man—"

"Ah, I could do the job real nice—"

Where most she satisfies; for vilest
things—

"—I mean, look at 'im. He's a facking mechanical—"

"So, I says, lookee here, bitch, I'll cut your—"

Become themselves in her

"—suck my cock or die! Whoopie! I'm on a hellbender, fellas!"

"—don't care. Murtaugh should string his ass from the welcome sign—"

"I met your Hicks. He was nothing really special." Piers blew a cloud of pungent clove exhaust, watched it eddy in the currents. "Thees circus freak of yours. He had a beeg mouth."

My head wobbled. "Always pegged him for the strong silent type. Ha, ha."

"No." Piers waved impatiently. "He had a beeg mouth. Drooled, how do you say?—Like an eediot. A fuck-ing eediot."

"Where?" I wheezed.

"Where? How do I know where? Ask the fuck-ing Professor. Maybe he knows where. The Professor knows everyone."

"There you are, darling," crooned Madame Octavia as if I had suddenly re-materialized. Her ponderous breasts pressed against my ribs. Her choice of scent brought tears to my eyes. "This gig is drying up, baby. It's a tourist trap. Ooh, Chi-Town is where the action is. Isn't Little Egypt a pistol? Hoochie-koochie baby!"

Red lights. White faces. Shadows spreading cracks.

I dropped the snifter from disconnected fingers. Thank goodness Octavia was there with a perfumed cloth to blot the splash. I was thinking, yes, indeed, a tragedy about Robert Louis; a step above the penny dreadfuls, but my hero nonetheless.

Where was Violet? Coupled to a banker? A sodbuster? Hoochie-koochie all night long.

"Excuse, me, Mr. Koenig." An unfamiliar voice, a visage in silhouette.

"Ah, Frankie, he's just laying about waiting for one of my girls—"

"Sheriff's business, Miss Octavia. Please, sir. We've been sent to escort you to the office. Levi, he's dead weight, get his other arm. You too, Dalton. There's a lad." The sheriff's boys each grabbed a limb and hoisted me up as if on angels' wings.

"The cavalry," I said.

Scattered applause. A bawdy ragtime tune. Hungry mouths hanging slack. And the muzzy lamps. Red. Black.

8.

"What do you call him?"

"Chemosh. Baal-Peeor. Belphegor. No big deal, the Moabites are dust. They won't mind if the title gits slaughtered by civilized folks."

"We're a fair piece from Moab."

"Belphegor speaks many tongues in many lands."

"A world traveler, eh?"

"That's right, Pinky."

"This friend of yours, he speaks to you through the shitter?"

"Yeah."

"Interesting. Seems a tad inelegant."

"Corruption begets corruption, Pinky," says Hicks. His eyes are brown, hard as baked earth. Gila monster's eyes. He once raised a four hundred pound stone above his head, balanced it in his palm to the cheers of mobs. Could reach across the table and crush my throat, even with the chains. Calcium deposits mar his fingers, distend from his elbows not unlike spurs. There is a suspicious lump under his limp hair, near the brow. He's sinewy and passive in the Chair of Questions. "What's more

lunatic than fallin' down before the image of a man tacked to a cross? Nothin'. You don't even git nothin' fun. I aim to have fun."

I'm fascinated by the wet mouth in the bronzed face. It works, yes indeed it articulates most functionally. Yet it yawns, slightly yawns, as if my captive strongman was victim of a palsy, or the reverse of lockjaw. Saliva beads and dangles on viscous threads. I gag on the carnivore's stench gusting from the wound. His teeth are chipped and dark as flint. Long, I ask, "What are you?"

"Holes close. Holes open. I'm an Opener. They Who Wait live through me. What about you?"

"I'm an atheist." That was a half-truth, but close enough for government work.

"Good on you, Pinky. You're on your way. And here's Tuttle." He indicates a prim lawyer in a crisp suit. "P. T. only hires the best. Adios, pal."

Three weeks later, when Hicks strolls out of Cedar Grove Sanitarium, I'm not surprised at the message he leaves—CLOSE A HOLE AND ANOTHER OPENS.

Funny, funny world. It's Tuttle who pays the freight for my hunting expedition into the American West.

9.

Deputy Levi called it protective custody. They dumped me on a cot in a cell. Murtaugh's orders to keep me from getting lynched by some of Jake's confederates. These confederates had been tying one on down at the Longrifle, scene of the late, lamented Jake's demise. Murtaugh wasn't sorry to see a "cockeyed snake like that little sonofabitch" get planted. The sheriff promised to chat with Trosper regarding the details of our interview. It'd be straightened out by breakfast.

I fell into the amber and drowned.

Things clumped together in a sticky collage—

Hicks leering through the bars, his grin as prodigious as a train tunnel.

Violet's wheat-blonde head bowed at my groin and me so whiskey-flaccid I can only sweat and watch a cockroach cast a juggernaut shadow beneath a kerosene lamp while the sheriff farts and snores at his desk.

Jake shits himself, screams soundlessly as my boot descends, hammer of the gods.

Lincoln waves to the people in the balconies. His eyes pass directly over me. I'm twenty-two, I'm hell on wheels. In three minutes I'll make my first kill. Late bloomer.

"I once was lost. Now I'm found. The Soldier's Friend, Sister M, had a hold on me, yes sir, yesiree."

"I give up the needle and took to the bottle like a babe at his mama's nipple."

"Never had a wife, never needed one. I took up the traveling life, got married to my gun."

A man in a suit doffs his top hat and places his head into the jaws of a bored lion. The jaws close.

A glossy pink labium quakes and begins to yield, an orchid brimming with ancient stars.

"How many men you killed, Jonah?" Violet strokes my superheated brow.

"Today?"

"No, silly! I mean, in all. The grand total."

"More than twenty. More every day."

Sun eats stars. Moon eats sun. Black hole eats Earth.

Hicks winks a gory eye, an idiot lizard, gives the sheriff a languid, slobbery kiss that glistens snail slime. When the sackcloth of ashes floats to oblivion and I can see again, the beast is gone, if he ever was.

The door creaks with the storm. Open. Shut.

Violet sighs against my sweaty chest, sleeps in reinvented innocence.

There's a crack in the ceiling and it's dripping.

10.

I did the expedient thing—holed up in my hotel room for a week, drinking the hair of the dog that bit me and screwing Violet senseless.

I learned her daddy was a miner who was blown to smithereens. No mother; no kin as would take in a coattail relation from the boondocks. But she had great teeth and a nice ass. Fresh meat for Madame Octavia's stable. She was eighteen and real popular with the gentlemen, Miss Violet was. Kept her earnings tucked in a sock, was gonna hop the mail train to San Francisco one of these fine days, work as a showgirl in an upscale dance hall. Heck, she might even ride the rail to Chicago, meet this Little Egypt who was the apple of the city's eye. Yeah.

She finally asked me if I'd ever been married—it was damned obvious I wasn't at present—and I said no. Why not? Lucky, I guessed.

"Mercy, Jonah, you got some mighty peculiar readin' here." Violet was lying on her belly, thumbing through my Latin version of the *Pseudomonarchia Daemonum*. Her hair was tangled; perspiration glowed on her ivory flanks.

I sprawled naked, propped against the headboard, smoking while I cleaned and oiled my Winchester Model 1886. Best rifle I'd ever owned; heavy enough to drop a buffalo, but perfect for men. It made me a tad wistful to consider that I wasn't likely to use it on Hicks. I figured him for close-quarters.

Gray and yellow out the window. Streets were a quagmire. I watched figures mucking about, dropping planks to make corduroy for the wagons. Occasionally a gun popped.

For ten dollars and an autograph, Deputy Levi had compiled a list of deaths and disappearances in Purdon and environs over the past four months, hand delivered it to my doorstep. Two pages long. Mostly unhelpful—routine shootings and stabbings, claim-jumping and bar brawls, a whole slew of accidents. I did mark the names of three prospectors who'd vanished. They worked claims separated by many miles of inhospitable terrain. Each had left a legacy of food, equipment and personal items—no money, though. No hard cash. No gold dust.

Violet gasped when she came to some unpleasant and rather florid illustrations.

"Lordy! That's...awful. You believe in demons and such, Jonah?" Curiosity and suspicion struggled to reconcile her tone.

"Nope. But other folks do."

"Tommy Mullen—he does?" Her eyes widened. I glimpsed Hicks, a gaunt satyr loitering in the Honeybee parlor while the girls drew lots to seal a fate.

"I expect he does." I slapped her pale haunch. "Come on over here, sweetness. It isn't for you to fret about." And to mitigate the dread transmitted through her trembling flesh, I said, "He's hightailed to the next territory. I'm wasting daylight in this burg." Her grateful mouth closed on me and her tongue moved, rough and supple. I grabbed the bed post. "Pardon me, not completely wasting it."

Three miners. Picture-clear, the cabins, lonely, isolated. A black shape sauntering from an open door left swinging in its wake. Crows chattering in poplar branches, throaty chuckle of a stream.

I drowsed. The hotel boy knocked and reported a Chinaman was waiting in the lobby. The man bore me an invitation from Langston Butler. Professor Butler, to his friends. The note, in handsome script, read:

Sashay on out to Forty-Mile Camp and I'll tell you how to snare the Iron Man. Cordially, L. Butler.

I dressed in a hurry. Violet groaned, started to rise, but I kissed her on the mouth and said to take the afternoon off. Indulging a bout of prescience, I left some money on the dresser. A lot of money. The money basically said, "If you're smart you'll be on the next train to San Francisco; next stop the Windy City."

I hoped Murtaugh had successfully smoothed all the feathers I'd ruffled.

This was my best suit and I sure didn't want to get any holes in it.

11.

Forty-Mile Camp was not, as its appellation suggested, forty miles from Purdon. The jolting ride in Hung Chan's supply wagon lasted under three hours by my pocket watch. Hung didn't speak to me at all. I rode shotgun, riveted by the payload of flour, sugar and sundries, not the least of which happened to include a case of weathered, leaky dynamite.

We wound along Anderson Creek Canyon, emerged in a hollow near some dredges and a mongrel collection of shacks. Cook-fires sputtered, monarch butterflies under cast-iron pots tended by women the color of ash. There were few children and no dogs. Any male old enough to handle pick, shovel or pan was among the clusters of men stolidly attacking the earth, wading in the frigid water, toiling among the rocky shelves above the encampment.

Nobody returned my friendly nod. Nobody even really looked at me except for two men who observed the proceedings from a copse of scraggly cottonwoods, single-shot rifles slung at half-mast. My hackles wouldn't lie down until Hung led me through the camp to a building that appeared to be three or four shanties in combination. He ushered me through a thick curtain and into a dim, moist realm pungent with body musk and opium tang.

"Koenig, at last. Pull up a rock." Butler lay on a pile of bear pelts near a guttering fire pit. He was wrapped in a Navajo blanket, but clearly emaciated. His misshapen skull resembled a chunk of anthracite sufficiently dense to crook his neck. His dark flesh had withered tight as rawhide and he appeared to be an eon older than his stentorian voice sounded. In short, he could've been a fossilized anthropoid at repose in Barnum's House of Curiosities.

Butler's attendant, a toothless crone with an evil squint, said, "*Mama die?*" She gently placed a long, slender pipe against his lips, waited for him to draw the load. She hooked another horrible glance my way and didn't offer to cook me a pill.

After a while Butler said, "You would've made a wonderful Templar."

"Except for the minor detail of suspecting Christianity is a pile of crap. Chopping down Saracens for fun and profit, that I could've done."

"You're a few centuries late. A modern-day crusader, then. An educated man, I presume?"

"Harvard, don't you know." I pronounced it Hah-vahd to maximize the irony.

"An *expensive* education; although, aren't they all. Still, a Pinkerton, tsk, tsk. Daddy was doubtless shamed beyond consolation."

"Papa Koenig was annoyed. One of the slickest New York lawyers you'll ever do battle with—came from a whole crabbed scroll of them. Said I was an ungrateful iconoclast before he disowned me. Hey, it's easier to shoot people than try to frame them, I've discovered."

"And now you've come to shoot poor Rueben Hicks."

"Rueben Hicks is a thief, a murderer and a cannibal. Seems prudent to put him down if I get the chance."

"Technically a cannibal is one that feeds on its own species."

I said, "Rueben doesn't qualify as a member?"

"That depends on your definition of human, Mr. Koenig." Butler said, and smiled. The contortion had a ghoulish effect on his face. "Because it goes on two legs and wears a coat and tie? Because it knows how to say please and thank you?"

"Why do I get the feeling this conversation is headed south? People were talking about you in town. You're a folk legend at the whorehouse."

"A peasant hero, as it were?"

"More like disgraced nobility. I can't figure what you're doing here. Could've picked a more pleasant climate to go to seed."

"I came to Purdon ages ago. Sailed from London where I had pursued a successful career in anthropology—flunked medical school, you see. Too squeamish. I dabbled in physics and astronomy, but primitive culture has always been my obsession. Its rituals, its primal energy."

"Plenty of primitive culture here."

"Quite."

"*Mama die?*" said the hag as she brandished the pipe.

Butler accepted the crone's ministrations. His milky eyes flared, and when he spoke, he spoke more deliberately. "I've been following your progress. You are capable, resourceful, tenacious. I fear Rueben will swallow you alive, but if anyone has a chance to put a stop to his wickedness it is you."

"Lead has a sobering effect on most folks." I said. "Strange to hear a debauched occultist like yourself fussing about wickedness. I take it you've got a personal stake in this manhunt. He must've hurt your feelings or something."

"Insomuch as I know he intends to use me as a blood sacrifice, I'm extremely interested."

"You ever thought of clearing out?"

"Impossible."

"Why impossible?"

"Gravity, Mr. Koenig." Butler took another hit. Eventually, he said in a dreamy tone, "I'm a neglectful host. Care to bang the gong?"

"Thanks, no."

"A reformed addict. How rare."

"I'll settle for being a drunk. What's your history with Hicks?"

"We were introduced in '78. I was in Philadelphia and had taken in the circus with some colleagues from the university. I fell in with a small group of the players after the show, Rueben being among this number. We landed in a tiny café, a decadent slice of gay Paris, and everybody was fabulously schnockered, to employ the argot. Rueben and I got to talking and we hit it off. I was amazed at the breadth, and I blush to admit, scandalous nature of his many adventures. He was remarkably cultured behind the provincial façade. I was intrigued. Smitten, too."

I said, "And here I thought Hicks was a ladies man."

"Rueben is an opportunist. We retired to my flat; all very much a night's work for me. Then…then after we'd consummated our mutual fascination, he said he wanted to show me something that would change my life. Something astounding."

"Do tell."

"We were eating mushrooms. A mysterious variety—Rueben stole them from P. T. and P. T. obtained them from this queer fellow who dealt in African imports. I hallucinated that Rueben caused a window to open in the bedroom wall, a portal into space. Boggling! Millions of stars blazed inches from my nose, a whole colossal bell-shaped galaxy of exploded gases and cosmic dust. The sight would've driven Copernicus insane. It was a trick, stage magic. Something he'd borrowed from his fellow performers. He asked me what I saw and I told him. His face…there was something wrong. Too rigid, too cold. For a moment, I thought he'd put on an extremely clever mask and I was terrified. And his mouth…His expression melted almost instantly, and he was just Rueben again. I knew better, though. And, unfortunately, my fascination intensified. Later, when he showed me the portal trick, this time sans hallucinogens, I realized he wasn't simply a circus performer. He claimed to be more than human, to have evolved into a superior iteration of the genus. A flawed analysis, but at least partially correct."

Hick's rubbery grin bobbed to the surface of my mind. "He's crazed, I'll give you that."

"Rueben suffers from a unique breed of mycosis—you've perhaps seen the tumors on his arms and legs, and especially along his spinal column? It's consuming him as a fungus consumes a tree. Perversely, it's this very parasitic influence that imbues him with numerous dreadful abilities. Evolution via slow digestion."

"Dreadful abilities? If he'd showed me a hole in the wall that looked on the moon's surface I might've figured he was a fakir, or Jesus' little brother, or what have you. He didn't. He didn't fly out of Cedar Grove, either."

"Scoff as you will. Ignorance is all the blessing we apes can hope for."

"What became of your torrid love affair?"

"He and I grew close. He confided many terrible things to me, unspeakable deeds. Ultimately I determined to venture here and visit his childhood haunts, to discover the wellspring of his vitality, the source of his preternatural affinities. He warned me, albeit such caveats were mere inducements to an inquisitive soul. I was so easily corrupted." Butler's voice trailed off as he was lost in reflection.

Corruption begets corruption, copper. "Sounds very romantic," I said. "What were you after? The gold? Nah, the gold is panned out or property of the companies. Mating practices of the natives?"

"I coveted knowledge, Mr. Koenig. Rueben whispered of a way to unlock the secrets of brain and blood, to lay bare the truth behind several of mankind's squalid superstitions. To walk the earth as a god. His mind is far from scientific, and but remotely curious. One could nearly categorize him as a victim of circumstance in this drama. I, however, presumably equipped with superior intellect, would profit all the more than my barbarous concubine. My potential seemed enormous."

"Yes, and look at you now, Professor," I said. "Do these people understand what you are?"

"What do you think I am, Detective?"

"A Satan-worshipping dope fiend."

"Wrong. I'm a naturalist. Would that I could reinvent my innocent dread of God and Satan, of supernatural phenomena. As for these yellow folk, they don't care what I am. I pay well for my upkeep and modest pleasures."

"For a man who's uncovered great secrets of existence, your accommodations lack couth."

"Behold the reward of hubris. I could've done as Rueben has—descended completely into the womb of an abominable mystery and evolved as a new and perfect savage. Too cowardly—I tasted the ichor of divinity and quailed, fled to this hovel and my drugs. My memories. Wisdom devours the weak." He shuddered and spat a singsong phrase that brought the old woman scuttling to feed him another load of dope. After he'd recovered, he produced a leather-bound book from beneath his pillow. The *Dictionnaire Infernal.* "A gift from our mutual acquaintance. Please, take it. These 'forbidden' tomes are surpassingly ludicrous."

I inspected the book; de Plancy's signature swooped across the title page. "Did Rueben travel all this way to fetch you a present and off a few hapless miners as a bonus?"

"Rueben has come home because he must, it is an integral component of his metamorphosis. Surely you've detected his quickening purpose, the apparent degeneration of his faculties, which is scarcely a symptom of decay, but rather a sign of fundamental alteration. Pupation. He has returned to this place to commune with his benefactor, to disgorge the red delights of his gruesome and sensuous escapades. Such is the pact between them. It is the pact all supplicants make. It was mine, before my defection."

My skin prickled at the matter-of-fact tone Butler affected. I said, "I don't get this, Professor. If you don't hold with demons and all that bunkum, what the hell are you worshipping?"

"Supplicating, dear boy. I didn't suggest we are alone in the cosmos. Certain monstrous examples of cryptogenetics serve the function of godhead well enough. That *scholars* invent fanciful titles and paint even more fanciful pictures does not diminish the essential reality of these organisms, only obscures it."

My suspicions about Butler's character were sharpening with the ebb and pulse of fire light. He lay coiled in his nest, a diamondback ready to strike. Not wanting an answer, I said, "Exactly what did you do to acquire this...knowledge?"

"I established communion with a primordial intelligence, a cyclopean plexus rooted below these hills and valleys. An unclassified mycoflora that might or might not be of terrestrial origin. There are rites to effect this dialogue. A variety of osmosis ancient as the sediment men first crawled from. Older! Most awful, I assure you."

"Christ, you've got holes in your brain from smoking way too much of the black O." I stood, covering my emotions with a grimace. "Next thing you'll tell me is Oberon came prancing from under his hill to sprinkle that magic fairy shit on you."

"You are the detective. Don't blame me if this little investigation uncovers things that discomfit your world view."

"Enough. Tell it to Charlie Darwin when you meet in hell. You want me to nail Hicks, stow the campfire tales and come across with his location."

"Rueben's visited infrequently since late spring. Most recently, three days ago. He promised to take me with him soon, to gaze once more upon the Father-Mother. Obviously I don't wish to make that pilgrimage. I'd rather die a nice peaceful death—being lit on fire, boiled in oil, staked to an ant hill. That sort of thing."

"Is he aware of my presence in Purdon?"

"Of course. He expected you weeks ago. I do believe he mentioned some casual harm to your person, opportunity permitting. Rest assured it never occurred to him that I might betray his interests, that I would dare. Frankly, I doubt he considers you a real threat—not here in his demesne. Delusion is part and parcel with his condition."

"Where is he right now?"

"Out and about. Satiating his appetites. Perhaps wallowing in the Presence. His ambit is wide and unpredictable. He may pop in tomorrow. He may appear in six months. Time means less and less to him. Time is a ring, and in the House of Belphegor that ring contracts like a muscle."

"The house?"

Butler's lips twitched at the corners. He said, "A cell in a black honeycomb. Rueben's father stumbled upon it during his missionary days. He had no idea what it was. The chamber existed before the continents split and the ice came over the world. The people that built it, long dust. I can give directions, but I humbly suggest you wait here for your nemesis. Safer."

"No harm in looking," I said.

"Oh, no, Mr. Koenig. There's more harm than you could ever dream."

"Enlighten me anyhow."

Butler seemed to have expected nothing less. Joyful as a sadist, he drew me a map.

12.

The cave wasn't far from camp.

Long-suffering Hung Chan and his younger brother Ha agreed to accompany me to the general area after a harangue from Butler and the exchange of American currency.

We essayed a thirty-minute hike through scrub and streams, then up a steep knoll littered with brush and treacherous rocks. Invisible from a distance, a limestone cliff face split vertically, formed a narrow gash about the height of the average man. The Chan brothers informed me through violent gestures and Pidgin English they'd await my return at the nearby riverbank. They retreated, snarling to themselves in their foreign dialect.

I crouched behind some rocks and cooled my heels for a lengthy spell. Nothing and more nothing. When I couldn't justify delaying any longer, I approached cautiously, in case Hicks was lying in ambush, rifle sights trained on the rugged slope. Immediately I noticed bizarre symbols scratched into the occasional boulder. Seasonal erosion had obliterated all save the deepest marks and these meant little to me, though it wasn't difficult to imagine they held some pagan significance. Also, whole skeletons of small animals—birds and squirrels—hung from low branches. Dozens of them, scattered like broken teeth across the hillside.

According to my pocket watch and the dull slant of sun through the clouds, I had nearly two hours of light. I'd creep close, have a peek and scurry back to the mining camp in time for supper. No way did I intend to navigate these backwoods after dark and risk breaking a leg, or worse. I was a city boy at heart.

I scrambled from boulder to boulder, pausing to see if anyone would emerge to take a pot shot. When I reached the summit I was sweating and my nerves twanged like violin strings.

The stench of spoiled meat, of curdled offal, emanated from the fissure; a slaughterhouse gone to the maggots. The vile odor stung my eyes, scourged deep into my throat. I knotted a balaclava from a handkerchief I'd appropriated from the Bumblebee Ranch, covered my mouth and nose.

A baby? I cocked my ears and didn't breathe until the throb of my pulse filled the universe. No baby. The soft moan of wind sucked through a chimney of granite.

I waited for my vision to clear and passed through the opening, pistol drawn

13.

so beautiful.

I

14.

stare at a wedge of darkening sky between the pines.

My cheeks burn, scorched with salt. I've been lying here in the shallows of a pebbly stream. I clutch the solid weight of my pistol in a death grip. The Chan brothers loom, hardly inscrutable. They are pale as flour. Their lips move silently. Their hands are on me. They drag me.

I keep staring at the sky, enjoy the vibration of my tongue as I hum. Tralalala.

The brothers release my arms, slowly edge away like automata over the crushed twigs. Their eyes are holes. Their mouths. I'm crouched, unsteady. My gun. Click. Click. Empty. But my knife my Jim Bowie special is here somewhere is in my hand. Ssaa! The brothers Chan are phantoms, loping. Deer. Mirages. My knife. Quivers in a tree trunk.

Why am I so happy. Why must I cover myself in the leaves and dirt.

Rain patters upon my roof.

15.

Time is a ring. Time is a muscle. It contracts.

16.

colloidal iris

17.

the pillar of faces

18.

migrant spores

19.

maggots

20.

glows my ecstasy in a sea of suns

21.

galactic parallax

22.

I had been eating leaves. Or at least there were leaves crammed in my mouth. Sunlight dribbled through the gleaming branches. I vomited leaves. I found a trickle of water, snuffled no prouder than a hog.

Everything was small and bright. Steam seeped from my muddy clothes. My shirt was starched with ejaculate, matted to my belly as second skin. I knelt in the damp needles and studied my filthy hands. My hands were shiny as metal on a casket.

Butler chortled from a spider-cocoon in the green limbs, "*Now you're seasoned for his palette. Best run, Pinkerton. You've been in the sauce. Chewed up and shat out. And if you live, in twenty years you'll be another walking Mouth.*" He faded into the woodwork.

I made a meticulous job of scrubbing the grime and blood from my hands. I washed my face in the ice water, hesitated at the sticky bur of my mustache and hair, finally dunked my head under. The shock brought comprehension crashing down around my ears.

I remembered crossing over a threshold.

Inside, the cave is larger than I'd supposed, and humid.

Water gurgling in rock. Musty roots the girth of sequoias.

Gargantuan statues embedded in wattles of amber.

The cave mouth a seam of brightness that rotates until it is a blurry hatch in the ceiling.

My boots losing contact with the ground, as if I were weightless.

Floating away from the light, towards a moist chasm, purple warmth.

Darkness blooms, vast and sweet.

Gibberish, after.

I walked back to Forty-Mile Camp, my thoughts pleasantly disjointed.

23.

Labor ground to a halt when I stumbled into their midst. None spoke. No one tried to stop me from hunching over a kettle and slopping fistfuls of boiled rice, gorging like a beast. Nor when I hefted a rusty spade and padded into Butler's hut to pay my respects. Not even when I emerged, winded, and tore through the crates of supplies and helped myself to several sticks of dynamite with all the trimmings.

I smiled hugely at them, couldn't think of anything to say.

They stood in a half-moon, stoic as carvings. I wandered off into the hills.

24.

The explosion was gratifying.

Dust billowed, a hammerhead cloud that soon collapsed under its own ambition. I thought of big sticks and bigger nests full of angry hornets. I wasn't even afraid, really.

Some open, others close.

25.

After I pounded on the door for ten minutes, a girl named Evelyn came out and found me on the front porch of the whorehouse, slumped across the swing and muttering nonsense. Dawn was breaking and the stars were so pretty.

I asked for Violet. Evelyn said she'd lit a shuck from the Bumblebee Ranch for parts unknown.

Octavia took in my frightful appearance and started snapping orders. She and a couple of the girls lugged me to a room and shoved me in a scalding bath. I didn't protest; somebody slapped a bottle of whiskey in my hand and lost the cork. Somebody else must've taken one look at the needle work on my arm and decided to snag some morphine from Doc Campion's bag of black magic. They shot me to the moon and reality melted into a slag of velvet and honey. I tumbled off the wagon and got crushed under its wheels.

"You going home one of these days?" Octavia squeezed water from a sponge over my shoulders. "Back to the Old States?" She smelled nice. Everything smelled of roses and lavender; nice.

I didn't know what day this was. Shadows clouded the teak panels. This place was firecracker hot back in the '50s. What a hoot it must've been while the West was yet wild. My lips were swollen. I was coming down hard, a piece of rock plunging from the sky. I said, "Uh, huh. You?" It occurred to me that I was fixating again, probably worse than when I originally acquired my dope habits. Every time my eyes dilated I was thrust into a Darwinian phantasm. A fugue state wherein the chain of humanity shuttered rapidly from the first incomprehensible amphibian creature to slop ashore, through myriad semi-erect sapiens slouching across chaotically shifting landscapes, unto the frantic masses in coats and dresses teeming about the stone and glass of Earth's megalopolises. I had vertigo.

"Any day now."

My ears still rang, might always.

Fading to a speck—the hilltop, decapitated in a thunderclap and a belch of dust. Boulders reduced to shattered bits, whizzing around me, a miracle I wasn't pulverized. Was that me, pitching like Samson before the Philistine army? More unreal with each drip of scented wax. My eyes were wet. I turned my head so Octavia wouldn't notice.

"Tommy Mullen came around today. You're still lookin' for Tommy. Right?"

"You see him?"

"Naw. Kavanaugh was talkin' to Dalton Beaumont, mentioned he saw Tommy on the street. Fella waved to him and went into an alley. Didn't come out again. Could be he's scared you'll get a bead on him."

"Could be."

Octavia said, "Glynna heard tell Langston Butler passed on. Died in his sleep. Guess the yellow boys held a ceremony. Reverend Fuller's talkin' 'bout ridin' to Forty-Mile, see that the Professor gets himself a Christian burial." She became quiet, kneading my neck with steely fingers. Then, "I'm powerful sad. The Professor was a decent man. You know he was the sawbones for three, four years? He did for the young 'uns as got themselves with child. Gentle as a father. Campion came along and the Professor fell to the coolie mud. Shame."

My smile was lye-hot and humorless. "He didn't limit his moonlighting to abortions. Butler did for the babies too, didn't he? The ones that were born here at the Ranch."

Octavia didn't answer.

All those whores' babies tossed into a pitchy shaft, tiny wails smothered in the great chthonian depths. I laughed, hollow. "The accidents. Don't see many orphanages this far north."

Octavia said, "How do you mean to settle your tab, by the by?" She was getting colder by the second. She must've gone through my empty wallet.

"For services rendered? Good question, lady."

"You gave your *whole* poke to Violet?" Her disbelief was tinged with scorn. "That's plain loco, mister. Why?"

The room was fuzzy. "I don't suppose I'll be needing it, where I'm going. I did an impetuous deed, Octavia. Can't take back the bet once it's on the table." Where was I going? Into a box into the ground, if I was lucky. The alternative was just too unhappy. I listened for the ticktock of transmogrifying cells that would indicate my descent into the realm of superhuman. Damnation; the bottle was dry. I dropped it into the sudsy water, watched it sink. Glowed there between my black and blue thighs.

"Musta been a heap of coin. You love her, or somethin'?"

I frowned. "Another excellent question. No, I reckon I don't love her. She's just too good for the likes of you, is all. Hate to see her spoil."

Octavia left without even a kiss goodbye.

26.

At least my clothes were washed and pressed and laid out properly.

I dressed with the ponderous calculation of a man on his way to a funeral. I cleaned my pistol, inspected the cylinder reflexively—it's easy to tell how many bullets are loaded by the weight of the weapon in your hand.

The whores had shaved me and I cut a respectable figure except for the bruises and the sagging flesh under my eyes. My legs were unsteady. I went by the back stairs, unwilling to list through the parlor where the piano crashed and the shouts of evening debauchery swelled to a frenzied peak.

It was raining again; be snowing in another week or so. The mud-caked board-walks stretched emptily before unlit shop windows. I shuffled, easily confused by the darkness and the rushing wind.

The hotel waited, tomb-dark and utterly desolate.

Like a man mounting the scaffold, I climbed the three flights of squeaking stairs to my room, turned the key in the lock after the fourth or fifth try, and knew what was what as I stepped through and long before anything began to happen.

The room stank like an abattoir. I lighted a lamp on the dresser and its frail luminance caught the edge of spikes and loops on the bathroom door. This scrawl read, *BELPHEGORBELPHEGORBELPHEGOR*.

The mirror shuddered. A mass of shadows unfolded in the corner, became a tower. Hicks whispered from a place behind and above my left shoulder, "Hello again, Pinky."

"Hello yourself." I turned and fired and somewhere between the yellow flash and the new hole in the ceiling He snatched my wrist and the pistol went car-oming across the floor. I dangled; my trigger finger was broken and my elbow dislocated, but I didn't feel a thing yet.

Hicks smiled almost kindly. He said, "I told you, Pinky. Close one hole, an-other opens." His face split at the seams, a terrible flower bending toward my light, my heat.

PROBOSCIS

1.

After the debacle in British Columbia, we decided to crash the Bluegrass festival. Not we—Cruz. Everybody else just shrugged and said yeah, whatever you say, dude. Like always. Cruz was the alpha-alpha of our motley pack.

We followed the handmade signs onto a dirt road and ended up in a muddy pasture with maybe a thousand other cars and beat-to-hell tourist buses. It was a regular extravaganza—pavilions, a massive stage, floodlights. A bit farther out, they'd built a bonfire, and Dead-Heads were writhing with pagan exuberance among the cinder-streaked shadows. The brisk air swirled heavy scents of marijuana and clove, of electricity and sex.

The amplified ukulele music was giving me a migraine. Too many people smashed together, limbs flailing in paroxysms. Too much white light followed by too much darkness. I'd gone a couple beers over my limit because my face was Novocain-numb and I found myself dancing with some sloe-eyed coed who'd fixed her hair in corn rows. Her shirt said *MILK*.

She was perhaps a bit prettier than the starlet I'd ruined my marriage with way back in the days of yore, but resembled her in a few details. What were the odds? I didn't even attempt to calculate. A drunken man cheek to cheek with a strange woman under the harvest moon was a tricky proposition.

"Lookin' for somebody, or just rubberneckin'?" The girl had to shout over the hi-fi jug band. Her breath was peppermint and whiskey.

"I lost my friends," I shouted back. A sea of bobbing heads beneath a gulf of night sky and none of them belonged to anyone I knew. Six of us had piled out of two cars and now I was alone. Last of the Mohicans.

The girl grinned and patted my cheek. "You ain't got no friends, Ray-bo."

I tried to ask how she came up with that, but she was squirming and pointing over my shoulder.

"My gawd, look at all those stars, will ya?"

Sure enough the stars were on parade; cold, cruel radiation bleeding across improbable distances. I was more interested in the bikers lurking near the stage and the beer garden. Creepy and mean, spoiling for trouble. I guessed Cruz and Hart would be nearby, copping the vibe, as it were.

The girl asked me what I did and I said I was an actor between jobs. Anything she'd seen? No, probably not. Then I asked her and she said something I didn't quite catch. It was either etymologist or entomologist. There was another thing, impossible to hear. She looked so serious I asked her to repeat it.

"Right through your meninges. Sorta like a siphon."

"What?" I said.

"I guess it's a delicacy. They say it don't hurt much, but I say nuts to that."

"A delicacy?"

She made a face. "I'm goin' to the garden. Want a beer?"

"No, thanks." As it was, my legs were ready to fold. The girl smiled, a wistful imp, and kissed me briefly, chastely. She was swallowed into the masses and I didn't see her again.

After a while I staggered to the car and collapsed. I tried to call Sylvia, wanted to reassure her and Carly that I was okay, but my cell wouldn't cooperate. Couldn't raise my watchdog friend, Rob in LA. He'd be going bonkers too. I might as well have been marooned on a desert island. Modern technology, my ass. I watched the windows shift through a foggy spectrum of pink and yellow. Lulled by the monotone thrum, I slept.

Dreamt of wasp nests and wasps. And rare orchids, coronas tilted towards the awesome bulk of clouds. The flowers were a battery of organic radio telescopes receiving a sibilant communiqué just below my threshold of comprehension.

A mosquito pricked me and when I crushed it, blood ran down my finger, hung from my nail.

2.

Cruz drove. He said, "I wanna see the Mima Mounds."

Hart said, "Who's Mima?" He rubbed the keloid on his beefy neck.

Bulletproof glass let in light from a blob of moon. I slumped in the tricked-out back seat, where our prisoner would've been if we'd managed to bring him home. I stared at the grille partition, the leg irons and the doors with no handles. A crusty vein traced black tributaries on the floorboard. Someone had scratched R+G and a fanciful depiction of Ronald Reagan's penis. This was an old car. It reeked of cigarette smoke, of stale beer, of a million exhalations.

Nobody asked my opinion. I'd melted into the background smear.

The brutes were smacked out of their gourds on junk they'd picked up on the Canadian side at the festival. Hart had tossed the bag of syringes and miscellaneous garbage off a bridge before we crossed the border. That was where we'd parted ways with the other guys—Leon, Rufus and Donnie. Donnie was the one who had gotten nicked by a stray bullet in Donkey Creek, earned himself bragging rights if nothing else. Jersey boys, the lot; they were going to take the high road home, maybe catch the rodeo in Montana.

Sunrise forged a pale seam above the distant mountains. We were rolling through certified boondocks, thumping across rickety wooden bridges that could've been thrown down around the Civil War. On either side of busted up two-lane blacktop were overgrown fields and hills dense with maples and poplar. Scotch broom reared on lean stalks, fire-yellow heads lolling hungrily. Scotch broom was Washington's rebuttal to kudzu. It was quietly everywhere, feeding in the cracks of the earth.

Road signs floated nearly extinct; letters faded, or bullet-raddled, dimmed by pollen and sap. Occasionally, dirt tracks cut through high grass to farmhouses. Cars passed us head-on, but not often, and usually local rigs—camouflage-green flatbeds with winches and trailers, two-tone pickups, decrepit jeeps. Nothing with out-of-state plates. I started thinking we'd missed a turn somewhere along the line. Not that I would've broached the subject. By then I'd learned to keep my mouth shut and let nature take its course.

"Do you even know where the hell they are?" Hart said. Hart was sour about the battle royal at the wharf. He figured it would give the bean counters an excuse to waffle about the payout for Piers' capture. I suspected he was correct.

"The Mima Mounds?"

"Yeah."

"Nope." Cruz rolled down the window, squirted beechnut over his shoulder, contributing another racing streak to the paint job. He twisted the radio dial and conjured Johnny Cash confessing that he'd "shot a man in Reno just to watch him die."

"Real man'd swallow," Hart said. "Like Josey Wales."

My cell beeped and I didn't catch Cruz's rejoinder. It was Carly. She'd seen the bust on the news and was worried, had been trying to reach me. The report mentioned shots fired and a wounded person, and I said yeah, one of our guys got clipped in the ankle, but he was okay, I was okay and the whole thing was over. We'd bagged the bad guy and all was right with the world. I promised to be home in a couple of days and told her to say hi to her mom. A wave of static drowned the connection.

I hadn't mentioned that the Canadians contemplated jailing us for various legal infractions and inciting mayhem. Her mother's blood pressure was already sky-high over what Sylvia called my "midlife adventure." Hard to blame her—it was my youthful "adventures" that set the torch to our unhappy marriage.

What Sylvia didn't know, couldn't know, because I lacked the grit to bare my soul at this late stage of our separation, was during the fifteen-martini lunch meeting with Hart, he'd showed me a few pictures to seal the deal. A roster of smiling teenage girls that could've been Carly's schoolmates. Hart explained in graphic detail what the bad man liked to do to these kids. Right there it became less of an adventure and more of a mini-crusade. I'd been an absentee father for fifteen years. Here was my chance to play Lancelot.

Cruz said he was hungry enough to eat the ass-end of a rhino and Hart said stop and buy breakfast at the greasy spoon coming up on the left, materializing as if by sorcery, so they pulled in and parked alongside a rusted-out Pontiac on blocks. Hart remembered to open the door for me that time. One glimpse of the diner's filthy windows and the coils of dogshit sprinkled across the unpaved lot convinced me I wasn't exactly keen on going in for the special.

But I did.

The place was stamped 1950s from the long counter with a row of shiny black swivel stools and the too-small window booths, dingy Formica peeling at the edges of the tables, to the bubble-screen TV wedged high up in a corner alcove. The TV was flickering with grainy black-and-white images of a talk show I didn't recognize and couldn't hear because the volume was turned way down. Mercifully I didn't see myself during the commercials.

I slouched at the counter and waited for the waitress to notice me. Took a while—she was busy flirting with Hart and Cruz, who'd squeezed themselves into a booth, and of course they wasted no time in regaling her with their latest exploits as hardcase bounty hunters. By now it was purely mechanical; rote bravado. They were pale as sheets and running on fumes of adrenaline and junk. Oh, how I dreaded the next twenty-four to thirty-six hours.

Their story was edited for heroic effect. My private version played a little differently.

We finally caught the desperado and his best girl in the Maple Leaf Country. After a bit of "slap and tickle," as Hart put it, we handed the miscreants over to the Canadians, more or less intact. Well, the Canadians more or less took possession of the pair.

The bad man was named Russell Piers, a convicted rapist and kidnaper who'd cut a nasty swath across the great Pacific Northwest and British Columbia. The girl was Penny Aldon, a runaway, an orphan, the details varied, but she wasn't important, didn't even drive; was along for the thrill, according to the reports. They fled to a river town, were loitering wharf-side, munching on a fish basket from one of six jillion Vietnamese vendors when the team descended.

Piers proved something of a Boy Scout—always prepared. He yanked a pistol from his waistband and started blazing, but one of him versus six of us only works in the movies and he went down under a swarm of blackjacks, Tasers and fists. I ran the hand-cam, got the whole jittering mess on film.

The film.

That was on my mind, sneaking around my subconscious like a night prowler. There was a moment during the scrum when a shiver of light distorted the scene, or I had a near-fainting spell, or who knows. The men on the sidewalk snapped and snarled, hyenas bringing down a wounded lion. Foam spattered the lens. I swayed, almost tumbled amid the violence. And Piers looked directly at me. Grinned at me. A big dude, even bigger than the troglodytes clinging to him, he had Cruz in a headlock, was ready to crush bones, to ravage flesh, to feast. A beast all right, with long, greasy hair, powerful hands scarred by prison tattoos, gold in his teeth. Inhuman, definitely. He wasn't a lion, though. I didn't know what kingdom he belonged to.

Somebody cold-cocked Piers behind the ear and he switched off, slumped like a mannequin that'd been bowled over by the holiday stampede.

Flutter, flutter and all was right with the world, relatively speaking. Except my bones ached and I was experiencing a not-so-mild wave of paranoia that hung on for hours. Never completely dissipated, even here in the sticks at a godforsaken hole-in-the-wall while my associates preened for an audience of one.

Cruz and Hart had starred on *Cops* and *America's Most Wanted;* they were celebrity experts. Too loud, the three of them honking and squawking, especially my ex-brother-in-law. Hart resembled a hog that decided to put on a dirty shirt and steel toe boots and go on its hind legs. Him being high as a kite wasn't helping. Sylvia tried to warn me; she'd known what her brother was about since they were kids knocking around on the wrong side of Des Moines.

I didn't listen. "*C'mon, Sylvie, there's a book in this. Hell, a Movie of the Week!*" Hart was on the inside of a rather seamy yet wholly marketable industry. He had a friend who had a friend who had a general idea where Mad Dog Piers was running. Money in the bank. See you in a few weeks, hold my calls.

"Watcha want, hon?" The waitress, a strapping lady with a tag spelling Victoria, poured translucent coffee into a cup that suggested the dishwasher wasn't quite up to snuff. Like all pro waitresses she pulled off this trick without looking away from my face. "I know you?" And when I politely smiled and reached for the sugar, she kept coming, frowning now as her brain began to labor. "You somebody? An actor or somethin'?"

I shrugged in defeat. "Uh, yeah. I was in a couple TV movies. Small roles. Long time ago."

Her face animated, a craggy talking tree. "Hey! You were on that comedy, one with the blind guy and his seein' eye dog. Only the guy was a con man or somethin', wasn't really blind and his dog was an alien or somethin', a robot, don't recall. Yeah, I remember you. What happened to that show?"

"Cancelled." I glanced longingly through the screen door to our ugly Chevy.

"Ray does shampoo ads," Hart said. He said something to Cruz and they cracked up.

"Milk of magnesia!" Cruz said. "And 'If you suffer from erectile dysfunction, now there's an answer!'" He delivered the last in a passable radio announcer's voice, although I'd heard him do better. He was hoarse.

The sun went behind a cloud, but Victoria still wanted my autograph, just in case I made a comeback, or got killed in a sensational fashion and then my signature would be worth something. She even dragged Sven the cook out to shake my hand and he did it with the dedication of a zombie following its mistress' instructions before shambling back to whip up eggs and hash for my comrades.

The coffee tasted like bleach.

The talk show ended and the next program opened with a still shot of a field covered by mossy hummocks and blackberry thickets. The black-and-white imagery threw me. For a moment I didn't recognize the car parked between mounds. Our boxy Chevy with the driver-side door hanging ajar, mud-encrusted plates, taillights blinking SOS.

A gray hand reached from inside, slammed the door. A hand? Or something like a hand? A B-movie prosthesis? Too blurry, too fast to be certain.

Victoria changed the channel to All My Children.

3.

Hart drove.

Cruz navigated. He tilted a road map, trying to follow the dots and dashes. Victoria had drawled a convoluted set of directions to the Mima Mounds, a one-star tourist attraction about thirty miles over. Cruise on through Poger Rock and head west. Real easy drive if you took the local shortcuts and suchlike.

Not an unreasonable detour; I-5 wasn't far from the site—we could do the tourist bit and still make the Portland night scene. That was Cruz's sales pitch. Kind of funny, really. I wondered at the man's sudden fixation on geological phenomena. He was a NASCAR and *Soldier of Fortune* magazine type personality. Hart fit the profile too, for that matter. Damned world was turning upside down.

It was getting hot. Cracks in the windshield dazzled and danced.

The boys debated cattle mutilations and the inarguable complicity of the Federal government regarding the Grey Question and how the moon landing was fake and remember that flick from the 1970s, *Capricorn One*, goddamned if O. J. wasn't one of the astronauts. Freakin' hilarious.

I unpacked the camera, thumbed the playback button, and relived the Donkey Creek fracas. Penny said to me, "*Reduviidae*—any of a species of large insects that feed on the blood of prey insects and some mammals. They are considered extremely beneficial by agricultural professionals." Her voice was made of tin and lagged behind her lip movements, like a badly dubbed foreign film. She stood on the periphery of the action, scrawny fingers pleating the wispy fabric of a blue sundress. She was smiling. "The indices of primate emotional thresholds indicate the [*click-click*] process is traumatic. However, point oh-two percent vertebrae harvest corresponds to non-[*click-click*] purposes. As an X haplotype you are a primary source of [*click-click*]. Lucky you!"

"Jesus!" I muttered, and dropped the camera on the seat. *Are you talkin' to me?* I stared at too many trees while Robert De Niro did his *Taxi Driver* schtick as a low frequency monologue in the corner of my mind. Unlike De Niro, I'd never carried a gun. The guys wouldn't even loan me a Taser.

"What?" Cruz said in a tone that suggested he'd almost jumped out of his skin.

He glared through the partition, olive features drained to ash. Giant drops of sweat sparkled and dripped from his broad cheeks. The light wrapped his skull, halo of an angry saint. Withdrawal's something fierce, I decided.

I shook my head, waited for the magnifying glass of his displeasure to swing back to the road map. When it was safe I hit the playback button. Same scene on the view panel. This time when Penny entered the frame she pointed at me and intoned in a robust, Slavic accent, "Supercalifragilisticexpialidocious is Latin for a death god of a primitive Mediterranean culture. Their civilization was buried in mudslides caused by unusual seismic activity. If you say it loud enough—" I hit the kill button. My stomach roiled with rancid coffee and incipient motion-sickness.

Third time's a charm, right? I played it back again. The entire sequence was erased. Nothing but deep-space black with jags of silvery light at the edges. In the middle, skimming by so swiftly I had to freeze things to get a clear image, was Piers with his lips nuzzling Cruz's ear, and Cruz's face was corpse-slack. And for an instant, a microsecond, the face was Hart's too; one of those three-dee poster illusions where the object changes depending on the angle. Then, more nothingness, and an odd feedback noise that faded in and out, like Gregorian monks chanting a litany in reverse.

Okay. ABC time.

I'd reviewed the footage shortly after the initial capture in Canada. There was nothing unusual about it. We spent a few hours at the police station answering a series of polite yet penetrating questions. I assumed our cameras would be confiscated, but the inspector simply examined our equipment in the presence of a couple suits from a legal office. Eventually the inspector handed everything back with a stern admonishment to leave dangerous criminals to the authorities. Amen to that.

Had a cop tampered with the camera, doctored it in some way? I wasn't a filmmaker, didn't know much more than point and shoot and change the batteries when the little red light started blinking. So, yeah, Horatio, it was possible someone had screwed with the recording. Was that likely? The answer was no—not unless they'd also managed to monkey with the television at the diner. More likely one of my associates had spiked the coffee with a miracle agent and I was hallucinating. Seemed out of character for those greedy bastards, even for the sake of a practical joke on their third wheel—dope was expensive and it wasn't like we were expecting a big payday.

The remaining options weren't very appealing.

My cell whined, a dentist's drill in my shirt pocket. It was Rob Fries from his patio office in Gardena. Rob was tall, bulky, pink on top and garbed according to his impression of what Miami vice cops might've worn in a bygone era, such as the '80s. Rob also had the notion he was my agent despite the fact I'd fired him ten years ago after he handed me one too many scripts for laxative testimonials. I almost broke into tears when I heard his voice on the buzzing line. "Man, am I glad you called!" I said loudly enough to elicit another scowl from Cruz.

"*Hola, compadre.* What a splash y'all made on page 16. *'American Yahoos Run Amok!'* goes the headline, which is a quote of the Calgary rag. Too bad the stupid bastards let our birds fly the coop. Woulda been better press if they fried 'em. Well, they don't have the death penalty, but you get the point. Even so, I see a major motion picture deal in the works. *Mucho dinero,* Ray, buddy!"

"Fly the coop? What are you talking about?"

"Uh, you haven't heard? Piers and the broad walked. Hell, they probably beat you outta town."

"You better fill me in." Indigestion was eating the lining of my esophagus.

"Real weird story. Some schmuck from Central Casting accidentally turned 'em loose. The paperwork got misfiled or somesuch bullshit. The muckety-mucks are p.o.'d. Blows your mind, don't it?"

"Right," I said in my actor's tone. I fell back on this when my mind was in neutral but etiquette dictated a polite response. Up front, Cruz and Hart were bickering, hadn't caught my exclamation. No way was I going to illuminate them regarding this development—Christ, they'd almost certainly consider pulling a U-turn and speeding back to Canada. The home office would be calling any second now to relay the news; probably had been trying to get through for hours—Hart hated phones, usually kept his stashed in the glovebox.

There was a burst of chittery static. "—returning your call. Keep getting the answering service. You won't believe it—I was having lunch with this chick used to be one of Johnny Carson's secretaries, yeah? And she said her best friend is shacking with an exec who just frickin' adored you in *Clancy & Spot.* Frickin' adored you! I told my gal pal to pass the word you were riding along on this bounty hunter gig, see what shakes loose."

"Oh, thanks, Rob. Which exec?"

"Lemmesee—uh, Harry Buford. Remember him? He floated deals for the *Alpha Team*, some other stuff. Nice as hell. Frickin' adores you, buddy."

"Harry Buford? Looks like the Elephant Man's older, fatter brother, loves pastels and lives in Mexico half the year because he's fond of underage Chicano girls? Did an exposé piece on the evils of Hollywood, got himself blackballed? That the guy?"

"Well, yeah. But he's still got an ear to the ground. And he frickin'—"

"Adores me. Got it. Tell your girlfriend we'll all do lunch, or whatever."

"Anywho, how you faring with the gorillas?"

"Um, great. We're on our way to see the Mima Mounds."

"What? You on a nature study?"

"Cruz's idea."

"The Mima Mounds. Wow. Never heard of them. Burial grounds, huh?"

"Earth heaves, I guess. They've got them all over the world—Norway, South America, Eastern Washington—I don't know where all. I lost the brochure."

"Cool." The silence hung for a long moment. "Your buddies wanna see some, whatchyacallem—?"

"Glacial deposits."

"They wanna look at some rocks instead of hitting a strip club? No bullshit?"

"Um, yeah."

It was easy to imagine Rob frowning at his flip-flops propped on the patio table while he stirred the ice in his rum and Coke and tried to do the math. "Have a swell time, then."

"You do me a favor?"

"Yo, bro'. Hit me."

"Go on the Net and look up 'X haplotype.' Do it right now, if you've got a minute."

"X-whatsis?"

I spelled it and said, "Call me back, okay? If I'm out of area, leave a message with the details."

"Be happy to." There was a pause as he scratched pen to pad. "Some kinda new meds, or what?"

"Or what, I think."

"Uh-huh. Well, I'm just happy the Canucks didn't make you an honorary citizen, eh. I'm dying to hear the scoop."

"I'm dying to dish it. I'm losing my signal, gotta sign off."

He said not to worry, bro', and we disconnected. I worried anyway.

4.

Sure enough, Hart's phone rang a bit later and he exploded in a stream of repetitious profanity and dented the dash with his ham hock of a fist. He was still bubbling when we pulled into Poger Rock for gas and fresh directions. Cruz, on the other hand, accepted the news of Russell Piers' "early parole" with a Zen detachment demonstrably contrary to his nature.

"Screw it. Let's drink," was his official comment.

Poger Rock was sunk in a hollow about fifteen miles south of the state capitol in Olympia. It wasn't impressive—a dozen or so antiquated buildings moldering along the banks of a shallow creek posted with NO SHOOTING signs. Everything was peeling, rusting or collapsing toward the center of the Earth. Only the elementary school loomed incongruously—a utopian brick and tile structure set back and slightly elevated, fresh paint glowing through the alders and dogwoods. Aliens might have landed and dedicated a monument.

Cruz filled up at a mom-and-pop gas station with the prehistoric pumps that took an eon to dribble forth their fuel. I bought some jerky and a carton of milk with a past-due expiration date to soothe my churning guts. The lady behind the counter had yellowish hair and wore a button with a fuzzy picture of a toddler in a bib. She smiled nervously as she punched keys and furiously smoked a Pall Mall. Didn't recognize me, thank God.

Cruz pushed through the door, setting off the ding-dong alarm. His gaze jumped all over the place and his chambray shirt was molded to his chest as if he'd been doused with a water hose. He crowded past me, trailing the odor of armpit funk and cheap cologne, grunted at the cashier and shoved his credit card across the counter.

I raised my hand to block the sun when I stepped outside. Hart was leaning on the hood. "We're gonna mosey over to the bar for a couple brewskis." He coughed his smoker's cough, spat in the gravel near a broken jar of marmalade. Bees darted among the wreckage.

"What about the Mima Mounds?"

"They ain't goin' anywhere. 'Sides, it ain't time, yet."

"Time?"

Hart's ferret-pink eyes narrowed and he smiled slightly. He finished his cigarette and lighted another from the smoldering butt. "Cruz says it ain't."

"Well, what does that mean? It 'ain't time'?"

"I dunno, Ray-bo. I dunno fuckall. Why'nchya ask Cruz?"

"Okay." I took a long pull of tepid milk while I considered the latest developments in what was becoming the most bizarre road trip of my life. "How are you feeling?"

"Groovy."

"You look like hell." I could still talk to him, after a fashion, when he was separated from Cruz. And I lied, "Sylvia's worried."

"What's she worried about?"

I shrugged, let it hang. Impossible to read his face, his swollen eyes. In truth, I wasn't sure I completely recognized him, this wasted hulk swaying against the car, features glazed into gargoyle contortions.

Hart nodded wisely, suddenly illuminated regarding a great and abiding mystery of the universe. His smile returned.

I glanced back, saw Cruz's murky shadow drifting in the station window.

"Man, what are we doing out here? We could be in Portland by three." What I wanted to say was, let's jump in the car and shag ass for California. Leave Cruz in the middle of the parking lot holding his pecker and swearing eternal vengeance for all I cared.

"Anxious to get going on your book, huh?"

"If there's a book. I'm not much of a writer. I don't even know if we'll get a movie out of this mess."

"Ain't much of an actor, either." He laughed and slapped my shoulder with an iron paw to show he was just kidding. "Hey, lemme tell'ya. Did'ya know Cruz studied geology at UCLA? He did. Real knowledgeable about glaciers an' rocks. All that good shit. Thought he was gonna work for the oil companies up in Alaska. Make some fat stacks. Ah, but you know how it goes, doncha, Ray-bo?"

"He graduated UCLA?" I tried not to sound astonished. It had been the University of Washington for me. The home of medicine, which wasn't my specialty, according to the proctors. Political science and drama were the last exits.

"Football scholarship. Hard hittin' safety with a nasty attitude. They fuckin' grow on trees in the ghetto."

That explained some things. I was inexplicably relieved.

Cruz emerged, cutting a plug of tobacco with his pocket knife. "C'mon, H. I'm parched." And precisely as a cowboy would unhitch his horse to ride across the street, he fired the engine and rumbled the one-quarter block to Moony's Tavern and parked in a diagonal slot between a hay truck and a station wagon plastered with anti-Democrat, pro-gun bumper stickers.

Hart asked if I planned on joining them and I replied maybe in a while, I wanted to stretch my legs. The idea of entering that sweltering cavern and bellying up to the bar with the lowlife regulars and mine own dear chums made my stomach even more unhappy.

I grabbed my valise from the car and started walking. I walked along the street, past a row of dented mailboxes, rust-red flags erect; an outboard motor repair shop with a dusty police cruiser in front; the Poger Rock Grange, which appeared abandoned because its windows were boarded and where they weren't, kids had broken them with rocks and bottles, and maybe the same kids had drawn 666 and other satanic symbols on the whitewashed planks, or maybe real live Satanists did the deed; Bob's Liquor Mart, which was a corrugated shed with bars on the tiny windows; the Laundromat, full of tired women in oversized tee-shirts, and screeching, dirty-faced kids racing among the machinery while an A.M. radio broadcast a Rush Limbaugh rerun; and a trailer loaded with half-rotted firewood for 75 BUCKS! I finally sat on a rickety bench under some trees near the lone stoplight, close enough to hear it clunk through its cycle.

I drew a manila envelope from the valise, spread sloppy typed police reports and disjointed photographs beside me. The breeze stirred and I used a rock for a paper weight.

A whole slew of the pictures featured Russell Piers in various poses, mostly mug shots, although a few had been snapped during more pleasant times. There was even one of him and a younger brother standing in front of the Space Needle. The remaining photos were of Piers' latest girlfriend—Penny Aldon, the girl from Allen Town. Skinny, pimply, mouthful of braces. A flower child with a suitably vacuous smirk.

Something cold and nasty turned over in me as I studied the haphazard data, the disheveled photo collection. I felt the pattern, unwholesome as damp cobwebs against my skin. Felt it, yet couldn't put a name to it, couldn't put my finger on it and my heart began pumping dangerously and I looked away, thought of Carly instead, and how I'd forgotten to call her on her seventh birthday because I was in Spain with some friends at a Lipizzaner exhibition. Except, I hadn't forgotten, I was wired for sound from a snort of primo Colombian blow and the thought of dialing that long string of international numbers was too much for my circuits.

Ancient history, as they say. Those days of fast-living and superstar dreams belonged to another man, and he was welcome to them.

Waiting for cars to drive past so I could count them, I had an epiphany. I realized the shabby buildings were cardboard and the people milling here and there at opportune junctures were macaroni and glue. Dull blue construction paper sky and cotton ball clouds. And I wasn't really who I thought of myself as—I was an ant left over from a picnic raid, awaiting some petulant child-god to put his boot down on my pathetic diorama existence.

My cell rang and an iceberg calved in my chest.

"Hey, Ray, you got any Indian in ya?" Rob asked.

I mulled that as a brand new Cadillac convertible paused at the light. A pair of yuppie tourists mildly argued about directions—a man behind the wheel in stylish wraparound shades and a polo shirt, and a woman wearing a floppy, wide-brimmed hat like the Queen Mum favored. They pretended not to notice me. The woman pointed right and they went right, leisurely, up the hill and beyond. "Comanche," I said. Next was a shiny green van loaded with Asian kids. Sign on the door said THE EVERGREEN STATE COLLEGE. It turned right and so did the one that came after. "About one thirty-second. Am I eligible for some reparation money? Did I inherit a casino?"

"Where the hell did the Comanche sneak in?"

"Great-grandma. Tough old bird. Didn't like me much. Sent me a straight razor for Christmas. I was nine."

Rob laughed. "Cra-zee. I did a search and came up with a bunch of listings for genetic research. Lemme check this…" He shuffled paper close to the receiver, cleared his throat. "Turns out this X haplogroup has to do with mitochondrial DNA, genes passed down on the maternal side—and an X haplogroup is a specific subdivision or cluster. The university wags are tryin' to use female lineage to trace tribal migrations and so forth. Something like three percent of Native Americans, Europeans and Basque belong to the X-group. Least, according to the stuff I thought looked reputable. Says here there's lots of controversy about its significance. Usual academic crap. Whatch you were after?"

"I don't know. Thanks, though."

"You okay, bud? You sound kinda odd."

"Shucks, Rob, I've been trapped in a car with two redneck psychos for weeks. Might be getting to me, I'll admit."

"Whoa, sorry. Sylvia called and started going on—"

"Everything's hunky-dory, all right?"

"Cool, bro." Rob's tone said nothing was truly cool, but he wasn't in any position to press the issue. There'd be a serious Q&A when I returned, no doubt about it.

Cruz's dad was Basque, wasn't he? Hart was definitely of good, solid German stock only a couple generations removed from the motherland.

Stop me if you've heard this one—a Spaniard, a German and a Comanche walk into a bar—

After we said goodbye, I dialed my ex and got her machine, caught myself and hung up as it was purring. It occurred to me then, what the pattern was, and I stared dumbly down at the fractured portraits of Penny and Piers as their faces were dappled by sunlight falling through a maze of leaves.

I laughed, bitter.

How in God's name had they ever fooled us into thinking they were people at all? The only things missing from this farce were strings and zippers, a boom mike.

I stuffed the photos and the reports into the valise, stood in the weeds at the edge of the asphalt. My blood still pulsed erratically. Shadows began to crawl deep and blue between the buildings and the trees and in the wake of low-gliding cumulus clouds. Moony's Tavern waited, back there in the golden dust, and Cruz's Chevy before it, stolid as a coffin on the altar.

Something was happening, wasn't it? This thing that was happening, had been happening, could it follow me home if I cut and ran? Would it follow me to Sylvia and Carly?

No way to be certain, no way to tell if I had simply fallen off my rocker—maybe the heat had cooked my brain, maybe I was having a long-overdue nervous breakdown. Maybe, shit. The sinister shape of the world contracted around me, gleamed like the curves of a great killing jar. I heard the lid screwing tight in the endless ultraviolet collisions, the white drone of insects.

I turned right and walked up the hill.

5.

About two hours later, a guy in a vintage farm truck stopped. The truck had cruised by me twice, once going toward town, then on the way back. And here it was again. I hesitated; nobody braked for hitchhikers unless the hitcher was a babe in tight jeans.

I thought of Piers and Penny, their expressions in the video, drinking us with their smiling mouths, marking us. And if that was true, we'd been weighed, measured and marked, what was the implication? Piers and Penny were two from among a swarm. Was it open season?

The driver studied me with unsettling intensity, his beady eyes obscured by thick, black-rimmed glasses. He beckoned.

My legs were tired already and the back of my neck itched with sunburn. Also, what did it matter anyway? If I were doing anything besides playing out the hand, I would've gone into Olympia and caught a southbound Greyhound. I climbed aboard.

George was a retired civil engineer. Looked the part—crewcut, angular face like a piece of rock, wore a dress shirt with a row of clipped pens and a tie flung over his shoulder, and polyester slacks. He kept NPR on the radio at a mumble. Gripped the wheel with both gnarled hands.

He seemed familiar—a figure dredged from memories of scientists and engineers of my grandfather's generation. He could've *been* my grandfather.

George asked me where I was headed. I said Los Angeles and he gave me a glance that said LA was in the opposite direction. I told him I wanted to visit the Mima Mounds—since I was in the neighborhood.

There was a heavy silence. A vast and unfathomable pressure built in the cab. At last George said, "Why, they're only a couple miles farther on. Do you know anything about them?"

I admitted that I didn't and he said he figured as much. He told me the mounds were declared a national monument back in the '60s; the subject of scholarly debate and wildly inaccurate hypotheses. He hoped I wouldn't be disappointed—they weren't glamorous compared to real natural wonders such as Niagara Falls, the Grand Canyon or the California Redwoods. The preserve was on the order of five hundred acres, but that was nothing. The Mounds had stretched for miles and miles in the old days. The land grabs of the 1890s reduced the phenomenon to a pocket, surrounded it with rundown farms, pastures and cows. The ruins of America's agrarian era.

I said that it would be impossible to disappoint me.

George turned at a wooden marker with a faded white arrow. A nicely paved single lane wound through temperate rain forest for a mile and looped into a parking lot occupied by the Evergreen vans and a few other vehicles. There was a fence with a gate and beyond that, the vague border of a clearing. Official bulletins were posted every six feet, prohibiting dogs, alcohol and firearms.

"Sure you want me to leave you here?"

"I'll be fine."

George rustled, his clothes chitin sloughing. "X marks the spot."

I didn't regard him, my hand frozen on the door handle, more than slightly afraid the door wouldn't open. Time slowed, got stuck in molasses. "I know a secret, George."

"What kind of secret?" George said, too close, as if he'd leaned in tight.

The hairs stiffened on the nape of my neck. I swallowed and closed my eyes. "I saw a picture in a biology textbook. There was this bug, looked exactly like a piece of bark, and it was barely touching a beetle with its nose. The one that resembled bark was what entomologists call an assassin bug and it was draining the beetle dry. Know how? It poked the beetle with a razor-sharp beak thingy—"

"A rostrum, you mean."

"Exactly. A rostrum, or a proboscis, depending on the species. Then the assassin bug injected digestive fluids, think hydrochloric acid, and sucked the beetle's insides out."

"How lovely," George said.

"No struggle, no fuss, just a couple bugs sitting on a branch. So I'm staring at this book and thinking the only reason the beetle got caught was because it fell for the old piece of bark trick, and then I realized that's how lots of predatory bugs operate. They camouflage themselves and sneak up on hapless critters to do their thing."

"Isn't that the way of the universe?"

"And I wondered if that theory only applied to insects."

"What do you suppose?"

"I suspect that theory applies to everything."

Zilch from George. Not even the rasp of his breath.

"Bye, George. Thanks for the ride." I pushed hard to open the door and jumped down; moved away without risking a backward glance. My knees were unsteady. After I passed through the gate and approached a bend in the path, I finally had the nerve to check the parking lot. George's truck was gone.

I kept going, almost falling forward.

The trees thinned to reveal the humpbacked plain from the TV picture. Nearby was a concrete bunker shaped like a squat mushroom—a park information kiosk and observation post. It was papered with articles and diagrams under plexiglass. Throngs of brightly clad Asian kids buzzed around the kiosk, laughing over the wrinkled flyers, pointing cameras and chattering enthusiastically. A shaggy guy in a hemp sweater, presumably the professor, lectured a couple of wind-burned ladies who obviously ran marathons in their spare time. The ladies were enthralled.

I mounted the stairs to the observation platform and scanned the environs. As George predicted, the view wasn't inspiring. The mounds spread beneath my vantage, none greater than five or six feet in height and largely engulfed in blackberry brambles. Collectively, the hillocks formed a dewdrop hemmed by mixed forest, and toward the narrowing end, a dilapidated trailer court, its structures rendered toys by perspective. The paved footpath coiled unto obscurity.

A radio-controlled airplane whirred in the trailer court airspace. The plane's engine throbbed, a shrill metronome. I squinted against the glare, couldn't discern the operator. My skull ached. I slumped, hugged the valise to my chest, pressed my cheek against damp concrete, and drowsed. Shoes scraped along the platform. Voices occasionally floated by. Nobody challenged me, my derelict posture. I hadn't thought they would. Who'd dare disturb the wildlife in this remote enclave?

My sluggish daydreams were phantoms of the field, negatives of its buckled hide and stealthy plants, and the whispered words *Eastern Washington, South America, Norway*. Scientists might speculate about the geological method of the mounds' creation until doomsday. I knew this place and its sisters were unnatural as monoliths hacked from rude stone by primitive hands and stacked like so many dominos in the uninhabited spaces of the globe. What were they? Breeding grounds, feeding grounds, shrines? Or something utterly alien, something utterly incomprehensible to match the blighted fascination that dragged me ever closer and consumed my will to flee.

Hart's call yanked me from the doldrums. He was drunk. "You shoulda stuck

around, Ray-bo. We been huntin' everywhere for you. Cruz ain't in a nice mood."
The connection was weak, a transmission from the dark side of Pluto. Batteries were dying.

"Where are you?" I rubbed my gummy eyes and stood.

"We're at the goddamned Mounds. Where are *you*?"

I spied a tiny glint of moving metal. The Chevy rolled across the way where the road and the mobile homes intersected. I smiled—Cruz hadn't been looking for me; he'd been trolling around on the wrong side of the park, frustrated because he'd missed the entrance. As I watched, the car slowed and idled in the middle of the road. "I'm here."

The cell phone began to click like a Geiger counter that'd hit the mother lode. Bits of fiddle music pierced the garble.

The car jolted from a savage tromp on the gas and listed ditchward. It accelerated, jounced and bounded into the field, described a haphazard arc in my direction. I had a momentary terror that they'd seen me atop the tower, were coming for me, were planning some unhinged brand of retribution. But no, the distance was too great. I was no more than a speck, if I was anything. Soon, the car lurched behind the slope of intervening hillocks and didn't emerge.

"Hart, are you there?"

The clicking intensified and abruptly chopped off, replaced by smooth, bottomless static. Deep sea squeals and warbles began to filter through. Bees humming. A castrati choir on a gramophone. Giggling. Someone, perhaps Cruz, whispering a Latin prayer. I was grateful when the phone made an electronic protest and expired. I hurled it over the side.

The college crowd had disappeared. Gone too, the professor and his admirers. I might've joined the migration if I hadn't spotted the cab of George's truck mostly hidden by a tree. It was the only rig in the parking lot. I couldn't tell if anyone was behind the wheel.

The sun hung low and fat, reddening as it sank. The breeze had cooled. It plucked at my hair, dried my sweat, chilled me a little. I listened for the roar of the Chevy, buried to the axles in loose dirt, high-centered on a stump; or perhaps they'd abandoned the vehicle. Thus I strained to pick my companions from among the blackberry patches and softly undulating clumps of scotch broom which had invaded this place too.

Quiet.

I went down the stairs and let the path take me. I went as a man in a stupor, my muscles lethargic with dread. The lizard subprocessor in my brain urged me to sprint for the highway, to scuttle into a burrow. It possessed a hint of what waited over the hill, had possibly witnessed this melodrama many times before. I whistled a dirge through clenched teeth and the mounds closed ranks behind me.

Ahead, came the dull clank of a slamming door.

The car was stalled at the foot of a steep slope, its hood buried in a tangle of brush. The windows were dark as a muddy aquarium and festooned with fleshy creepers and algid scum.

I took root a few yards from the car, noting that the engine was dead, yet the vehicle rocked on its springs from some vigorous activity. A rhythmic motion that caused metal to complain. The brake lights stuttered.

Hart's doughy face materialized on the passenger side, bumped against the glass with the dispassion of a pale, exotic fish, and withdrew, descending into a marine trench. His forehead left a starry impact. Someone's palm smacked the rear window, hung there, fingers twitching.

I retreated. Ran, more like. I may have shrieked. Somewhere along the line the valise flew open and its contents spilled—a welter of files, the argyle socks Carly gave me for Father's Day, my toiletries. A handful of photographs pinwheeled in a gust. I dropped the bag. Ungainly, panicked, I didn't get far, tripped and collapsed as the sky blackened and a high-pitched keening erupted from several locations simultaneously. In moments all ambient light had been sucked away; I couldn't see the thorny bush gouging my neck as I wriggled for cover, couldn't make out my own hand before my eyes.

The keening ceased. Peculiar echoes bounced in its wake, gave me the absurd sensation of lying on a sound stage with the kliegs shut off. I received the impression of movement around my hunkered self, although I didn't hear footsteps. I shuddered, pressed my face deeper into musty soil. Ants investigated my pants cuffs.

Cruz called my name from the throat of a distant tunnel. I knew it wasn't him and kept silent. He cursed me and giggled the unpleasant giggle I'd heard on the phone. Hart tried to coax me out, but this imitation was even worse. They went down the entire list and despite everything I was tempted to answer when Carly began crying and hiccupping and begging me to help her, Daddy please, in a baby girl voice she hadn't owned for several years. I stuffed my fist in my mouth, held on while the chorus drifted here and there and eventually receded into the buzz and chirr of field life.

The sun flickered on and the world was restored piecemeal—one root, one stump, one hill at a time. My head swam; reminded me of waking from anesthesia.

Dusk was blooming when I crept from the bushes and tasted the air, cocked an ear for predators. The Chevy was there, shimmering in the twilight. Motionless now.

I could've crouched in my blind forever, wild-eyed as a hare run to ground in a ruined shirt and piss-stained slacks. But it was getting cold and I was thirsty, so I slunk across the park at an angle that took me to the road near the trailer court. I went, casting glances over my shoulder for pursuit that never came.

6.

I told a retiree sipping ice tea in a lawn chair that my car had broken down and he let me use his phone to call a taxi. If he witnessed Cruz crash the Chevy into the mounds, he wasn't saying. The police didn't show while I waited and that said enough about the situation.

The taxi driver was a stolid Samoan who proved not the least bit interested in my frightful appearance or talking. He drove way too fast for comfort, if I'd been in a rational frame of mind, and dropped me at the Greyhound depot in downtown Olympia.

I wandered inside past the ragtag gaggle of modern gypsies which inevitably haunted these terminals, studied the big board while the ticket agent pursed her lips in distaste. Her expression certified me as one of the unwashed mob.

I picked Seattle at random, bought a ticket. The ticket got me the key to the restroom, where I splashed my welted flesh, combed cat tails from my hair and looked almost human again. Almost. The fluorescent tube crackled and sizzled, threatened to plunge the crummy toilet into darkness, and in the discotheque flashes, my haggard face seemed strange.

The bus arrived an hour late and it was crammed. I shared a seat with a middle-aged woman wearing a shawl and scads of costume jewelry. Her ivory skin was hard and she smelled of chlorine. I didn't imagine she wanted to sit by me, judging from the flare of her nostrils, the crimp of her over-glossed mouth.

Soon the bus was chugging into the wasteland of night and the lights clicked off row by row as passengers succumbed to sleep. Except some guy near the front who left his overhead lamp on to read, and me. I was too exhausted to close my eyes.

I surprised myself by crying.

And the woman surprised me again by murmuring, "Hush, hush, dear. Hush, hush." She patted my trembling shoulder. Her hand lingered.

HALLUCIGENIA

And I remembered the cry of the peacocks.
—Wallace Stevens

1.

The Bentley nosed into the weeds along the shoulder of the road and died. No fuss, no rising steam, nothing. Just the tick, tick, tick of cooling metal, the abrupt silence of the car's occupants. Outside was the shimmering country road, a desolate field and a universe of humidity and suffocating heat.

Delaney was at the wheel, playing chauffeur for the Boss and the Boss' wife, Helen. He said to Helen, "She does this when it's hot. Vapor lock, probably." He yanked the lever, got out and lighted a cigarette. His greased crewcut, distorted by the curve of the windshield, ducked beneath the hood.

Helen twisted, smiled at Wallace. "Let's walk around." She waggled her camera and did the eyebrow thing.

"Who are you, Helmut Newton?" Wallace was frying in the backseat, sweating like a bull, khakis welded to his hocks, thinking maybe he had married an alien. His big, lumpen nose was peeling. He was cranky.

Fresh from Arizona, Helen loved the bloody heat; loved tramping in briars and blackberry tangles where there were no lurking scorpions or snakes. She was a dynamo. Meanwhile, Wallace suffered the inevitable lobster sunburns of his Irish heritage. Bugs were furiously attracted to him. Strange plants gave him rashes. He wondered how fate could be as sadistic to arrange such a pairing.

Maybe Dad had been right. When he received the news of the impending nuptials, Wallace's father had worn an expression of a man who has been stabbed in the back and was mostly pained by the fact his own son's hand gripped the dagger. Paxton women were off-limits! The families, though distanced by geography, were intertwined, dating back to when Dalton Smith and George Paxton served as officers during WWII. Dalton quailed at the very notion of his maverick sons mucking about with George's beloved granddaughter and obliterating a familial alliance decades in the forging. Well, maybe brother Payton could bag one, Payton was at least respectable, although that was hardly indemnity against

119

foolishness—after all, *his* French actress was a neurotic mess. But Wallace? Out of the question entirely. Wallace Smith, eldest scion of the former senior senator of Washington State was modestly wealthy from birth by virtue of a trust fund and no mean allowance from his father. Wallace, while having no particular interest in amassing a fortune, had always rankled at the notion he was anything less than a self-made man and proved utterly ingenious in the wide world of high finance and speculation. He dabbled in an assortment of ventures, but made his killing in real estate development. Most of his investments occurred offshore in poor, Asian countries like Viet Nam and Thailand and Korea where dirt was cheap but not as cheap as the lives of peasant tenants who were inevitably dispossessed by their own hungry governments to make way for American-controlled shoe factories, four-star hotels and high-class casinos.

The trouble was, Wallace had been too successful too soon; he had lived the early life of any ten normal men. He had done the great white hunter bit in the heart of darkest Africa; had floated the Yellow River and hiked across the Gobi desert; climbed glaciers in Alaska and went skin diving in Polynesia. The whole time he just kept getting richer and the feats and stunts and adventures went cold for him, bit by bit, each mountain conquered. Eventually he pulled in his horns and became alarmingly sedentary and complacent. In a manner of speaking, he became fat and content. Oh, the handsome, charismatic man of action was there, the high-stakes gambler, the financial lion, the exotic lover—they were simply buried under forty extra pounds of suet following a decade of rich food and boredom. It was that professional ennui which provoked a midlife crisis and led him into the reckless pursuits of avocations best reserved for youngsters. Surfing and sweat lodges. Avant-garde poetry and experimental art. Psychedelic drugs, and plenty of them. He went so far as to have his dick pierced while under the influence. Most reckless of all, love. Specifically love for a college girl with world-beater ambitions. A college girl who could have been a daughter in another life.

Wallace returned Helen's smile in an act of will. "Why not? But I'm not doing anything kinky, no matter how much you pay me."

"Shucks," Helen said, and bounced. Dressed in faded blue overalls she resembled a slightly oversized Christmas elf.

Wallace grunted and followed. Hot as a kiln; humidity slapped him across florid jowls, doubled his vision momentarily. He absently unglued his tropical shirt from his paunch and took a survey. On the passenger side, below the gravel slope and rail, spread the field: A dead farm overrun with brittle grass and mustard-yellow clusters of dandelions on tall stalks. Centered in the morass, a solitary barn, reduced to postcard dimensions, half-collapsed. Farther on, more forest and hills.

He had lived around these parts, just west of Olympia, for ages. The field and its decaying barn were foreign. This was a spur, a scenic detour through a valley of failed farmland. He did not come this way often, had not ever really looked.

It had been Helen's idea. She was eager to travel every back road, see what was over every new hill. They were not in a hurry—cocktails with the Langans at The Mud Shack were not for another hour and it was nothing formal. No business; Helen forbade it on this, their pseudo-honeymoon. The real deal would come in August, hopefully. Wallace's wrangling with certain offshore accounts and recalcitrant foreign officials had delayed the works long enough, which was why he did not argue, did not press his luck. They could do a loop on the Alcan if it made her happy.

Caw-ca-caw! A crow drifted toward the pucker brush. Wallace tracked it with his index finger and cocked thumb.

"You think somebody owns that?" Helen swept the field with a gesture. She uncapped the camera. Beneath denim straps her muscular shoulders shone slick as walnut.

"Yeah." Wallace was pretty sure what was coming. He glanced at his Gucci loafers with a trace of sadness. He called to Delaney. "What d'ya got, Dee?" Stalling.

Delaney muttered something about crabs. Then, "It ain't a vapor lock. Grab my tools. They're by the spare."

Wallace sprang the trunk, found the oily rag with the wrenches. He went around front, where a scowling Delaney sucked on another cigarette. The short, dusky man accepted the tools without comment. Greasy fingerprints marred his trousers. His lucky disco pants, tragically.

"Want me to call a wrecker?" Wallace tapped the cell phone at his hip. He made a note to send Delaney's pants to Mr. Woo, owner of the best dry cleaners this side of Tacoma. Mr. Woo was a magician with solvents.

Delaney considered, dismissed the idea with a shrug. "Screw it. I've got some electric tape, I'll fix it. If not, we'll get Triple-A out here in a bit."

"What can I do?"

"Stand there looking sexy, Boss. Or corral your woman before she wanders off into the woods."

Wallace noticed that his darling wife waded waist-deep in the grass, halfway across the clearing, her braids flopping merrily. He sighed, rolled his shoulders and started trudging. Yelling at this distance was undignified. Lord, keeping track of her was worse than raising a puppy.

The crumbling grade almost tripped him. At the bottom, remnants of a fence—rotted posts, snares of wire. Barbs dug a red zigzag in his calf. He cursed, lumbered into the grass. It rose, coarse and brown, slapped his legs and buttocks. A dry breeze awoke and the yellow dandelion blooms swayed toward him.

Wallace's breath came too hard too quickly. Every step crackled. Bad place to drop a match. He remembered staring, mesmerized, at a California brushfire in the news. No way on God's green earth—or in His dead grass sea—a walrus in loafers would outrace such a blaze. "Helen!" The shout emerged as a wheeze.

The barn loomed, blanked a span of the sky. Gray planks, roof gone to seed wherever it hadn't crumpled. Jagged windows. In its long shadow lay the tottered frame of a truck, mostly disintegrated and entangled in brambles. Wallace shaded his eyes, looking for the ruins of the house that must be nearby, spotted a foundation several yards away where the weeds thinned. Nothing left but shattered concrete and charred bits of timber.

No sign of Helen.

Wallace wiped his face, hoped she had not fallen into a hole. He opened his mouth to call again and stopped. Something gleamed near his feet, small and white. Squirrel bones caught in a bush. A mild surprise that the skeleton was intact. From his hunting experience, scavengers reliably scattered such remains.

Wallace stood still then. Became aware of the silence, the pulse in his temple. Thirst gnawed him He suddenly, completely, craved a drink. Whiskey.

And now it struck him, the absence of insects. He strained to detect the hum of bees among the flowers, the drone of flies among the droppings. Zero. The old world had receded, deposited him into a sterile microcosm of itself, a Chinese puzzle box. Over Wallace's shoulder, Delaney and the car glinted, miniature images on a miniature screen. A few dusty clouds dragged shadows across the field. The field flickered, flickered.

"Hey, Old Man River, you having a heart attack, or what?" Helen materialized in the vicinity of the defunct truck. The silver camera was welded to her right eye. *Click, click.*

"Don't make me sorry I bought that little toy of yours." Wallace shielded his eyes to catch her expression. "Unless maybe you're planning to ditch poetry and shoot a spread for *National Geographic.*"

Helen snapped another picture. "Why, yes. I'm photographing the albino boor in its native habitat." She smiled coyly.

"Yah, okay. We came, we saw, we got rubbed by poison sumac. Time to move along before we bake our brains."

"I didn't see any sumac."

"Like you'd recognize it if it bit you on the ass, lady."

"Oh, I would, I would. I wanna take some pictures of that." Helen thrust the camera at the barn. Here was her indefatigable fascination—the girl collected relics and fragments, then let the images of sinister Americana stew in her brain until inspiration gave birth to something essay-worthy. The formula worked, without question. She was on her way to the top, according to the buzz. *Harper's*; *Poetry*; *The New Yorker* and *Granta*—she was a force to be reckoned with and it was early in the game.

"There it is, fire when ready."

"I want to go inside, for a quick peek."

"Ah, shit on that." Wallace's nose itched. The folds of his neck hung loose and raw. A migraine laid bricks in the base of his skull. "It isn't safe. I bet there's some big honking spiders, too. Black widows." He hissed feebly and made pinching motions.

"Well, yeah. That's why I want you to come with me, sweetness. Protect me from the giant, honking spiders."

"What's in it for me?"

She batted her lashes.

"A quick peek, you say."

"Two shakes of a lamb's tail," she said.

"Oh, in that case." Wallace approached the barn. "Interesting."

"What." Helen sounded preoccupied. She fiddled with the camera, frowning. "This thing is going hinky on me—I hope my batteries aren't dying."

"Huh. There's the driveway, and it's been used recently." The track was overgrown. It curved across the field like a hidden scar and joined the main road yonder. Boot prints sank into softer ground near the barn, tire treads and faint marks, as if something flat had swept the area incompletely. The boot prints were impressive—Wallace wore a 13-Wide and his shoe resembled a child's alongside one.

"Kids. Bet this is a groovy spot to party," Helen said. "My senior year in high school, we used to cruise out to the gravel pits after dark and have bonfire parties. Mmm-mm, Black Label and Coors Light. I can still taste the vomit!"

Wallace did not see any cans, or bottles, or cigarette butts. "Yeah, guess so," he said. "Saw a squirrel skeleton. Damned thing was in one piece, too."

"Really. There're bird bones all over the place, just hanging in the bushes."

"Whole birds?"

"Yup. I shot pictures of a couple. Kinda weird, huh?"

Wallace hesitated at the entrance of the barn, peering through a wedge between the slat doors. The wood smelled of ancient tar, its warps steeped in decades of smoke and brutal sunlight, marinated in manure and urine. Another odor lurked beneath this—ripe and sharp. The interior was a blue-black aquarium. Dust revolved in sluggish shafts.

Helen nudged him and they crossed over.

The structure was immense. Beams ribbed the roof like a cathedral. Squared posts provided additional support. The dirt floor was packed tight as asphalt and littered with withered straw and boards. Obscured by gloom, a partition divided the vault; beyond that the murky impression of a hayloft.

"My god, this is amazing." Helen turned a circle, drinking in the ambience, her face butter-soft.

Along the near wall were ranks of shelves and cabinets. Fouled implements cluttered the pegboard and hooks—pitchforks, shovels, double-headed axes, mattocks, a scythe; all manner of equipment, much of it caked in the gray sediment of antiquity and unrecognizable. Wallace studied what he took to be a curiously shaped bear trap, knew its serrated teeth could pulp a man's thighbone. Rust welded its mouth shut. He had seen traps like it in Argentina and Bengal. A diesel generator squatted in a notch between shelves, bolted to a concrete foot. Fresh grease welled in the battered case.

Was it cooler in here? Sweat dried on Wallace's face, his nipples stiffened magically. He shivered. His eyes traveled up and fixed upon letters chalked above the main doors. Thin and spiky and black, they spelled:

THEY WHO DWELL IN THE CRACKS

"Whoa," Wallace said. There was more, the writing was everywhere. Some blurred by grease and grit, some clear as:

FOOL

Or:

LUCTOR ET EMERGO

And corroded gibberish:

GODOFBLOATCHEMOSHBAALPEEORBELPHEGOR

"Honey? Yoo-hoo?" Wallace backed away from the yokel graffiti. He was sweating again. It oozed, stung his lips. His guts sloshed and prickles chased across his body. Kids partying? He thought not. Not kids.

"Wallace, come here!" Helen called from the opposite side of the partition. "You gotta check this out!"

He went, forcing his gaze from the profane and disturbing phrases. Had to watch for boards, some were studded with nails and wouldn't that take the cake, to get tetanus from this madcap adventure. "Helen, it's time to go."

"Okay, but look. I mean, Jesus." Her tone was flat.

He passed through a pool of light thrown down from a gap in the roof. Blue sky filled the hole. A sucker hole, that's what pilots called them. Sucker holes.

The stench thickened.

Three low stone pylons were erected as a triangle that marked the perimeter of a shallow depression. The pylons were rude phalluses carved with lunatic symbols. Within the hollow, a dead horse lay on its side, mired in filthy, stagnant water. The reek of feces was magnificently awful.

Helen touched his shoulder and pointed. Up.

The progenitor of all wasp nests sprawled across the ceiling like a fantastic alien city. An inverse complex of domes and humps and dangling paper streamers. Wallace estimated the hive to be fully twelve feet in diameter. A prodigy of nature, a primordial specimen miraculously preserved in the depths of the barn. The depending strands jiggled from a swirl of air through a broken window. Some were pink as flesh; others a rich scarlet or lusterless purple-black like the bed of a crushed thumbnail.

Oddly, no wasps darted among the convolutions of the nest, nor did flies or beetles make merry among the feculent quagmire or upon the carcass of the horse. Silence ruled this roost surely as it did the field.

Wallace wished for a flashlight, because the longer he squinted the more he became convinced he was not looking at a wasp nest. This was a polyp, as if the very fabric of the wooden ceiling had nurtured a cancer, a tumor swollen on the bloody juices of unspeakable feasts. The texture was translucent in portions, and its membranous girth enfolded a mass of indistinct shapes. Knotty loops of rope, gourds, hanks of kelp.

Click, click.

Helen knelt on the rim of the hollow, aiming her camera at the horse. Her mouth was a slit in a pallid mask. Her exposed eye rolled.

Wallace pivoted slowly, too slowly, as though slogging through wet concrete. *She shouldn't be doing that. We really should be going.*

Click, click.

The horse trembled. Wallace groaned a warning. The horse kicked Helen in the face. She sat down hard, legs splayed, forehead a dented eggshell. And the horse was thrashing now, heeling over, breaching in its shallow cistern, a blackened whale, legs churning, hooves whipping. It shrieked from a dripping muzzle bound in razor wire. Wallace made an ungainly leap for his wife as she toppled sideways into the threshing chaos. A sledgehammer caught him in the hip and the barn began turning, its many gaps of light spinning like a carousel. He flung a hand out.

Blood and shit and mud, flowing. The sucker holes closed, one by one.

2.

"You're a violent man," Helen said without emphasis. *Her eyes were large and cool.* *"Ever hurt anyone?"*

Wallace had barely recovered his wits from sex. Their first time, and in a hot tub no less. He was certainly a little drunk, more than a little adrenalized, flushed and heaving. They had eventually clambered onto the deck and lay as the stars whirled.

Helen pinched him, hard. "Don't you even think about lying to me," she hissed. "Who was it?"

"It's going to be you if you do that again," he growled.

She pinched him again, left a purple thumbprint on his bicep.

Wallace yelled, put her in a mock headlock, kissed her.

Helen said, "I'm serious. Who was it?"

"It's not important."

Helen sat up, wrapped herself in a towel. "I'm going inside."

"What?"

"I'm going inside."

"Harold Carter. We were dorm mates," Wallace said, finally. He was sinking into himself, then, seeing it again with the clarity of fire. "Friend of ours hosted an off-campus poker club. Harold took me once. I wasn't a gambler and it was a rough crowd aiming to trim the fat off rich college kids like ourselves. I wouldn't go back, but Harold did. He went two, three nights a week, sometimes spent the entire weekend. Lost his shirt. Deeper he got, the harder he clawed. Addiction, right? After a while, his dad's checks weren't enough. He borrowed money—from me, from his other buddies, his sister. Still not enough. One day, when he was very desperate, he stole my wallet. It was the week after Christmas vacation and I had three hundred bucks. He blew it at a strip club. Didn't even pay off his gambling marker. I remember

waiting up for him when he straggled in at dawn, looking pale and beat. He had glitter on his cheeks from the dancers, for God's sake. He smiled at me with the game face, said hi, and I busted him in the mouth. He lost his uppers, needed stitches. I drove him to the hospital. Only time I ever punched anyone." Which skirted being a lie only by definition. He had flattened a porter in Kenya with the butt of a rifle and smashed a big, dumb Briton in the face with a bottle of Jameson during a pub brawl in Dublin. They had it coming. The porter tried to abscond with some money and an antique Bowie knife. The Brit was just plain crazy-mean and drunk as a bull in rut. Wallace was not going to talk about that, though.

They lay, watching constellations burn. Helen said, "I'll go to Washington, if I'm still invited."

"Yes! What changed your mind?"

She didn't say anything for a while. When she spoke, her tone was troubled. "You're a magnet. Arizona sucks. It just feels right."

"Don't sound so happy about it."

"It's not that. My parents hate you. Mother ordered me to dump your ass, find somebody not waiting in line for a heart bypass. Not in those words, but there it was." Helen laughed. "So let's get the hell out of here tomorrow—don't tell anybody. I'll call my folks after we settle in."

Wallace's chest ballooned with such joy he was afraid his eyes were going to spring leaks. "Sounds good," he said gruffly. "Sounds good."

Wallace stood in the gaping cargo door of a Huey. The helicopter cruised above a sandy coast, perhaps the thin edge of a desert. The sea was rigid blue like a watercolor. A white car rolled on the winding road and the rotor shadow chopped it in half. He recognized the car as his own from college—he had sold it to an Iranian immigrant for seventy-five dollars, had forgotten to retrieve a bag of grass from the trunk and spent a few sweaty months praying the Iranian would not know what it was if he ever found it. Was Delaney driving? Wallace wondered why a Huey—he had never served in the military, not even the reserves or the Coast Guard. Too young by a couple of years for Viet Nam, and too old for anything that came about during the bitter end of the Cold War. Then he remembered—after the horse broke his leg, he had been airlifted to Harbor View in Seattle.

Soundless, except for Mr. Woo's voice, coming from everywhere and nowhere. God had acquired a Cantonese accent, apparently.

"Mr. Wallace, you are very unlucky in love, I think," Mr. Woo said from the shining air. He was not unkind.

"Three strikes," Wallace said with a smile. He smiled constantly. No one mentioned it, but he was aware. His face ached and he could not stop. "Gracie divorced me. Right out of college, so it doesn't count. A practice run. Beth was hell on wheels. She skinned me alive for what—ten years? If I'd known what kind of chicks glom onto real estate tycoons, I would've jumped a freight train and lived the hobo life. You have no idea, my friend. I didn't really divorce her, I escaped. After Beth, I made a solemn vow to never marry again. Every few years I'd just find some mean, ugly woman and buy her a house. Helen's different. The real deal."

"Oh, Mr. Wallace? I thought you live in big house in Olympia."

"I owned several, in the old days. She took the villa in Cancun. Too warm for me anyway."

"But this one, this young girl. You killed her."

"She's not dead. The doctors say she might come 'round any day. Besides, she's faster than I am. I can't keep up."

"A young girl needs discipline, Mr. Wallace. You must watch over her like a child. She should not be permitted to wander. You are very unlucky."

The chopper melted. Mr. Woo's wrinkled hands appeared first, then a plastic bag with Wallace's suit on a hanger. A wobbly fan rattled above the counter. "Here is your ticket, Mr. Wallace. Here is some Reishi mushroom for Mrs. Wallace. Take it, please."

"Thanks, Woo." Wallace carefully accepted his clothes, carried them from the dingy, chemical-rich shop with the ginger gait of a man bearing holy artifacts. It was a ritual he clung to as the universe quaked around him. With so much shaking and quaking he wondered how the birds balanced on the wire, how leaves stayed green upon their branches.

Delaney met him at the car, took the clothes and held the door. He handed Wallace his walking stick, waited for him to settle in the passenger seat. Delaney had bought Wallace an Irish blackthorn as a welcome home present. An elegant cane, it made Wallace appear more distinguished than he deserved, Delaney said. Wallace had to agree—his flesh sagged like a cheap gorilla suit, minus the hair, and his bones were too prominent. His eyes were the color of bad liver, and his broad face was a garden of broken veins.

There were reasons. Two hip operations, a brutal physical therapy regimen. Pain was a faithful companion. Except, what was with the angry weals on his neck and shoulders? Keloid stripes, reminiscent of burns or lashes. Helen was similarly afflicted; one had festered on her scalp and taken a swath of hair. Their origin was on the tip of Wallace's tongue, but his mind was in neutral, gears stripped, belts whirring, and nothing stuck. He knocked back a quart of vodka a day, no problem, and had started smoking again. A pack here or there—who was counting? He only ate when Delaney forced the issue. Hells-bells, if he drank enough martinis he could live on the olives.

Delaney drove him home. They did not talk. Their relationship had evolved far beyond the necessity of conversation. Wallace stared at the trees, the buildings. These familiar things seemed brand new each time he revisited them. The details were exquisitely rendered, but did not con him into accepting the fishbowl. Artificial: the trees, the houses, the windup people on the shaded streets. Wallace examined his hands; artificial too. The sinews, the soft tissues and skeletal framework were right there in the X-ray sunlight. He was Death waiting to dance as the guest of honor at *Día de los Muertos*.

Wallace was no longer in the car. The car melted. It did not perturb him. He was accustomed to jump-cuts, seamless transitions, waking dreams. Doctor Green said he required more sleep or the hallucinatory episodes would intensify, destroy his ability to function. Wallace wondered if he ever slept at all. There was no way to be certain. The gaps in his short-term memory were chasms.

He was at home in the big house his fortune built, seated stiffly on the sofa Beth, ex-wife number two, procured from Malaysia along with numerous throw rugs, vases and some disturbing artwork depicting fertility goddesses and hapless mortals. He did not like the décor, had never gotten around to selling it at auction. Funny that Beth took half of everything and abandoned these items so punctiliously selected and obtained at prohibitive expense. Wallace's closest friend, Skip Arden, suggested that Beth always hoped things would change for the better, that she might regain favor. Skip offered to burn the collection for him.

Wallace's house was a distorted reflection of the home he had grown up in, a kind of anti-mirror. This modern house was designed by a famous German architect that Beth read of in a foreign art directory. Multi-tiered in the fashion of an antique citadel, and as a proper citadel, it occupied a hill. There was an ivy-covered wall, a garden and maple trees. Mt. Rainier fumed patiently in its quarter of the horizon. At night, lights twinkled in the town and inched along the highway. Wallace's personal possessions countered the overwhelming Baroque overtones—his hunting trophies, which included a den crammed with the mounted heads of wild boars, jaguars and gazelles; and his gun collection, a formidable floor-to-ceiling chestnut-paneled cabinet that contained a brace of armament ranging from an assortment of knives and daggers native to three dozen nationalities, to an even greater array of guns—from WWII American issue Browning .45 automatics up to show-stopping big-game rifles, the Model 76 African .416 and his pride and joy, a Holland & Holland .500, which had come to him from the private collection of a certain Indian prince, and was capable of sitting a bull elephant on its ass. Littered throughout the rambling mansion was the photographic evidence of his rough and wild youth; mostly black and white and shot by compatriots long dead or succumbed to stultified existences similar to his own. The weapons and the photographs grounded his little hot air balloon of sanity, but they also led to *thinking* and he had never been one to dwell on the past, to suffer introspection. They were damning, these fly-buzz whispers that built and built with each stroke of the minute hand, each wallowing undulation of the ice in his drink. *You always wanted to be Hemingway. Run with the bulls; fire big guns and drink the cantinas dry. Maybe you'll end up like the old man, after all. Let's look at those pistols again, hmm?* And when such thoughts grew too noisy, he took another snort of bourbon and quieted the crowd in his skull.

Outside his skull, all was peaceful. Just Wallace, Helen, Helen's aides, Cecil and

Kate, Delaney, and Bruno and Thor, a pair of mastiffs that had been trained by Earl Hutchison out in Yelm. The dogs were quietly ubiquitous as they patrolled the house and the grounds. The gardener called on Friday; the housecleaner and her team every other weekend. They had keys; no one else bothered Wallace except Wallace's friends.

These friends came and went unexpectedly. Ghosts flapping in skins. Who? Skip and Randy Freeman made frequent guest appearances. Barret and Macy Langan; Manfred and Elizabeth Steiner. Wallace thought he had seen his own father, though that was unlikely. Dad divided his time between the VFW, the Masonic Temple and the Elks Lodge, and according to reports, his participation at social gatherings was relegated to playing canasta, drinking gin and rambling about "The Big One" as if he had jubilantly kissed a nurse in Time Square to celebrate V-J Day only last week.

"She's getting worse," Skip said as he helped himself to Wallace's liquor. "You should ship her to Saint Pete's and be done with it. Or send her home to ma and pa. Whatever you've got to do to get out from under this mess." He was talking about Helen, although he could have been discussing a prize Hereford, or an expensive piece of furniture. His own wife hated him and refused to live under his roof, it was said. Skip, a reformed attorney-at-law, was older and fatter than Wallace. Skip drank more too, but somehow appeared to be in much better shape. His craggy features were ruddy as Satan under thick, white hair. Egregiously blunt, he got away with tons of indiscretions because he was a basso profundo who made Perry Mason sound like a Vienna choirboy. Jaws slackened when he started rumbling.

"Is she?" Wallace nodded abstractedly. "I hadn't noticed."

"Yes she is, and yes you have," said Randy Freeman, the radical biologist. Radical was accurate—he had bought *The Anarchist Cookbook* and conducted some experiments in a gravel pit up past the Mima Mounds. Which was how he had blown off his right hand. His flesh-tone prosthesis was nice, but it was not fooling anybody. He had recently completed a study of the behavior of crows in urban environments and planned to write a book. Randy was a proponent of human cloning for spare parts.

Skip said, "Nine months. Enough is enough, for the love of Pete, you could've given birth. Pull yourself together, get back on the horse. Uh, so to speak. You should work." He gestured broadly. "Do *something* besides grow roots on your couch and gawk."

"Yeah," said Randy.

"I do things, Skip. Look, I got my dry cleaning. Here it is. I pick it up every Thursday." Wallace patted the crinkly plastic, rubbed it between his fingers.

"You're taking those pills Green prescribed."

"Sure, sure," Wallace said. Delaney sorted the pills and brought them with a glass of water at the right hour. Good thing, too. There were so many, Wallace would have been confused as to which, where and when.

"Well, stop taking them. Now."

"Okay." It was all the same to Wallace.

"He can't stop taking them—not all at once," Randy said. "Wallace, what you gotta do is cut back. I'll talk to Delaney."

"We'll talk to Delaney about this, all right. That crap is eating your brain," Skip said. "I'll give you some more free advice. You sue those sonsofbitches that own that Black Hills property. Jerry Premus is champing at the bit to file a claim."

"Yeah…he keeps calling me," Wallace said. "I'm not suing anybody. We shouldn't have been there."

"Go on thinking that, Sparky. Premus will keep the papers warm in case your goddamned senses return," Skip said.

Wallace said, "She *is* getting worse. I hear strange noises at night, too." It was more that strange noises, wasn't it? What about the figure he glimpsed in the garden after dusk? A hulking shadow in a robe and a tall, conical hat. The getup was similar to, but infinitely worse, than the ceremonial garb a Grand Dragon of the Ku Klux Klan might wear. The costumed figure blurred in his mind and he was not certain if it existed as anything other than a hallucination, an amalgam of childhood demons, trauma and drugs.

He looked from his reflection in the dark window and his friends were already gone, slipped away while he was gathering wool. Ice cubes collapsed in his glass. The glass tilted slackly in his hand. "Nine months. Maybe Skipperoo's got a point. Maybe I need to wheel and deal, get into the old groove. What do you think, Mr. Smith?" Wallace spoke to his glum reflection and his reflection was stonily silent.

"Mr. Smith?" Cecil's voice crackled over the intercom, eerily distorted. They had installed the system long ago, but never used it much until after the accident. It was handy, despite the fact it almost gave Wallace a coronary whenever it started unexpectedly broadcasting. "Do you want to see Helen?"

Wallace said, "Yes; be right up," although he was sickened by the prospect. Helen's face was a mess, a terrible, terrible mess, and it was not the only thing. Whenever Wallace looked at her, if he really looked at her a bit more closely after the initial knee-jerk revulsion, the clouds in his memory began to dissolve. Wallace did not like that, did not like the funhouse parade of disjointed imagery, the shocking volume of the animal's screams, the phantom reek of putrescence. The triple pop of Delaney's nickel-plated automatic as he fired into the horse's head. Wallace preferred his thick comforter of pill- and alcohol-fueled numbness.

Dalton had asked him, *You really love this girl? She isn't like one of your chippies you can bang for a few years and buy off with a divorce settlement. This is serious, sonny boy.*

Yeah, Dad. Course, I do.

She a trophy? Better goddamn well not be. Don't shit where you eat.

Dad, I love her.

Good God. You must have it bad. Never heard a Smith say that before...

Wallace pressed the button again. "Is she awake?"

"Uh, yes. I just finished feeding her."

"Oh, good." Wallace walked slowly, not acknowledging Delaney's sudden presence at his elbow. Delaney was afraid he would fall, shatter his fragile hip.

One of Wallace's private contractors had converted a guestroom into Helen's quarters. A rectangular suite with a long terrace over the garden. Hardwood floors and vaulted ceilings. They needed ample space to house her therapy equipment—the hydraulic lift and cargo net to transport her into the changing room, the prototype stander which was a device designed to prevent muscle atrophy by elevating her to a vertical plane on a rectangular board. She screamed torture when they did this every other afternoon and wouldn't quit until Cecil stuck headphones over her ears and piped in Disney music.

Helen lay in bed, propped by a rubber wedge and pillows. During the accident, her brain was deprived of sufficient oxygen for several minutes. Coupled with the initial blunt trauma, skull fractures and bacterial contamination, the effects were devastating. Essentially, the accident had rendered Helen an adult fetus. Her right hand, curled tight as a hardwood knot, was callused from habitual gnawing. She possessed minimal control of her left hand, could gesture randomly and convulsively grasp objects. Cecil splinted it a few hours a day, as he did her twisted feet, to prevent her tendons from shortening. Her lack of a swallow reflex made tube-feeding a necessity. She choked on drool. It was often impossible to tell if she could distinguish one visitor from another, or if she could see anything at all. Cortical blindness, the doctors said. The worst part was the staph infection she contracted from her open head wound. The dent in her skull would not heal. It refused to scab and was constantly inflamed. The doctors kept changing her medication and predicting a breakthrough, but Wallace could tell they were worried. She had caught a strain resistant to antibiotics and was essentially screwed.

"Hi, Mr. Smith." Cecil carefully placed the feeding apparatus into a dish tub. He was a rugged fellow, close to Helen's age. Built like a linebacker, he was surprisingly gentle and unobtrusive. He faithfully performed his myriad duties and retreated into the adjoining chamber. It was always him or his counterpart, the RN Kate, a burly woman who said even less than Cecil. She dressed in an official starched white pinafore over her conservative dresses and a white hat. Wallace always knew when she was around because she favored quaint, polished wooden shoes that click-clocked on the bare floors. Ginger Rogers, he privately called her. Ginger Rogers tapping through the halls.

Helen flinched and moaned when Wallace took her hand. Startle reflex, was the medical term. She smiled flaccidly, eyes vacant as buttons. She smelled of baby powder and antiseptic.

Wallace heard himself say, "Hey, darling, how was dinner?" Meanwhile, it was the raw wound in her forehead that commanded his attention, drew him with grim certainty, compounded his sense of futility and doom.

Abruptly exhausted, he whispered farewell to Helen and shuffled upstairs and crawled into bed.

3.

After the world waned fuzzy and velvet-dim, he was roused by the noises he had mentioned to Skip and Randy. The night noises.

He pretended it was a dream—the blankets were heavy, his flesh was heavy, he was paralyzed but for the darting of his eyes, the staccato drum roll in his chest. The noises came through the walls and surrounded his bed. Faint sounds, muffled sounds. Scratching and scrabbling, hiccupping and slithering. Soft, hoarse laughter floated up to his window from the garden.

Wallace stashed a .357 magnum in the dresser an arm length from his bed. He could grab that pistol and unload it at the awful giant he imagined was prowling among the rosebushes and forsythia and snowball trees. He closed his eyes and made fists. Could not raise them to his ears. The room became black as pitch and settled over him and pressed down upon him like a leaden shroud. Grains of plaster dusted the coverlet. *Pitter-pat, pitter-pat.*

4.

Detective Adams caught Wallace on a good morning. It was Wallace's fifty-first birthday and unseasonably cold, with a threat of rain. Wallace was killing a bottle of Hennessy Private Reserve he'd received from Skip as an early present and shaking from a chill that had no name. However, Wallace was coherent for the first time in months. Delaney had reduced the pills per Skip's orders and it was working. He was death-warmed-over, but his faculties were tripping along the tracks right on schedule. He toyed with the idea of strangling Delaney, of hanging him by the heels. His mood was mitigated solely by the fact he was not scheduled for therapy until Thursday. Possibly he hated therapy more than poor shrieking Helen did.

Detective Adams arrived unannounced and joined Wallace on the garden patio at the glass table with the forlorn umbrella. Adams actually resembled a cop to Wallace, which meant he dressed like the homicide cops on the television dramas. He wore a gray wool coat that matched the streaks in his hair. A square guy, sturdy and genial, though it was plain this latter was an affectation, an icebreaker. His stony eyes were too frank for any implication of friendliness to survive long. He flicked a glance at the mostly empty bottle by Wallace's wrist. "Hey there, Mr. Smith, you're looking better every time I swing by. Seriously though, it's cold. Sure you should be hanging around like this? You might get pneumonia or something. My aunt lives over in Jersey. She almost croaked a couple years ago."

"Pneumonia?"

"Nah, breast cancer. Her cousin died of pneumonia. Longshoreman."

Wallace was smoking unfiltered Cheyenne cigarettes in his plushest tiger-striped bathrobe. His feet were tinged blue as day-old fish. His teeth chattered. "Just when you think spring is here, winter comes back to whack us in the balls. One for the road, eh?"

Detective Adams smiled. "How's everything? Your hip…?"

"Mostly better. Bones are healed, so they say. Hurts like hell."

"How's your wife?"

"Helen's parents are angry. They want me to send her to Arizona, pay for a home. They're…yeah, it's screwed up."

"Ah. Are you planning to do that?"

"Do what?"

"Send her home."

"She's got a lot of family in the southwest…Lot of family." Wallace lighted another cigarette after a few false starts.

"Maybe sending your wife to Arizona is a good idea, Mr. Smith. Heck, a familiar setting with familiar faces, she might snap out of this. Never know."

Wallace smoked. "Fuck 'em. What's new with you, Detective?"

"Not a darned thing, which is pretty normal in my field. I just thought I'd touch base, see if any more details had occurred to you since our last palaver."

"When was that?"

"Huh? Oh, let me check." Adams flipped open a notebook. "About three weeks. You don't remember."

"I do now," Wallace said. "I'm still a little mixed up, you see. My brain is kind of woozy."

"Yeah," Adams turned up the wattage of his smile. "I boxed some. Know what you mean."

"You talk to Delaney? Delaney saw the whole thing."

"I've spoken to everyone. But, to be perfectly clear, Delaney didn't actually see *everything*. Did he?"

"Delaney shot the horse."

"Yes, I saw the casings. A fine job under pressure."

This had also been present in each interview; an undercurrent of suspicion. Wallace said, "So, Detective, I wonder. You think I smashed her head in with a mallet, or what?"

"Then broke your own hip and somehow disposed of the weapon before Mr. Delaney made the scene? Oh, I don't suppose I think anything along those lines. The case bothers me, is all. It's a burr under my saddle blanket, heh. We examined the scene thoroughly. And…without a horse carcass, we're kinda stuck."

"You think Delaney did it." Wallace nodded and took a drag. "You think me and Delaney are in it together. Hey, maybe we're lovers and Helen was cramping our style. Or maybe I wanted Helen's money. Oops, I have plenty of my own. Let me ponder this, I'll come up with a motive." He chuckled and lighted another cigarette from the dwindling stub of his current smoke.

Wallace's humor must have been contagious. Detective Adams laughed wryly. He raised his blocky cop hands. "Peace, Mr. Smith. Nothing like that. The evidence was crystal—that horse, wherever it went, just about did for the two of you. Lucky things turned out as well as they did."

"I don't feel so lucky, Detective."

"I guess not. My problem is, well, heck, it's not actually a problem. There's something odd about what happened to you, Mr. Smith. Something weird about that property. It's pretty easy to forget how it was, standing in there, in the barn, screening the area for evidence. Too easy. Those pylons were a trip. Boy howdy!"

"Don't," Wallace said. He did not want to consider the pylons, the traps or the graffiti. The imagery played havoc with his guts.

"Lately, I get the feeling someone is messing with my investigation."

"Please don't," Wallace said, louder.

"My report was altered, Mr. Smith. Know what that means? Somebody went into the files and rewrote portions of the paperwork. That doesn't happen at the department. Ever."

"Goddamn it!" Wallace slammed his fist on the table, sent the bottle clattering. His mind went crashing back to the barn where he had regained consciousness for several seconds—Helen beside him in the muck, dark blood pulsing over her exposed brain, surging with her heartbeat. He covered his eyes. "Sorry. But I can't handle talking about this. I don't like to think about what happened. I do whatever I can to not think about it."

"Don't be offended—I need to ask this." Adams was implacable as an android, or a good telemarketer. "You aren't into any sort of cult activity, are you? Rich folks get bored, sometimes they get mixed up with stuff they shouldn't. I've seen it before. There's a history in these parts."

"There's history wherever you go, Detective. You ought to ask the people who own that property—"

"The Choates. Morgan Choate."

"They're the ones with all the freaky cult bullshit going on."

"Believe me, I'd love to find Anton LaVey's nephew was shacking there, something like that. Solve all my headaches. The Choate place was foreclosed on three years ago. Developer from Snoqualmie holds the deed. This guy doesn't know squat—he bought the land at auction, never set foot on it in his life. Anybody could be messing around out there."

Wallace did not give a tinker's damn about who or what might be going on, he was simply grateful they would be grinding that barn into dust and fairly soon.

Detective Adams waited a moment. Then, softly as a conspirator, "Strange business is going on, Mr. Smith. Like I said—we checked your story very carefully. The Smith name carries weight in this neck of the woods, I assure you. My boss would have my balls if I hassled you."

"Come on, my pappy isn't a senator anymore. I'm not exactly his favorite, anyway."

"Just doing my job, and all that."

"I understand, Detective. Hell, bad apples even fell off the Kennedy tree. Right?"

"I'm sure you're not a bad apple. You seem to be a solid citizen. You pay your taxes, you hire locally and you give to charity."

"Don't forget, I donated to the Policeman's Ball five years running."

"That's a write-off, sure, but it's worth what you paid. Ask me, your involvement is purely happenstance. You're a victim. I don't understand the whole picture, yet. If there's anything you haven't told me, if you saw something…Well, I'd appreciate any help you might give me."

Wallace lifted his head, studied Adams closely. The cop was frayed—bulging eyes latticed with red veins, a twitch, cheeks rough as Brillo. Adams' cologne masked the sour musk of hard liquor. His clothes were wrinkled as if he'd slept in them. Wallace said, "As far as I'm concerned, it's over. I want to move on."

"Understandable, Mr. Smith. You've got my number. You know the drill." The detective stood, peered across the landscaped grounds to the forest. A peacock strutted back and forth. A neighbor raised them in the distant past; the man lost his farm and the peacocks escaped into the wild. The remaining few haunted the woods. The bird's movements were mechanical. Back and forth. "Do me a favor. Be careful, Mr. Smith. It's a mean world."

Wallace watched Adams climb into a brown sedan, drive off with the caution of an elderly woman. The brake lights flashed, and Adams leaned from the window and appeared to vomit.

Daylight drained fast after that.

5.

Wallace pulled on the loosest fitting suit in his wardrobe, which was not difficult considering how the pounds had melted from him during his long recovery. He knotted a tie and splashed his face with cologne and crippled his way downstairs to the liquor cabinet and fixed himself a double scotch on the rocks. He downed that and decided on another for the road. Sweat dripped from him and his shirt stuck to the small of his back and hips. He sweated nonstop, it seemed, as if the house were a giant sauna and yet he routinely dialed the thermostat down to the point where he could see his own breath.

Pain nibbled at him, worried at his will. He resisted the urge to swallow some of the heavy-duty pills in his coat pocket—promises to keep. Then he went somewhat unsteadily to the foyer with its granite tiles and a marble statue of some nameless Greek wrestler and the chandelier on its black chain, a mass of tiered crystal as unwieldy as any that ever graced the ballroom of a Transylvanian castle or a doomed luxury liner, and reported to Delaney. Delaney eyed him critically, dusted lint from his shoulder and straightened his tie while Wallace dabbed his face with a silk, monogrammed handkerchief, one of a trove received on birthdays and Christmases past, and still the sweat rilled from his brow and his neck and he wilted in his handsome suit. Delaney finally opened the front door and escorted him to the car. The air was cold and tasted of smog from the distant highway. Delaney started the engine and drove via the darkened back roads into Olympia. They crossed the new Fourth Avenue Bridge with its extra-wide sidewalks and faux Gaslight Era lampposts that conveyed a gauzy and oh-so-cozy glow and continued downtown past unlit shop windows and locked doors to a swanky restaurant called The Marlin. The Marlin was old as money and had been the *It* spot of discerning socialites since Wallace's esteemed father was a junior senator taking lobbyists and fellow lawmakers out for highballs and graft.

Everyone was waiting inside at a collection of candlelit tables near the recessed end of the great varnished bar. People, already flushed with their martinis and bourbons and cocktails, rose to shake his hand and clap his back or hug him outright and they reeked of booze and perfume and hairspray and cigarettes and talked too loudly as they jostled for position around him. The Johnsons and Steiners attended as a unit, which made sense since so many of their kids were intermarried, it was exceedingly difficult to determine where the branches and the roots of the respective family trees ended or began; Barb and Michael Cotter; Mel Redfield, the former California poet laureate; old man Bloom, the former city councilman, and his nephew Regis, a tobacco lobbyist who kept rubbing his eyes and professing irritation at all the secondhand smoke; Skip Arden, doing his best John Huston as The Man from the South, in a vanilla suit hand-sewn by a Hong Kong tailor of legendary distinction; Jacob Wilson, recent heir to the Wilson fortune, who matched Skip in girth and verbosity, if not in taste or wit, and Jacob's bodyguard, Frank, a swarthy man in a bomber jacket who sat at the bar with Delaney and pretended inattentiveness to anything but the lone Rolling Rock beer he would order for the duration of the evening; Randy Freeman, wild-eyed behind rimless glasses and dressed way down in a wrinkled polo shirt, khaki pants and sandals and his lovely, staid wife, Janice; the Jenson twins down from Bellevue, Ted and Russell who worked for Microsoft's public relations department—they were smooth as honey and slippery as eels; Jerry Premus, Wallace's hired gun in matters legal, who was twice as smooth and twice as slippery as the Jenson brothers combined; a couple of youngish unidentified women with big hair, skimpy gowns and glittering with the kind of semi-valuable jewelry Malloy's on State Avenue might rent by the evening; Wallace forgot their names on contact and figured they must be with a couple of the unattached men; and dear old Dad himself lurched from the confusion to kiss his cheek and mutter a gruff, how do ye do? Wallace looked over Dalton Smith's shoulder, counting faces and there were another half-dozen that he did not recognize and who knew if they were hangers-on or if his faculties were still utterly short-circuited. He decided to play it safe and put on his biggest movie-star grin for all concerned and bluff his way to the finish line.

Skip took charge of the event, dinging his glass of champagne to summon collective attention. He proposed a toast to Wallace's regenerative capabilities, his abundance of stalwart comrades and his continued speedy recovery, upon which all assembled cried, "Hear, hear!" and drank. No one mentioned Helen. She sat amongst them, nonetheless. Wallace, ensconced at the head of the main table like a king, with his most loyal advisers, Skip and Randy at either hand, saw her shadow in the faces that smiled too merrily and then concentrated with abject diligence on their salmon and baked potatoes in sour cream, or in the pitying expressions blocked by swiftly raised glasses of wine or the backs of hands as heads swiveled to engage neighbors in hushed conversation. Not that such clandestine tactics were necessary: Wallace's exhaustion, his entrenched apathy, precluded any intemperate outburst and Skip's thunderous elocution mercifully drowned out the details anyway.

Wallace was fairly saturated and so nursed his drink and picked at his birthday prime rib and tried to appear at least a ghost of his former gregarious self. Matters were proceeding apace until the fifth or six round of drinks arrived and Manny Steiner started in on Viet Nam and the encroachment of French and American factories upon traditional indigenous agrarian cultures. Wallace suddenly feared he might do something rash. He set aside his glimmering knife, grinned and told Manny to hold that thought. He lurched to his feet, miraculously without upsetting a flotilla of tableware and half-full glasses, and made for the restrooms farther back where it was sure to be dim and quiet. Delaney, alert as any guard dog, cocked his head and then rose to follow, and subsided at a look from Wallace.

Wallace hesitated at the men's room, limped past it and pushed through the big metal door that let into the alley. The exit landing faced a narrow, dirty street and the sooty, featureless rear wall of Gossen's Fine Furniture. A sodium lamp illuminated a dumpster and a mound of black garbage bags piled at the bottom of the metal stairs. He sagged against the railing, fumbled out his cigarettes, got one going and smoked it almost convulsively. Restaurant noises pulsed dimly through the wall. Water dripped from the gutters and occasionally car horns echoed from blocks farther off, tires screeched and a woman laughed, high and maniacal—the mating cry of the hopelessly sloshed female.

He finished his cigarette and began another and was almost human again when someone called to him.

"Hey." The voice floated from the thicker shadows of the alley. It was a husky voice, its sex muted by the acoustics of the asphalt and concrete. "Hey, mister."

Wallace dragged on his cigarette and peered into the darkness. The muscles in his neck and shoulders bunched. His hand shook. He opened his mouth to answer that odd, muffled voice and could not speak. His throat was too tight. What did it remind him of? Something bad, something tickling the periphery of his consciousness, a warning. A certain quality of the voice, its inflection and cadence, harkened recollections of hunting for tigers in the high grass in India, of chopping like Pizarro through the Peruvian jungles on the trail of jaguars—of *being* hunted.

"Mister." The voice was close now. "I can see you. Please. *Prease.*" The last word emerged in a patently affected accent, a mockery of the Asian dialect. A low, wheezy chuckle accompanied this. "*Prease, mistuh. You put a hotel in my rice paddy, mistuh.*"

Wallace dropped his cigarette. He turned and groped for the door handle and it was slick with condensation. He pushed hard and the handle refused to budge. Locked. "Ah, sonofabitch!" He slumped against the door, face to the alley, and clutched his cane, wished like hell he had not been too lazy and vain to strap on one of his revolvers, which he never carried after the accident because the weight dragged on his shoulder. His heart lay thick and heavy. He gulped to catch his breath.

The sodium lamp dimmed. "*Mistuh Smith. Where you goin' Mistuh Smith?*" Someone stood across the way, partially hidden by the angle of the building.

Jesus Christ, what is he wearing? Wallace could not quite resolve the details because everything was mired in varying shades of black, but the figure loomed very tall and very broad and was most definitely crowned with bizarre headgear reminiscent of a miter or a witch's hat. Wallace's drunkenness and terror peeled back in an instant of horrible clarity. Here was the figure which had appeared in his fever dreams—the ghastly, robed specter haunting the grounds of his estate. The lamp flickered and snuffed and Wallace was trapped in a cold black box. He reached back and began to slap the door feebly with his left hand.

"Wally. It is *soo* nice to meet you in the flesh." The voice emanated from a spot near Wallace's foot and it was easy to imagine the flabby, deranged face of a country bumpkin grinning up between the stairs. "Are you afraid? Are you afraid, sweetheart? Don't be afraid…*boss man.* They're about to cut the cake."

Wallace slapped the door, slapped the door. It was as futile as tapping the hull of a battleship. A rancid odor wafted to him—the stench of fleshy rot and blood blackening in the belly of a sluice. "W-what do you want?"

"I want to show you something beautiful."

"I'm—I'm not interested. No cash."

"Father saw you that day. What Father sees, He covets. He covets you, Wally-dear."

Wallace's stomach dropped into his shoes. "Who are you?"

The other laughed, a low, moist chuckle of unwholesome satisfaction. "Me? A sorcerer. The shade of Tommy Tune. The Devil's left hand. One of the inheritors of the Earth." Something rattled on the steps. Fingernails, perhaps. "I am a digger of holes, an opener of doors. I am here to usher in the dark." The odor grew more pungent. Glutted intestines left to swell in greenhouse heat; a city stockyard in July. Flies droned and complained. Flies were suddenly everywhere. "He lives in the cracks, Wally. The ones that run through everything. In the cracks between yesterday and tomorrow. Crawl into the dark, and there He is, waiting…."

"Look, I—just leave me alone, okay. Okay?" Wallace brushed flies from his hair, his lips and nose. "Don't push me, fella."

"Wifey met Him and you shall too. Everyone shall meet Him in good, sweet time. You'll scream a hymn to the black joy He brings."

Wallace lunged and thrust at the voice with his cane and struck a yielding surface. The cane was wrenched from his fingers with such violence his hand tore and bled. He stumbled and his traitorous hip gave way. He went to his knees, bruised them on the grating. Pain telescoped from his hip and stabbed his eyes—not quite the sense of broken bone, but it hurt, Christ did it ever. Fingers clamped onto his wrist and yanked him flat. The hand was huge and impossibly powerful and Wallace was stuck fast, his arm stretched over the edge of the landing and to the limits of his shoulder socket, his cheek pressed against metal. The dying remnants of his cigarette smoldered several inches from his eye. Sloppy, avaricious lips opened against his palm. The tongue was clammy and large as a preposterously gravid slug and it lapped between Wallace's fingers and sucked them into a cavernous mouth.

Wallace thrashed and lowed like a cow that has been hamstrung. Teeth nicked him, might have snipped his fingers at the knuckle, he could tell from the size and sharpness of them. A great, Neolithic cannibal was making love to his hand. Then his hand slipped deeper, as the beast grunted and gulped and the mouth closed softly over his forearm, his elbow, and this couldn't be possible, no way the esophageal sheath of a monstrous throat constricted around his biceps with such force his bones creaked together, no way that he was being swallowed alive, that he was going to disappear into the belly of a giant—

The world skewed out of focus.

The door jarred open and light and music surged from the restaurant interior. "Boss, they want to cut the cake...Boss! What the hell?" Delaney knelt beside him and rolled him over.

Wallace clutched his slick fingers against the breast of his suit and laughed hysterically. "I dropped my cane," he said.

"What are you doing out here?" Delaney gripped Wallace's forearms and lifted him to his feet. "You okay? Oh, jeez—you're bleeding! You break anything?"

"Needed some air...I'm fine." Wallace smiled weakly and sneaked a glance at the alley as he hurriedly wiped his face with his left sleeve. The lamp was still dead and the wedge of light from the open door did not travel far. He considered spilling his guts. Delaney would call the cops and the cops would find what? Nothing and then they would ask to see his prescription and probably ask if he should be mixing Demerol with ten different kinds of booze. Oh, and by the way, what really happened in that barn. Go on: you can tell us. "I'm okay. Slipped is all."

Delaney leaned over the railing and peered down. "I'll go find your cane—"

"No! I, uh, busted it. Cheap wood."

"Cheap wood! Know what I shelled out for that?"

"No, really. I'm freezing. We'll get a new one tomorrow."

Delaney did not appear convinced. "It broke?"

"Yeah. C'mon, Dee. Let's go and get this party over with, huh?"

"That's the spirit, Mr. S," Delaney steadied him and said no more, but Wallace noticed he did not remove his hand from his pocket until they were safely inside and among friends.

6.

The remainder of the evening dragged to pieces like old fearful Hector come undone behind Achilles' cart and eventually Wallace was home and unpacked from the car. He collapsed into bed and was asleep before Delaney clicked off the lights.

Wallace dreamt of making love to Helen again.

They occupied a rocky shelf above Sun Devil Stadium, screwing like animals on a scratchy Navajo blanket. It was dusk, the stadium was deserted. Helen muttered into the blanket. Wallace pulled her ponytail to raise her head, because he thought he heard a familiar syllable or phrase. Something guttural, something darksome. His passion cooled to a ball of pig iron in his belly. The night air grew bitter, the stars sharp.

Helen said in a metallic voice, *There is a hole no man can fill.*

Wallace flew awake and sat pop-eyed and gasping. Clock said 3:39 A.M. He got out of bed, switched on the lamp and slumped in its bell of dull light, right hand tucked against his chest. His hand was thickly bandaged and it itched. The contours of the bedroom seemed slightly warped, window frames and doorways were too skinny and pointy. The floor was cold. The lamp bulb imploded, with a sizzle that nearly stopped his heart and darkness rushed in like black water filling a muddy boot print.

He did not feel welcome.

Delaney stood in the kitchen eating a sandwich over the sink. He was stripped to the waist. "You want me to fix you one?" He asked when Wallace padded in. He lived in the old gardener's cottage, used a second key to come and go as he pleased. Wallace had contemplated asking him to move into the downstairs guestroom and decided it was too much of an imposition. Delaney had women over from the clubs; he enjoyed loud music. Best to leave him at the end of a long leash.

Wallace waved him off, awkwardly poured a glass of milk with his left hand, sloshed in some rum from an emergency bottle in a counter drawer. He held his glass with trembling fingers, eyeballing the slimy bubbles before they slid into his mouth; poured another. He leaned against the stainless steel refrigerator. The kitchen was designed for professional use—Beth had retained a chef on the payroll for awhile. That was when the Smith House was the epicenter of cocktail socials and formal banquets. The mayor and his entourage had attended on several occasions. The middleweight champion of the world. A porn star and his best girl. With people like that dropping in, you had better have a chef.

Anymore, Delaney did the cooking. Delaney, king of cold cuts.

Wallace said, "How'd you get that one?" He meant the puckered welt on Delaney's ribcage.

Delaney scraped his plate in the sink, ran the tap. "I was a pretty stupid kid," he said.

"And all that's changed?"

Delaney said, "Des Moines is a tough town. We were tough kids. A big crew. We caused some trouble. People got hurt."

Wallace knew about Delaney's record, his history of violence, the prisons he had toured. He knew all that in a peripheral way, but had never pried into Delaney's past, never dug up the nitty-gritty details. Guys like him, you left well enough alone. The confession did not surprise him. It was Delaney's nature and a large reason why Wallace hired him when the investment money began to attract unwanted attention. Delaney knew exactly how to deal with people who gave Wallace grief.

Delaney sat on a stool, arms crossed. He directed his gaze at the solid black window, which gave back only curved reflections of the room and its haggard occupants. "Most of us went to the pen, or died. Lots of drinking, lots of dope. Everybody carried. I got shot for the first time when I was sixteen. We knocked over this pool hall on the South End—me and Lonnie Chavez and Ruby Pharaoh. Some guy popped up and put two .32 slugs through my chest. The hospital was a no-go, so Ruby Pharaoh and Chavez loaded me in Ruby's caddy and took me to a field. Chavez's dad was an Army corpsman; he lifted some of his old man's meds and performed home surgery." The small man shook his head with a wry grin. "Hell, it was like the old Saturday matinee westerns we watched as kids—Chavez heating up his knife with a Zippo and Ruby pouring Wild Turkey all over my chest. Hurt like a sonofabitch, let me say. Chavez hid me in a chicken coop until the whole thing blew over. I was real weak, so he fed me. Changed my bandages, brought me comic books and cigs. I never had a brother."

"Me neither," Wallace said. "Mine was too young and I left home before he got outta diapers. But I gotta be honest, I always thought of you as a son."

"You ain't my daddy, Mr. S. You're too rich to be my daddy. You like the young pussy, though. He did too and it caused him no end of trouble."

"That cop was by today."

"Yeah."

"He seems edgy. Seems worried."

"Yeah."

"Dee, when you came into the barn, did you see anything, I don't know, weird?" Wallace hesitated. "Besides the obvious, I mean. These burns on my back; I can't figure how I got them. And what happened to the horse?"

Delaney shrugged. "What's the matter, Mr. S? Cop got you spooked too?"

"I don't need him for that." Wallace placed his glass in the sink. "What happened to the horse, Dee?"

"I blew its head off, Boss." Delaney lighted a cigarette, passed it to Wallace, fired another and smoked it between his middle and fourth fingers, palm slightly cupped to his lips. During the reign of Beth, smoking had been forbidden in the house. Didn't matter anymore.

"I want cameras in tomorrow. Get Savage over here, tell him I've seen the light," Wallace said.

"Cameras, huh."

"Look...I've seen somebody sneaking around at night. I suspected I was hallucinating and maybe that's all it is. I think one of the Choates is around."

"Dogs woulda ripped his balls off."

"I want the cameras. That's it."

"Okay. Where?"

"Where...the gate, for certain. Front door. Pool building. Back yard. We don't use the tool shed. Savage can run everything through there. Guess I'll need to hire a security guy—"

"A couple of guys."

"A couple of guys, right. Savage can take care of that too."

"It'll be a job. A few days, at least."

"Yeah? Well, sooner he gets started...."

"Okay. Is that all?"

Wallace nodded. "For now. I haven't decided. Night, Dee."

"Night, Boss."

7.

Billy Savage of Savage and Sons came in before noon the following day and talked to Delaney about Wallace's latest security needs. Savage had silver, greased down hair, a golfer's tan and a denture-perfect smile. Wallace watched from his office window as Savage and Delaney walked around the property. Savage took notes on a palm-sized computer while Delaney pointed at things. It took about an hour. Savage left and returned after lunch with three vans loaded with men and equipment. Delaney came into the office and gave Wallace a status report. The guys would be around for two or three days if all went according to plan. Savage had provided him a list of reliable candidates for security guards. Wallace nodded blearily. He was deep into a bottle of blue label Stoli by then. He'd told Delaney he trusted his judgment—*Hire whoever you want, Dee. Tell Cecil to leave Helen be for a while. I'm sick of that screaming.*

She's asleep, Mr. S. They doped her up last night and she's been dead to the world ever since.

Oh. Wallace rubbed his eyes and it was night again. He lolled in his leather pilot's chair and stared out at the cruel stars and the shadows of the trees. "You have to do something, Wally, old bean. You really do." He nodded solemnly and took another swig. He fumbled around in the dark for the phone and finally managed to thumb the right number on his speed dialer. Lance Pride, of the infamous Pride Agency, sounded as if he had been going a few rounds with a bottle himself. But the man sobered rather swiftly when he realized who had called him at this *god-awful* hour. "Wallace. What's wrong?"

Wallace said, "It's about the accident."

"Yeah. I thought it might be." And after nearly thirty seconds of silence, Pride said, "Exactly what do you want? Maybe we should do this in person—"

"No, no, nothing heavy," Wallace said. "Write me the book on the Choates. Forward and back."

Pride laughed bleakly and replied that would make for some unpleasant bedtime reading, but not to worry. "Are we looking at…ahem, payback?" He had visited the hospital, sent flowers, etcetera. Back in the olden days, when Wallace was between wives and Pride had only gotten started, they frequented a few of the same seedy haunts and closed down their share. Of course, if Wallace wanted satisfaction over what had happened to Helen, he need but ask. Friend discount and everything. The detective was not a strong-arm specialist per se, however he had a reputation for diligence and adaptation. Before the arrival of Delaney, Wallace had employed him to acquire the goods on more than one recalcitrant landowner—and run off a couple that became overly vengeful. Pride was not fussy about his methods; a quality that rendered him indispensable. "I'll skin your cat, all right," was his motto.

Wallace thanked him and disconnected. He stared into darkness, listening for the strange, intermittent cries from his wife's room.

8.

It was a busy week. On Tuesday, Doctor Green paid a visit, shined a light in his eyes and took his pulse and asked him a lot of pointed questions and wrote a prescription for sleeping pills and valium. Doctor. Green wagged his finger and admonished him to return to physical therapy—Hesse, the massively thewed therapist at the Drover Clinic had tattled regarding Wallace's spotty attendance. Wednesday, the hospital sent a private ambulance for Helen and whisked her off to her monthly neurological examination. She came home in the afternoon with a heart monitor attached to her chest. Kate told Wallace it was strictly routine, they simply wanted to collect data. She smiled a fake smile when she said it and he was grateful.

He sat with Helen for a couple of hours in the afternoons while Kate did laundry and made the bed and filled out the reams of paperwork necessary to the documentation of Helen's health care service. Helen was losing weight. There were circles beneath her vacant eyes and she smelled sick in the way an animal does when it stops eating and begins to waste from the inside. There was also the crack in her face. The original small fracture had elongated into a moist fissure. Wallace gazed in queasy fascination at the pink, crusty furrow that began at her hairline and closed her right eye and blighted her cheekbone. The doctors had no explanation for the wound or its steady encroachment. They had taken more blood and run more scans, changed some medications and increased the dosage of others and indicated in the elegant manner of professional bearers of bad tidings that it was a crap shoot.

Meanwhile, men in coveralls traipsed all over the grounds setting up alarms and cameras; Delaney interviewed a dozen or so security guard applicants from the agency Billy Savage recommended.

Wallace observed from the wings, ear glued to the phone while his subordinates in Seattle and abroad informed him about the status of his various acquisitions and investments. His team was soldiering on quite adequately and he found his attention wandering to more immediate matters: securing his property from the depredations of that ghoulish figure and getting to the bottom of the Choate mystery.

Pride had the instincts of a blue ribbon bird dog and he did not disappoint Wallace's expectations. The detective only required three days to track down an eyewitness to history, one Kurt Bruenig of the Otter Creek Bruenigs.

"The Choates were unsavory, you bet." Kurt Bruenig wiped his mustache, took a long sip of ice tea. A barrel of a man, with blunt fingers, his name stitched on the breast of an oil-stained coverall. His wrecker was parked outside their window booth of the Lucky Bucket in downtown Olympia. "Nasty folk, if you must know. Why *do* you want to know, Mr. Smith?"

Wallace's skull felt like a soccer ball. He cracked the seal on a packet of aspirin and stirred seltzer water in a shabby plastic drinking glass. He swallowed the aspirin and chased them with the seltzer and held on tight while his guts seesawed into the base of his throat.

"Somethin' wrong?"

"How's your lunch?" Wallace gestured at the man's demolished fish and chips basket.

"Fine."

"Yes? How's the fat check you got in your pocket? Look, there's more in it for you, but I'm asking, and my business is mine." Wallace caught Delaney's eye at the bar, and Delaney resumed watching the Dodgers clobber the Red Sox on the big screen.

"Hey, no problem." Bruenig shrugged affably. Tow truck drivers dealt with madmen on a daily basis. "The Choates...our homestead was the next one over, butted up against Otter Creek."

"Pretty area," Wallace said. He placed a small recorder on the table and adjusted the volume. "Please speak clearly, Mr. Bruenig. You don't mind, do you?"

"Uh, no. Sure. It went to hell. Anyways, they were around before us, 'bout 1895. My great-granddaddy pitched his tent in 1910. Those old boys were cats 'n' dogs from the get-go. The Choates were Jews—claimed to be Jews. Had some peculiar customs that didn't sit well with my kin, what with my kin bein' Baptists and all. Not that my great-granddaddy was the salt of the earth, mind you—he swindled his way into our land from what I've been told. I suppose a fair amount of chicanery watered my family tree. We come from Oklahoma and Texas, originally. Those as stayed behind got rich off of cattle and oil. Those of us as headed west, you see what we did with ourselves." He nodded at the wrecker, wiped his greasy fingers on a napkin. "My dad and his tried their hands at farmin'. Pumpkins, cabbage. Had a Christmas tree farm for a few years. Nothin' ever came of it. My sister inherited when my dad passed away. She decided it wasn't worth much, sold out to an East Coast fella. Same as bought the Choate place. But the Choates, they packed it in first. Back in '83—right after their house burned down. We heard one of 'em got drunk and knocked over a lantern. Only thing survived was the barn. Like us, there weren't many of them around at the end. Morgan, he was the eldest. His kids, Hank and Carlotta—they were middle-aged, dead now. Didn't see 'em much. Then there was Josh and Tyler. I was in school with those two. Big, big boys. They played line on a couple football teams that took state."

"How big would you say they were?" Wallace asked.

"Aw, that's hard to say. Josh, he was the older one, the biggest. Damned near seven foot tall. And thick—pig farmers. I remember bumpin' into Josh at the fillin' station, probably four years outta high school. He was a monster. I saw him load a fifty-five-gallon drum into the back of his flatbed. Hugged it to his chest and dropped it on the tailgate like nothin'. He moved out to the Midwest, somewhere. Lost his job when the brewery went tits-up. Tyler, he's doin' a hard stretch in Walla Walla. Used to be a deputy in the Thurston County Sheriff's department. Got nailed for accessory to murder and child pornography. You remember that brouhaha about the ring of devil worshipers supposed to operate all over Olympia and Centralia? They say a quarter of the department was involved, though most of it got hushed by the powers that be. He was one of those unlucky assholes they let dangle in the wind."

Wallace hadn't paid much attention to that scandal. In those days he had been in the throes of empire building and messy divorces. He said, "That's what you meant by nasty folk?"

"I mean they were dirty. Not dirt under the nails from honest labor, either. I'm talkin' 'bout sour—piss and blood and old grotty shit on their coveralls. Josh and Tyler came to school smellin' half dead, like they'd slaughtered pigs over the weekend and not bothered to change. Nobody wanted to handle their filthy money when they paid down to the feed store. As for the devil worshiping, maybe it's true, maybe not. The Satanist rap was sort of the cherry on top, you might say. The family patriarch, Kaleb Choate, was a scientist, graduated from a university in Europe. It was a big deal in the 1890s and people in these parts were leery on account of that. A Jew *and* a scientist? That was askin' a bit much. He worked with Tesla—y'know, the Tesla coil guy. My understanding is Tesla brought him to America to work in his laboratory and didn't cotton to him and they had a fallin' out, but I dunno much about all that. One more weird fact, y'know? Wasn't long before rumors were circulatin' 'bout how old man Choate was robbin' crypts down to the Oddfellows Cemetery and performin' unnatural

experiments on farm animals and Chinamen. We had a whole community of
those Chinese and they weren't popular, so nobody got too riled if one turned
up missin', or what-have-you. And a bunch of 'em did disappear. Authorities
claimed they moved to Seattle and Tacoma where the big Chinese communities
were, or that they sailed back to China and just forgot to tell anybody, or that
they ran off and got themselves killed trespassing. Still, there were rumors and
by the time my great-granddaddy arrived, Kaleb Choate's farm was considered
off limits for good honest Christians. 'Course there was more. Some people took
it into their heads that Choate was a wizard or a warlock, that he came from a
long line of black magicians. There were a few, like the Teagues on Waddel Creek
and the Bakkers over to the eastern Knob Hills, who swore he could mesmerize
a fella by lookin' into his eyes, that he could fly, that he fed those Chinamen to
demons in return for…well, there it kinda falls apart. The Choates had land
and that was about it. They were dirt poor when I was a kid—sorta fallen into
ruin, y'might say. If Old Poger made a bargain with 'em, then they got royally
screwed from the looks of it. I wonder 'bout the flyin' part on account of my
sister and her boyfriend, Wooly Clark, claimed Josh could levitate like those
yogis in the Far East, swore to Jesus they saw him do it in the woods behind the
school once when they were necking. But hell, I dunno. My sister, she's a little
soft in the brain, so there's no tellin' what she did or didn't see…

"Anyhow, the Bruenigs and the Choates had this sort of simmerin' feud
through the years—Kaleb kicked the bucket in the '40s, but our families kept
fightin'. Property squabbles, mainly. Their pigs caused some problems, came
onto our land and destroyed my grandma's garden more than once. The kids
on both sides liked to cause trouble, beat hell out of each other whenever they
could. I guess the grown men pulled that too. My uncles got in a brawl with
some of the Choates at the Lucky Badger; all of 'em were eighty-six'd for life
and Uncle Clover did a month in the county lockup for bustin' a guy over the
noggin with a chair."

Wallace said, "So, did you ever notice anything unusual going on?"

"You mean, like was the deal with Tyler an isolated incident or were the old
rumors all true? Maybe we had a bona fide witch coven next door?" Bruenig
shook his head. "There were some strange happenin's, I'll grant. More complicated than witches, though."

"Complicated?"

"That's right, partner. Look at the history, you'll notice a few of the Choates
were eggheads. Heck of a deal to be an egghead yet spend your whole life on a
farm, isn't it? Buncha friggin' cloistered monks—unnatural. You had Kaleb's son,
Morgan, he owned the land until they sold out and he was a recluse, nobody
ever saw him, but I heard tell he was an astronomer, wrote a book or somethin'.
Then you got Paul Choate—Dr. Creepy, the kids called him; he taught physics
at Evergreen in the '70s and did some research for NASA. But he wasn't even
the smartest of the litter. We knew at least three more of those guys coulda

done the same. Hell, Josh was a genius in school. He just hated class; bored him. Me, I always thought they were contacted by aliens. That's why they all acted so weird."

"You're shitting me," Wallace said.

"No, sir. You gonna sit there and tell me you don't believe in the ETs? This is the twenty-first century, pal. You oughta read Carl Sagan."

"You read Carl Sagan?"

"'Cause I drive a wrecker I'm a dumbass? Read Sagan, there's plenty of funky stuff goin' on in the universe."

"Okay, okay," Wallace said. "Tell me about the aliens."

"Like I said, it goes all the way back to the beginnin', if you pay attention. Within a decade of Kaleb Choate's arrival, folks started reportin' peculiar sightin's. Goat men in the Waddel Creek area, two-headed calves, lights over the Capitol Forest—no airplanes to explain that away. Not then. People saw UFOs floatin' around the Choate fields month after month in 1915 and 1916, right when the action in Europe was gettin' heavy. Some of it's in the papers, some it was recorded by the police department and private citizens, the library. It's a puzzle. You find a piece here and there, pretty quick things take shape. Anyhow, this went on into the '50s and '60s, but by then the entire country was in the middle of the saucer scare, so the authorities assumed mass hysteria. There were still disappearances too, except now it wasn't the Chinese—the Chinese had moseyed to greener pastures by the late '40s. Nope, this was mostly run-of-the-mill, God-fearin' townies. Don't get me wrong, we aren't talking 'bout bus loads. Three or four kids, a couple wives, a game warden and a census taker, some campers. More than our share of bums dropped off the face of the earth, but you know that didn't amount to a hill of beans. These disappearances are spread thin. Like somebody, or somethin' was bein' damn careful not to rouse the natives.

"Of course, as a kid I was all-fired curious 'bout morbid crap, pestered my dad constantly. I pried a little out of him; more I learned Hardy Boys style. Got to tell you, my daddy wouldn't talk 'bout the Choates if he could help it; he'd spit when someone mentioned 'em. Me and my sister got ambitious and dug into the dirty laundry. We even spied on 'em. Mighty funny how often they used to get visitors from town. Rich folks. Suits from the Capitol drove out there. Real odd, considerin' the Choates have always been looked down on as white trash—homegrown eggheads or not. That's what got me thinkin'. That and I saw Morgan and his boys diggin' in their fields at night."

"Mass graves?" Wallace said dryly.

Bruenig barked a wad of phlegm into his basket. "Huh! Better believe it crossed my mind. Told my pappy and his eyes got hard. Seems granddad saw 'em doin' the same thing in *his* day. Near as we could tell they were laying pipe or cable, all across their property. They owned about three thousand acres, so there's miles of it, whatever it is. Then there were the pylons—"

"Pylons. Where'd you see those?" Wallace's interest sharpened.

"Farther back on their land. Long time ago a road wound around there—it's overgrown now, but when it was cleared there were these rocks sittin' out in the middle of nowhere. Sorta like that Stonehenge deal, except it was just one or two in each field. Jesse, my sister, counted twenty of 'em scattered 'round. She said they looked like peckers, and I have to admit they did bear a resemblance."

"Any idea who made them?"

"No. I mentioned it to a young geologist fella, worked for the BLM. He got interested, said he was gonna interview the Choates, see if they'd built on tribal grounds. Never heard from him again, though. He was barkin' up the wrong tree anyway. Those rocks are huge; least two tons each. How the Indians supposed to move that kinda load? Otter Creek—*puhlease.* Not in your lifetime. Plus, I never seen rock looked like those pylons. We don't have obsidian 'round here. Naw, those things are ancient and the ETs shipped 'em in from somewhere else. Probably markers, like pyramids and crop circles. Then the Choates come along and use 'em to communicate with the aliens. Help 'em with their cattle mutilations and their abductions. Don't ask me why the aliens need accomplices. No way we'll ever understand what makes a Gray tick."

Wallace turned off the recorder, slipped it in his pocket. "Is that all, Mr. Bruenig? Anything else you want to add that I might find useful?"

"Well, sir, I reckon I don't truly know what that could be. My advice is to steer clear of the Choate place, if you're thinkin' of muckin' 'round that way. You aren't gonna find any arrowheads or souvenirs worth your time. Don't know that I hold with curses, but that land's gotta shadow over it. I sure as hell don't poke my nose around there."

9.

Wallace's favorite was the dead woman on the rocker.

Beth had hated it, said the artist, a local celebrity named Miranda Carson, used too much wax. The sculpture was indeed heavy, it required two burly movers to install it in the gallery. Wallace did not care, he took morbid pleasure in admiring the milky eyes, the tangled strands of real hair the artist collected from her combs. In low light, the wax figure animated, transformed into a young woman, knees drawn to chin, meditating upon the woods behind the house, the peacocks and the other things that lurked. Wallace once loaned the piece, entitled *Remembrance*, to the UW library; brought it home after an earthquake shattered an arm and damaged the torso. Carson had even driven over and performed a hasty repair job. The cracks were still evident, like scars. Macabre and beautiful.

The gallery was populated by a dozen other sculptures, a menagerie orphaned by Beth's departure and Wallace's general disinterest. Wallace wandered among them, cell phone glued to his ear, partially aware of Skip's buzzing baritone. Wallace thought the split in the dead girl's body seemed deeper. More jagged.

"—so Randy and I'll go today. Unless you want to come. Might be what you need."

"Say again?" Wallace allowed himself to be drawn into the cathode. It dawned on him that he had made a serious tactical error in confiding the Bruenig interview to Skip. They had discussed the Choate legend over drinks the prior evening and Wallace more than half-expected his friend to laugh, shake his snowy head and call him a damn fool for chasing his tail. Instead, Skip had kept mum and sat stroking his beard with a grim, thoughtful expression. Now, after a night's sleep, the story had gestated and hatched as a rather dubious scheme to nip Wallace's anxieties at their roots.

"Randy and I'll scope out that property this afternoon. He wants to see that nest you were going on about at the hospital. He said it sounds weird. I told him it's dried up. He refuses to listen, of course."

"Wait-wait." Wallace rubbed his temple. "You plan to go to the barn."

"Uh-hmm, right."

"To what—look at the nest?"

"That's what I've been saying. I'm thinking noon, one o'clock. We'll have dinner at the Oyster House. It's lobster night."

"Lobster night, yeah. Skip?"

"What?"

"Forget about the nest. You're right, it won't be there, they migrate, I think. And the barn's condemnable, man. It's dangerous. Scary people hang around—maybe druggies, I dunno. Bad types." Wallace's hand was slippery. He was afraid he might drop the phone.

"Oh yeah? Well it just so happens I called Lyle Ferguson—your old pal Lyle, remember him? He landed the bid and he says they're planning to commence tearing down the barn and all that sort of thing on Monday or Tuesday. So time is of the essence, as they say."

"Skip—"

"Hey, Wally. I'm driving here. You don't want to come with us?" Skip's voice crackled.

"No. Uh, say hi to Fergie, if you see him."

"Okay, buddy. I'm driving, I gotta go. Call you tomorrow." *Click.*

"Uh, huh." Wallace regarded a bust on a plinth. It was the half-finished head of a woman wearing thick lipstick. A crack had begun to divide the plaster face.

He had had Pride check into Bruenig's story about the BLM geologist and the monoliths. The geologist was named Chuck Doolittle and he abruptly quit his post six years ago, dropped everything and departed the state of Washington, although nobody at the department had a handle on where he might have emigrated. As for the so-called monoliths, the bureau disavowed knowledge of any such structures and while the former Choate property did overlap tribal grounds, it had long ago been legally ceded to the county. No mystery at all.

The only hitch, insomuch as Pride was concerned, was the fact certain records pertaining to the Choate farm were missing from the county clerk's office. According to a truncated file index, the Choate folder once contained numerous photos of unidentified geological formations, or possibly manmade constructs of unknown origin. The series began in 1927, the latter photographs being dated as late as 1971. Pride located eight black-and-white pictures taken in 1954 through 1959 that displayed some boulders and indistinct earth heaves akin to the Mima Mounds. Unfortunately, the remainder of the series, some ninety-eight photos, was missing and unaccounted for since an office fire at the old courthouse in '79.

Wallace went into Helen's suite, waited near the door while Cecil massaged Helen's cramped thigh muscles. Kate had arrived early. The burly nurse dabbed Helen's brow with a wash cloth and murmured encouragement. Helen's fish-black eyes rolled with blindness and fear. There was nothing of comprehension or sanity in them and the cleft in her forehead and cheek was livid as a gangrenous brand. She howled and howled without inflection, the flat repeating utterance of an institutionalized mind.

Wallace limped upstairs to his office, turned up the radio. His hip throbbed fiercely; sympathy pangs. His hand itched with fading scabs. What had happened to him that night in the alley behind the Marlin? What was happening now? He found some Quaaludes in a drawer, chased them with a healthy belt of JD and put his head down in his arms, a kindergartner again.

10.

Wallace was standing in Skip's dining room. Wallace's feet were nailed down with railroad spikes.

"Why'd you let them go?" Delaney asked. He slouched against a cabinet and smoked a cigarette.

Watery light washed out the details. Randy's prosthesis shined upon the table, plastic fingers blooming in a vase. A two-inch crack separated the fancy tiled ceiling. There was movement inside. Squirming.

Skip swaggered from the kitchen and plunged oversized hands into a bowl of limp, yellow noodles. He drew forth a clump, steaming and dripping, plopped it on his head as a wig. Grinned the wacky grin of a five-year-old stoned out of his gourd on cough syrup.

"Why are you doing that?" Wallace tried to modulate his voice; his voice was scratchy, was traitorously shrill.

Skip drooled and capered, shook fistfuls of noodles like pompoms.

Wallace said, "Where's Randy? Skip, is Randy here?"

"Nope."

"Where is he?"

"With the god of the barn-b-barn—b-barn barn barn barn!"

"Skip, where's Randy?"

"In the barn with Bay-el, Bay-el, Bay-el. Playing a game." Skip hummed a ditty to his noodles, cast Wallace a sidelong glance of infinite slyness. "Snufalupagus LOVES raw spaghetti. No sauce, no way! I pretend it's worms. Worms get big, Wallace. You wouldn't believe how big some worms get. Worms crawl inside your guts and make babies. They crawl up your nose, your ears, into your mouth. If somebody grinds you into itty-bitty pieces and a worm eats you, it'll know all the stuff you did." He lowered his voice. "They can crawl up your butt and make ya do the hula dance and jabber like Margie Thatcher on crank!"

"Where's Randy?"

"Playing sock puppets." Skip began ramming noodles down his throat. "He's Kermit de Frog!"

"Should've stopped them, Boss. Now they've stirred up the wasps' nest. You're fucked." Delaney stubbed his cigarette and walked through the wall.

Wallace awoke in darkness, fearful and disoriented. He had drunkenly migrated to his bedroom at some fuzzy period and burrowed into the covers. He remembered long, narrow corridors, bloody nebulas splattered against leaded glass and Kirlian figures scorched into the walls: skeletal fragments of clawing hands and gaping mouths.

Wallace, Helen said. She was there with him in the room, wedged high in the corner of the walls where they joined the ceiling. She gleamed white as bone and her eyes and mouth and the crack in her face were black as the pits between the stars. *There's a hole you can't fill,* she said.

Wallace screamed in his throat, a mangled, pathetic cry. The clouds moved across the moon and reshaped the shadows on the wall and Helen was not hanging there with her black black eyes, her covetous mouth, or the stygian worm that fed on her face. There were only moonbeams and the reflections of branches like skinned fingers against the plaster.

Wallace lay trembling. Eventually he drifted away and slept with the covers over his head. He flinched at the chorus of night sounds, each knock upon the door.

11.

"Skip. Are you eating? Where've you been?"

"Nothing, Wallace. I'm tired."

"Skip, it's three. I've been calling for hours. Why don't you come over."

"Ahh, no thanks. I'm gonna sleep a while. I'm tired."

"Skip."

"Yeah?"

"Where's Randy? He doesn't answer his phone."

"Dunno. Try him at the office. Little bastard's always working late."

"I tried his office, Skip."

"Okay. That's right. He's out of town. On business."

"Business. What kind of business?"

"Dunno. Business."

"Where did he go, exactly? Skip? Skip, you still there?"

"Dunno. He won't be around much, I guess. There's a lot of business."

"Skip—"

"Wallace, I gotta sleep, now. Talk to you later. I'm very tired."

12.

Wallace sat on the steps, new cane across his knees, Bruno and Thor poised at his flanks like statuary come alive. The sun bled red and gold. The trees would be getting green buds any day now. He listened to the birds mating in the branches. The graveyard-shift security guard, a gray, melancholy fellow named Tom, was going off-duty. He came over to smoke a cigarette and introduce himself to his new boss. He was a talker, this dour, gaunt Tom. He used to drive school buses until his back went south—lower lumbar was a killer, yessiree. He was an expert security technician. Twenty-four years on the job; he had seen everything. The other two guys, Charlie and Dante, were kids, according to Tom. He promised to keep an eye on them for Wallace, make certain they were up to standard. Wallace said thanks and asked Tom to bring him the nightly surveillance video. The guard asked if he meant all four of them and Wallace considered that a moment before deciding, no, only the video feed from the garden area. Tom fetched it from the guard shack and handed it over without comment. The look on his face sufficed—he was working for a lunatic.

Wallace plugged the CD into the player on his theater-sized plasma television in the den. He called Randy's house and talked to Janice while silent, grainy night images flickered on the screen. Janice said Randy had left a cryptic message on the answering machine and nothing since. He had rambled about taking a trip and signed off by yelling, *Hallucigenia! Hallucigenia sparsa! It's a piece of something bigger—waaay bigger, honey!* Janice was unhappy. Randy had pulled crazy stunts before. He dodged lengthy stays in Federal penitentiaries as a college student and she had been there for the entire, wild ride. She expected the phone to ring at any moment and him to be in prison, or a hospital. What if he tried to sneak into Cuba again? What if he blew off his other hand? Who was going to wipe his ass then? Wallace reassured her that nothing of the sort was going to happen and made her promise to call when she heard anything.

Lance Pride dropped in to report his progress. Pride was lanky, a one-time NBA benchwarmer back in the '70s. He dressed in stale tweeds and emanated a palpable sense of repressed viciousness. His eyes were hard and small. He glanced at the video on the television and did not comment.

Pride confessed Joshua Choate appeared to be a dead end. His last known residence was a trailer court on the West Side of Olympia and he had abandoned the premises about three years ago. The former Ph.D. farm boy had not applied for a driver's license, a credit card, a job application or anything else. Maybe he was living on the street somewhere, maybe he had skipped the country, maybe he was dead. Nobody had seen him lately, of that much Pride was certain.

Pride strewed a bundle of newspaper clippings on the coffee table, artifacts he had unearthed pertaining to Paul, Tyler and Josh: stories detailing the promotion of Tyler Choate and a file picture of the young deputy sheriff grinning as he loomed near a Thurston County police cruiser and another of him shackled and bracketed by guards after he had been exposed as a mastermind cultist; a shot of Joshua when he had been selected as an all-American tackle—his wide, flabby face was nearly identical to his brother's; articles from the mid-'60s following Paul Choate's hiring at the newly founded Evergreen State College and his brief and largely undocumented collaboration with NASA regarding cosmic microwave background radiation. There were school records for Tyler and Josh—four-point-oh students and standout football players. Major universities had courted them with every brand of scholarship. Tyler did his time at Washington State, majored in psychology, perfect grades, but no sports, and joined the sheriff's department. Meanwhile, Josh earned a degree in physics at Northwestern, advanced degrees in theoretical physics from Caltech and MIT and then dropped off the radar forever. Tyler eventually became implicated in a never fully explained scandal involving Satanism and rape and got dropped in a deep, dark hole. The only other curious detail regarding the younger brothers was the fact both of them had been banned from every casino within two hundred miles of Olympia. None of the joints ever caught them cheating, but they were unstoppable at the blackjack tables and the houses became convinced the boys counted cards.

None of it seemed too useful and Wallace barely skimmed the surface items before conceding defeat and shoving the pile aside. Pride just smiled dryly and said he'd make another pass at things. He had a lead on the company that had sold the Choates a ton of fabricated metals in the '60s and '70s. Unfortunately the company had gone under, but he was looking into former employees. He told Wallace to hang onto the newspaper clippings and left with a promise to check in soon.

Wallace moped around the house, mixing his vodka with lots of orange juice in a feeble genuflection toward sobriety. He picked up the newspaper photo of Josh Choate aged seventeen, in profile with his shoulder pads on. He wore a slight smile and his pixilated eye was inscrutable. *I am a loyal son. I am here to usher in the dark.*

The day was bright and hot like it often was in Western Washington during the spring. The garden filled the television with static gloom. Upstairs, Helen began to scream. Wallace was out of orange juice.

He called Lyle Ferguson. The contractor was cordial as ever. He was moving crews into the Otter Creek Housing Development, AKA the old Choate place as of that morning. Yeah, Skip Arden had called him, sure; asked whether he could nose around the property. No problem, Ferguson had said, just don't trip and break anything. Pylons? Oh, yeah they found some rocks on the site. Nothing a bulldozer couldn't handle....

13.

The next day Wallace became impatient and had Delaney drive him to the branch office of Fish and Wildlife. Short visit. Randy Freeman's supervisor told Wallace that Randy had two months vacation saved. The lady thought perhaps he had gone to Canada. Next, he phoned the number Detective Adams gave him and got the answering machine. He hit the number for the front desk and was told Detective Adams was on sick leave—would he care to leave a message or talk to another officer?

Wallace sat in the rear of the Bentley, forehead pressed against the glass as they waited in traffic beside Sylvester Park. Two lean, sun-dried prostitutes washed each other's hair in the public drinking fountain. Nearby, beat cops with faces the shade of raw flank steak loomed over a shirtless man sprawled in the grass. The man laughed and flipped the cops off and a pug dog yapped raucously at the end of a rope tied to the man's belt.

Delaney chewed on a toothpick. He said, "Boss, where are we going with this?"

Wallace shrugged and wiped his face, his neck. His thoughts were shrill and inchoate.

"Well, I don't think it's a good idea," Delaney said.

"You should've kept feeding me my pills. Then we wouldn't be sitting here."

"You need to see a shrink. This is what they call the grieving process."

"Think I'm in the denial stage?"

"I don't know what stage to call it. You aren't doing so hot. You're running in circles." The car moved again. Delaney drove with the window rolled down, his arm on the frame. "Your wife isn't going to recover. It's a bitch and it hurts, I know. But she isn't going to come around, Mr. S. She won't ever be the woman you married. And you got to face that fact, look it dead in the eye. 'Cause, till you do, whatever screws are rattling loose in your head are going to keep on rattling." He glanced over at Wallace. "I'm sorry to say that. I'm real sorry."

"Don't be sorry." Wallace smiled, thin and sad. "Just stick with me if you can. I'll talk to that Swedish psychiatrist Green recommended. Ha, I've been ducking that guy since I got out of the hospital. I'll do that, but there's something else. I have to find out what the Choates were doing on that property."

"Pit bull, aren't you, Boss?" There was admiration mixed with the melancholy.

"Bruenig said the man moved out of state. He's wrong. Choate's in the neighborhood. Maybe he lives here, maybe he's visiting, hiding under a bridge. Whatever. I saw his tracks at the barn and I think he's been creeping around the garden. I told you." *Saw him in the alley, too, didn't you, Wally?* He shuddered at the recollection of that febrile mouth closing on him.

"Yup, you saw tracks. Almost a year ago," Delaney said. "If they were even his."

"Trust me, they were. Pride's running skips on him, although I'm getting the feeling this fellow isn't the type who's easy to find. That's why I've got Pride tracking down whoever sold the Choates the materials for their projects in the back forty. Maybe you can call in a favor with the Marconi boys, or Cortez, see if you can't turn up some names. I gotta know."

"Maybe you don't wanna know."

"Dee…something's wrong. People are dying."

Delaney looked at him in the rearview mirror.

"You better believe it," Wallace said. "Stop acting like my wet nurse, damn it."

Delaney stared straight ahead. "Okay," he said.

"Thank you," Wallace said, slightly ashamed. He lighted a cigarette as a distraction.

They went to Skip's home, idled at the gate. Delaney leaned out and pressed on the buzzer until, finally, a butler emerged with apologies from the master of the house. The servant, a rigid, ramrod of a bloke, doubtless imported directly from the finest Hampton school of butlery, requested that they vacate the premises at once. Wallace waited until the butler was inside. He climbed out of the car and hurled a brandy flask Skip gave him some birthday past, watched with sullen pleasure as it punched a hole through a parlor window. Delaney laughed in amazement, shoved Wallace into the car, left rubber smoking on the breeze.

14.

Wallace and Delaney were sitting in the study playing cards and eating a dinner of tuna fish sandwiches and Guinness when Lyle Ferguson called to say the barn had been razed. Ferguson hoped Helen would be more at peace. There was an awkward silence and then the men exchanged meaningless pleasantries and hung up.

"It's done," Wallace said. He drank the last of his beer and set the dead soldier near its mates.

Delaney dragged on his cigarette and tossed his cards down. He said, "Thing is, no matter how much you cut, cancer always comes back."

Wallace chose not to acknowledge that. "Next week, I'll hunt for the rest of those pylons, the ones in the woods, and take a jackhammer to them. I'll dynamite them if it comes to that."

"Not big on respecting cultural artifacts, are we?"

"I have a sneaking suspicion that it's better for us whatever culture they belong to is dead and in the ground." Wallace missed his little brother. The kid was an ace; he would have known what was what with Bruenig's story, the crazy altar in the barn, the pylons.

"I saw Janice yesterday. She's losing her marbles. Randy was supposed to take her and the kids to Yellowstone for spring vacation. She called the cops."

"I have two postcards from him." What Wallace didn't say was that there was something strange about the cards. They were unstamped, for one. And they seemed too old, somehow, their picturesque photographs of Mount Rainier and the Mima Mounds yellowing at the edges, as if they'd lingered on a gift shop rack for decades. Which, in fact, made sense when he checked the photo copyrights and saw the dates 1958 and 1971.

"Sure you do." Delaney dropped his butt into an empty bottle, pulled another cigarette from behind his ear and lighted it. His eyes were bloodshot. "Hate to admit it…but I was a little stoned that day. When everything happened. Nothing major—I wasn't impaired, I mean."

"Hey, it doesn't matter. I'm not going to bust your chops over something stupid like that."

"No. It's important. I wasn't totally fucked up, but I don't completely trust my recollections either. Not *completely*."

"What're you talking about?"

"I pulled you out of the barn first. Then I ran in for Mrs. S. You're not supposed to move a person with injuries. Know why I moved her?"

Wallace's mouth was full of sand. He shook his head.

"Because it took the horse, Mr. S. The horse was already trussed like a fly in a spider web and hanging. I still see its hooves twitching. I didn't look too close. Figured I wouldn't have the balls to go under there and grab your wife." Delaney's mouth turned down. "That wasp nest of yours…it had a face," he said, and looked away. "An old man's face."

"Dee—"

"Randy was an okay dude. He deserves a pyre. You gonna deal, or what?"

15.

Night seeped down. It rained. The power came and went, stuttered in the wires. Wallace picked up on the second ring. The caller ID said, UNKNOWN NAME-UNKNOWN NUMBER.

"Hi, Wally. Your friend is right." The mouth on the other end was too close to the receiver, was full, sensual and malicious.

Wallace's face stiffened. "Josh?"

"Cancer always returns because time is a ring. And a ring…well, that's just a piece of metal around a hole." A wave of crackling interference drowned the connection.

"Josh!" No answer; only low, angry static.

The display said, THEREISAHOLENOMANCANFILLTHEREISAHOLENO-MANCANFILLTHEREISAHOLENOMANCANFILL. Then nothing.

16.

Friday morning, Charlie, the dayshift security guard, brought Wallace a densely wrapped parcel from Lance Pride. The shipping address was a small town in Eastern Washington called Drummond and it had been written in a thin, backward-slanting style that Wallace didn't recognize.

Wallace cut the package open and found a tape cassette and a battered shoebox jammed with musty papers—personal correspondence from the appearance. It bothered him, this delivery from Pride. Why not in person? Why not a phone call, at least? Goosebumps covered his arms.

Wallace retreated to his office. He made a drink and sat at his desk near the window that looked across the manicured lawn, the sleeping garden, and far out into the woods. He finished his drink without tasting it and fixed another and drank that too. Then he filled his glass again, no ice this time, no frills, and put the tape in the machine and pressed the button. The wall above his desk shifted from red to maroon and a chill breeze fluttered drapes. The afternoon light slid toward the edge of the Earth.

After seconds of static and muffled curses, Pride cleared his throat and began to speak.

"Wallace, hi. This is Wednesday evening and...where am I. Uh, I'm at the Lone Tree Motel outside of Drummond on Highway 32 and I recently finished interviewing Tyler Choate. It's about two in the A.M. and I haven't slept since I dunno, so cut me slack if this starts to drag. The guards had confiscated my tape recorder at the door, but Tyler gave me a note pad so I could write it down for later. He wanted to be certain you got your money's worth...I'll try to hit the highlights as best I can. Bear with me...

"Okay, I went looking for the manufacturer that might've sold the Choates aluminum tubes, pipes or what have you. I called some people, did some digging and came up with a name—Elijah Salter. Salter was a marine, vet of the Korean War; rode with the cavalry as a gunner and engineering specialist—survived Operation Mousetrap and had the Bronze Star and Ike's signature to prove it. This leatherneck Bronze Star-winner came home after the war, started a nice family and went back to school where he discovered he was a real whizz-bang mechanical engineer. He graduated and signed on with a metal fabrication plant over in Poulsbo. Calaban Industries. This plant makes all kinds of interesting stuff, mostly for aerospace companies and a certain east coast college that was rigging a twenty-mile-long atom-smasher—more on that later.

"Well, old Sergeant Salter climbed the ladder to plant manager, got the keys to the executive washroom, the Club Med package, free dental. They gave him plenty of slack and he jumped at it, opened a sideline with his own, special clientele—among these, the Choates. Struck me as a tad eerie, this overseer of a high-tech company keeping a group of hicks in his black book and I decided to run it to ground. Wasn't tough to track Salter, he'd retired in '84, renovated a villa near here. I kid you not, a dyed-in-the-wool Spanish villa like where Imperial-era nobility cooled their heels. I couldn't believe my ex-jarhead could afford a spread that posh—guy had palm trees, marble fountains, you name it. You woulda been jealous. Tell you what: his sidelines musta been lucrative.

"Made it big, made it real big, and after Salter got over the shock of meeting me in his den with my revolver pointed at his gut, he offered me a scotch and soda and praised Kaleb Choate to the heavens. Claimed not to know any of the rest of the clan that was still alive. Oh, he knew *of* them, he'd corresponded with Paul Choate occasionally, but they hadn't ever met in person or anything like that. I didn't get it—Kaleb's been in the ground since 1947, but what the hell.

"The sergeant had gone soft, the way a lion in a cage goes soft—he still had that bloody gleam in his eye when he gestured at the house and said his patrons took care of their own.

"Patrons? The way it slithered out of his mouth, way he sneered when he said it, didn't make me too comfortable. Also, when he's bragging about all the wonderful things these patrons did for him, I noticed a painting hanging over the piano. Damned thing was so dark it was almost black and that's why it took me a while to make out it wasn't actually a portrait, it was a picture of a demon. Or something. Guy in a suit like muckety-mucks wore in the Roaring Twenties, but his head was sort of, well, deformed, I guess is the best way to put it. Like I said, though, the oil was so dark I couldn't quite figure what I was seeing—just that it reminded me of a beehive sittin' on a man's neck. That, and the hands were about as long as my forearm. Reminded me of spooky stories my granny used to tell about Australia during the Depression. The aborigines have this legend about desert spirits called the Mimis. The Mimis are so thin they turn sideways and slip through a crack in the wall. They grab snotty kids, drag 'em underground. Don't know why I thought of that—maybe the long, snaky hands rang a bell. Granny used to scare the holy shit outta us kids with her campfire tales.

"Now I'm studying Salter's décor a bit more closely and, yep, he's got funky Gothic crap going on everywhere. Salter goes, sure, ya, ya betcha, we laid some aluminum cables on the Choate property; set up a few other gadgets too—but these projects were simply improvements on systems that had been in place for decades. I asked him what the idea was behind these cables, and he titters something about flytraps and keyholes. Kaleb Choate had been investigating alternate forms of energy and that's why he buried pipes and wires everywhere; he was building a superconductor, although his version was different, a breakthrough because it operated at high temperature. He used it to develop a whole bunch of toys. Salter used the word *squid* to describe them, except I don't think that's quite right either. Here it is—superconducting quantum interference device. SQUID, that's cute, huh. Oh, yeah…about the weird rocks you saw. Those pylons scattered around the area have been there for thousands of years. Some ancient tribe set 'em up to achieve a prehistoric version of Kaleb's machine, kinda like the Pyramids were before their time. Those rocks are highly radioactive—but Salter said the radiation is of unknown origin, something today's science boys haven't classified, even.

"Said if I want to know the *dirty details* I should speak with the Choate brothers. I didn't appreciate that answer much, so I bopped him around. He starts babbling at me in a foreign language—dunno *what* language, probably Korean, but it made my skin prickle—this old savage on his belly by the pool, grinning and yammering and leaking from his nose. Then Salter just stops all of a sudden and stares at me and he's obviously disgusted. I got a gun on him, I ain't afraid to hurt him a little or a lot, and here he is shaking his head as if I'm some brat whose shat his diaper at a dinner party. He says he hopes I live so long as to bear witness and join the great revelry. Says my skin will fly from a flagpole. And all the pistol-whipping in the world wouldn't encourage him to say anything else. Not in English, anyhow. I ransacked his house, found a shoebox of letters and postcards from P., M., and T. Choate to Salter dated 1967 through 2002 and there were some drawings of things the Choates were building; blueprints...Oh, and I swiped a rolodex chock full of interesting names. Creepy bastard had the Lieutenant Governor's home number, I kid you not. Guy's handwriting was goddamned sloppy, but I spotted one for Tyler Choate, the ex-sheriff's deputy. I decided Salter was right—best to have a chat with Tyler, get it straight from the source.

"Choate was my only choice. According to the records, Tyler and Joshua were the last of the breed, discounting obscure family branches, illegitimate kids, and so on. Since I'd been striking out with Josh, and Tyler's doing twenty to life in the state pen, I went the easy route.

"Tyler's not at Walla Walla anymore; there'd been some razzle-dazzle with the paperwork and he got transferred north to a max security facility. Place called Station 3, between Lind and Marengo on the Rattlesnake Flat.

"Choate surprised me. Friendly. Real damned friendly. Strange accent; spoke very distinctly, as if he were a 'right proper' gentleman not a con nabbed for assorted nastiness. In fact, I got the impression he was eager for my visit. Lonely. Didn't care what I was after, either. I gave him a cockamamie story, naturally, but I needn't have bothered. Sonofabitch was rubbing his hands together over the phone.

"It was a date. Long drive and I hate going east. Once you climb over the mountains it's nothing but wheat fields, desert and blowing dust. This Station 3 was on the outskirts of the Hanford Nuclear Reservation. It sat at the end of a dirt road in the middle of a prairie. The earth is black in those parts; salt deposits. Humongous black rocks and pine trees scattered around. Coyotes, jackrabbits and rattlesnakes.

"I went by an Indian reservation; heard there's a pretty nice casino, but I didn't check. The Station itself was depressing—a bunch of crappy concrete houses inside a storm fence with rusty rolls of barbwire on top. Some buses were parked near the loading docks, the kind that are painted gray and black with mesh on the windows, said FRANKLIN COUNTY CORRECTIONS in big letters. A reject military base is how it looked.

"Way, way out in a field men were hoeing rows in biblical tradition; seems the prison industry, such as it is, revolves around selling potatoes and carrots to the local tribe. A dozen cons in jumpsuits milled in the yard, pulling weeds, busting asphalt to make way for the new parking lot. Don't know why they needed one—the screws and admin parked in a garage and there were maybe three cars in front, counting mine.

"After handing my I.D. to the guards in the gatehouse, they buzzed me through to a short, uncovered promenade. Heavy gauge chain link made a funnel toward the main complex and as I walked I noticed there's graffiti on the concrete walls. Some of it'd been whitewashed, but only some. I saw SHAITAN IS THE MASTER and PRAISE BELIAL. BOW TO CHEMOSH O MAGGOTS. THE OLD ONE IS COMING. Frankly, it gave me the willies. Told myself they hadn't gotten around to scrubbing those sections. They'd missed a spot or two. Uh-huh.

"I was beginning to regret my impulsive nature. Not as if I'm green, or anything; I'd been locked inside the kit kat for a minor beef. More than the graffiti was playing on my nerves, though. The guards seemed off-key. The whole bunch of them were sluggish as hornets drunk on hard cider. Swear to God one was jacking off up in the tower; his rifle kinda bounced on its shoulder strap.

"Warden Loveless, he's this pencil-dick bean counter with thick glasses; he didn't blink while we were jawing. Sounded like one of my undergrad English lit profs, droned through his nose. Don't recall his little list of rules and regs, but I can't forget him drooling on his collar. He kept dabbing it with a fancy handkerchief. I tried not to stare, but damn.

"The warden says he's glad I made it, he thought I had changed my mind, and he sounded relieved, joked about sending some of the boys to bring me in if I hadn't come. Warden Loveless says Tyler Choate is expecting me, that we should go visit him right away, and let me tell you the only reason I didn't turn on my heel and walk out was there were several men holding carbines at half-mast and staring at me with zombie eyes, and I think some of them were drooling too. See, I coulda sworn Loveless said *Master* instead of Tyler. Acoustics were pretty screwed up in there, though.

"Loveless takes me on a walking tour of the prison. Place probably hadn't been remodeled since the '40s or '50s, exposed pipe and those grilled-in bulbs. Damp and foul as a latrine, mildew creeping in every joint. Damned dark; seemed like most of the lights had been busted and never replaced. Another odd detail—three-quarters of the cells were empty. We've got the planet's most crowded prison system and this place is deserted.

"We rode an elevator to the sublevels, a steel cage like coal miners crowd into. Down, way down. The cage rattled and groaned and I never realized before that I'm claustrophobic. Okay, something funny happened to me. The walls closed in and my collar got tight. I…started seeing things. No sound, only images, clear as day, like my mind was the Bijou running a matinee horror flick.

"That goddamned barn of yours. My mom and pop squirming in a lake of worms. Helen grinning at me. Jellyfish. I hate those things. Got stung once in Virginia when I spent the summer with my cousin. I nearly drowned. Goddamned things. I saw other stuff, stuff I don't want to remember. So damn real I got vertigo, thought the floor was gonna drop from under me.

"Maybe I'm not claustrophobic, maybe it was something else. Fumes. Stress. My daddy had shellshock when he came home from the war. Flipped his wig every so often, beat the hell outta his fellow drunks at the tavern. When he was like that, he'd sit in his rocker till the A.M., cleaning his Winchester and staring at nothing, face of a china plate. Said he saw the gooks coming, too many, not enough bullets, stabbed so many his bayonet got dull as a butter knife. My old man drank wood grain alcohol through a funnel; smelled like a refinery before he died.

"Riding down in that elevator, I bet my face looked like his when he was fighting ghosts. I played it cool, gritted my teeth and thought about the Red Sox batting order, getting laid by the chick who used to come by the Mud Shack every Thursday with her sister, whatever happy shit I could dream up on short notice. The vertigo and the visions went away when we hit bottom. A broken circuit. After a few steps it was easy to think the whole episode was a brain fart, my bout with the pink elephants. Yeah, I had DT's. Been trying to kick the sauce and you know how that is... My hands were doing the Parkinson's polka.

"Loveless called this level the Isolation Ward; told me to follow the lights to H Block; said he'd wait for me. No rush. Choate didn't entertain every day.

"More graffiti. More by a thousandfold. Numbers, symbols, gibberish. It covered the tunnel walls, ceiling, the cell bars. Probably inside the cells too, but those things were black as a well-digger's asshole. Kicker is, I saw one of the fellas responsible for the artwork—this scrawny man in filthy dungarees was doing the honors. Must've been eighty years old; his ribs stuck out and his eyes were milky. Blind as hell. He carted a couple buckets of black and white paint and was slapping brushloads onto the concrete. After he'd made a nice mess, he'd get a different brush to start turning the shapeless gobs into letters and such. Precise as a surgeon, too. Kind of fascinating except for the parts I could read were little gems like: WORMS OF THE MAW WILL FEED ON THY LIVER and INFIDELS WILL CHOKE ON THE MASTER'S SHIT.

"There was a guard station and a gate. While the gate was grinding open I heard music up ahead, distorted by the echoes of clanging metal and my heart. Thought I was gonna have a coronary right there. A bloody glow oozed from the mouth of a cell. It was the only light after the wimpy fluorescent strip in the guard shack.

"Tyler Choate had himself a cozy pad there in the bowels of Station 3. They'd even removed the door; it was lying farther down the hall, as if somebody had chucked it aside for the recycling man. Chinese paper lamps were everywhere, floating in the dark; that's what gave off the red glow. The bunks had been ripped out, replaced by a hammock and some chairs. Bamboo. Oriental rugs, a humongous vase with a dead fern. Big wooden cabinets loaded with knick-knacks, bric-a-bracs and liquor. Sweet Jesus, the old boy loves his liquor. Found out later most of the doodads were from China, the Polynesian Islands, a bunch of places I can't pronounce. Who would've guessed this hick deputy for a traveling man, right?

"Music was coming from an antique record player—the type with a horn and a hand crank. A French diva sang the blues and Tyler Choate soaked her up in a big reed chair, feet propped, eyes closed. Real long hair; oily black in a pony tail looped around his neck. He looked like a Satanic Buddha—skinny on the ends and bloated in the middle.

"I noticed the shoe collection. Dozens and dozens of shoes and boots, lined up neat as you please along the wall and into the shadows of the adjoining cell where the red light didn't quite reach. None of them were the right size for Choate—his slippers were enormous; the size of snowshoes, easy. Tailor-made for sure.

"Then he says to me, *Welcome to the Mandarin Suite, Mr. Pride. Take off your shoes.* His voice was lispy, like the queers that hang around beauty parlors. But not like that either. This was different. He sounded…amused. Smug.

"The elevator ride had rattled me, sure, sure, but not enough to account for the dread that fell on me as I stood in that dungeon and gawped at him. I felt woozy again, same as the elevator, worse than the elevator. Swear, he coulda been beaming these terrible thoughts into my head. I kept seeing Randy Freeman's face, all splattered and buried in mud. Why would I see such a thing, Wally? Doesn't make sense.

"When Choate stood to shake my hand, I nearly crapped my pants. I knew from the files the Choate brothers were tall, but I swear he wasn't much shy of eight feet, and axe-handle broad. He wore a white silk shirt with stains around the pits. He smelled rank. Rank as sewage, a pail of fish guts gone to the maggots. A fly landed on his wrist, crawled into his sleeve. Bruenig wasn't jiving about those kids being filthy.

"My hand disappeared into Choate's and I decided that I'd really and truly screwed up. Like sticking my hand into a crack in the earth and watching it shut. Except, he didn't pulp my bones, didn't yank me in close for a hillbilly waltz, nothing like that. He said he was happy to meet a real live P.I., made me sit in the best chair and poured Johnny Walker Black in greasy shot glasses, drank to my health. All very cordial and civilized. He asked if I had met his brother, and I said no, but Josh was hanging around your house and it really had to stop. He agreed that Josh was on the rude side—he'd always been a touch wild. Choate asked what you thought about the barn, if you'd figured it out yet. I said no and he laughed, said since you hadn't blown your brains out, you must not know the whole truth, which, to me, sounded like some more hocus pocus crap was in the offing. I wasn't wrong on that count. Did I know anything about String Theory? He thought I looked like a guy who might dabble in particle physics between trailing unfaithful husbands and busting people's heads. I told him I'm more of a Yeats man and he said poetry was an inferior expression of the True Art. What about molecular biology; surely I craved to understand how we apes rose from primordial slime. No? Supersymmetry? Hell no, says I, and he chuckled and filled my glass. Guess the Bruenig spiel was right about a few things. The Choate men were scientists, always have been interested in the stars and nature, time travel and all sorts of esoteric shit. Mostly they studied how animals and insects live, how, lemmesee…how *biological organisms adapt and evolve in deep quantum time. The very nature of space time itself.* Choate said the family patriarchs had been prying into that particular branch of scientific research since before the Dark Ages.

"What was Kaleb's interest? Tyler said, *Hypermutation and punctuated equilibrium.* Started in on those SQUIDs Salter told me about. Kaleb wanted to accelerate his own genetic evolution. He grafted these homemade SQUIDs onto his brain and that jumpstarted the process. I can just imagine the operation. *Brrr.* He survived without lobotomizing himself and it was a roaring success. The implant heightened his mental acuity by an incredible degree, which led to more inventions—*Devices Tesla never dreamt of—never dared!* Jesus Louise…shoulda seen Tyler Choate's face when he said that. He leered at me like he intended to make me his *numero uno* bitch.

"What kind of devices, you may be asking. See, Grandpa figured there was a way to configure electromagnetic pulses to create a black hole, or a kind of controlled tear in subatomic matter, and I heard some think-tank guys in Boston tried the very same thing a few years ago, so between you and me, maybe the geezer wasn't totally bonkers, but anyhow. Kaleb wanted to use this black hole, or what ever the hell it's supposed to be, to access a special radioactive energy. They'd detected traces of it in the pylons, like Salter said, and Tyler confirmed the radiation doesn't exist anywhere in the known spectrum.

"I'm blitzed and feeling a bit kamikaze, so I ask, where's it come from, then? *Out there,* is how Tyler put it. *Out there in the great Dark.* So picture this: this friggin' psycho hillbilly leaning over me with his face painted like blood in the lamplight, sneering about *ineffable mysteries* and flexing his monster hands as if he's practicing to choke a camel. He grins and says Grandpa Kaleb bored a hole in space and crawled through. Tyler started spouting truly wild-ass stuff. Some bizarre mumbo-jumbo about a vast rift, the cosmic version of the Marianas Trench. He said very old and truly awful things are drifting in the dark and it's damned lucky for us apes that these huge, blind things haven't taken any notice of planet Earth.

"Tyler said Kaleb became *The door and the bridge. The mouth of the pit.* And if that wasn't enough, Tyler and Josh are hanging around because the rest of Kaleb's heirs have been taken to His bosom, rejoined the fold. Tyler and Josh had been left with us chickens to, I dunno, guard the henhouse or something. To make things ready. Ready for what? *For the Old Man, of course. For His return.* I didn't press him on that.

Another thing…The bonus effect of Kaleb's gizmo's electromagnetic pulse is it's real nifty for shutting off car engines and stranding people near the ol' farm…I asked why they wanted to strand people near their property and he just looked at me. Scary, man. He said, *Why? Because it gives Him tremendous pleasure to meet new and interesting people. Grandfather always liked people. Now He loves them. Sadly, folks don't drop by too often. We keep Him company as best we can. We're good boys like that.*

"By this point I was pretty much past wasted and I know he went on and on, but most of it flew over my head. One thing that stuck with me as I got ready to stagger outta there, is he clamped one giant paw on my shoulder and said with that creepy smile of his, '*Out there' is a relative term, it's closer than you might think. Oh my, the great Dark is only as far away as your closet when you kill the light…as your reflection when it thinks you aren't looking. Bye, bye and see you soon.*

"I beat it topside. Barefoot. Bastard kept my shoes…." Pride's narrative faltered and was replaced by a thumping noise in the background. A chair squeaked. He spoke from a distance, perhaps the motel room door. "Yeah? Oh, hey—" His voice degenerated into jags of a garbled conversation followed by a long, blank gap; then a wheeze like water gurgling in a hose. Another gap. Someone coughed and chuckled. Then silence.

17.

Wallace gazed at the rolling wheels as dead air hissed through the speaker. He emptied the dingy shoebox on his desk, pushed the yellow papers like a man shuffling dominos or tarot cards. He poured another drink from the dwindling bottle, squinted at the cramped script done in bleeding ink, whole paragraphs deformed by water stains and stains of other kinds and the depredations of silverfish. There were schematics, as Delaney had promised—arcane, incomprehensible figures with foreign notations.

The house was dark but for the lamp on Wallace's desk. The walls shuddered from a blast of wind. Rain smacked hard against the windows. Floorboards creaked heavily and Wallace strained to detect the other fleeing sound—a rustling, a whisper, an inhalation like a soft, weak moan. He wiped his face and listened, but there was nothing except whistling pipes. He poured another drink and now the bottle was dry.

He sifted through the letters, sprinkling them with vodka because his hands were trembling. He studied one dated February 1971. It was somewhat legible:

Eli,

The expedition has gone remarkably well, thanks to your timely assistance. It is indeed as Grandfather says, "Per aspera ad astra that we seek communion and grace from our patrons of antiquity." I shall keep you apprised of developments. Yours, P. Choate.

Another, from June 1971:

Grandfather has sent word from the gulf, Ab ovo, as it were. It is as they promised…and more. His words to me: "Non sum qualis eram." It is the truth. He is the door and the bridge and we are grateful. On the day all doors are thrown open, you shall be remembered and honored for your service to the Grand Estate. Thank you, dear friend. Yours, P. Choate.

He counted roughly three dozen others, including some photographs, mostly ruined. He paused at a warped and faded postcard picturing a ramshackle barn in a field. It was unclear whether this was an etching or an actual photograph—the perspective featured the southeast face of the barn and the road in the distance. He could barely make out the Bentley on the shoulder, a man working under the raised hood. The back of the card was unstamped and grimy with fingerprints. It had been addressed to Mr. Wallace Smith of 1313 Vineland Drive. October 6, 1926:

Hello, Wallace.

Helen wishes you were here.

Regards, K. Choate.

Wallace's belly sank into itself. What could it possibly mean?

Grandfather always liked people. Now He loves them.

The house shook again and Wallace dropped the card. He was nauseated. "*Mr. Smith?*" The intercom squawked and he almost pissed himself. "*—to say good night?*" Kate was nearly unintelligible over the intercom.

"What!" He nearly shattered the plastic from the force of his blow. He took a breath, said in a more reasonable tone, "I'll be there in a minute."

The desk lamp flickered. *I am here to usher in the dark.* Wallace dialed Pride's cell number and received no answer. He pushed away from the desk, stood, and shuffled in a dream to the hallway. A draft ran cold around his ankles and when he thumbed the switch, the lights hesitated in their sockets, grudgingly ignited and shone dim and milky. Shadows spread across the floor and climbed the walls.

Wallace plodded forward and ended up at Helen's door. Helen's door was made of thick oak and decorated with filigreed panels. He stood before the oak door and breathed through his mouth, blowing like a dray horse.

Cancer always returns.

Wallace turned the knob and pushed into Helen's apartment. He slapped the switch and nothing happened. The dimensions were all wrong; the room had become an undersea cavern where a whale had bloated on its gasses and putrefied. Objects assumed phantom shapes in the sleepy murk: the therapy table and its glinting buckles; a pinewood armoire; a scattering of chairs; the unmade bed, a wedge of ivory sheets and iron lattice near the opaque window.

Wallace detected a hushed, sticky sound. The muffled squelch of a piglet snuffling its mother's teat, smacking and slobbering with primal greed. As he turned toward the disturbance, something damp and slender tickled the back of his neck. Then his scalp, his left ear, his cheek. Something like moist jelly strands entangled him. These tendrils floated everywhere, a veritable hanging garden of angel's hair gently undulating in the crosshatched light from the hallway. Wallace cried out and batted the strands like a man flailing at cobwebs.

He gaped up into the blue-black shadows and did not comprehend the puzzle of dangling feet, one in a shoe, the other encased in hosiery; or the legs, also wrapped in nylon hose that terminated at the hem of a skirt. Wallace did not recognize the mannequin extremities, jittering feebly with each impulse of a live current. The left shoe, a square, wooden thing with a blunt nose, plopped onto the hardwood as the legs quivered and slid upward, vanishing to mid-thigh attended by the sound of a squishing sponge.

Wallace was confused; his mind twittered with half-formed memories, fragmented pictures. All circuits busy, please try again. He thought, *Kate's shoe. Kate's shoe is on the floor. Kate's legs. Where's the rest of her. Where oh where oh fuck me.* He beheld it then, an elephantine mass lodged in the ceiling, an obscene scribble of shivering tapioca and multi-jointed limbs. A gory fissure traversed its axis and disgorged the myriad glutinous threads. The behemoth wore a wicked old man's face with a clotted Vandyke, a hooked nose and wet, staring eyes that shone like cinders of dead stars. The old man patiently sucked Kate the Nurse into his mouth. Ropes of viscid yolk dripped from the corners of the old man's lips and pattered on the floor. Wallace thought with hysterical glee, *Gulper eel, gulper eel!* Which was an eel that lived in the greatest depths and could quite handily unhinge its skull to swallow large prey.

Wallace reeled.

The bloody fissure throbbed and seeped; and tracking the convulsion, he discovered the abomination's second head. He glimpsed Helen's pallid torso, her drooping breasts and slack face—an alto-relievo sculpted from wax at the apex of the monstrous coagulation of her body. The crack nearly divided her face and skull and it fractured the ceiling with a jagged chasm that traveled far beyond the scope of any light.

Helen opened her eyes and smiled at Wallace. Her smile was sweet and infinitely mindless. Her mouth formed a perfect black circle that began to dilate fantastically and she craned her overlong neck as if to kiss him.

Wallace screamed and stumbled away. He was a man slogging in mud. The vermiculate tendrils boiled around him, coiled in his hair, draped his shoulders and slithered down the collar of his shirt.

He was still screaming when he staggered into the hall and yanked the door shut. He crabbed two steps sideways and tottered. His legs gave way and the floor and walls rolled and then he was prone with his right arm flung out before him in a ghastly imitation of a breast stroke.

A wave of lassitude suffused him, as if the doctor had given him a yeoman's dose of morphine, and in its wake, pins and needles, and hollowness. Countless tendrils had oozed through the doorjamb, the spaces between the hinges, the keyhole, and burrowed into him so snugly he was vaguely aware of their insistent twitches and tugs. Dozens were buried in the back of his hand and arm, reshaping the veins and arteries; more filaments nested in his back, neck and skull, everywhere. As he watched, unable to blink, their translucence flushed a rich crimson that flowed back toward their source, drawn inexorably by an imponderable suction.

He went under.

18.

Wallace regained consciousness.

The veins in his hand had collapsed and the flesh was pale and sunken like the cracked hand of a mummy. Near his cheek rested a sandal that surely belonged to a giant. The sandal was caked in filth and blood.

"Are you sleeping, brother Wallace?" Josh said. "I want to show you something beautiful." He opened the door. Wallace's eyes rolled up as he was steadily drawn across the threshold and into darkness.

Oh, sweetheart, Helen said eagerly.

19.

Delaney came in that morning and boiled himself a cup of instant coffee and poured a bowl of cereal and had finished both before he realized something was wrong. The house lay vast and quiet except for small sounds. Where was the hubbub of daily routine? Helen had usually begun shrieking by now, and Cecil inevitably put on one of the old classical heavies like Mozart or Beethoven in hopes of calming her down. Not today—today nothing stirred except the periodic rush of air through the ducts.

Delaney lighted a cigarette and smoked and tried to convince himself he was jumpy over nothing. He went upstairs and found Wallace's bedroom empty. Near Helen's suite, he came across a muddy track. The shoe print was freakishly large. Delaney pulled a switchblade from his pocket and snicked it open. He put his hand on the door knob and now his nerves were jangling full alarm like they sometimes had back in the bad old days of gang battles and liquor store hold-ups and dodging Johnny Law. The air was supercharged. And the doorknob was sticky. He stepped back and regarded, stoic as a wolf in the face of the unknown, his red fingers. A fly hummed and circled his head.

He bounced the switchblade in his palm and decided, to hell with it, he was going in, and then a woman giggled and whispered something and part of the something contained *Delaney*. He knew that voice. It had been months since he heard it last. "Screw this noise," he said very matter of fact. He turned and loped for the stairs.

Delaney calmed by degrees once he was outside, and walked swiftly across the waterlogged grounds to his cottage where he threw a few essentials into his ancient sea bag—the very one his daddy brought home from the service—checked his automatic and stuffed it under his shirt. He started his Cadillac and rolled to the gate. His breathing had slowed, he had combed his hair and gotten a grip and was almost normal on the surface. At least his hands had stopped shaking. He forced a cool, detached smile. The smile that said, *Hello, officer. Why, yes, everything is fine.*

Charlie the guard was a pimply twenty-something with disheveled hair and an ill-fitting uniform. He was obviously hung-over and scarcely glanced up at Delaney as he buzzed the gate. "See ya, Mr. Dee."

"Hey, any trouble lately? Ya know—anything on the cameras?"

Charlie shrugged. "Nah. Well, uh, the feed's been kinda wonky off 'n' on. "

"Wonky?"

"Nothin' to worry 'bout, Mr. Dee. We ain't seen any prowlers."

"What about the night fella?"

"Uh, Tom. He woulda said somethin' if there was a problem. Why?"

"No reason. I figured as much. You take care, partner." Delaney pushed his sunglasses into place and gave the guard a little two-finger salute. He cast a quick, final glance at the house in his rearview mirror, but the view was spoiled by a crack in the glass. Had that been there before? He tacked it on his list of things-to-do once he got wherever he was going. Where was he going? Far away, that was certain.

Delaney gunned the engine and cruised down the driveway. He vanished around the bend as Charlie set aside his copy of *Sports Illustrated* to answer the phone. "Uh, yeah. Oh, mornin', Mr. Smith. Uh…Okay, sure. Right now? Yessir!" Charlie hung up with a worried expression. It was only his second week on the job. He walked briskly to the big house, opened the door and hurried inside.

PARALLAX

EXCERPTED FROM NEWS 6 COVERAGE OF JACK CARSON BRIEFING (by Ron Jones—6/6/99):

JC: ...and thank you to all the people involved in the search. The Olympia Police Department, the fire department, the Washington Highway Patrol, all the volunteers. The media. You've worked tirelessly to bring Miranda back to us safe and sound. Thank you.

RJ: Is there anything you would care to add, Mr. Carson?

JC: Yes. Miranda, honey. I love you. Please come home.

I see Miranda in the endless chain of faces.

After six years they're all starting to resemble her. Which is kind of funny since I often forget what she looks like until I spot her on a bus; in line at the bank; at a sidewalk café, scanning the *Daily O*, a Rottweiler at her feet, and wham. My heart knocks, my hands shake as if I quit the sauce only yesterday.

Six years, already?

Six years and I still can't touch Crown Royal, can't stomach the diesel taint. Six years and I hate the sound of ice slurring in a glass: makes me flinch and resurrects an image of icebergs in miniature on slate. I'm done with ice cubes, iceboxes, all of it. Sometimes I don't brave the kitchen for weeks.

Six years as of Saturday. Saturday Marchland pays a visit. He barges into the house, drunk and alone. They kicked him off the force, I don't recall when. The brute has time to kill. Crosses my mind it's *me* he's come to kill after the pussyfooting around. That thought is a catalyst. It starts the cookie crumbling.

What's he waiting for, for Christ's sake? That's easy. He's been waiting for the coroner's report to confirm his suspicions about the body they found near Yelm six months ago. It's not that the deadly dull pathologists have a flair for the dramatic as much as there's a logjam at the forensics lab. Government cutbacks are a real bitch.

Six months, six years, six bullets in a .38 revolver. Marchland wants to be certain; of course he does. They confiscated his gun along with the badge, but that's not a problem; he got another piece at the pawn shop. He showed me once.

I ask how his partner Fisher is doing. Nothing doing.

Marchland lumbers to my liquor cabinet, grabs a dusty bottle of the best. He says to me, "Happy anniversary, Jack." Then he knocks back his whiskey and slops another. He trembles as he swallows, shudders like it's poison going down the hatch. His tics pronounce themselves most eloquently. His left eye is an agate. The right eye, the good eye, flickers like a shutter.

He's a wild boar, a crocodile, a basilisk. He smacks his lips as if he wishes it were my blood in his mouth.

Six years and Marchland won't quit. Good for him. I'm numb to his animal pathos. I've turned a stone ear to his dumb anguish. I'm tuned to the music of the stars, radio free Tau Ceti. No interest in act I of *Hamlet*. Let's jump to long knives and good-night speeches. Let's bring the curtain down already.

I turn away and stare through the window at the field where the scotch broom creeps yellow as hell toward my doorstep. Six years and it has advanced from the hinterlands to the picket fence in the back yard. Six more years and it will have chewed this house to the foundation, braided my bones in its hair.

I think nothing changes because thunderheads roll like wheels. I think of wheels in wheels, the threshing scythes in the hubs of clattering chariots, and I think hasn't this gone on long enough?

But Marchland doesn't shoot me. He drains the tumbler, watches me watching the yellow field. When he leaves, he closes the door softly.

EXCERPTED FROM *THE MAKING OF ULTRAGOTHIC: BEHIND THE DOCUMENTARY*. INTERVIEW OF JUDITH PEIRCE (by William Tucker—3/19/02):

WT: What did you call your artist community—Penny Royal?

JP: That's right.

WT: Kind of a traveling show.

JP: More of an artist support group that toured Europe. A networking project. We put on exhibitions.

WT: Who was involved?

JP: Oh, me and Jack. Freddy Snopes, Larry Torrence. Joe Adams—he went into computers, does fractal art. Miranda, of course. There were others; the group was pretty huge at times, but we were the core, the nucleus.

WT: There have been a lot of rumors about Penny Royal. Is it true that members of Penny Royal indulged in heavy drug use, attended orgies and held Satanic rituals?

JP: Satanic rituals?

Judy is ready to rumble.

It's the same argument—the only argument—we ever have.

There are variations on the theme, but this is how it usually goes with Judy when she's drunk enough or stoned enough to grab the bull by the horns. Tonight she's both.

"Why do you stay, Jack? Why, in God's name, do you stay in this house?" And believe me, she's shrill when she's in the mood. She's got the cast-iron lungs of a professional activist, a cactus for a liver.

We've been friends since Cambridge. Since the magical, apocalyptic fairy-tale days of starving in exotic cities, sustained by youth, cheap grass and cheaper wine, the kindness of strangers. Suffering was beautiful then, as is any addiction at the threshold of the honeymoon bungalow. Judy was the den mother of our brood, a select confab of like-minded *artistes*. She was savagely glamorous in her impoverishment, fearless as a martyr. Attrition ground up and blew away our comrades; turned them into bankers and graphic designers, housewives with fruiting ovaries and dutiful husbands hanged by their own neckties. I would've gone down too, except she kept me treading water until Miranda and the Muses and Lady Luck carried me home.

Judy's suffering doesn't seem so hip anymore. That youthful euphoria has evaporated. Her lean, bronze face sags with the effects of too much too fast, changes as if a lamp had briefly illuminated the planes and creases. Sad, she looks horribly sad. Looks like she's been guzzling kerosene.

Thank God Judy is an old-school lesbian, else I'd be stuck on the notion she did away with Miranda to get with me. I almost ask her if she loved Miranda with the love that dare not speak its name. Almost, except that's the easy way out. And it's another question I probably don't want answered.

"I like my house. I'm attached to it," I say.

"Yeah, but, isn't it creepy?"

"Creepy? No." It is, indeed. Am I going to admit that?

She wags her head. "Hell yeah it's creepy. Only a psycho or a robot could sleep in this place knowing what you know. You act like a robot sometimes. Serious."

"Gee, thanks."

It's a really expensive house, a huge house with lots of artifacts cluttering the vaulted rooms, although none of the artifacts are mine. Correction, I kept one personal reminder of life with Miranda—a great ceramic bust of Achilles that I once hollowed in the throes of demonic possession or whatever it is the ancients took as the author of genius. This bust gapes from the window of my study. The old Greek's fractured skull is a palace for the silverfish, a repository of dust and dreams.

The remainder of my stuff has been reduced to splinters, ashes, pulverized. It took me three weeks to accomplish the feat. The big items went fast. The small items were tedious. I organized piles in the driveway, sat cross-legged as a swami, sorting them with maniacal devotion. I'd collected so many more things than seemed possible! The project was worth the effort, though. My wife's treasures deserve ample negative space.

I've converted my office into a gallery of Miranda's wax sculptures—the drowned woman; the cancer victim on the gurney we swiped from Saint Pete's; the seagull mobile; the Native American-style death masque in the window; a basket of petrified apples and pears oozing beneath a glaze of paraffin; a fruit fly graveyard in the embalming oils. These remnants of her portfolio, these fragments I have gathered to my breast, are a paean to her gothic sensibilities.

Everything is heavy or awkward or fragile. The notion of touching any of it makes me nauseous. I framed the article in *Smithsonian*, the one with the picture of her at the fabled museum accepting a pile of grant cash and a handshake from some fossil in a suit. I don't look at it much because it makes me nauseous too.

Then there's the Norman Rockwell yard, and the Norman Rockwell field, and those trees could've been painted by him as well. Everything turns green and red this time of year. It's a postcard outside my window.

I say, "Where am I supposed to go? Even psycho robots gotta sleep."

"You're loaded; you could go anywhere. Buy an island, become dictator of a banana republic, whatever, man. The only decent thing to do is burn it to the ground, blow it to hell and gone. Donate it, turn it into a fawkin' museum and sell tickets, whatever. Your call, Jack."

I sip my off-brand cola and force a smile. "I'm not loaded—you are."

"Ha, ha."

"But see, I can't leave."

"Why can't you?"

"What if she comes back?"

"Here we go. Here we fawkin' go. I need some more booze. Fast."

"What if she does?"

"Jack."

"What if the old girl strolls through the door one day with an explanation for everything?"

"Jack—"

"Hi, baby, sorry I'm late, I was abducted by the Greys'; or, 'holy shit, you wouldn't believe the line at Wal-Mart—'"

"Jack. Jack, for Chrissake...She wouldn't shop at Wal-Mart and she isn't going to come back. You gotta sell this house and move on. Serious. You aren't well, buddy. Uh, uh."

"I can't do that."

"Jack—"

"Judy, no."

"Ja-ack." Her voice cracks to pieces at this point.

I just sip my cola and wait for the storm to break.

"Yes, you can. Jack, man. Why can't you?"

I won't tell Judy the reason, the honest-to-Betsy reason. I won't tell her I wake up every other night with an iron band around my chest, bad dreams rattling in my attic. I wake up like a beast in the woods that's scented something it can't quite identify. I wake up with this premonition, as if any second now I'm going to receive the ultimate clue, that I'm finally going to find out what happened to my wife. Like the end of the cliffhanger serial is one commercial break away.

Instead, I tell Judy to have another snort and wipe her nose, because she's bawling into her gin and tonic. We don't discuss the fact the cops might be watching me again, that the phone is probably tapped and God knows what's coming next.

I change the subject to sports, the weather.

EXCERPTED FROM THE *ALAMOGORDO DAILY TELEGRAPH* (6/9/87):

HONEYMOON COUPLE FOUND SAFE—Jack and Miranda Carson, presumed missing since their rental car was reported abandoned on Highway 70 near the White Sands National Monument on June 6, were found Tuesday at the Diamond Inn Resort. The resort is located 150 miles west of White Sands.

Mr. Carson, an acclaimed modern artist from Olympia, Washington, expressed surprise at being the subject of a missing persons report. "We're not missing, we're on our honeymoon!" Mr. Carson said. It was his opinion that the vehicle had been stolen and he had neglected to note its absence.

Further confusion arose from the fact that the Carsons signed the Diamond Inn register on June 8, prompting the Otero County Sheriff's Office to question the couple's whereabouts during the preceding thirty-six to forty-two hours. Mr. Carson, known for his flamboyant promotional style, denied any involvement in a publicity hoax, saying, "Publicity? Why would I want publicity on my honeymoon? We've been in our room or at the bar since we got here."

Patty Angstrom, spokesperson for the Sheriff's Office, declined comment pending further investigation.

Sunday is a coma. Sunday's dreamscape is a long, pale sweep of desert.

My dreams are cinematic and exaggerated as spaghetti westerns. A lopsided V of Search & Rescue choppers crawls along the horizon. Mountains are jagged teeth of a cannibal cowboy. The wind hums the hum of bees in bleached skull hives; a discordant harmonica tune.

A plastic hand claws from the earth, the hand of a mannequin severed at the wrist. It's feminine, and the ring on its finger is the ring I gave Miranda, the one from the flea market in New Mexico, not far from some proving grounds we read about in a tacky brochure. The ring matches the one she gave me.

Mesas and dunes blur, ruinous Luna gapes as the sun founders in her wake.

Home again. Miranda on the living room sofa. She's wearing my ancient rugby sweater; her brown hair's a glorious mess. She's daubing her nails and humming that old Sinatra song we first danced to in the Cloud Room. The light collects on her shoulder. I kiss her and walk through the door to the kitchen, try not to stumble. I drag my black double like a wrecking ball.

I'm fixing drinks; hair of the dog that bit us. I'm chopping at an ice block, trying not to botch the job, because my belly is queasy and the gong in my skull makes it tricky to concentrate.

The ice pick falls from my hand, rocks in a semicircle on the counter. The ice becomes a white-gold lake. The numbers on the microwave flicker forward two minutes. White light pours into my eyes. My head erupts.

No OFF button. I know this is only a movie, but I'm buckled to the theater seat. Once it starts, it won't stop; the hits keep on coming. The memory of the event is like a splash of indelible ink, a bloodstain.

Cicadas chirr in the flowerbox. An unseasonably crisp breeze pushes the tall grass. Sparks gather in black-hearted clouds. The stink of fire. Then silence. Miranda isn't humming, isn't making any sound. The only noise is the soft gasp of air forced through a vent near my feet. And something else, something vast and running on a frequency that scrambles the neurons in my brain. My personal supernova.

Then it's night. Gauzy, crystal-studded, immense.

I'm behind the wheel of a speeding luxury car—leather interior, power everything. Miranda's riding shotgun, sipping Bacardi and trailing her arm out the window, laughing. Gods, what a sweet sound; it sends an electric spike through me, curls my toes. We're on the road to Vegas. Ricardo Montalbán's disembodied voice congratulates my excellent taste in driving machines and women. The car isn't moving, it's at full stop. There's a big exit hole in the windshield. Vacuum moans as it sucks away the atmosphere, pulls my smile into a stroke victim's grimace.

The harmonica keens and Miranda's missing again.

I float up from the abyss, regard her side of the bed. Her pillow is drenched crimson by radio-clock light. You'd think I'd wake screaming, except that's fiction. Shaking, sweating, blinded by rocketing blood pressure, yes. But no screaming.

Why should I? It's utter phantasmagoria, anyway. I've never been in a car crash, never owned a car that plush, never had such a desire. A road trip to Vegas? New Mexico was desert enough for me.

We got married in a historic trading post. Or in a cathedral by a priest named Dominic. Doves floating; Miranda's white train dragging in the good clean Catholic dust.

Which was it?

There was that ordained minister and his wife who stayed in the room across the way at the resort. We played golf once; backgammon, something. He'd offered to marry us in the chapel or the Cloud Room, hadn't he? Damn—I don't remember at the moment and the moment is slipping away.

I stumble into the bathroom.

Water circles in the toilet. The stars march circles in a wedge of pebbled glass. They never seem quite right anymore. They hang differently from when Miranda and I used to lay on a blanket and do the romantic thing where you count them. They don't seem very romantic now.

I peer into the gloom of the yard, through the tall trees and taller shadows. A truck that resembles Marchland's flatbed Ford is parked at the end of the driveway. Like the Flying Dutchman, it materializes in that spot when I least expect. It's been there on and off for months, for ages. The dome light silhouettes Marchland's torso, his massive head.

Perhaps I should offer him a nightcap, or a cup of tea. There's lots of Miranda's herbal tea leftover in the pantry. Never been much of a tea man, myself.

I drop the blinds, return to bed.

On Monday I'm among my people.

Judy has the studio unlocked and the lights burning when I arrive with Kern. Judy warns me that someone has left twenty-or so hang-ups on the machine over the weekend. The *Seattle Post Intelligencer* wants to do an interview. A friendly retrospective. There have been no anonymous death threats for going on a year; that's a record. Miranda's mom died of cancer a while back. Her dad got himself killed on a ski slope in Italy and maybe that explains the drought. Why the hell does a retiree need to take up skiing anyway? My largesse is the culprit—after I got famous we sent scads of cash to Miranda's parents. Getting rich late in life would do in just about anyone.

If Judy is the long-suffering Kato to my Green Hornet, Kern is my evil apprentice who longs to usurp my title as art world wunderkind. He's a brilliant conniver, bound for glory. They love each other a few degrees shy of homicide.

Kern met me at the China Clipper for breakfast and we talked about the Seattle exhibition upcoming next month. Kern did the talking. Can't say I heard much of it—hope I bobbed my head in the right places.

The exhibition is of tremendous importance to Kern—it's his chance to hob-nob with future patrons. We've got well-heeled boys and girls from New York, San Francisco and Chicago on the guest list.

I drift. The bulky pieces are done and packed up for shipment. My mind is free to spiral into its pit.

Kern doesn't fathom my indifference to the minutia. Once, I was the king of flash. I paid for rock bands and fireworks, bought ad space in the *New York Times*, made a spectacle of myself on network television; choked smug journalists with my bare hands; whatever it took to spread the word. He can't grasp this fundamental shift. He's also my disciple and his disapproval remains oblique. Plus, I've loaned him three hundred dollars and my old Datsun. Kern's got a big mouth and a canary ass. This proved to be an unfortunate combination when he swaggered into the local watering hole one fateful Western Swing Night. The local bullyboys totaled Kern's Volkswagen and went to work on him. An overhand blow from an aluminum bat spoiled his designer-model looks just a tad, and he's been humble pie since.

I won't lift a finger today.

Judy handles the bills and the maintenance people, coordinates with the lawyers and the galleries, keeps my head screwed on straight. She's a champ. Kern sweats the details in the forges.

I gnaw my nails, stare at the poster board with the billion memos, the press clippings curled as dried leaves. My eye is dragged to a photo of me and Miranda holding hands beneath the ceramic colossus of Achilles I erected in Pioneer Square. I've just won the bet between us about who'd hit the jackpot first, but we're smiling. Miranda didn't have it in her to be bitter. That statue bought me a ticket to ride, as the boys from Liverpool said. We appear insignificant in its shadow.

Coffee rings and ink drippings mar the draft book near my left hand; fishhook doodles, random letters that have nearly eaten through the paper, the number 6 and the words ORDO TEMPLI ORIENTIS; PARALLAX; MIRANDA. No designs, however. I haven't managed a real design since *Achilles*, and if not for stamping my name on Kern's drawings I'd be staring down the barrel of artistic obscurity.

Kern and Judy don't want me to wither on the vine. I'm the franchise, the label on the jar that seals the deal. If I go down, Judy may as well start hunting for secretarial positions and Kern will be shaking his ass for dollars at the Long Horn Lounge.

Inertia takes me in its jaws, pads outside this cement igloo, strands me in the middle of the parking lot. Truthfully, I am waiting for Marchland to come and maintain his customary vigil, the police-drama surveillance he obviously took to heart back in the academy. I do this every morning, although today is the first time in a great while that I have admitted as much to myself.

I gaze down the hill across the bridge at Olympia, its crescent of waterfront warehouses and high-tension wires giving way at the center to clumps of brownstones and hoary maples. Yeah, there's a few trees over there, they haven't hacked down the last of them yet.

I want to smoke, but I gave up smoking when I kicked the hooch. Since Miranda's disappearance, the simple expedient has been to deny myself all semblance of pleasure—as if dogged asceticism will pull the picture into focus, will pay off the vengeful fortune teller.

The neon marquee of the Samovar Inn fizzes to gray.

The last time I had sex was in that very hotel: room 6. That was something on the order of a year ago. The woman wasn't my wife, obviously, and I'd wondered beforehand, as I folded my clothes and drank tap water because my mouth was too dry, if this made me an adulterer. I wasn't driven by physical need. Biological imperatives had been submerged long before the Samovar rendezvous. Polar caps cover that territory. I obeyed the impulse to plummet from a high place, the impulse that quickens when we gaze over the edge of a cliff. I'd wanted to prove at least one of the theories about my character. I wanted to send this train off the tracks, just to watch the wreck.

The girl I met at the hotel was named Gina, or Jenna, something with a soft *g*. Her hair was brown, just like Miranda's; she was an art student too, knew the book on me front and back. I can't remember much about her, except she wore sandals and purple eyeliner. She is a ghost among the throng of ghosts I seem to be collecting.

I wonder how Gina, or whoever she is, is doing. Has anybody seen her since then? This is how I indulge my latent masochism—entertaining macabre lines of thought, speculating about blackouts, schizophrenia, mysterious gaps in time. I'm into self-mutilation in a big way.

Judy is of that opinion.

Judy says so during our weekly conclaves at the Millstone when we sneak away and leave Kern to his machinations. Judy says it without opening her mouth—it's in her expression as she casually lines up the eight ball, the way she studies her toothpick after steak and red wine, or when she's chambering another round in her trusty Winchester rifle at the club.

Thing is, Judy's loyal. She doesn't care about finding the truth. She's the main reason I stopped seeing my psychiatrist and flushed the happy pills down the drain. Hell, I'd pretty much flushed everything else down there.

Too bad none of it is enough.

Marchland cruises by in his battered truck. He's wearing a ten-gallon hat, tinted glasses. He parks down the block where he can watch the studio from three directions, same as always.

Today is different. Today is the straw upon a mighty heap of straws. Today the straw has found a vein and the bad blood is rushing out.

I wave at him and begin walking across the lot, end up in my car before I formulate the intent to go anywhere. When I roll out and cruise north on Legion, my thoughts are flies buzzing in a bottle.

After the third traffic light I know.

EXCERPTED FROM *THE MAKING OF ULTRAGOTHIC: BEHIND THE DOCU-MENTARY*. INTERVIEW WITH HOMICIDE DETECTIVE MARTIN FISHER (by William Tucker—4/4/02):

WT: During the timeframe of Mr. Carson's visit to Italy in 1983-84 how many women were reported missing?

MF: Approximately four. That's our best information.

WT: You contacted Interpol regarding Mr. Carson's activities in Europe...

MF: Uh, yes. In the process of investigating Miranda Carson's disappearance. Well, and the FBI kept a file on some of the members of Penny Royal. Uh, a couple of them had ties to ELF—

WT: Environmental Life Force. The so-called eco-terrorists. Saboteurs, not murderers...

MF: Yes, but it clarifies a pattern of behavior. These folks didn't necessarily mature with age. A couple were very sympathetic to ELF, and the Bureau shared information with us. There was also evidence that some of the members of Penny Royal dabbled in the occult. Mr. Carson corresponded with a former intimate of the late Aleister Crowley—one Mason Barnes. Mr. Barnes was an investment banker from Oakland, and a chapter leader of the Ordo Templi Orientis. He owned several properties in the United States and Europe and the Carsons were among those who availed themselves of Mr. Barnes' amenities on numerous occasions.

WT: Isn't it a fact that Mason Barnes and associates were instrumental in promoting Jack Carson's early work?

MF: Yes—that's correct. They financed him, arranged for an exclusive show in a major gallery. Launched him. Barnes went to prison in 1993 on multiple counts of extortion, kidnapping, sexual assault, and drug distribution. Whether Jack Carson was fully aware of Mr. Barnes' cult activity is unknown. Of course we looked at this in connection with the vanished women—and a possible motive for kidnapping or murder of Miranda Carson. And, obviously, we pursued the Italian leads. But this didn't go anywhere.

WT: Why not?

MF: One of the missing women, a secretary at a utilities office in Palermo, was subsequently found to be living in Venezuela. Local authorities did not consider foul play a plausible concern regarding the other women. Interpol treated it as a closed case.

WT: The local investigators declined to reopen the case.

MF: They declined. There simply wasn't enough to go on.

WT: Were the other three women ever located?

MF: No, they were not.

Whenever I think about That Day the images spill forth like negatives on a reel, like my guts coiling around my throat. The first thing I always remember is the migraine.

I hadn't been hit with a migraine since my college years. Those were humdingers, though—real knuckle-whiteners. The kind that bring tears to your eyes, bring up your lunch. The kind that can put you on your knees whimpering for God, mom, or whoever will listen. I'd almost forgotten.

This one wasn't like those. This was worse, and it came with special effects.

There I was, chopping ice in the kitchen. The migraine slammed me behind my left eye. I thought I'd been stabbed. Vertigo staggered me, and I dropped the ice pick and clutched my head. White light flooded through the multiplying windows. White light hit me in a wave and then receded and shrank, left me blinking at fractured afterimages. The kitchen door divided into a paper chain of kitchen doors and wrapped the bizarrely off-kilter room. Objects elongated and deformed and swapped places. This was a world made of warm taffy or the stuff inside a lava lamp. The worst of it was watching the scotch broom in the field cycle from yellow to white to black and back. The scotch broom undulated as if the field was a sea trough during a hurricane.

The sky shuddered and went white like an eye rolling up and back.

And then, everything was fine. Somebody released my skull from the vice. The scenery wobbled into place. I sagged against the counter, grateful the merry-go-round had let me off in one piece, that the vessels in my brain hadn't decided to rupture then and there. Just a migraine; not an aneurysm, not a stroke.

The merry-go-round hadn't stopped, though.

It took me a few moments to catch on, but I did soon enough. Silence spread like a riptide. Doom doesn't require fanfare when all it has to do is cup your balls and slowly squeeze. I got the message.

—Honey? Exactly like the movies. And, as in the movies, I tried again, poised at the lip of a chasm that widened with each synaptic detonation.

I searched everywhere. I tore the house to pieces.

The air was warm with her breath. Her perfume collided with particles of dust. She gazed from half a dozen photographs. We'd gone to the Capitol Theatre the night before, to catch the premiere of *Annie Get Your Gun*, and Miranda's stockings were draped across a chair in the bathroom. Her purse, her credit cards, her jewelry, her clothes, present and accounted—everything whole and untouched.

Every door was safely shut.

On the sofa by the window, I found a creased copy of *Ladies' Home Journal*. On the coffee table by the sofa, I found an open bottle of cherry nail polish and a brush. Three red droplets etched a crescent upon the coffee table glass. The fumes were strong.

It got dark. I never found her.

The cops came; took my picture, took my story. Took me apart.

Detective Marchland wrote in a ledger. He had thick, mason's fingers with dirt under the nails. He exuded a medieval tang, as if his rumpled suit should've been a leather apron soaked in hog blood.

Detective Fisher smiled hatefully as he picked up knickknacks, caressed the spines of our many books. A lanky man in a cheap suit, he was positively dapper next to his partner.

—Love your house, Mr. Carson. Throw parties here, do you?

My mind was in slowdown. My gray matter had been nearly suffocated in the first hours of panic.

—Parties?

—We hear you have some real shindigs, Detective Marchland said. He kept scribbling and I realized that neither of them was exactly looking me in the eye.

—Lotta drugs at these parties, Mr. Carson? I bet there are.

—You can tell us, Detective Fisher said, weighing a musty copy of *The Decameron* in his palm.

—She just…vanished, you say? Poof, like that? Left everything she owns. Maybe somebody took her, you think?

—Know who might want to take your wife, Mr. Carson? Anybody asking for money, that sort of thing? You see, sir, people don't just disappear. Usually there's a reason. Sometimes they have help.

I understood where this was headed, could see them placing the dynamite, the blasting caps.

Parties? Oh my, yes. After *Achilles* we'd gone wild. Three-day parties, two hundred-car parties. Big bands, boom boxes, dj's, drug dealers, and hip-hop gangstas. Rock stars, track stars, porn stars. Limousine loads of them. We'd run the gamut, we'd done it up right. Most of it a bright, blobby fuse that I'd relegated to the trunk of ancient history.

The cops kicked that trunk over and rummaged through the dirty linen with unrestrained glee. No patrons of the arts here. It didn't do them any good. They never found her either. However, they did find some bloody rags stuffed inside a coffee can in Miranda's studio. She'd cut her hand on a piece of scrap metal. Nothing sinister, boys.

Cue the trial of the new century.

During the trial of the new century I learned that Marchland slept with my future wife pretty much their entire senior year in high school. They'd even considered getting hitched. Talk about a surprise to the prosecution. We won't talk about what gastrointestinal effects the revelation had on me. For a micromoment I leaped to the inspiration it was him who'd done the deed. He'd snuck into the house past the alarm, the locks, and two snoozing Rottweilers, chloroformed my beloved, kidnapped her under my nose. No go. The day Miranda disappeared, my rival, the ex-cop, was making the rounds with his partner.

Even so, Marchland's omission of this prior relationship sank the prosecution. The trial quickly raveled into a small-town soap opera.

Thank goodness for that—it's what eventually saved me from a prolonged stay at the crossbar hotel. It was the LAPD-O.J. Simpson fiasco all over again. Of course, that doesn't shock, that part's common knowledge. All of the dirt is in the public domain. Anybody who got CNN could keep score. There's a DVD documentary at Blockbuster, and I hear the grad student who filmed it is the toast of Tinsel Town. He spliced bits of courtroom testimony with my prior appearances on the *Tonight Show* and *Oprah*. The kid even got his mitts on security camera footage from my midnight demolition of *Achilles* with a sledgehammer, the madcap foot pursuit and arrest. Yes indeed, that screaming face squashed against the cruiser's window is mine.

Those prison-interview tapes are priceless. Good grief, I am positively scary in an orange jumpsuit. See me fidget, cast furtive glances at the cameraman with my slippery, Cro-Magnon eyes. And those questions. I love how they fire the questions.

—Are you guilty, Mr. Carson?

What they mean is, just admit it.

EXCERPTED FROM *THE MAKING OF ULTRAGOTHIC: BEHIND THE DOCU-MENTARY*. INTERVIEW WITH FORMER HOMICIDE DETECTIVE KURT MARCHLAND (by William Tucker—4/12/02):

WT: *Bundy. Ridgeway. Yates.*

KM: *(nods).*

WT: *Serial killers who stalked the Pacific Northwest.*

KM: *Yes.*

WT: *Washington State is a magnet for these guys, isn't it?*

KM: *Frankly, Bill, it…well, that's a myth. There's no link between geography and serial killers. Makes good copy, though.*

WT: *Bianchi, Russell, Dodd…*

KM: *Right. That's right.*

WT: And of course, the ones we don't know about.

KM: (chuckles).

WT: Jack Carson?

KM: Jack Carson...I think so. Yes.

WT: But no proof. No body.

KM: The circumstantial evidence, the other incidents in the past. There's a history there. I mean, we found a lot of blood in that workshop.

WT: Would you characterize him as the one who got away?

KM: (long pause) I like to think...his day is coming.

WT: Some people have compared you with Mark Fuhrman.

KM: Yes.

WT: You've been criticized for...quote, "torpedoing" the Carson case.

KM: Yes.

WT: Is that fair?

KM: I made a mistake. My career was destroyed. The guy murdered his wife and walked. I paid for that mistake. I was ruined.

WT: A powerful indictment. He was found not-guilty, however.

KM: The jury was forced to disregard my testimony. It cast doubt on everything the prosecution had built.

WT: Because of a technicality. So, it was unfair.

KM: Ask Miranda Carson. Ask her about what's fair.

I drive deep into the country, past the dairy and the sod fields, past a busload of migrant laborers pulling weeds along the outer track; keep going until I cross an iron bridge with green moss eating alive the girders, and turn onto a rutted lane. Brush scrapes the door panels and squeaks against the windows. The claustrophobic lane opens into a valley of evergreens, none more than eight feet tall, the whole interlaced by dirt paths in the manner of a fishing net. I park on the ridge, get out and stretch my legs, inhale the musk of shorn fir boughs.

Miranda adored Schneider's Christmas Tree Farm. We brought the dogs here on many a lazy summer evening, let them careen after rabbits through the serried ranks of baby Douglas firs. I'd sit on the hood of our car, puffing a cigarette while the blue sky burnt to black. Miranda, she'd chase the dogs, snap pictures of birds with her disposable camera. Sometimes she'd find the carcass of a blue jay or a robin and wrap it in a kerchief, pack the smelly bundle home for one of her sculptures. Once, she created a wax mobile of decayed seagulls, showed it at a local art festival to the horror and consternation of our less cosmopolitan associates. Nobody ever expected a sweet, wholesome girl to possess such an edge.

When Marchland arrives he shuts off his engine and sits there until I begin to wonder if he will actually climb out and confront whatever it is I have in mind.

The sun hangs directly overhead.

"Don't be afraid," I say. I'm slumped against the bumper of my car. I'm thinking of nothing. I'm on autopilot. My mouth works and discharges a prerecorded message. "I figured this would be a good place. Surprised no one ever thought to look." I bare my teeth to really sell it. "Except somebody did finally look. That body they found—it was in a shallow grave about a mile from here. Rotted away to bone fragments and sinews. They know it's a woman, at least."

Marchland's face is hidden by the brim of his hat.

I plow on, jabbing the bee's nest. "What happened, Kurt? After high school, I mean. You weren't bright enough for the big leagues, were you, my friend?"

Marchland doesn't say anything. Doesn't have to.

"So, she bops off to college and meets me. Horror of horrors. I had drugs, talent, oodles of charisma. Means and opportunity. You were basically screwed. Life is unfair, eh? Course, this time we had us a twist ending—a little bitter-sweet vindication for the blue collar slob, isn't that right?" Sure it is. My stalker is no man of mystery; I have become intimate with the squalid details of his wasted life—his lost love, stolen love, if one prefers; the procession of failed marriages; the ruined career, you name it.

Tit for tat.

I used to think Marchland's rage was fueled by simple jealousy, by frustration and sorrow of this melancholy end to an adolescent romance. Now, I get the feeling things are way more complicated.

He carefully adjusts the wing mirror with a hand shaped for the handle of an axe. His knuckles are disfigured; they've been broken in saloon brawls, backroom interrogations. Still, he says nothing. Stewing.

I'm nodding, mesmerized by my own invention. I'm catching my stride. I stand between the vehicles, my legs bowed like a gunfighter bracing to slap leather. "Yeah, you were right. You, your partner, the media ghouls. I'm fucking guilty. Haven't you always known that? Problem is, you're a coward." Is it true? Even I don't know anymore what it is I have or haven't done. The crush of popular opinion has asserted its peculiar laws upon me.

Marchland caresses the mirror, runs his thumb back and forth as if he's testing the edge of a knife, as if he's searching for a pulse.

I curse him then. I scream at him with such fierceness my throat constricts and my eyeballs quiver. Profanities, accusations, a stream of vitriolic gibberish that doesn't sound a bit like me. Hoarse and shaken, I deliver the *coup de grâce*, "She never mentioned you. Ever." I show him a zero with thumb and forefinger. I wait and wait and nothing happens except the trees stir and dust settles. Then I get into my car and drive away. Marchland doesn't give chase, doesn't do anything except sit dead in the road. His truck dwindles and is lost when I round the bend.

I'm jacked to the gills on nature's fight or flight chemicals. I can't see straight; the scenery jitters. Phantom trees, pale disc of sun, the gravel road a molted snakeskin beneath these tires. None of it solid, none of it substantial, two-dimensional flatness to every angle, every blurred outline washed in polychromatic glare.

Cramps lock my fingers on the wheel; my tongue is too fat. I might as well have stared down the drain pipe of a gun, the way my body throbs in the aftermath. I don't know what to do with myself; I hadn't planned this far ahead.

What did I expect, anyway? That if only I pushed enough buttons Marchland would explode like Krakatoa, put a bullet in my brain? Or maybe that wasn't the point of this exercise. Maybe I wanted to sting him like I was stung when they dropped the bomb on me during the trial. Maybe revenge is all this was and the rest could be filed under minor details.

I swing onto the blacktop, get almost to the moss-encrusted bridge when the grille of Marchland's Ford rushes in, fills my rearview mirror.

Clank.

Many moons before the D.A. decided The People had a case, I hired this private eye to look into things. Naturally, public opinion was I only did it to clear my name. To that I say, well, hell, at least I wasn't cooling my heels on a golf course.

Money was easy, I hired the best I could find. Lance Pride, owner-operator of the Pride Agency. I could have gone bigger, could have gone to one of those corporate outfits with international connections, two hundred agents on the ground kicking trashcans, crunching data. The fact I went small and local wasn't lost on my detractors. To them, the vocal majority, it simply demonstrated a token effort, a face-saving maneuver. Demonstrated that I knew the whole search was a farce.

They were right, if for the wrong reasons. A buddy of mine named Marvin Cortez, a strong-arm guy who memorized Plato and Machiavelli, once hypothesized the universe is comprised of nothing more, nothing less than information, that the Kabbalists are on the money with their tetragrams and all that other esoteric magic square shit—the meaning of everything is in a lost equation. Miranda wasn't missing; she'd been subtracted, swallowed whole by some quantum boa constrictor.

I went to Pride because Pride was a bloodhound and because Pride was a checkered-past fellow and he promised to help me put holes in the sonofabitch who kidnapped Miranda—if there *was* a sonofabitch. He couldn't dismiss the possibility she'd decided to take a powder. People bailed on their lives by the thousands, every year. My chums the homicide dicks could attest that tons of missing persons weren't missing, they were on the lam from abusive spouses, debts, their humdrum routines.

Miranda wouldn't have bailed. Abandoned her mom and dad and beloved older brother who was a dentist with three kids that called her auntie and begged to visit our lovely country home every time we saw them. She wouldn't have left me hung out to dry, facing a murder rap. Miranda wouldn't do that, no way.

Then what of those photos from an airport in South America, about eight months after her disappearance? The picture of a woman in a flower-print dress going through customs. Hard to tell with the fugitive-from-Hollywood glasses and the hat and all, but that woman sure looked a lot like Miranda. Surely did indeed. Too bad the mystery woman melted into the great, old continent before anybody could ask her some questions.

It went like that for years. Periodically there'd be a Miranda sighting—a tourist in Delhi, a face in a train window, a grainy still from some camera in some Midwest department store, a blurry image in a crowd of a back-page newspaper story. Tips—ah, all those anonymous tips. I kept a file cabinet just for the letters and emails. Pride received hundreds of phone calls, and I guess the police did too. I had to guess because they didn't talk to me.

Most of it was garbage, easy to see it was garbage. Even in my state of mind I saw through it. Occasionally though, once in a blue moon, as they say, Pride handed me a picture and my pulse would stutter—because it was her staring back at me. The name would be wrong, the hair different, the face older, but unmistakably hers. Twice, Pride bought tickets and flew with me to the places these photos had been taken.

First we visited a town in the rust belt, had a chat with a woman who called herself Macy and worked in a five and dime. Macy drawled, seemed functionally illiterate and was completely charming, guileless as a kitten.

Second time it was a suburban housewife in Oregon who drove a mammoth SUV and had four kids. This one was married to the local high school softball coach. Not so charming, not so guileless, and not the woman I married—metaphorically or otherwise.

Neither of the women knew me, although when they put two and two together, that I was that *other* infamous uxoricidal brute loose for lack of evidence, their eyes turned into saucers. If either was Miranda gone underground, she should've won an Academy Award.

They weren't actresses. They were a couple of people with a fluke resemblance to my wife and that was that. Everybody has a twin, out there in the world, a doppelgänger. The beat went on.

After a while, a long while, even Pride threw in the towel, left me to chase the next fata morgana on my own. He begged off on our business lunches, became too busy to return my calls, eventually stopped cashing my checks. By the end I think he was wondering about me, wondering if I had somehow fooled him. Bundy fooled Anne Rule, he surely did. There was a precedent. I think Pride worried the rest of the world knew something he didn't.

That made two of us.

EXCERPTED FROM THE JOURNAL OF INMATE XX-201957. LOCATION, WASHINGTON STATE CORRECTIONAL FACILITY (7/13/2013):

You never would've caught me.

i was bored. So i stopped. Stopped taking precautions, stopped covering my tracks. Don't think you're clever.

You should've seen your faces.

If they mean to stick me with the needle in the morning, guess i can come clean and tell the truth. Sing for my last supper.

Who tells the truth and nothing but the truth, so help them GOD? People who think GOD's watching the show, that He's got His Hand on the switch, that's who.

The truth is fine, a ripping yarn is better. Assholes who wrote the Holy Book knew that everybody is looking for a good read.

Bugs, mongrel puppies, teenage prostitutes. GOD don't seem to give a goddamn about none of them. Folks say you were a COP how could you? i say there is no such thing.

Folks ask me how many, how many, really? Did you take that one, and it's the famous one they mean. My smile may seem sly, but it's not sly it's patronizing. Only a fool hears a line like "bugs, mongrel puppies, and teenage prostitutes" and assumes one thing naturally leads to another.

MIRANDA wasn't a whore, now was she? She's disqualified. i was in the office with a dozen witnesses the day she went the way of joseph force crater. Do your homework. Do your damn math.

Besides, i picked up the hobby later in life. Didn't even start until i left the department, my third divorce. Sour days, baby. i needed something to keep my hands busy.

carson's the one to ask. i always said so and i still do. That sneaky sonofabitch. Takes one to know one. Those college girls in france and italy, the ones who vanished while he was doing his backpack tour of europe. Coincidence? You all love coincidences, don't you? That girl who washed out of evergreen and then dropped off the planet, i hear he banged her. Quite the grieving widower, ain't he? Know what i think? i think he was a no-talent trust fund hippie who married better than he deserved. i think he sold his soul to rock n' roll and one day the Devil called in the marker.

Face it, boys—when it comes to women that bastard is the bermuda triangle.

Wheels turn. Stop.

Heads turn.

Miranda has just entered the Cloud Room to the muted strains of "That Old Black Magic" and she's decked out in her elegant but provocative red dress, the strapless number that smashes my rational side to jelly. She takes my hand and we start to dance by the light of the full moon, a glitter ball.

The glitter ball, a globe of pale fire, flickers, strobes, incandesces.

Judy blinks into existence and says, "Why were you out there, Jack?"

No Cloud Room. I'm in a bed and the walls are close. Stark green walls. Coffin walls.

Of course, what I hear first is, "Why'd you kill her, Jack?" I'm thinking "*Et tu, Brute?*", before the truth registers in the low, awful chord of a bag pipe dirge.

The room darkens, a noose constricts around us and Judy's sad, florid face wavers in the candle flicker, recedes down a long, flexible tunnel—a ventilation tube. Her lips move and I think she needs to speak up because she sounds like the ocean in a sea shell.

Oh, right. The tree. I hit the tree, or the tree hit me. I drove off the shoulder and rammed a monster oak near a pasture. Cows chewing, vacuously watching me bleed, the car burn.

Judy wavers, disintegrates.

A man in white enters the frame, says a few words, mostly unintelligible, and shines a light in my eyes. I do catch the word *coma* and something about cerebral hemorrhaging. Guy must be a doctor. About the second I figure this out, he's warped off into the fuzzy nimbus at the edge of my vision.

"How ya doin', Michelangelo?" This from the doctor's replacement, a haggard man with a bleach-blond mustache. This isn't a state trooper, or an Olympia traffic cop, no sir. It's my long lost pal Detective Fisher hoping for a deathbed confession. Homicide dicks need hope too—it's no secret they're just janitors with gold badges.

The detective looks awful in the sunlight leaking through the window slot. He's aged these past six years. Not quite so poorly as Marchland, but poorly enough I'd almost pity him if I didn't despise California beach boys with such profound intensity. I'd bet dollars to doughnuts the sorry jerk keeps a surfboard stashed in the closet, Sex Waxed and ready to go.

We don't get do-overs on those Halcyon Days; Fisher won't be hanging ten anytime soon, won't be doing the lambada with Annette Funicello. He's been hitting the bottle and the bottle has been counterpunching. He reaches down to smooth my blanket and a wedding band catches the light. His touch is gentle, as if I'm a sick child.

When Fisher speaks I'm distracted by the shimmer of his ring, his cellophane-flesh, the teletype scrawl moving across his brow, the hollows of his cheeks. He was fresh when he'd been attached to the first Green River Killer task force, eons ago. The task force that never actually caught anyone. A John Wayne wannabe made the collar, swilled up the glory and wrote a bestseller during the fifteen-minute joyride. Ran for Congress; the works. Some cops always get their man. Some never do.

"Sod farmer pulled you out. Saved your ass. What's left of it."

I can't talk, not with the respirator and the tubes, but I'm beginning to see the shape of things through the lifting fog. I recall a stranger in a plaid coat, his hands passing before my eyes, falling upon my shoulders. Trees and greasy clouds switch places. The burning car, the placid cows. And the stranger's wizened face swinging over mine in low orbit. Takes me a moment to decipher what he says. He mouths, *Killer.* Then his face becomes insubstantial, its atoms fracture to the four corners. The press and thump of machinery, the glint of Fisher's ring fill the margins.

Fisher is still here, digging in. "They say you're done. I can hardly buy that until I see it. Guys like you don't stop ticking until the warden turns on the gas, do they, Jack?"

Obviously Detective Fisher hasn't abandoned his pet theory. He'd been superb as a witness for the state, desperate not to let another maniac slip through his clutches. Not so down in the heel back then, either; charming as a snake-oil salesman, Fisher dressed the part of an Ivy Leaguer even if the farthest east he'd ever been was LA. Few things are more compelling than a handsome cop in a crisp suit pointing a steady finger at a prisoner wearing shackles.

Ah, if they could see him now.

Fisher says, "Even if you do squeak through, I don't guess you're gonna be walkin' around much. Not gonna be climbin' around any scaffolds, either. You can get yourself one of those deluxe rigs with the hydraulics and all that. Oxygen tanks strapped to the back. A hefty male nurse to change your diapers. Maybe do some whittlin' in your chair." He seems well-pleased at my evident paraplegia, and I don't blame him. If the best revenge is living well, second best has to be watching your enemy shrivel like a worm on the end of a hook.

"Damned tragedy, you getting in a car crash after losing your wife and all. I bet you were crying your eyes out to Hank Williams or somethin'—didn't see the curve until it was too late. Damned tragedy." He shakes his head. "Oh, I noticed a dent in your bumper. Was that paint from another car? Guess you backed into somebody and didn't report the accident. No worries. Olympia PD has better things to do than hassle you on a misdemeanor hit-and-run beef. I put in a good word for you."

The doctor appears from stage left. He taps Fisher on the shoulder and harangues him in Esperanto or Cantonese. Fisher laughs the good-natured laugh of a career cynic, raises his palms to ward invisible blows. He pauses at the curtain, says, "Hey, we got the results on that Jane Doe. She's not a Jane Doe anymore. You busy sonofagun—we found a few of her friends. Made yourself a whore graveyard."

I'm getting sick to my stomach. I see the choppers, the hounds, burly men in windbreakers muttering into handsets. Not a desert in Nevada or New Mexico, but a green Pacific Northwest divide lumped with unmarked graves.

The burning car, the placid cows. Marchland observing his handiwork from the road. He tugs the brim of his hat to shade his Devil's face, although for a tick his face could've been anyone's, even mine.

A full tank of gas could've taken Marchland halfway to the moon. Or to a lonesome stretch of the I-5 Corridor where girls of all ages hawk their services along the archipelago of strip malls and truck stops, motels and casinos. A savage border where a grimy three-foot-high concrete buttress holds back the woods and the night.

I can't even twitch my fingers. Getting sleepy.

Fisher keeps talking, he's got a mouthful of static. My eyes close. I'm thinking of cats in boxes, radioactive elements, and one simple question. As long as the cat stays boxed the answer is maybe.

Violins and horns scratch my cerebrum, catch fire.

I'm dancing with Miranda under the glitter ball. The band has Old Blue Eyes down cold. If I don't look at the detective, the song will go on and on, perhaps forever. If I don't hear Fisher's words Miranda and I can keep on dancing until the champagne runs dry and the ball dims to a cinder.

The glitter ball pulses. It's the white exit of a black entrance, mouth of an event horizon, the hole at the heart of everything. In moments it has filled all space, has compressed all time to a point.

The possibilities are infinite.

This must be a seizure.

There is no warning. The pressure in the room changes.

The wallop of pain strikes her temple like a mallet, causes her to cease humming, to discard the nail brush, scattering droplets of cherry enamel, to curl in the center of the room, trembling. She has never heard of a seizure causing pain. There shouldn't be pain. She can't coordinate her thoughts to assail this incongruity and it circles down the drain.

The world falls silent. Dull light curdles against the window, foams in her hair, reveals her delicate skull inside translucent flesh, traces the kaleidoscope of veins and nerves. She struggles to her feet and gropes toward the kitchen like a drowning swimmer.

The great, physical silence throbs and builds. White light fuses her vision and then recedes like a wave. She sways before the kitchen door. But there are too many doors. They shift and flex. Light and dark flicker through them. The light and the dark are cold and vast and the room distends, balloonlike, beyond its natural circumference. The doors distend also. Vertigo begins to crush her spine. The room is an inescapable gravity well.

Then, it's finished. The pain withdraws its hooks and clamps and leaves her shaken, but otherwise unmarked. She wipes her eyes and everything is restored to its proper place and perspective. Yet, yet, something has changed. The house is different now. An ant farm suddenly, terminally decolonized.

She finds the kitchen empty.

A block of ice in bits, drips, drips. The ice pick is balanced on the counter edge, its point a morning flame. The microwave clock nictitates indecipherable fragments of numerals, of words, a dying signal.

She smells the musk of his aftershave, the warmth of his smoky exhalations yet hanging in a gulf of dust motes. It's as if he dropped through a sprung trap door.

She says, "Jack? Honey?"

Out there, the scotch broom nods, nods.

EXCERPTED FROM THE ACTION 9 COVERAGE OF MIRANDA CARSON BRIEFING (by Rod Jones—6/9/99):

MC: ...and in closing I just want to thank everyone involved with the search for Jack. There are so many people who have given their time...I thank all of you for the cards and letters. It means so much to us.

And to whoever is holding my husband: please, let him come home. Take him to a hospital or a fire station. Please, from the bottom of my heart, I beg you to do the right thing. Please let Jack come home to his family. You have the power.

Jack, I love you. We won't stop looking.

THE ROYAL ZOO IS CLOSED

Sweeney smeared a bloody thumbprint on the refrigerator. He stared at it, studied it, at length. Stared as if he'd discovered a roadmap of a foreign country, stared like it was going to show him the quickest means to apprehend some territory he hadn't thought of—not aloud, not yet.

He stared at that thumbprint, his thumbprint, but already alien, already drying from red to black. He thought, *Why did I think of a map, it's a completely different shape—a cockroach, a butterfly, two butterflies fucking. And fuck me, it's changing.*

Actually, several hundred-thousand thoughts were crashing in the supercollider of his cerebrum; asteroids caroming off a cortex loaded to the steerage with memories of pancakes, prison, premature ejaculations and continental drift. How in the Beginning the whole wobbly volcanic mass had two heads, Laurasia and Gondwanaland, and J. W. Booth was captured in a barn, and how Underdog and Popeye couldn't fight their way out of a paper bag until they'd had their fix. However, it was the Rorschach-eats-Escher quality of his own fleshly warps and whorls in bas-relief that set his synapses ablaze, shot alarm pings across the radar screen.

Sweeney stepped away too fast, the instinct of a man caught out by a truck speeding through the crosswalk, the convulsive jerk that gives a pious soul pause to genuflect, elicits lips to a crucifix, or a rosary, the antenna-twitch of a bug in the descending shadow of some colossal hand. An orchestra tuned off-key instruments in the pit of Sweeney's belly.

Just a bloody thumbprint on a white background. Just that. Only the fridge humming and the window rattling from the traffic on the street. He checked the clock, watched it tick into a new hour. He gathered his papers from the kitchen table, stuffed them into his briefcase with the mindless preoccupation of an animal scavenging for winter. Now his heart was quiet in its cage and he was feeling better and also a little stupid. The last time this happened he spent three hours gaping at the filament of the bathroom light, paralyzed with an unshakable conviction that it suddenly represented the last dying spark in a universe of frozen ash.

He walked out of the apartment and was waiting at the bus stop for the 76 when it occurred to him to wonder how he cut his hand. He flexed his fingers searching for a wound that wasn't there and considered if the department head would buy stigmata.

Sweeny's portfolio was spattered in blood and probably ruined, but it didn't matter—the machines and the cockroaches would doubtless inherit everything precisely as Hawking always promised. And anyway, this was his last day at work.

Riding from the University District to downtown in the morning meant crowds. Crowds meant nothing to Sweeney. He was a veteran of the city, the first one off the platform and perched on a seat above the wheel-well, briefcase across his knees. He looked out the window at the skyline, chromatic super-structures strung by blinking lights. Dusty haze coiled within the sunrise. The Needle slid past on the starboard side. Quite apropos, since this city was the West Coast plexus of the Heroin Nebula. Sweeney hadn't bought a ticket to the revolving crown of the famous tower, not in thirty years—and wouldn't ever. Every morning he half-expected to watch it flare like a firecracker and rocket into space.

Stop and go in the freeway crush lasted twenty minutes. It always seemed like an hour packed tight as olives on the stinking bus with the blue-haired new-wave lawyers, twitching nosebleeds of all sexes on the double to their doctors, and the transients in Technicolor rags, polyester business suits and garbage bags, smelling of ammonia and microwaved meat.

One guy, a fat guy in a coat and tie with an Adam's apple that truly resembled an apple, a Washington Golden Delicious, muttered a monologue about passenger pigeons. Nobody could shrink away from him, nor escape his encyclopedic recitation; there was no space to squeeze. Sweeney might as well have been trapped aboard a mail train stalled on the outskirts of The Third World, waiting for a smashup to wipe the excess of human cargo from the tracks, except here there were no chickens, no soldiers with fingers inside trigger guards, and the heat wasn't hammer and tongs yet. It was still coming.

A fire engine revved its klaxon, bullied past them, crawling upstream through columns of stalled metal, and Sweeney considered how in the dimness of his childhood he had wanted to be a fireman, to wear the helm with the symbol, the black and yellow turnout coat, to wield the ax.

Sweeney wouldn't take the job if they paid him triple. He wouldn't be a cop either. Or a teacher. Christ, he wouldn't set foot inside a high school, they were shooting galleries these days.

The bus disgorged in the tunnel. Worker ants poured from the barrel, flowed up the escalators into the street. Sweeney led the surge, chin in his chest, striding past the Korean espresso stand, the all-star a cappella rappers, and the heavies with their hats out. A radio sputtered static. Jimmy Swaggart shrieking on full automatic, accompanied by a horn section, the hiss-boom-bah of the hometown coliseum, a cymbal clash. Jesus wasn't dead, just in hiding like Cousin Waldo. Maybe they were shacking with Noriega at a Vatican safehouse.

Fresh graffiti slashed across green mailboxes, a dog bristled at Sweeney's approach, practically slavered to take a piece of his ankle, but didn't. A bum wearing a Seahawks parka and a monogrammed sock cap he'd likely ripped off called the dog back, gave it a pat with a hand most of the skin had curled from, like scales on the dirt-blacked talon of some large, flightless bird. Sweeney hurried on. He was going places.

He was thinking and obsessing about the graffiti on the mailboxes, the brick walls of the buildings, and everywhere it splattered and proliferated; a specialized urban life form, human kudzu bred in the caverns of a hive mind that chanted slogans like FREE WILL, and INDEPENDENCE, and REVOLLUTION. And spelled it incorrectly, mostly.

What was encrypted in the glyphs of the modern age, what did it mean? Certainly a cipher, as was the ancient Cockney, invented as the argot of the disenfranchised, the disaffected, the cant of thieves who crept into darkened homes and ate the peanut butter and drank the beer and put their greasy mitts on your daughter, if you had one, and pretty soon she'd be following them around, learning how to do loop-de-loops on a skateboard, a bullring in her nose, or wherever, a satellite in a decaying orbit. She might wander off to Hollywood, do a tour in the trenches, wind up on the casting coach hoping to become the next Norma Jean bursting from a cake to serenade the knights of Camelot, another domesticated seal; thoroughly modern though, because her tattoos said as much. A cipher by any other name and *I'm sorry Mr. & Mrs. So & So, we found her in a ditch.* That's where the smart money was in the whole degenerate crap shoot.

Sweeney, consumed with graffiti, recollected graffiti artists he had known. Jacks of the trade, as it were. The best of them always went armed with a pithy salvo, inscrutable as a ghetto to the sleek banker rolling in an SUV.

When you're outta crack, the crack of dawn will do, so said a former would-be sumo named Confucius, Confucius Alexander Trey, or Cat for short. A college buddy, a drinking buddy, the one who went the wrong way down the track, although these days Sweeney wasn't so certain of that estimation. Cat was a sure-enough Michelangelo with a spray can or a magic marker and his canvases of preference were the temples of wealth and avarice—as defined by the book of C. He didn't make it far, geologically speaking. He died in '99, shotgunned in the face outside a shelter in Pioneer Square. Closed coffin, open circuit, and there's no apothegm to counter that, so shovel on the dirt. Karma, brothers and sisters, has a mouth as big as the world.

Sweeney glimpsed Confucius smirking, here and there, not every time, but with sufficient regularity to warrant suspicion, and it was another thing to worry about. Confucius knew something, obviously. Maybe it was true—the handwriting was on the wall.

Things were getting too complicated. In the eighteenth century when the Cockney slang was in flower, blokes trundling along Buck's Row weren't worried about Big Bangs or ICBMs pointed at their bedrooms, or String Theories tweaking the chords of high-strung theological violins. They didn't give a fig about Stephen Hawking, or nanotech out-sprinting human evolution to the brass ring, or wristwatches. The world wasn't on its last legs in 1788, wasn't sucking in its last breath, wasn't ready to topple from the roof of heaven into an abyss, even if a few critics thought it might, or that it should. The prophecies were shouted lowercase.

Today of all days, the graffiti held a message for Sweeney that had lurked there from the beginning, astride the mortar and the calculus.

Sweeney read HELL between the isosceles, ellipses and hoops. He read EAT OR BE EATEN and THE END IS HERE. He read SWEENEY CALL HOME. And he read no further. He went on his way, wearing the stunned expression of a man who has forgotten something important. A man fumbling in his pocket for keys to a car he doesn't own, a house he's never lived in.

Sweeney gazed into the branches of the plum trees planted at intervals along the sidewalk. The trees were pleasant; it was much safer than touring the country where animals rustled among the woodwork. These trees were innocent of inhabitants—the rats only lived in them at night. Sometimes earnest dollars amounted to more than a hill of beans in a world of spoons. Sometimes someone had taste. Sometimes someone showed restraint—plum trees, glitzy fountains and the billion acres of grass you're not supposed to walk on under penalty of death. Propriety, decency, common sense were tragically underrepresented, as was exhibited by the Hammering Man looming near the SAM, the pregnant nude bronzed between a library and a Lutheran daycare, or Lenin glowering in Fremont, the self-styled Left Bank, the so-called Center of the Universe. Fremont could have him if they wanted. Stalin too—why not? Grab a shovel; shit isn't always free, just cheap. Sweeney thought they were trying a bit too hard.

Sweeney was, as ever, early. He ducked into a diner, seized the lone deserted table with remnants of the Last Breakfast—cigarette butts interred in the co-agulated gravy, wadded napkins on the floor, pieces of change under a plastic cup. Brand new curses lovingly scribed into Formica, a hunk of gum with veins. He sat on calcified vinyl, watching for the waitress. Sort of a sport.

MAGGY, said her tag. Everyone was tagged. The fish in the stream, and the polar bear on the ice floe. This was the Information Age. Knowing What's What was half the game.

MAGGY asked him what he wanted. She did it telepathically, hand on hip, the interrogative frown a trademark of stoics and customer service personnel in any epoch. She'd seen Sweeney every weekday morning of several burned up calendars, and still she made the query, for it was possibly the height of professional courtesy to obey such rituals.

He said coffee, she poured it and rolled onward, appraising other mouths in the herd. She too was going places. Itzhak Bentov, the esteemed, albeit informal, poet physicist might've commented that she was already there.

Sweeney tried to read the paper, found his focus dilated telescopically. He couldn't grasp those paragraphs of multitudinous complexity, the small-town soap opera plot of places and events blown out of proportion, intumescent and malignant, somewhat staggering, yet squalid, as a drunk sailor on shore leave, or Saint Vitus wavering in a mural shot through a digital camera in the drunken sailor's paw. The typeset conspired with the graffiti. The implications were cosmic. He speculated for milliseconds what the plan was, couldn't begin to perceive its contours, much less the details, and gave up. He fixated on the pictures. Thus modern man was brought full circle to the chronicles of habit carved by hominids hunkered around tiny fires in limestone dens way back when.

Across the ocean, a medieval metropolis was catching hell. Domes burned. Thunderheads boiled atop black pillars. Panic. Chaos. Live coverage at 11. A sign read THE ROYAL ZOO IS CLOSED.

They got a grainy shot of a zookeeper in a dirty turban, face buried in his blackened hands. An emaciated tiger pressed its ribs against a cage door, appeared as if it could slip right through the bars. Its fur as matted as indoor-outdoor carpet, its eyes were sleepy. The tiger licked cracks in the concrete. Bandits had stolen the gorillas, the snakes and the elephants.

The Coalition couldn't get the water going. There was no power. There was no food. There was, however, plenty of hope. A child on a stretcher lost his parents in the shelling; people were searching for them, and incidentally, his arms had come off and nobody could find them either. He was smiling. In the background, a mob pulverized the Dictator's statue with sledgehammers, bulldozing a plot for the Golden Arches, a five-star hotel, something commercially utilitarian and ineffably American.

Sweeney flipped to the sports page. The Mariners were in spring training; they would take the West easy. He brought fifty dollars for the pool at the office. Suckers. His coffee was done. Sweeney folded the paper neatly. Like so, and so, and so.

—IMPREZIO—

The week before his last day at the office, Sweeney visited the doctor. Sweeney suffered cold sweats, heart palpitations, nausea, a whole laundry list. He was panicky, delusional, irritated, sometimes enraged, sometimes overcome with inchoate grief regarding events he couldn't quite recall and worse to come and it was nearly enough to drive a grown man to tears. Somebody somewhere once told him a good cry was as a lance to a boil. A good cry would set him right as rain.

Sweeney never cried, never shouted, never stuck a pencil in anybody's neck despite the often overwhelming compulsion to homicide engendered by modern life; nonetheless, things were not remotely copasetic. Of late, that being the last decade, give or take, Sweeney had devolved into an emotional oscillator. From moment to moment he wanted to swig sake and fly his Zero into an aircraft carrier; kick some teeth; flog his dog; flog the noisy neighbor; slit his own throat; start a fire; shoot his boss; quit his job; do heavy drugs, preferably peyote, or maybe mash-Allah in a hash-house in Amsterdam, or an authentic buffalo-skin teepee on the Great Plains and receive a vision quest; quit being a slave to cigarettes; send a letter bomb to P. Morris; get right with Jesus; join the cult of the homeless; screw a starlet, even an ugly one; or say screw everything and go home and hide under the covers until everything blew over. In the vernacular, Sweeney was freaking out.

The conversation between Sweeney and the doctor went as follows.

—Doc, I've got problems. I'm impotent, and I think I may be a racist.

—Why do you assume you're impotent?

—This woman moved in across the hall. And she's a hottie, see. She prances around in harem pants and a g-string, and yeah I want to, well, uh, know her. Biblically. God, I'm old enough to be her father. But, uh, well, that's not the problem, the problem is this: The attraction is purely intellectual, a friggin' computer algorithm—you aren't hungry, but you see some shortcake, it makes your mouth water and you know you must want it 'cause you haven't had shortcake since Oppy split the atom. I look at that chick in the harem pants and want a piece of shortcake all right, but, uh, nothing's happening with me physically. It's like a psychotic Zen nightmare and I don't even know how to repair a goddamned motorcycle.

—Stress, Sweeney. It's all in your mind. I'll write you a prescription. Why do you think you're racist?

—'Cause I'm afraid of foreigners. Not the ones who live here, not unless they're wearing turbans and carrying satchels, ha-ha. I guess what it is, what I meant was, I'm afraid of other countries.

—Ah. Which ones in particular?

—I don't know. Which ones got the bomb or are getting it? China, Russia, North Korea, Iran, India, Pakistan for starters. Hell, France, Israel, good old U.S.A. A reformed coke fiend with a finger on the button; yeah I get scared of Texans, even the transplants, and their stupid hats, their baseball teams and Brahma bulls. They speak a different language. Call information sometime, you'll see what I mean. I guess it's irrational. Yeah.

—You're not just a racist, Sweeney. You're a xenophobe. I can help; here's another prescription. Allow me to refer you to a very fine psychiatric professional. I send all the doozies to him. Here's his card.

—What? No can do, Doc. I read the small print in the insurance manual. They only cover up to seventy percent of the couch time, no promises either. I'll shrink my head next year, when I can afford it. There's one thing though, maybe you can tell me if I'm schizophrenic. Or if I'm a paranoid schizophrenic. Can you be one and not the other, or is it always both?

—Perhaps you'd better tell me more.

—I see patterns lately. Everywhere. Clouds with cherub faces, dry leaves murmuring Chinese herbal secrets, paint peeled to make a symbol, a drop of blood trickling counterclockwise from the mouth of a dying pigeon. A car horn confuses me, makes me think big Gabe is blowing his trumpet. Shit like that.

—Oh, me too, Sweeney. Me too. Take a couple bottles of these, though. Just in case.

The mantra of Millennial anxiety: Mass Hysteria. Mass Hypnosis. Mass Production. Mass Transit. Mass Murder. Mass Media. Massacre. Mass Exodus. Mass Extinction.

Pundits said Hitler and Pol Pot gelded the term Genocide. That the Holocaust exhausted the fat muscles of pathos and empathy, unyoked them from their central gravity, sent them chasing after every rabbit, and gave the collective consciousness a callous. After Ted B. and Jeff D. the whole multiple homicide shtick was positively ho-hum. Social outrage was quarantined and relegated to splinter cells, underground presses, leftist political organizations and charities. Humanity was immunized against anguish. Horror was white noise, Misery the Muzak of a strip-mall culture. Everyone was terrorized and utterly fearless.

It may have been true, every bleeding syllable, except that morning in Pioneer Square, first a few, then many, woke up to the cold facts. Glaciers scraped these valleys; meteorites once studded the clay like a lunatic design on a masochist's tongue, excavated holes and trenches at the bottom of the ocean, added their traces of background radiation. Had civilization forgotten Vesuvius and Krakatoa? That Mother Nature likes to eat her children on occasion? No consequence—shortly, citizens of the empire were raw nerves on the hoof.

Sweeney didn't make it to the office. When he breached the plaza where the fruit market, the fiddle shop, and the Memorial lived, and Starbucks, ubiquitous as scotch broom, the trip was rendered pointless. The sky began to open its wide, toothless mouth, and that mouth slobbered the phosphorescent slime of prehistoric seabeds.

Doors were shutting, metal curtains dropping, police cruisers trolling, staccato blats of authoritarian comfort crackling from bullhorns and mouths gone flaccid with shock that pierced even the cops' shiny blue hearts. Janitors wearing sad masks emerged from recesses to take down the sandwich boards, spear the trash, sweep detritus from the stage. The big curtain began to drop, black on black.

The sun flickered, an oblong dwarf, and it seemed a little underdone, a soft yolk. The air acquired somber tints as if filtered by the lens of an artless cinematographer.

Tak Fujimoto wept.

A shudder passed through the city, the girders and the skeletons, and into bedrock. Afterward, a sound. A deep, abiding sigh as of vast lungs deflated. People walked in widening circles. People tripped over stalled cars. People vomited and cackled. People hugged their babies and their bibles. Atheists too. Dogs fell sideways and scratched until they foamed at the muzzle, bled from the eyes; pigeons heaved up on strings and smashed through plate glass, painted wet mosaics on granite. Stoplights shifted through their spectrums.

Sweeney tried to understand. He was puzzled why action figures were windmilling as they drifted from high-rise ledges; why billboards flashed random numbers; why small, hungry fires flickered in faults and crevices; why flocks of paper money whirled in funnels while seagulls plummeted in sheaves; why no one seemed to care. It was a recording. None of it was happening. Orson Welles, take your bow and sit down. Enough is enough.

Sweeney gazed into a salon on the ground floor of a hotel some local celebrity once nearly torched with a cigarette in bed after too much vodka. Beehive dryers were unoccupied; the drones had vanished, buzzed off. The TV blared. He fastened upon an image. A chasm opened, so he looked. The image fastened upon him. The chasm returned his glance. There was a brief struggle. Then it was finished. The dead German laughed.

—CODA—

Sweeney struggled home. A treacherous five-mile hike under cracked overpasses and through demolished neighborhoods. No vehicles moved. No birds sang, no children screamed. Nothing and nothing; just the erratic thud of blood in his neck and infrequent thunder that resonated far off without clouds. The air bruised purple. It filled the rippling sky; it was swelling.

Sweeney wasn't in a hurry. He was steady as she goes. He was a tortoise, and happy for it. His wingtip shoes were dirty and unlaced. He stumbled. The asphalt grew sticky.

He remembered nothing of substance. He remembered a Frenchman and his submarine. Jellyfish. Portuguese Man o' War was a predator by committee. The Man o' War wore its stomachs on its sleeve, trailed whips and stingers in dragnets, ate its prey squirming. If the sky, by sinister alchemy, or diabolical prestidigitation, transformed into a mirror of the mother sea, the primordial cradle; and if leviathans swam that breadth and hovered, softly undulating over the teeming habitations of the globe, feasting; what should you wear?

He sweated. His thoughts trickled, disjointed, timid. He decided the poets and the painters, the sculptors and the writers, the crackpot theologians and their excommunicated kin, and the mystics had it right. Reality was a makeshift prop, an amalgamation of agreed-upon conjecture, a consensus of self-limiting parameters and paradigms made palatable by endless speculation fueled by madness and hope and no mean amount of good dope. Rubber science, bouncing like a handball off the nonexistent wall of a metaphysical gulag.

The sun? Scratch the surface and reveal a skull courtesy of Dali's brush, Lovecraft's eye peeping through the socket, H. P.'s cruel dead lips whispering he warned us; he wrote the book.

The moon? No moon, only a sound stage in the Arizona desert. Stars were bullet holes in the galactic canvas. The day dark matter quavered in the pudding cup would be the universal gloaming of life as it's ordered. Today, in fact.

Sweeney didn't spy any looters and he wondered. Natural or unnatural? Did such nomenclature properly exist? Then he was at his building. He climbed the stairs, one by one, and entered his stark room. So small, artificial as a Hollywood set.

The light failed, the dim thunder faded into a well of silence. Remote and subterranean, a whale kept calling for its pod. Sweeney pulled the blinds and lighted candles; the electricity had fizzled and retreated into its maze of wires. The radio clicked and clicked and clicked and became too eerie, so Sweeney killed the switch.

Obeying an impulse good enough for a mayfly, an ancient biological imperative, he pressed his vanity across the hall with his nubile neighbor, the hot girl in harem pants. Sweeney, being theoretically the last man on Earth, vowed not to flounder as Prufrock, but to brave rebuff with a ballsy grin and pick the bugs from his teeth as necessary. He brandished a murky bottle of wine he'd saved since forever, buried in a cabinet for emergency maneuvers.

He combed his hair. Knocked. No answer. He tried the door and beheld not a supple, buxom example of testosterone-aggravated fantasy, but a fawn-eyed old man in horn-rim glasses who resembled, exactly, Woody Allen, sprawled in a recliner, legs to the shins in a bucket of gray water. He appeared as melancholy as Sweeney felt. Each to each, they grunted apologetically. As Sweeney retreated, dignity in shambles, the old man said nothing; his face was overrun by shadow until just his glasses hung, gleaming.

Sweeney ground pills from three bottles in a salad bowl. The bowl was a Christmas present from his mother. He sloshed it to the brim with wine. Hail Socrates, Napoleon and Alexander, he swallowed.

He waited for another epiphany, impatiently at first. Dull reverberations made silverware hiss, a nest of adders. Came the dumb groan of the foundation. In the proximate below, scores of apartment doors slammed like a chain of collapsing dominoes. Now silence.

Nothing came to him. He yawned. For want of inspiration, he grabbed a spoon and meticulously carved his name and the date into the plaster. Below those, he wrote:

HERE LIES A SUPERNUMERARY WHO DESPISED THE OPERA

And a postscript:
KILROY IS DEAD

Sweeney crawled into bed and stared at the ceiling. He couldn't sleep, so he made shadow puppets on the wall. He made tigers and elephants, churches and church steeples and Polyphemus shaking his fist at the gods until the candlewick sighed and swooned into the wax and he lost the light. Then there was darkness and Sweeney began to snore.

THE IMAGO SEQUENCE

Imago. Imago. Imago.
—Wallace Stevens

1.

Like the Shroud of Turin, the disfigured shape in the photograph was a face waiting to be born. An inhuman face, in this instance. The Devil, abstracted, or a black-mouthed sunflower arrested mid-bloom. Definitely an object to be regarded with morbid appreciation, and then followed by a double scotch to quash the heebie-jeebies.

I went to Jacob Wilson's Christmas party to see his uncle's last acquisition, one that old man Theodore hadn't stuck around to enjoy. A *natural Rorschach*, Jacob said of the photo. It had been hanging in the Seattle Art Museum for months, pending release at the end of its show. Jacob was feeling enigmatic when he called about the invitation three days before Christmas and would say no more. No need—the hook was set.

I hadn't talked to Jacob since the funeral. I almost skipped his party despite that guilt, aware of the kind of people who would attend. Whip-thin socialites with quick, sharp tongues, iron-haired lawyers from colonial families and sardonic literati dredged from resident theater groups. Sleek, wealthy and voracious; they inhabited spheres far removed from mine. As per custom, I would occupy the post of the educated savage in Jacob's court. An orangutan dressed for a calendar shoot, propped in the corner to brood artfully. Perhaps I could entertain them with my rough charm, my lowbrow anecdotes. It wasn't appealing. Nonetheless, I went because I always went, and because Carol gave me her sweetest frown when I hesitated; the one that hinted of typhoons and earthquakes.

The ride from my loft in downtown Olympia served to prepare my game face. I took the 101 north, turned onto Delphi Road and followed it through the deep, dark Capitol Forest and up into the Black Hills. Carol chattered on her cell, ignoring me, so I drove too fast. I always drove too fast these days.

The party was at full steam as I rolled along the mansion's circle drive and angled my rusty, four-door Chrysler into a slot among the acres of Porsches, Jaguars and Mercedes. Teddy Wilson might've only been a couple of months in his grave, but Jacob was no neophyte host of galas. He attracted the cream, all right.

Bing Crosby and a big band were hitting their stride when the front doors gave way. A teenage hood in a spiffy white suit grabbed our coats. I automatically kept one hand over my wallet. The bluebloods congregated in a parlor dominated by a fiery synthetic tree. A slew of the doorman's white-tuxedoed brethren circulated with trays of champagne and hors d'oeuvres. The atmosphere was that of a cast party on the set of *Casablanca*. Jarring the illusion was Wayne Newton's body double slumped on the bench of the baby grand, his pinky ring winking against the keys. I didn't think he was playing; a haphazard pyramid of shot glasses teetered near his leg and he looked more or less dead.

Guests milled, mixing gleeful ennui with bad martinis. Many were sufficiently drunk to sand down the veneer of civility and start getting nasty. Jacob presided, half seas over, as the Cockney used to say, lolling before his subjects and sycophants in Byzantine splendor. I thought, *Good god, he's wearing a cape!* His attire was a silken clash of maroon and mustard, complete with ruffles, a V-neck shirt ripped from the back of a Portuguese corsair, billowing pantaloons and wooden sandals that hooked at the toe. A white and gold cape spread beneath his bulk, and he fanned himself with a tri-corner hat. Fortunately, he wasn't wearing the hat.

Carol glided off to mingle, stranding me without a backward glance. I tried not to take it personally. If not for a misfortune of birth, this could have been her tribe.

Meanwhile, I spotted the poster-sized photograph upon its easel, fixed in the center of the parlor. Heavy as a black hole, the photograph dragged me forward on wires. Shot on black and white, it detailed a slab of rock, which I assumed was subterranean. Lacking a broader frame of reference, it was impossible to know. The finer aspects of geology escaped me, but I was fascinated by the surreal quality of this glazed wall, its calcified ridges, webbed spirals and bubbles. The inkblot at its heart was humanoid, head twisted to regard the viewer. The ambient light had created a blur not unlike a halo, or horns, depending on the angle. This apish thing possessed a broad mouth slackened as an unequal ellipse. A horrible silhouette; lumpy, misshapen and dead for epochs. Hopefully dead. Other pockets of half-realized darkness orbited the formation; fragments splintered from the core. More cavemen, devils, or dragons.

Hosts occurred to me.

A chunky kid in a turtleneck said it actually resembled a monstrous jellyfish snared in flowstone, but was undoubtedly simple discoloration. Certainly not any figure—human or otherwise. He asked Jacob his opinion. Jacob squinted and declared he saw only the warp and woof of amber shaved bare and burned by a pop flash. Supposedly another guest had witnessed an image of Jesus on

Golgotha. This might have been a joke; Jacob had demolished the contents of his late uncle's liquor cabinet and was acting surly.

I seldom drank at Jacob's cocktail socials, preferring to undertake such solemn duty in the privacy of my home. But I made a Christmas exception, and I paid. Tumblers began clicking in my head. A queasy jolt nearly loosened my grip on my drink, bringing sharper focus to the photograph and its spectral face in stone. The crowd shrank, shivered as dying leaves, became pictographs carved into a smoky cave wall.

A dung fire sputtered against the encroaching well of night, and farther along the cave wall, scored with its Paleolithic characters, a cleft sank into the humid earth. Flies buzzed, roaches scuttled. A reed pipe wheedled an almost familiar tune—

My gorge tasted alkaline; my knees buckled.

This moment of dislocation expanded and burst, revealing the parlor still full of low lamplight and cigarette smog, its mob of sullen revelers intact. Jacob sprawled on his leather sofa, regarding me. His expression instantly subsided into a mask of flabby diffidence. It happened so smoothly and I was so shaken I let it go. Carol didn't notice; she was curled up by the fireplace laughing too loudly with a guy in a Norwegian sweater. The roses in their cheeks were brick-red and the sweater guy kept slopping liquor on the rug when he gestured.

Jacob waved. "You look shitty, Marvin. Come on, I've got medicine in the study."

"And you look like the Sun King."

He laughed. "Seriously, there's some grass left. Or some Vicodin, if you prefer."

No way I was going to risk Jacob's weed if it had in any way influenced his fashion sense. On the other hand, Vicodin sounded too good to be true. "Thanks. My bones are giving me hell." The dull ache in my spine had sharpened to a railroad spike as it always did during the rainy season. After we had retreated to the library and poured fresh drinks, I leaned against a bookcase to support my back. "What's it called?"

He sloshed whiskey over yellow teeth. "*Parallax Alpha*. Part one of a trio entitled the *Imago Sequence*—if I could lay my hands on *Parallax Beta* and *Imago* I'd throw a *real* party." His voice reverberated in the rich, slurred tones of a professional speaker who'd shrugged off the worst body blows a bottle of malt scotch could offer.

"There are two others!"

"You like."

"Nope, I'm repulsed." I had gathered my nerves into one jangling bundle; sufficient to emote a semblance of calm.

"Yet fascinated." His left eyelid drooped in a wink. "Me too. I'd kill to see the rest. Each is a sister of this piece—subtle perspective variances, different fields of depth, but quite approximate."

"Who's got them—anybody I know?"

"*Parallax Beta* is on loan to a San Francisco gallery by the munificence of a collector named Anselm Thornton. A trust fund brat turned recluse. It's presumed he has *Imago*. Nobody is sure about that one, though. We'll get back to it in a minute."

"Jake—what do you see in that photo?"

"I'm not sure. A tech acquaintance of mine at UW analyzed it. 'Inconclusive,' she said. *Something's* there."

"Spill the tale."

"Heard of Maurice Ammon?"

I shook my head.

"He's obscure. The fellow was a photographer attached to the Royal University of London back in the '40s and '50s. He served as chief shutterbug for pissant expeditions in the West Indies and Africa. Competent work, though not Sotheby material. The old boy was a craftsman. He didn't pretend to be an artist."

"Except for the *Imago* series."

"Bingo. *Parallax Alpha*, for example, transcends journeyman photography, which is why Uncle Teddy was so, dare I say, obsessed." Jacob chortled, pressed the glass to his cheek. His giant, red-rimmed eye leered at me. "Cecil Eaton was the first to recognize what Ammon had accomplished. Eaton was a Texas oil baron and devoted chum of Ammon's. Like a few others, he suspected the photos were of a hominid. He purchased the series in '55. Apparently, misfortune befell him and his estate was auctioned. Since then the series has changed hands several times and gotten scattered from Hades to breakfast. Teddy located this piece last year at an exhibit in Seattle. The owner got committed to Grable and the family was eager to sell. Teddy caught it on the hop."

"Define obsession for me." I must've sounded hurt, being kept in the dark about one of Teddy's eccentric passions, of which he'd possessed legion, because Jacob looked slightly abashed.

"Sorry, Marvo. It wasn't a big deal—I never thought it was important, anyway. But...Teddy was on the hunt since 1987. He blew maybe a quarter mil traveling around following rumors and whatnot. The pieces moved way too often. He said it was like trying to grab water."

"Anybody ever try to buy the whole enchilada?"

"The series has been fragmented since Ammon originally sold two to Eaton and kept the last for himself—incidentally, no one knows much about the final photograph, *Imago*. Ammon never showed it around and it didn't turn up in his effects."

"Where'd they come from?"

"There's the weird part. Ammon kept the photos' origin a secret. He refused to say where he took them, or what they represented."

"Okay. Maybe he was pumping up interest by working the element of mystery." I'd watched enough artists in action to harbor my share of cynicism.

Jacob let it go. "Our man Maurice was an odd duck. Consorted with shady folks, had peculiar habits. There's no telling where his mind was."

"Peculiar habits? Do tell."

"I don't know the details. He was smitten with primitive culture, especially obscure primitive religions—and most especially the holy pharmaceuticals that accompany certain rites." He feigned taking a deep drag from a nonexistent pipe.

"Sounds like a funky dude. He lived happily ever after?"

"Alas, he died in a plane crash in '57. Well, his plane disappeared over Nairobi. Same difference. Bigwigs from the university examined his journals, but the journals didn't shed any light." Jacob knocked back his drink and lowered his voice for dramatic effect. "Indeed, some of those scholars hinted that the journals were extremely cryptic. Gave them the willies, as the campfire tales go. I gather Ammon was doubtful of humanity's long term survival; didn't believe we were equipped to adapt with technological and sociological changes looming on the horizon. He admired reptiles and insects—had a real fixation on them.

"The series went into private-collector limbo before it was subjected to much scrutiny. Experts debunked the hominid notion. Ammon's contemporaries suggested he was a misanthropic kook, that he created the illusion to perpetrate an intricate hoax."

Something in the way Jacob said this last part caused my ears to prick up. "The experts only satisfy four out of five customers," I said.

He studied his drink, smiled his dark smile. "Doubtless. However, several reputable anthropologists gave credence to its possible authenticity. They maintained official silence for fear of being ostracized by their peers, of being labeled crackpots. But if someone proved them correct…"

"The photos' value would soar. Their owner would be a celebrity, too, I suppose." Finally, Jacob's motives crystallized.

"Good god, yes! Imagine the scavenger hunt. Every swinging dick with a passport and a shovel would descend upon all the remote sites Ammon ever set foot. And let me say, he got around."

I sat back, calculating the angles through a thickening alcoholic haze. "Are the anthropologists alive; the guys who bought this theory?"

"I can beat that. Ammon kept an assistant, an American grad student. After Ammon died, the student faded into the woodwork. Guess who it turns out to be?—The hermit art collector in California. Anselm Thornton ditched the graduate program, jumped the counterculture wave in Cali—drove his upper-crust, Dixie-loving family nuts, too. If anybody knows the truth about the series I'm betting it's him."

"Thornton's a southern gentleman."

"He's of southern stock, anyhow. Texas Panhandle. His daddy was a cattle rancher."

"Longhorns?"

"Charbray."

"Ooh, classy." I crunched ice to distract myself from mounting tension in my back. "Think papa Thornton was thick with that Eaton guy? An oil baron and a cattle baron—real live American royalty. The wildcatter, a pal to the mysterious British photographer; the Duke, with a son as the photographer's protégé. Next we'll discover they're all Masons conspiring to hide the missing link. They aren't Masons, are they?"

"Money loves money. Maybe it's relevant, maybe not. The relevant thing is Thornton Jr. may have information I desire."

I didn't need to ask where he had gathered this data. Chuck Shepherd was the Wilson clan's pet investigator. He worked from an office in Seattle. Sober as a mortician, meticulous and smooth on the phone. I said, "Hermits aren't chatty folk."

"Enter Marvin Cortez, my favorite ambassador." Jacob leaned close enough to club me with his whiskey breath and squeezed my shoulder. "Two things. I want the location of this hominid, if there is a hominid. There probably isn't, but you know what I mean. Then, figure out if Thornton is connected to…the business with my uncle."

I raised my brows. "Does Shep think so?"

"I don't know what Shep thinks. I do know Teddy contacted Thornton. They briefly corresponded. A few weeks later, Teddy's gone."

"Damn, Jake, that's a stretch—never mind. How'd they make contact?"

Jacob shrugged. "Teddy mentioned it in passing. I wasn't taking notes."

"Ever call Thornton yourself, do any follow up?"

"We searched Teddy's papers, pulled his phone records. No number for Thornton, no physical address, except for this card—the Weston Gallery, which is the one that has *Parallax Beta*. The director blew me off—some chump named Renfro. Sounded like a nut job, actually. I wrote Thornton a letter around Thanksgiving, sent it care of the gallery. He hasn't replied. I wanted the police to shake a few answers out of the gallery, but they gave me the runaround. Case closed, let's get some doughnuts, boys!"

"Turn Shep loose. A pro like him will do this a lot faster."

"Faster? I don't give a damn about faster. I want answers. The kind of answers you get by asking questions with a lead pipe. That isn't up Shep's alley."

I envisioned the investigator's soft, pink hands. Banker's hands. My own were broad and heavy, and hard as marble. Butcher's hands.

Jacob said, "I'll cover expenses. And that issue with King…"

"It'll dry up and blow away?" Rudolph King was a contractor on the West Side; he moonlighted as a loan shark, ran a pool hall and several neat little rackets from the local hippie college. I occasionally collected for him. A job went sour; he reneged on our arrangement, so I shut his fingers in a filing cabinet—a bit rough, but there were proprietary interests at stake. Jacob crossed certain palms with silver, saved me from making a return appearance at Walla Walla. Previously, I did nine months there on a vehicular assault charge for running over a wise-mouth pimp named Leon Berens. Berens had been muscling in on the wrong territory—a deputy sheriff's, in fact, which was the main reason I only did a short hitch. The kicker was, after he recovered, Berens landed the head bartender gig at the Happy Tiger, a prestigious lounge in the basement of the Sheraton. He was ecstatic because the Happy Tiger was in a prime spot three blocks from the Capitol Dome. Hustling a string of five-hundred-dollars-a-night call girls for the stuffed shirts was definitely a vertical career move. He fixed me up with dinner and drinks whenever I wandered in.

"Poof."

Silence stretched between us. Jacob pretended to stare at his glass and I pretended to consider his proposal. We knew there was no escape clause in our contract. I owed him and the marker was on the table. I said, "I'll make some calls, see if I can track him down. You still want me to visit him…well, we'll talk again. All right?"

"Thanks, Marvin."

"Also, I want to look at Teddy's papers myself. I'll swing by in a day or two."

"No problem."

We ambled back to the party. A five-piece band from the Capitol Theatre was gearing up for a set. I went to locate more scotch. When I returned, Jacob was surrounded by a school of liberal arts piranhas, the lot of them swimming in a pool of smoke from clove cigarettes.

I melted into the scenery and spent three hours nursing a bottle of Dewar's, avoiding eye contact with anyone who looked ready for conversation. I tried not to sneak too many glances at the photograph. No need to have worried on that score; by then, everyone else had lost complete interest.

Around midnight Carol keeled over beside the artificial tree. The guy in the Norwegian sweater moved on to a blonde in a shiny dress. I packed Carol in the car and drove home, grateful to escape another Jacob Wilson Christmas party without rearranging somebody's face.

2.

Nobody knew if Theodore Wilson was dead, it was simply the safe way to bet. One knife-bright October morning the Coast Guard had received a truncated distress signal from his yacht, *Pandora*, north of the San Juans. He'd been on a day trip to his lover's island home. Divers combed the area for two weeks before calling it quits. They found no wreckage, no body. The odds of a man surviving more than forty minutes in that frigid water were minimal, however. Teddy never slowed down to raise a family, so Jacob inherited a thirteen-million-dollar estate for Christmas. It should've been a nice present for me as well—I'd been Jake's asshole buddy since our time at State.

College with Jacob had been movie-of-the-week material—the blue-collar superjock meets the royal wastrel. Me on a full wrestling scholarship and Jacob starring as the fat rich boy who had discovered superior financial status did not always garner what he craved most—adulation. Thick as ticks, we shared a dorm, went on road trips to Vegas, spent holidays at the Wilson House. Eventually he convinced his globetrotting uncle to support my Olympic bid. It was a hard sell—the elder Wilson had no use for contemporary athletic competition. Descended from nineteenth century New England gentry, he favored the refined pursuits of amateur archeology, ancient philology and sailing—but young Jacob was glib and the deal was made. Never mind that I was a second-rate talent blown up on steroids and hype, or that two of my collegiate titles were fixed by thick-jowled Irishmen who drank boilermakers for breakfast and insisted wrestling was a pansy sport.

Teddy dropped me more than ten years ago. He lost a bucket of cash and a serious amount of face among his peers when I tanked in '90 before the Olympic Trials. The Ukrainian super heavyweight champion broke my back in two places during an exhibition match. Sounded like an elephant stepping on a stick of wet kindling.

Bye, bye macho, patriotic career. Hello physician-prescribed dope, self-prescribed booze and a lifetime of migraines that would poleax a mule.

Really, it was a goddamned relief.

I got familiar with body casts, neck braces and pity. Lately, the bitter dregs of a savings account kept a roof over my head and steak in my belly. A piecemeal contract to unload trucks for a couple Thurston County museums satisfied a minor art fetish. Mama had majored in sculpture, got me hooked as a lad. Collecting debts for the local "moneylenders" was mainly a hobby—just like dear old pop before somebody capped him at a dogfight. I was a real Renaissance man.

I met Carol while I was politely leaning on her then boyfriend, a BMW salesman with a taste for long-shot ponies and hard luck basketball teams. Carol worked as a data specialist for the department of corrections. She found the whole failed-athlete turned arm-breaker routine erotic. What should've been a weekend fling developed into a bad habit that I hadn't decided the best way to quit.

The day after the party I asked her what she thought of Jacob's photograph. She was stepping out of the shower, dripping hair wrapped in a towel. "What photograph?" She asked.

I stared at her.

She didn't smile, too busy searching for her earrings. Probably as hung-over as I was. "Oh, that piece of crap his uncle bought off that crazy bitch in Seattle. I didn't like it. Piece of crap. Where are my goddamned earrings."

"Did you even look at it?"

"Sure."

"Notice anything unusual?"

"It was unusually crappy. Here we go." She retrieved her earrings from the carpet near her discarded stockings. "Why, he try to sell it to you? For god's sake, don't buy the ugly thing. It's crap."

"Not likely. Jacob wants me to do a little research."

Carol applied her lipstick with expert slashes, eyed me in her vanity while she worked. "Research, huh?"

"Research, baby," I said.

"Don't do anything too stupid." She shrugged on her coat, grabbed an umbrella. It was pouring out there.

"Yeah," I said.

"Yeah, right. And don't buy that crappy photo." She pecked my cheek, left me sneezing in a cloud of perfume and hairspray.

New Year's Eve sneaked up on me. I stopped dragging my feet and made calls to friends of friends in the Bay Area, hoping to get a line on the enigmatic Mr. Thornton. No dice. However, the name triggered interesting matches on the Internet. According to his former associates, a couple of whom were wards of the federal penal system, Thornton had been a flower child; an advocate of free love, free wine and free thinking. Yeah, yeah, yeah.

Shep's intelligence was more thorough. After quitting grad school Thornton organized a commune in San Francisco in the '60s, penned psychedelic tracts about the nature of faith and divine cosmology, appeared on local talk radio and did cameos in film documentaries. He'd also gotten himself charged with kidnapping and contributing to the delinquency of minors. Disgruntled parents accused him of operating a cult and brainwashing runaway teens. Nothing stuck. His house burned down in '74 and the commune disbanded, or migrated; reports were fuzzy.

Thornton resurfaced in 1981 to purchase *Parallax Beta* at an estate sale in Manitoba. Its owner, a furrier named Robespierre, had come to an unfortunate fate—Robespierre got raving drunk at a party, roared off in his brand new Italian sports car and plunged into a ravine. Authorities located the smashed guardrail, but no further trace of the car or its drunken occupant.

Thornton's relatives were either dead or had disowned him. There was a loyal cousin in Cleveland, but the lady suffered from Alzheimer's, thus tracking him through family was a no-go. Shep confirmed getting stonewalled by the Weston Gallery. Ah, a dead end; my work here was done.

Except, it wasn't.

It began as the traditional New Year's routine. I drank and contemplated my navel about a wasted youth. I drank and contemplated the gutted carcass of my prospects. I drank and contemplated what *Parallax Alpha* was doing to my peace of mind.

Initially, I wrote it off as interest due on multiple fractures and damaged nerves. My lower back went into spasms; pain banged its Viking drum. I chased a bunch of pills with a bunch more eighty-proof and hallucinated. With sleep came ferocious nightmares that left welts under my eyes. *Dinosaurs trumpeting, roaches clattering across the hulks of crumbling skyscrapers. Dead stars in a dead sky. Skull-yellow planets caught in amber—a vast, twinkling necklace of dried knuckles.*

The beast in the photograph opening its mouth to batten on my face. I was getting this nightmare, and ones like it, with increasing frequency.

I wasn't superstitious. Okay, the series had a bizarre history that got stranger the deeper I dug; bad things dogged its owners—early graves, retirement to asylums, disappearances. And yeah, the one picture I had viewed gave me a creepy vibe. But I wasn't buying into any sort of paranormal explanation. I didn't believe in curses. I believed in alcoholism, drug addiction and paranoid delusion. Put them in a shaker and you were bound to lose your marbles now and again.

Then one evening, while sifting Teddy's personal effects—going through the motions to get Jacob off my back—I found a dented ammo box. The box was stuffed with three decades' worth of photographs, although the majority were wartime shots.

Whenever he had a few drinks under his belt, Jacob was pleased to expound upon the grittier side of his favorite uncle. Jolly Saint Teddy had not always been a simple playboy multimillionaire. Oh, no, Teddy served in Vietnam as an intelligence officer; spooks, the boys called them. Predictable as taxes, really—he'd recently graduated from Dartmouth and there was a war on. A police action, if you wanted to get picky, but everybody knew what it was.

The snapshots were mainly of field hijinks with the troops and a few of Saigon R&R exploits. From what I could discern, when they were in the rear areas, all the intelligence guys dressed like Hollywood celebrities auditioning for a game show—tinted shooting glasses, Hawaiian shirts, frosty Coke bottles with teeny umbrellas at hand, a girl on each arm; the whole bit. Amusing, in a morbid sense. One of the field shots caught my attention and held it. It was not amusing in any sense.

The faded caption read, *Mekong D. 1967.* A platoon of marines decked out in full combat gear, mouths grinning in olive-black faces. Behind them were two men dressed in civilian clothes. I had no problem recognizing Anselm Thornton from Shep's portfolio, which included newspaper clippings, class albums from Texas A&M, and a jittery video-taped chronicle of the beatniks. Thornton's image was fuzzy—a pith helmet obscured his eyes, and a bulky, complicated camera was slung over one shoulder; sweat stains made half-moons under his armpits. Had he been with the press corps? No, the records didn't lie. During Nam Thornton had been dropping LSD and poaching chicks outside of Candlestick Park.

Teddy, the old, exquisitely corpulent Teddy I knew, stood near him, incomprehensibly juxtaposed with these child-warriors. He wore a double-breasted suit a South American tailor had made recently. The suit restrained a once powerful frame sliding to blubber. Below a prominent brow, his face shone a mottled ivory; his eyes were sockets. His mouth gaped happily, smoldering with dust and cobwebs. A structure loomed beyond the marines. Screened by foliage, a battered marquee took shape. The marquee spelled AL D IN. The building was canted at an alarming angle; greasy smoke mushroomed from the roof.

That gave me pause. The Aladdin used to be Teddy's residence of choice when he visited Vegas. It was in a back room of that sacred hotel he once shook hands with his hero, the inestimable Dean Martin—who, in his opinion, was the better half of the Lewis & Martin act—during a high-stakes poker game reserved for the *crème de la crème* of big-shot gamblers. Teddy didn't qualify as a whale, as they referred to those suckers who routinely lost half a mil in one night, but he dropped his share of iron at the tables, and he always did have a knack for being at the heart of the action. I squinted at that photo until my eyes crossed—it was the Aladdin, no question. Yet an Aladdin even Teddy might not have recognized. Gray smudges in the windows were faces gazing down upon the razed jungle. Many of them were laughing or screaming.

I couldn't figure out what the hell I was seeing. I pawed through the box by the light of a Tiffany lamp while a strong winter rain bashed at the windows. More of the same; nearly 300 pictures, all out of kilter, many in ways I never did quite understand. The latest seemed to contain medical imagery—some kind of surgery in progress. Overexposed, they formed a ruddy patina that was maddeningly obscure: Teddy's face streaked with blood as someone stitched his scalp in near darkness; coils of achromatic motion and pale hands with thick, dirty nails; a close-up of a wound, or a flower's corona; white, pink and black. It was impossible to identify the action.

I stopped looking after that, hedged around the issue with Jacob, asked him in an oblique way if his uncle might've known Thornton, during the halcyon days. Jacob was skeptical; he was certain such a fact would've come to light during Teddy's quest for the *Imago Sequence*. I didn't tell him about the ammo box; at that point it seemed wiser to keep my mouth shut. Either I was losing my sanity, or something else was happening. Regardless, the pattern around Jacob's inherited art piece was woven much tighter than I had suspected. The whole mess stank and I could only speculate how ripe it would become.

3.

I drove to Bellevue for an interview with Mrs. Florence Monson Chin, previous owner of *Parallax Alpha*. Her family had placed her in Grable, the best that money, a heap of money, could buy. Intimates referred to it as the Grable Hotel or Club Grable. These days, her presence there was an open secret thanks to the insatiable press. No matter; the hospital had a closed-doors policy and an iron fist in dealing with staff members who might choose to blab. Any news was old news.

Mrs. Chin was heiress to the estate of a naturalized Chinese businessman who'd made his fortune breeding rhesus monkeys for medical research. His associates called him the Monkey King. After her elderly husband passed on, Mrs. Chin resumed her debutante ways, club-hopping from Seattle to the French Riviera, screwing bullfighters, boxers and a couple foreign dignitaries, snorting coke and buying abstract art—the more abstract, the more exquisitely provincial, the better. The folks at *Art News* didn't take her seriously as a collector, but it seemed a black AmEx card and a mean streak opened plenty of doors. She partied on the wild and wooly side of high society right up until she flipped her wig and got clapped in the funny farm.

I knew this because it was in all the tabloids. What I didn't know was if she would talk to me. Jacob made nice with her father, got me a direct line to her at the institution. She preferred to meet in person, but gave no indication she was particularly interested in discussing *Parallax Alpha*. She didn't sound too whacko on the phone, thank god.

Grable loomed at the terminus of a long gravel lane. Massive and Victorian, the institution had been freshly updated in tones of green and brown. The grounds were hemmed by a fieldstone wall and a spiral maze of orchards, parks and vacant farmland. I'd picked a poor time of year to visit; everything was dead and moldering.

The staff oozed courtesy; it catered to a universally wealthy and powerful clientele. I might've looked like a schlep, nonetheless, far safer to kiss each and every ass that walked through the door. An androgynous receptionist processed my information, loaned me a visitor's tag and an escort named Hugo. Hugo deposited me in a cozy antechamber decorated with matching wicker chairs, an antique vase, prints of Mount Rainier and Puget Sound, and a worn Persian rug. The prints were remarkably cheap and crappy, in my humble opinion. Although, I was far from an art critic. I favored statues over paintings any day. I twiddled my thumbs and pondered how the miracle of electroshock therapy had been replaced by cable television and self-help manuals. The wicker chair put a crick in my neck, so I paced.

Mrs. Chin sauntered in, dressed in a superfluous baby-blue sports bra with matching headband and chromatic spandex pants. Her face gleamed, stiff as a native death mask; her rangy frame reminded me of an adolescent mummy without the wrapper. I read in *US* that she turned forty-five in the spring; her orange skin was speckled with plum-dark liver spots that formed clusters and constellations. She tested the air with predatory tongue-flicks. "Mr. Cortez, you are the most magnificently ugly man I have seen since papa had our gardener deported to Argentina. Let me tell you what a shame that was."

"Hey, the light isn't doing you any favors either, lady," I said.

She went into her suite, left the door ajar. "Tea?" She rummaged through kitchen drawers. A faucet gurgled and then a microwave hummed.

"No thanks." I glanced around. It was similar to the antechamber, except more furniture and artwork—she liked O'Keefe and Bosch. There were numerous oil paintings I didn't recognize; anonymous nature photographs, a Mayan calendar, and a smattering of southwestern pottery. She had a nice view of the grounds. Joggers trundled cobble paths; a peacock fan of pastel umbrellas cluttered the commons. The place definitely appeared more an English country club than a hospital. "Great digs, Mrs. Chin. I'm surprised they let you committed types handle sharp objects." I stood near a mahogany rolltop and played with a curved ceremonial knife that doubled as a paperweight.

"I'm rich. I do whatever I want." She returned with cups and a Tupperware dish of steaming water. "This isn't a prison, you know. Sit."

I sat across from her at a small table with a centerpiece of wilted geraniums and a fruit bowl containing a single overripe pear. A fat bluebottle fly crept about the weeping flesh of the pear.

Mrs. Chin crumbled green tea into china cups, added hot water, then honey from a stick with an expert motion, and leaned back without touching hers. "Hemorrhoids, Mr. Cortez?"

"Excuse me?"

"You look uncomfortable."

"Uh, back trouble. Aches and pains galore from a misspent youth."

"Try shark cartilage. It's all the rage. I have a taste every day."

"Nummy. I'll pass. New Age health regimens don't grab me."

"Sharks grow new teeth." Mrs. Chin said. "Replacements. Teeth are a problem for humans—dentistry helps, but if an otherwise healthy man has them all removed, say because of thin enamel, he loses a decade, perhaps more. The jaw shortens, the mouth cavity shrinks, the brain is fooled. A general shutdown begins to occur. How much happier our lives would be, with the shark's simple restorative capability." This spooled from her tongue like an infomercial clip.

"Wow." I gave her an indulgent smile, took a cautious sip of tea. "You didn't slip any in here, did you?"

"No, my stash is far too expensive to waste on the likes of you, Mr. Cortez. Delightful name—are you a ruthless, modern day conqueror? Did you come to ravish my secrets from me?"

"I'm a self-serving sonofabitch if that counts for anything. I don't even speak Spanish. English will get you by in most places, and that's good enough for me. What secrets?"

"I'm a sex addict."

"Now that's not exactly a secret, is it?" It wasn't. Her exploits were legendary among the worldwide underground, as I had learned. She was fortunate to be alive. "How do they treat that, anyway?"

"Pills, buckets of pills. Diversion therapy. They replace negative things with positive things. They watch me—there are cameras everywhere in this building. Does the treatment work?" Here she winked theatrically. "I am permitted to exercise whenever I please. I love to exercise—endorphins keep me going."

"Sad stuff. Tell me about *Parallax Alpha*." I produced a notebook, uncapped a pen.

"Are you so confident that I will?" She said, amused.

"You're a lonely woman, I've a sympathetic ear. Consider it free counseling."

"Pretty. Very pretty. Papa had to sell a few of my things, balance the books. Did you acquire the photograph?"

"A friend of mine. He wants me to find out more about it."

"You should tell your friend to go to hell."

"Really."

"Really." She picked up the pear, brushed the fly off, took a large bite. Juice glistened in her teeth, dripped from her chin. She dabbed it with a napkin. Very ladylike. "You don't have money, Mr. Cortez."

"I'm a pauper, it is true."

"Your friend has many uses for a man like you, I'm sure. Well, the history of the *Imago Sequence* is chock full of awful things befalling rich people. Does that interest you?"

"I'm not overly fond of the upper class. This is a favor."

"A big favor." Mrs. Chin took another huge bite, to accent the point. The lump traveled slowly down her throat—a pig disappearing into an anaconda. "I purchased *Parallax Alpha* on a lark at a seedy auction house in Mexico City. That was years ago; my husband was on his last legs—emphysema. The cigarette companies are making a killing in China. I was bored; a worldly stranger invited me to tour the galleries, take in a party. I didn't speak Spanish either, but my date knew the brokers, landed me a fair deal. The joke was on me, of course. My escort was a man named Anselm Thornton. Later, I learned of his connection to the series. You are aware that he owns the other two in the collection?"

"I am."

"They're bait. That's why he loans them to galleries, encourages people with lots of friends to buy them and put them on display."

"Bait?"

"Yes, bait. The photographs radiate a certain allure; they draw people like flies. He's always hunting for the sweetmeats." She chuckled ruefully. "I was sweet, but not quite sweet enough to end up in the fold. *Alpha* was mine, though. Not much later, I viewed *Beta*. By then the reaction, whatever it was, had started inside me, was consuming me, altering me in ways I could scarcely dream. I craved more. God, how I begged to see *Imago*! Anselm laughed—laughed, Mr. Cortez. He laughed and said that it was too early in the game for me to reintegrate. He also told me there's no *Imago*. No *Imago*, no El Dorado, no Santa Claus." Her eyes were hard and yellow. "The bastard was lying, though. *Imago* exists, perhaps not as a photograph. But it exists."

"Reintegrate with what, Mrs. Chin?"

"He wouldn't elaborate. He said, 'We are born, we absorb, we are absorbed. Therein lies the function of all sentient beings.' It's a mantra of his. Anselm held that thought doesn't originate in the mind. Our brains are rather like meaty receivers. Isn't that a wild concept? Humans as nothing more than complicated sensors, or mayhap walking sponges. Such is the path to ultimate, libertine anarchy. And one might as well live it up, because there is no escape from the cycle, no circumvention of the ultimate, messy conclusion; in fact, it's already happened a trillion times over. The glacier is coming and no power will hold it in abeyance."

I didn't bother writing any of that down; I was plenty spooked before she came across with that booby-hatch monologue. I said, "It sounds like extremely convenient rationale for psychopathic behavior. He dumped you after your romp?"

"Frankly, I'm a lucky girl. Anselm deemed me more useful at large, spreading his influence. I brought *Parallax Alpha* stateside—that was the bargain, my part in the grand drama. Life went on."

"You got together in Mexico?"

"Yes. The resort threw a ball, a singles event, and Roy Fulcher made the introductions. Fulcher was a radical, a former chemist—Caltech, I believe. Struck me as a naturalist gone feral. A little bird informed me the CIA had him under surveillance—he seemed primed to blow something up, maybe spike a city reservoir. At the outset I suspected Fulcher was approaching me about funding for some leftist cause. People warned me about him. Not that I needed their advice. I had oodles of card-carrying revolutionaries buzzing in my hair at the time. Soon, I absolutely abhorred the notion of traveling in Latin America. Fuck the guerillas, fuck the republic, I just want a margarita. Fulcher wasn't after cash, though. He was Anselm's closest friend. A disciple."

"Disciple, gotcha." I scribbled it in my trusty notebook. "What's Thornton call his philosophy? Cultist Christianity? Rogue Buddhism? Crystal worship? What's he into?"

She smiled, stretched, and tossed the remains of her fruit in a waste basket shaped like an elephant foot. "Anselm's into pleasure. I think it fair to designate him the reigning king of sybarites. I was moderately wicked when I met him. He finished me off. Go mucking about his business and he'll do for you too."

"Right. He's Satan, then. How did he ruin you, Mrs. Chin? Did he hook you on drugs, sex, or both?"

Her smile withered. "Satan may not exist, but Anselm surely does. Drugs were never the issue. I could always take them or leave them, and it's more profound than sex. I speak of a different thing entirely. There exists a quality of corruption you would not be familiar with—not on the level or to the degree that I have seen, have lived." She stopped, studied me. Her yellow eyes brightened. "Or, I'm mistaken. Did you enjoy it? Did you enjoy looking at *Parallax Alpha*? That's the first sign. It's a special person who does; the kind Anselm drools over."

"No, Mrs. Chin. I think it sucks."

"It frightened you. Poor baby. And why not? There are things to be frightened of in that picture. Enlightenment isn't necessarily a clean process. Enlightenment can be filthy, degenerate, dangerous. Enlightenment is its own reward, its own punishment. You begin to see so much more. And so much more sees you."

I said, "I take it this was in the late '80s, when you met Thornton? Rumor has it he's a hermit. Not much of a high-society player. Yet you say he was in Mexico, doing the playboy shtick."

"Even trapdoor spiders emerge from their lairs. Anselm travels in circles that will not publicize his movements."

"How would I go about contacting him? Maybe get things from the horse's mouth."

"We're not in touch. But those who wish to find him...find him. Be certain you wish to find him, Mr. Cortez."

"Okay. What about Fulcher? Do you know where he is?"

"Oh, ick. Creepy fellow. I pretended he didn't exist, I'm afraid."

"Thanks for your time, Mrs. Chin. And the tea." I started to rise.

"No more questions?"

"I'm fresh out, Mrs. Chin."

"Wait, if you please. There's a final item I'd like to show you." She went away and returned with a slim photo album. She pushed it across the table and watched me with a lizard smile to match her lizard eyes. "Can I trust you, Mr. Cortez?"

I shrugged.

She spoke softly. "The staff censors my mail, examines my belongings. There are periodic inspections. Backsliding will not be tolerated. They don't know about these. These are of my vacation in Mexico; a present from Anselm. Fulcher took them from the rafters of the cathedral. Go on, open it."

I did. There weren't many photos and I had to study them closely because each was a section of a larger whole. The cathedral must've been huge; an ancient vault lit by torches and lanterns. Obviously Fulcher had taken pains to get the sequence right—Mrs. Chin instructed me to remove eight of them from the protective plastic, place them in order on the table. An image took root and unfolded. A strange carpet, stained rose and peach, spread across shadowy counterchange tiles, snaked around immense gothic pillars and statuary. The carpet gleamed and blurred in patches, as if it were a living thing.

"That's me right about there," Mrs. Chin tapped the third photo from the top. "Thrilling, to enact the writhing of the Ouroboros!"

"Jesus Christ," I muttered. At least a thousand people coupled upon the cathedral floor. A great, quaking mass of oiled flesh, immortalized by Fulcher's lens. "Why did you show me this?" I looked away from the pictures and caught her smile, cruel as barbed wire. There was my answer. The institution was powerless to eradicate *all* of her pleasures.

"Goodbye, Mr. Cortez. Goodbye, now."

Leaving, I noticed another overripe pear in the fruit bowl, as if Mrs. Chin had replaced it by sleight of hand. A fly sat atop, rubbing its legs together, wearing my image in its prism eyes.

I wasn't feeling well.

I awoke at 2 A.M., slick and trembling, from yet another nightmare. My head roared with blood. I rose, trying to avoid disturbing Carol, who slept with her arm shielding her eyes, my dog-eared copy of *The Prince* clutched in her fingers. I staggered into the kitchen for a handful of aspirin and a glass of cold milk. There was a beer left over from dinner, so I drank that too. It was while standing there, washed in the unearthly radiance of the refrigerator light, that I realized the orgy in Mrs. Chin's photographs had been orchestrated to achieve a specific configuration. The monumental daisy chain made a nearly perfect double helix.

4.

In the middle of January I decided to cruise down to San Francisco and spend a weekend beating the bushes.

I met Jacob for early dinner on the waterfront at an upscale grille called The Marlin. Back in the day, Teddy treated us there when he was being especially avuncular, although he had preferred to hang around the yacht club or fly to Seattle where his cronies played. Jacob handed me the Weston Gallery's business card and a roll of cash for expenses. We didn't discuss figures for Thornton's successful interrogation. The envelope would be fat and the goodwill of a wealthy, bored man would continue to flow freely. Nor did he question my sudden eagerness to locate the hermit art collector. Still, he must have noticed the damage to my appearance that suggested worse than a simple New Year's bender.

Following dinner, I drove out in the country to a farmhouse near Yelm for tequila and cigars with Earl Hutchinson, a buddy of mine since high school. He'd been a small, tough kid from Iowa; a so-called bad seed. He looked the part: slicked hair, switchblade in his sock, a cigarette behind his ear, a way of standing that suggested trouble. Hutch hadn't changed, only drank a little more and got harder around the eyes.

We relaxed on the porch; it was a decent night with icy stars sprinkled among the gaps. Hutch was an entrepreneur; while I was away in college he hooked up in the arms trade—he'd served as an artillery specialist in the Army, forged connections within the underbelly of America's war machine. He amassed an impressive stockpile before the anti-assault weapon laws put the kibosh on legal sales; there were dozens of AK-47s, M16s and Uzis buried in the pasture behind his house. I'd helped him dig.

These days it was guard dogs. He trained shepherds for security, did a comfortable business with local companies. I noticed his kennels were empty except for a brood bitch named Gerta and some pups. Hutch said demand was brisk, what with the rise of terrorism and the sagging economy. Burglaries always spiked during recessions. Eventually the conversation swung around to my California trip. He walked into the house, came out with a .357 and a box of shells. I peeled four hundred bucks from my brand new roll, watched him press the bills into his shirt pocket. Hutch poured more tequila and we finished our cigars, reminiscing about happy times. Lied about shit, mainly.

I went home and packed a suitcase from college, bringing the essentials—winter clothes, pain pills, toiletries. I watered the plants and left a terse message on Carol's answering service. She'd flown to Spokane to visit her mother. She generally found a good reason to bug out for the high country when I got piss-drunk and prowled the apartment like a bear with a toothache.

I told her I'd be gone for a few days, feed the fish. Then I headed south.

The truth is, I volunteered for the California job to see the rest of the *Imago Sequence*. As if viewing the first had not done ample harm. In addition to solving Teddy's vanishing act, I meant to ask Thornton some questions of my own.

I attempted to drive through the night. Tough sledding—my back knotted from hunching behind the wheel. A dose of Vicodin had no effect. I needed sleep. Unfortunately, the prospect of dreaming scared the hell out of me.

I drove as long as my nerve held. Not fast, but methodically as a nail sinking into heartwood, popping Yellowjackets and blasting the radio. In the end the pain beat me down. I took a short detour on a dirt road and rented a motel room south of Redding. I tried to catch a couple hours of rest. It was a ter-rible idea.

Parallax Alpha ate its way into my dreams again.

The motel ceiling jiggled, tapioca pudding with stars revolving in its depths. The blackened figure at *Parallax Alpha*'s center seeped forth. I opened my mouth, but my mouth was already a rictus. The ceiling swallowed me, bones and all.

—*I squatted in a cavernous vault, chilled despite the rank, humid darkness pressing my flesh. Stench burrowed into my nose and throat. Maggots, green meat, rotten bone. Thick, sloppy noises, as wet rope smacking rock drew closer. A cow gave birth, an eruption. The calf mewled—blind, terrified. Old, old water dripped. An army of roaches began to march; a battalion of worms plowed into a mountain of offal; the frenetic drone of flies in glass; an embryonic bulk uncoiling in its cyst—*

I awakened, muscles twitching in metronome to the shuttering numbers of the radio clock. Since Christmas my longest stretch of uninterrupted sleep was three hours and change. I almost relished the notion of a grapeshot tumor gestating in my brain as the source of all that was evil. It didn't wash; too easy. So said my puckered balls, the bunched hackles of my neck. Paleontologists, anthropologists, ordained priests, or who-the-hell-ever could debate the au-thenticity of Ammon's handiwork until the cows came home. My clenched guts and arrhythmic heart harbored no doubt that he had snapped a photo of someone or something truly unpleasant. Worse, I couldn't shake the feel-ing that Mrs. Chin was correct: it had looked right back at me. It was looking for me now.

I got on the road; left a red fantail of dust hanging.

Midmorning crawled over the Frisco skyline, gin blossom clouds piling upon the bay. I drove to the address on the card, a homely warehouse across from a

Mexican restaurant and a mortgage office that had been victimized by graffiti artists, and parked in the alley. Inside the warehouse were glass walls and blue shadows broken by giant ferns.

I lifted a brochure from a kiosk in the foyer; a slick, multicolored pamphlet with headshots of the director and his chief cronies. I slipped it into my blazer pocket and forged ahead. The lady behind the front desk wore a prison-orange jumpsuit. Her hair was pulled back so tightly it forced her to smile when she shook my hand. I asked for Director Stanley Renfro and was informed that Mr. Renfro was on vacation.

Could I please speak to the acting director? She motioned me beyond shadowbox panels to the rear of the gallery where a crew of Hispanic and Vietnamese day laborers sweated to dismantle an installation of a scale city park complete with fiberglass fruit trees, benches and a working gothic fountain. I picked my way across the mess of tarps, coax and sawdust. Motes hung in the too-bright wash of stage lights. A Teutonic symphony shrilled counterpoint to arc welders.

Acting director Clarke was a lanky man with a spade-shaped face. A serious whitebread bastard with no interest in fielding questions about Thornton or his photograph. Clarke was sated with the power rush of his new executive position; I sensed I wouldn't be able to slip him a few bills to grease the rails and I'd already decided to save breaking his head as a last resort.

I used charm, opening with a throwaway remark about the genius of Maurice Ammon.

Clarke gave my haggard, sloppy self the once-over. "Ammon was a hack." His eyes slightly crossed and he talked like a man punching typewriter keys. "Topless native women suckling their babies; bone-through-the-nose savages leaning on spears. Tourist swill. His specialty."

"Yeah? Don't tell me the Weston Gallery is in the business of showcasing hacks?"

"We feature only the highest-caliber work." Clarke paused to drone pidgin Spanish at one of the laborers. When he looked up at me again his sneer hardened. "I dislike the *Imago Sequence*. But one cannot deny its…resonance. Ammon got lucky. Doesn't overcome a portfolio of mediocrity."

No, he didn't like the series at all. I read that plainly from the brief bulge of his eyes similar to a horse getting a whiff of smoke for the first time. The reaction seemed reasonable. "A three-hit wonder." I tried to sound amiable.

It was wasted. "Are you a cop, Mr. Cortez?"

"What, I look like a cop to you?"

"Most citizens don't have so many busted knuckles. A private eye, then."

"I'm a tourist. Do you think Ammon actually photographed a fossilized cave man?"

"That's absurd. The so-called figures are geological formations. Ask the experts."

"Wish I had nothing else to do with my life. You don't buy it, eh?"

"The hominid theory is titillation." He smirked. "It does sell tickets."

"He got bored with native titties and went for abstract art? Sure looks like a troglodyte to me."

"Well, pardon my saying you don't know squat about photography and I think you're here on bad business. Did the toad send you?"

I chuckled. "You've met Teddy."

"Never had the pleasure. I saw him in September, sniffing around the photo, practically wetting his pants. Figured he was trying to collect the set. I'll tell *you* exactly what Renfro told *him*: *Parallax Beta* is not for sale and its owner is not interested in discussing the matter."

"Renfro said that to Teddy, did he? Seems I'm chasing my tail then." He had said what I hoped to hear. "By the way, where did Mr. Renfro go for his vacation? Somewhere warm, I hope."

Clarke's sneer broadened. "He's on sabbatical." From the pleasure in his tone he did not expect his former patron to return.

"Well, thanks for your time."

"Adios, Mr. Cortez. Since you came for a peek at *Parallax Beta*, stop by the Natural History display."

"Blessings to you and your children, Herr Director." I went where he pointed, trying to act casual. The prospect of viewing the second photograph filled me with elation and dread. There it was, hanging between the Grand Tetons and the caldera of slumbering Mt. Saint Helens.

Parallax Beta was the same photograph as *Alpha*, magnified tenfold. The amber background had acquired a coarser quality, its attendant clots and scars were more distinct, yet more distinctly ambiguous. They congealed to form asteroid belts, bell-shaped celestial gases, volcanic moons. The hominid's howling mouth encompassed the majority of the picture. It seemed capable of biting off my head, of blasting my eardrums with its guttural scream.

My vision tunneled and I tore myself away with the convulsive reflex of a man awakened from a dream of falling. *Panpipes, clashing cymbals, strobes of meteoric rain. Dogs snarling, a bleating goat. Buzzing flies, worms snuggling in musty soil.* All faded as I lurched away, routed from the field.

I made it to the lobby and drank from the water fountain, splashing my face until the floor stopped tilting. The lady in the jumpsuit perched behind her desk, vulture-talons poised near the phone. She extended another wintry smile as I retreated from the building into the hard white glare.

Eleven A.M. and next to zero accomplished, which meant I was basically on schedule. I was an amateur kneecap man, not a PI. My local connections were limited to a bookie, a sports agent who might or might not be under indictment for money laundering, and the owner of a modest chain of gymnasiums. I adjourned to a biker grille called the Hog and downed several weak Bloody Marys with a basket of deep-fried oysters. The lunch crowd consisted of two leathery old timers sipping draft beer, their Harley Davidson knockoffs parked on the curb; a brutish man in a wife beater t-shirt at the bar doing his taxes on a short form; and the bartender who had so much pomade in his hair it gleamed like a steel helmet. The geriatric bikers were sniping over the big NFC championship game coming up between the Niners and the Cowboys.

Between drinks, I borrowed the bartender's ratty phonebook. Half the pages were ripped out, but I found a listing for S. Renfro, which improved my mood for about three seconds. I tried ringing him from the payphone next to the men's room. A recorded message declared that the number was not in service, please try again. Following Hog tradition, I tore out the page and saved it for later.

I called Jacob collect. After he accepted charges, I said, "Were you around Teddy before he disappeared?"

"Eh? We've been over this."

"Be nice, I'm slow."

Several static-laden beats passed. Then, "Um, not so much. Teddy's always been secretive, though."

"Okay, was he *more* or *less* secretive those last few weeks?"

He coughed in a phlegmy way that suggested I had prodded him from the slumber of the indolent rich. "I don't know, Marv. I got used to him sneaking around. What's going on?"

"I haven't figured that out yet. Did his habits change? And I mean even an iota."

"No—wait. He dressed oddly. Yeah. Well, more than usual, if you want to split hairs."

"I'm listening."

"Give me a sec…" Jacob cursed, knocked something off a shelf, cursed again. A metallic snick was followed by a scratchy drag into the receiver. "He wore winter clothes a lot at the end. Inside, too, the few times I saw him. You know—sock cap, mackinaw and boots. He looked like a Canadian longshoreman. Said he was cold. But, what's that? Teddy dressed for safari half the time. He was eccentric."

"Thin blood. Too many years in the tropics," I said.

"You have anything yet?"

"Nope. I'm just trying to cover all the bases." I wondered if dear, departed Theodore had suffered night sweats, if he had ever lain in bed staring at a maw of darkness that grinned toothless as a sphincter. I wondered if Jacob did.

Jacob said, "You don't think he was mixing with a rough element, right?"

"Probably not. He was going batty, fell into the drink. Stuff like this happens to seniors. They find them wandering around race tracks or shopping malls. Happens every day."

"Keep digging anyway."

"I'll hit you back when I find more. Bye, bye." I broke the connection, rubbed sweat from my cheek. I needed a shave.

The last call was to my bookie friend. I took the Cowboys and the points because I hoped to counter the growing sense of inevitability hanging over my head like Damocles' least favorite pig sticker. Come Sunday night I owed the bookie fifteen hundred bucks.

5.

Stanley Renfro's house drank the late afternoon glow. Far from imposing; simply one of many brick and timber colonials bunkered in the surrounding hills. It was painted in conservative tones and set back from the street, windows blank. A blue sedan was parked in the drive, splattered with enough seagull shit to make me suspect it hadn't moved lately. Half a dozen rolled newspapers decomposed on the shaggy lawn. The grass was shin-high and climbing.

I did not want to walk up the block and enter that house.

My belly churned with indigestion. A scream had recently interrupted my fitful doze. This scream devolved into the dwindling complaints of a bus horn. Minutes later when the sodium lamps caught fire and Renfro's house remained black, I decided he was dead.

This leap of intuition could not be proved by yellow papers or flourishing weeds. *Nah, the illustrious director might be taking a nap. No need to turn the lights on. Maybe he's not even inside. Maybe he's in Borneo stealing objets d'art from the natives. He left his car because a crony gave him a lift to the airport. He forgot to cancel the newspaper. Somebody else forgot to cut the grass.* Sure. The house reminded me of a corpse that hadn't quite begun to fester. I retrieved a flashlight from the glove compartment. Thick, and made of steel, like cops use. It felt nice in my hand.

I climbed from the Chrysler, leaned against the frame until my neck loosened and I could rotate my head without catching a fireworks show. No one appeared to notice when I hiked through Renfro's yard, although a small dog barked nearby. The alarm system was cake—being predicated on pressure, all I needed to do was smash a kitchen window and climb through without disturbing the frame. This turned out to be unnecessary. The power was down and the alarm's emergency battery had died.

The kitchen smelled foul despite its antiseptic appearance. Street light spread my shadow into monstrous proportions. Water drooled around the base of the refrigerator. Distant traffic vibrated china in its cabinet. Everything reeked of mildew and decaying fruit.

I clicked on the flashlight as I proceeded deeper into the house. The ceilings were low. I determined within a few steps that the man was a bachelor. That relieved me. Beyond the kitchen, a narrow hall of dusky paneling absorbed my light beam. The décor was not extraordinary considering it belonged to the director of an art gallery—obscure oil paintings, antique vases and ceramic sculptures. Undoubtedly the truly expensive bric-a-brac was stashed in a safe or strong room. I didn't care about that; I was hunting for a name, a name certain to be scribbled in Renfro's personal files.

The shipwrecked living room was a blow to my composure. However, even before I entered that demolished area, my wind was up. I felt as a man tiptoeing through a diorama blown to life-size. As if the outer reaches of the house were a façade that had not quite encompassed the yard.

Mr. Renfro had been on a working vacation, by the evidence. Mounds of wet dirt were heaped around a crater. Uprooted boards lay in haphazard stacks. Sawed joists gleamed like exposed ribs. The pit was deep and ugly—a cavity. I turned away and released a sluice of vodka, tomato juice and oyster chunks. Purged, I felt better than I had in days.

I skirted the destruction, mounted the stairs to the second floor. Naked footprints scarred the carpet, merging into a muddy path—the trail a beast might pound with its blundering mass. If Renfro made the prints, I figured him for around 6', 240. Not quite in my league, but hefty enough that I was happy to grip the sturdy flashlight. A metal bucket was discarded on the landing. Inside the upper bathroom, the clawfoot tub had cracked, overflowing dirt and nails. The sink was shattered. Symbols had been scrawled above the toilet with mud, but the flowery paper hung in shreds. I deciphered the letters MAG and MMON. A cockroach clambered up the wall, fell, started again. Its giant, horned silhouette crossed mine. I didn't linger.

I peeked in the master bedroom to be thorough. It too was victim of hurricane savagery. The bed was stripped, sheets wadded on the floor amid drifts of clothes. A set of designer luggage had barely survived; buckles and zippers sprung, meticulously packed articles disgorged like intestines. I got the distinct impression Renfro had planned a trip before whatever happened, happened.

Renfro had converted the spare bedroom to an office. Here were toppled oak file cabinets, contents strewn and stomped. My prize was a semi-collapsed desk, buried in a landslide of paper. Its sides bore gouges and impact marks. Thankfully Renfro hadn't filled this room with dirt. I searched for his Rolodex amid the chaos, keeping an eye on the door. The house was empty, obviously the house was empty. Renfro wasn't likely to be lurking in a closet. He wasn't likely to come shambling into the office, caked with mud and blood and fondling a hatchet. I still kept an eye on the door.

A drawer contained more file hangers. Inside the R-T folder was an index card with A. THORNTON (*Imago Colony*) written in precise block letters, a Purdon address which was probably a drop box, a list of names that meant nothing to me, and an unmarked cassette tape. Actually the label had been smudged. I stuck the card and the tape in my pocket. On impulse I checked the Ws and found a listing for T. WILSON. *Parallax Alpha* was penned in the margin. Below that, in fresher ink—*Provender?*

Mission accomplished, I was eager to saddle up and get the hell out of Tombstone. Then my light illuminated the edge of a wrinkled photograph of Stanford lacrosse players assembled on a field. A dated shot, but I recognized a younger Renfro from the brochure in my pocket. He knelt front and center, sporting a permed Afro and a butterfly collar. His eyes and mouth were holes. They reminded me of how Teddy's mouth looked in his war pictures. They also reminded me of the pit Renfro had excavated in his living room. Behind the team, where campus buildings should logically be, reared the basalt ridge of a mountain. A flinty spine wreathed by primordial steam.

This was Teddy's photo collection redux. And there were more delights. I considered vomiting again.

I stared for a bit, turning the photo this way and that. Concentration was difficult, because my fingers shook. I sorted the papers again, including the pile on the floor, examining the various photographs and postcards that were salted through the general mess. Some framed, some not. Wallet-sized, to the kind grandma hangs above the mantle. This time I actually *looked* and beheld a pattern that my subconscious had recognized already. Each picture was warped, each was distorted. Each was a fake, a fabrication designed to unnerve the viewer. What other purpose could they serve?

I checked for splice marks, hints of computer grafting, as if my untrained eye could've helped. Nothing to explain the mechanics of the hoax. The terrain was wrong in all of these. Very wrong. The sky was not quite the same sky we walked around under every day. No, the sky in the more peculiar photos appeared somewhat viscous with bubbles and spot discoloration—the sky was a solid. As a matter of fact, it kind of resembled amber. Shapes that might've been blimps hovered at the periphery, pressed against the fabric of the sky.

This was enough spooky bullshit for me. I beat feet.

Downstairs, I hesitated at the pit. I shined my lonely beam into the gloom. It was about twelve feet deep; the sides crumbled and seeped groundwater. A nasty thought had been ticking in my brain. *Where is Renfro? In the hole, of course.*

Which suggested he was hiding—*or lying in wait.* I didn't actually want to find him either way. Thornton's information was in my pocket. Assuming it panned out, there were many hours of driving ahead. But the nasty thought was ticking louder, getting closer. *Why is Renfro digging a hole under his very nice house? Wow, I wonder if it's related to his screwed up picture collection? And, oh, do you think it has anything to do with a certain photograph on loan to his precious gallery? Do you suppose he spent long, long hours in front of that picture, fixated, neglecting his duties until his people sent him on a little vacation? Don't call us, we'll call you.*

There was a lot of debris at the bottom of that hole. A lot of debris and the light was dimming as its batteries gave up the ghost and I couldn't be one hundred percent sure, but I glimpsed an earthen lump down there, right where the darkness thickened. A man-sized lump. At its head was a damp depression in which a small object glinted. When I hit it with the light, it flickered. Blinked, blinked.

6.

I wanted to turn around and bolt for home, get back to my beer and cartoons. I headed for Purdon instead. A Mastodon sinking in a tar pit.

Purdon was a failed mill town several hours northeast of San Francisco—victim of the rise of environmentalism in the latter '90s. A mountainous region bracketed by a national park and a reservation. Rural and impoverished as all hell. Plenty of pot plantations, militia compounds and dead mining camps; all of it crisscrossed with a few thousand miles of logging roads slowly being eaten by forest. An easy place to vanish from the planet.

My mind had been switched off for the last hundred miles.

I switched it off because I was tired of thinking about the events at Renfro's house. Tired of considering the implications. It occurred to me, not for the first time, that I had fallen down the rabbit hole and would awaken at any moment. Unfortunately, I had brought a couple of the suspect photos and they remained steadfastly bizarre. Combined with Teddy's, did this not suggest a supernatural force at work?

Thoughts like that are why I shut my mind off.

Better to stick with problems at hand. Problems such as motoring into the sticks looking for a man I had seen in ancient clippings and a jerky movie frame shot three decades prior. A man who was probably a certifiable lunatic if he had owned the *Imago Sequence* for so many years. Whether he might know the whereabouts of a petrified hominid, or the truth about the disappearance of a thoroughly modern human, no longer seemed important. The only matter of importance was finding a way to kill the nightmares. And if Thornton couldn't help me? Best not to scrutinize that possibility too closely. I could almost taste the cold, oily barrel of my revolver.

I played Renfro's tape. The recording was damaged—portions were garbled, others were missing entirely, comprised of clicking and deep sea warbles. The intelligible segments featured a male lecturer. "—*satiation is the natural inclination. One is likely to spend centuries glutting primitive appetites, wreaking havoc on enemies, and so forth. What then? That depends on the personality. Few would seek the godhead, I think. Such a pursuit would require tremendous imagination, determination…resources. Provender would be an issue. It is difficult to conceive the acquisition of so much ripe flesh. No, the majority will be content with leisurely hedonism—*"

The Chrysler groaned as it climbed. Night paled and the rain slackened into gray drizzle. Big hills, big trees, everything dripping and foggy. Signs grew sparse and the road fell apart. I had to pay attention lest my car be hurled into a ravine.

"—*consumption of accelerated brainmatter being one proven catalyst. Immersion in a protyle sink is significantly more efficacious, albeit infinitely more perilous. Best avoided.*" Laughter. The recording petered to static.

I reached Purdon in time for church. Instead, I filled my tank at the Union 76 next to the defunct lumber mill, washed and changed clothes in the cramped bathroom. At the liquor store I bought a bottle of cheap whiskey. Here was my indemnity from coming nightmares. Then I ate a huge breakfast at the Hardpan

Café. The waitress, who might also have been the proprietor, was a shrewd-eyed Russian. There were a lot of Russian immigrants in the area, I discovered. She didn't care for my looks, but she kept my coffee cup level and her thoughts to herself while I stared out the window and plotted my next move.

Not much to see—narrow streets crowded with warped 1920s salt box houses. FOR LEASE signs plastered dark windows. A few people, mostly hung-over men, prowled the sidewalks. Everybody appeared to wear flannel and drive dented pickups. Most of the trucks had full gun racks.

I asked the Russian woman about finding a room and was directed to the Pine Valley Motel, which was less lovely than it sounded—unless you were thinking pine box, and then, yeah, that was more accurate, in an esthetic sense. The motel sprawled in a gravel lot at the edge of town, northernmost wing gutted by a recent fire and draped with rust-stained tarps. Mine was the sole car parked in front.

A stoic senior citizen missing two fingers of his right hand took my money and produced the key. His stained ballcap read: PURDON MILL—AN AMERI-CAN COMPANY! For fun, I asked if he knew anything about Anselm Thornton or the Imago Colony and received a glassy stare as he honked his nose into a handkerchief.

The walls of No. 32 were balsa-thin and the bed creaked ominously, but I didn't see any cockroaches. I counted myself lucky as I cracked the seal on the whiskey. I made it to within a pinky of the bottom before the curtain dropped.

Ants.

I shared a picnic with a woman who was the composite of several women, all of them attractive, all of them wanton yet motherly, like the new Betty Crocker. She spoke words that held no weight and so fluttered away on the breeze with a vapor trail of pollen. Our feast was laid upon the requisite checkerboard blanket beneath a flowering tree with the grass and the sun and all that. With all that and the chirping birds and the painfully blue sky and the goddamned ants; I didn't notice the ants until the woman held a slice of bread to my lips and as I opened my mouth to accept the bread I saw an ant trapped in the honey. Too late, my mouth closed and I swallowed and I looked down and beheld them everywhere upon the checker cloth, these ants. Formicating. I rose up, a behemoth enraged, and trampled them in shallow puffs of dust. They died in their numbers, complaining in small voices as their works were conculcated—their wagon trains and caravans, their miniature Hippodromes and coliseums, their monuments and toy superstructures, all crashed, all toppled, all ablaze. I threw my head back to bellow curses and noticed the sun had become a pinhole. The hole openedopendopened—

Open.

I stared at the ceiling and realized that I now slept with my eyes wide and glazed. Marbles, the last of my marbles.

Shadows flowed swiftly along the decrepit wallpaper of No. 32, shrinking from the muzzy glare of the sun as it wallowed behind clouds. The thermostat was set at body temperature and the room steamed. I didn't recall waking to do that. I had slept for eighteen hours. *Eighteen hours!* It was a bloody miracle! I dressed, avoiding the mirror.

There were various stratagems available, a couple of them clever. I wasn't feeling clever, though. In fact, my skull felt like a pot of mush.

I flashed a snapshot of Teddy at the locals, finally got a bite from the mechanic at the gas station. He remembered Teddy from the previous September—*Heavy guy, yeah; drivin' a foreign car, passin' through. North, I suppose, 'cause he asked where Little Egypt was. We get that a lot. Tourists want to fool around the mines. Ain't shit-all left, though. I checked his brakes—these roads are hell on brakes. He paid cash.*

No surprises, the jigsaw was taking its form.

I measured the dwindling girth of my money clip and dealt a portion of it to Rod, the pimply badger of a clerk at the post office. It went down smoothly after I told him I was working for a family who believed their baby girl had joined a cult. Oh, this sweaty, mutton-chopped fellow became a regular Samaritan once the folding green was in his pocket. He came across with the goods—names and descriptions of the people who regularly accessed Thornton's box. He'd never seen Thornton, didn't know much about him and didn't want to. The Imago Colony? Zip. Thornton's group numbered about forty, although who knew?—what with tourist season and the influx of visitors come spring. They occupied mining claims somewhere on Little Egypt; kept to themselves. Mormons, or some shit. Weird folk, but nobody had heard about them causing trouble before. He let me look at a topographical map that showed Little Egypt was, in fact, a sizeable chunk of real estate. Thornton's camp could be any one of a dozen claims scattered throughout the area. I slipped him another fifty bucks to keep mum about our conversation.

Satisfied, I retreated to the Hardpan Café, which commanded an unobstructed view of the post office. I settled in to wait for my hippie friends to make the scene. The Russian lady was overjoyed.

Thornton's people arrived on Thursday. Two rough men dressed in greatcoats; they drove around town in a clanking two-ton truck with a canvas top. A military surplus vehicle capable of serious off-road travel. The U.S. Army star was mud-splattered.

I compared them to my list. One, a redhead, was a nobody. The other man was middling sized, with a dented forehead, pebbly eyes and a long beard that would've made Fidel Castro jealous. Roy Fulcher, larger and uglier than life. Still playing henchman to Thornton in the new century. Loyal as a dog; how sweet.

If any of the locals tipped the men that I had been asking about their operation, it was not evident. They nonchalantly gathered supplies while I lurked in the background. Toward evening Fulcher pointed the truck north and rumbled off with a load of dry goods, fuel, and mail. I trailed.

Eventually, the truck turned onto a gravel road. A bullet-raddled sign read: LITTLE EGYPT RD. The metal pole was bent nearly double, victim of unknown violence. Rough country here; patches of concrete-hard snow gleamed under scraggly trees. In a few miles gravel gave way to a mud track and the ruts were too deep for the Chrysler. I pulled over, shouldered a satchel I'd bought at the Purdon Thrifty Saver and started walking, carefully picking my way as twilight grew moss and the stars glittered like caltrops. As the air cooled, mist cloaked the branches and brambles.

The hills got steep fast, draining the strength from my legs. My back protested. I shook most of the bottle of aspirin into my mouth to stay on the safe side, and rested frequently. When the track forked, I shined my flashlight to orient on the freshest ruts. It wasn't difficult; it was like following a bulldozer up the mountain. I clicked the light off quickly, hoping to conceal my position, and continued trudging.

I checked my watch to gauge the mileage and discovered it had died at 6:32 P.M. Much later, my legs got too heavy and I slumped under a lonely pine. Clouds snuffed the stars.

7.

The gray light swam as it brightened; rocks and brush solidified all around. Two inches of snow dusted the landscape like the face of a corpse.

My back had seized up. It hurt in a profound way. *Like a bitch,* as my pop would've said. The aspirin was gone, the whiskey too. It seemed impossible that I would ever stand. But I rose, among a shower of black motes and silvery comets. Rose with the chuffing sob of a steer as it is goaded onto the gangway. Then I hugged my homely little tree, pissed on my boots and trembled with nausea. I needed a drink.

The road curved upward in a series of switchbacks. The snow disintegrated to brown sludge. I staggered along the shoulder, avoiding the quagmire. My feet got wet anyway. I clutched at exposed roots and outcroppings. A bird scolded me.

Cresting a saddle in the hills I gazed upon the flank of a mountain about a quarter mile off. Shacks were scattered beneath the crags—tin roofs bled orange tracks in the snow. The truck Fulcher had driven was parked alongside two battered jeeps near a Quonset hut. Wood smoke coiled above the camp, chugged forth from several stacks. A knot of muddy pigs huddled in a paddock. Nothing else moved.

My glance fell upon a trio of silhouetted formations farther along the mountainside; too far to discern clearly. Pylons? The instant I spotted them a whisper of unease urged me to look elsewhere. To flee, yes. I patted the bulk of the revolver in my pocket and the whispers died away.

I gulped air and wished I'd thought to bring field glasses for this expedition. Keeping to the brush, I swung a wide northwest circle. Drawing closer to the pylons it registered that about a dozen jutted randomly above the stony field. Crows danced atop them, squawking their hideous argot. An unpleasant sensation of primitive familiarity rooted me in my tracks. The objects were made of milled poles planted at angles like king-sized Xs, each twice the height of a man. Symbols were carved into them. Latin? The farthest structure had something caught at its apex—a bundle of rags.

"Marvin!"

I turned. A man in a billowing poncho strode from the direction of the camp. He waved and I waved back automatically. The brush must not have concealed me so well after all. He walked swiftly, a stop-motion figure on grainy film. The haze had a spaghetti-western effect—it made him taller and shorter by turns and cast his face in gloom.

"Mr. Thornton?" I said when he halted before me. God, he was tall. I was no midget and I had to crane my neck at him.

"Welcome to the Pleasure Dome. Glad you could make it. We seldom receive visitors during the winter season." He sounded British and wore an Australian-style drover's hat pulled low over jagged brows and scaly eyes. Potbellied and thick through the hips, yet gangly and muscular the way a well-fed raptor is muscular. His enormous hands hung loosely. A thin-lipped mouth threatened to bisect his broad, sallow face. Lots and lots of stained, crooked teeth were revealed by his huge smile. "It has you, I see. Ticktock go the mitochondria—a nova in bloom. Marvelous, marvelous."

I stared at him and decided he was far too spry for a fellow pushing seventy-five. His movements were quick and powerful. His doll-smooth flesh radiated youthful heat. "Who told you I was coming?" I suspected someone at the Weston Gallery had phoned with the news. Were there phones up here?

Thornton hesitated as if he actually meant to answer the question. "Come back to the house. The ground is unsafe."

"Unsafe, how?"

"Not all the shafts are properly sealed. Holes everywhere. Periodically someone disappears—they come poking around for souvenirs or gold and…well one misstep is all it takes. Teenagers, usually. Or tourists."

I nodded in idiot silence, grappling with my instincts—my mind was a cacophony of ghostly exhortations to rap this man's head while we were away from his presumed horde of disciples, to put him on his knees with the gun barrel under his jaw and pry loose the answers to a dozen pertinent questions. I recalled the lumpish shape at the bottom of Renfro's hole, how it shuddered and quaked, and my hand dipped into my pocket—

"How's Jacob, anyway?" Thornton had already turned his back. Maybe he was grinning. His dry, Victorian accent quavered up the register toward that of a crone's.

"Jacob." It seemed to be getting darker by the second in that desolate valley.

"The fellow who sent you to break my legs and whatnot. He misses his uncle.

Kidding, kidding. Do you miss Teddy? Does anyone? It would be decent."

"You know Jacob?"

"Not really. His uncle and I were friends, once. Teddy lived on the edge of my circle. I never gathered the impression he spoke of me to anyone…uninitiated. Jacob would not suit my purposes."

"I'm here to find out what happened to Teddy."

"Truly? I supposed you came because of the *Sequence*."

"See, I'm kind of stuck on the chicken or the egg theory. I'll take whatever I can get. So give."

"Teddy vanished. A boating accident, wasn't it?"

"After visiting you."

"Teddy was a big boy. Big enough for both of us. Remove your hand from the gun, Marvin. Harm me and you'll never get what you came for."

My lungs burned. "Harm you. There's no reason. Is there?"

"For some men, there is always a reason. It's what you do well, hurting. You're a terrier. I know everything about you, Marvin. I smell meanness cooking in your blood. The blood on your hands. I ask, do you want blood from me, or knowledge? Here is a crossroads."

"I want to know about the photographs. I need to understand what's happening to me." I said this simply, even humbly. I removed my hand from the revolver.

"It's not only happening to you. It's happening to everyone, everywhere. *You're* tuned in to the correct frequency, and therein lies the difference." Thornton twisted his oversized head to regard me without shifting his shoulders. His face was milky. A face of unwholesome flexibility; and yes, his grin fetched to mind sickles and horns. "Let's amble—we'll do lunch, we'll chat. I'll show you my gallery. It's an amazing gallery. I'll show you *Imago*. You'll enjoy it, Marvin. You'll sleep again. Sleep without nightmares." He was walking before he finished, beckoning with a casual twitch of his hand. His oilskin poncho slithered in his wake not unlike a tail.

I followed on wooden legs. Crows argued behind us.

The Quonset hut was so old its floor was a sunken mass of caramelized wood and dirt. An arch in the rear opened to darkness. Moth-eaten banners of curiously medieval design hung from the rafters, casting fluttery shadows upon the long table where I mechanically chewed a ham sandwich and drank a sour beer that Roy Fulcher had fetched. Thornton had departed, promising a swift return. He asked Fulcher to attend my needs.

Light oozed through window glass that sagged and pooled at the bottom of rotten frames. Crates made pyramids against the walls, alongside boxes, barrels and stacks of curling newspapers. Homey.

Fulcher watched me eat. His features were vulpine and his lank beard was stained yellow-brown around the mouth. He smelled ripe. Farther off, a group of fellow colonists played at a ping-pong table. They cast sly glances our way and chuckled with suppressed brutality. Four men, two women, ages indeterminate. They were scrawny, haggard and unwashed. Several more came and went, shuffling. Zombies but for a merry spark in their eyes, satisfied smirks.

I said, "Here's the million-dollar question—where's the caveman buried?"

"Caveman? I don't think there's a caveman." Fulcher's was an earthy accent, a nasal drawl that smacked of coal mines and tarpaper shanties.

"All this trouble and no caveman?"

"Sorry."

"It's okay. Jacob will get over it," I said. "I don't suppose you'll tell me where Ammon took the *Imago Sequence?* That won't hurt anything, if there's no caveman."

Fulcher leaned in. "Take a spoon and dig a hole in your chest. That's where he made his pictures."

I pushed my plate aside. I wiped my lips with a dingy cloth towel. I stared at him, long and steadily. I said, "If you won't talk about Ammon, tell me about your colony. Love what you've done with the place. What do you guys do for fun in these parts?" I'd cultivated a talent for reading people, weighing them at a glance, separating shepherds from sheep. It was nothing special; a basic survival technique—but it came up dry now. These people confounded my expectations. Was I in a commune or a militia compound? Were these hippie cultists, leftwing anarchists, or something else? I gave one of the more brazen ping-pong players— the redhead from town—a hard look. Fulcher had called him Clint. Clint's grin vanished and he concentrated on his game. Human, at least.

"You know," Fulcher said.

"I hate word games, Roy. They make me hostile."

"Ask Anselm."

"I'm asking you."

"It brought you to us—one from multitudes. You still question what our work is here?"

"It? If you mean the *Imago Sequence*, then yeah, I'm full of questions."

"Anselm will answer your *questions* in due course."

"Well, Roy, problem is, I'm kind of stupid. People usually need to repeat stuff."

Fulcher's expression grew rigid. "You don't want to see. Surprise—it's too late. The fictions you've invented, your false assumptions, your pretenses, will soon be blown apart. I doubt it will profit you in the least. You're a thug."

"Story of my life; nobody likes me. I guess you'd be willing to show me the big picture. Shoot me down with your intellectual superiority."

"Anselm will show you the cosmic picture, Mr. Cortez."

"Isn't it customary for you religious zealots to have pamphlets lying around? Betcha there's a printing press somewhere in this Taj Mahal. Surely you've got propaganda for the recruits? And beads? I like beads."

"No pamphlets, no recruits. This is *Imago Colony*. Religion doesn't apply."

"Oh, no? What's with all the faux Roman crucifixes in the back forty?"

"The crucifixes? Those are authentic. Anselm imported them."

I tried to wrap my mind around that concept. The implications eluded me. I said, "Bullshit. What the hell for?"

"The obvious—sport. Anselm has exotic tastes. He enjoys aspects of cultural antiquity."

"Yeah, so I hear. And he has a thing about bugs, I guess; sort of similar to his mentor. Seems to be a reliable pattern with lunatics. An imago is an insect, right?"

"It's symbolic."

"Oh. I thought the bug thing was cute."

"An imago is not *any* insect. The final instar of an insect, its supreme incarnation. Care for another beer?"

"I'm good." I gestured at the ping-pong tournament. "Weedy crowd, Roy. Somebody told me there were forty, fifty of you in this camp."

"Far less, these days. Attrition."

"Uh, huh."

"You've come during harvest season, Mr. Cortez. That's what we do in the cold months. The others are engaged, those who remain. Things will quicken in the spring. People seem to be more driven to enlightenment during sandal weather. Spiritualists, nature enthusiasts, software engineers on holiday with wives and kiddies. We get all kinds."

"Thornton is off to play plantation overseer, eh? I wonder what you kids harvest in these parts—poppies? Opium is Afghanistan's chief export—ask the Taliban what it paid for its military hardware, the light bills in its palaces. The climate around here is about goddamned ideal. You'd be millionaires. I've got a couple pals, line you right out for a piece of the pie."

Fulcher rubbed his dented brow, smiled. "What wonderful irony! We do love to trip. You have me there. Poppies, that's very funny. I almost miss those days. I stick with cigarettes anymore."

"Lay your gimmick on me."

"Evolution."

"You and everybody else."

"What do people want?" Fulcher raised his grimy hand to forestall my answer. "What do people truly want—what would induce a man to sell his soul?"

"To be healthy, wealthy and wise." I said with mild sarcasm. Mild because as I uttered the punch line to the children's rhyme, coldness began to unfold in my bones. The tumblers in my head were turning again.

"Bravo, Mr. Cortez. Power, wisdom, immortality." His expression altered. "We have found something that will afford us…longevity, at least. With longevity comes everything else."

"The Fountain of Youth?" *In the deep mountain woods a mossy statue spurted black water. Congregations of hillbillies in coveralls bathed in its viscid pool. A bonfire, a forest of uncured pelts swaying. A piper.* I shuddered. "Dancing girls, winning lotto tickets?"

"A catalyst. A mechanism that compresses aeons of future human evolution. Although future is a relative term."

"Ammon's photographs." It seemed obvious. Everything seemed patently obvious, except that the room was undulating and I couldn't figure out who was playing the flute. A panpipe, actually; high, thin, discordant. It pierced my brain.

Fulcher ignored the music. He flushed, warming to my edification. "The *Imago Sequence* is a trigger. If you've got the right genes you might already be a winner."

I rubbed my ear; the pipe raised unpleasant specters to mind, set them gibbering. *The monstrous hominid opened its mouth wider, wider.* "How does that shit work?"

"Take a picture of God, tack it on the wall and see who bows. Recognition is the key. It doesn't make a difference what you comprehend intellectually, only what stirs on a cellular level, what awakens when it recognizes the wellspring of creation."

"Don't tell me you believe the caveman is God."

"I said there's no caveman. Look deeper, friend. Reality lies beyond the surface. It's not the Devil in the details, it's God."

"Aha! You *are* a bunch of Christian cultists."

"We do not exist to worship an incomprehensible being. A being which assuredly lacks the means to appreciate slavish devotion."

"Seems pointless to have a god at all, when you put it like that."

"Do you supplicate plutonium? Do you sing hymns to uranium? We bask in the corona of an insensate majesty. In its sway we seek to lay the foundation blocks of a new city, a new civilization. We're pioneers. Our frontier is the grand wasteland between Alpha and Omega."

"Will you transform into a being of pure energy and migrate to Alpha Centauri?"

"Quite opposite. Successful animal organisms are enduring organisms. Enduring organisms are extremely basic, extremely efficient. Tarantulas. Scorpions. Reptiles. Flies."

"Don't forget cockroaches. They're going to inherit the earth." I laughed, began coughing. The room wobbled. "So Thornton is what—the messiah helping you become the best imago you can be?"

"Anselm is the Imago. We are maggots. We are provender."

"I get it. He does the transcending and you get the slops."

"It is good to have a purpose in life. To be an integral part of the great and terrible cycle." Fulcher shook his head. "As I serve him, he served Ammon and Ammon served the one before him down through time gone to dust. *'By sating the image of the Power they fulfill their fleshly contract. By suckling the teat of godliness the worthy shall earn their reward.*' Thus it is written in a book much more venerable than the Bible. For we who survive to remake ourselves in the image of the Power, all risks are acceptable."

"Reverend Jones rides again! Pass the grape Kool-Aid!"

"Hysterical, much?"

"Naw, just lately." I took a breath. "I wonder though, what does a guy do after he reaches the top of the ol' ladder? Live in a cave and compose epic poetry? Answer riddles? Pick up a sword and lay waste to Rome?"

"Caligula was one of us, actually."

I didn't know what to say to that. I plowed ahead. "Well?"

"Basic organisms require basic pleasures."

"Basic pleasures?" The chilly sensation linked hands with vertigo and did a Scottish jig. I was as a figurine in that enormous room.

"Subsistence and copulation. That's what the good life boils down to, my friend. Eating and fucking. Whoever you want, whatever you want, whenever you want."

The mouth opening, opening—

"Power to the people." I was slurring. Why was I slurring?

"Ready to go?" Fulcher rose, still smiling through his matted beard. We walked through the tall archway. He lightly gripped my elbow to steady me. One beer and I was drunk as a sailor on the third day of shore leave. The corridor expanded in the best Escher fashion, telescoping into infinite shadow. There were ragged tapestries at intervals, disfigured statues, a well-trammeled carpet with astrological designs. The corridor branched and branched again at grand arches marred by ages of smoke. At one fork, a kerosene lamp swung on a sooty chain. Behind a massive iron door the piping shrilled, died, shrilled. Hoarse screams of the primordial sex act, exhausted sobs, laughter and applause. Mrs. Chin's photograph haunted me.

"The gallery," Fulcher said.

I recognized the musk upon him, finally. For a horrible moment I thought we would go through that door. We continued down the other hall.

Fulcher brought me to a dingy chamber lit by a single dirty bulb in an overhead cage. The room was windowless and bare except for a large chair made of wood and iron. The chair had arm straps and leg shackles; an artifact from the Spanish Inquisition. It was not difficult to picture the fallen bishops, the heretical nobles who had shrieked in its embrace.

"Please, make yourself comfortable." Fulcher helped me along with a shove.

I slumped in the strange chair, my head heavy as a wrecking ball, and watched as he produced a nasty looking bowie knife and expertly sliced off my clothes. When he encountered the revolver he emptied the cylinder, slid the weapon into his waistband without comment. He cinched my arms and legs; his fingers glowed, dragging tracers as they adjusted buckles and straps. Seemingly he had grown extra arms. I could only gawk at this phantasm; I felt quite docile. "Wow, Roy. What was in my beer? I feel terrific."

"One should hope. You ingested several hundred milligrams of synthetic mescaline—enough to launch a rhinoceros into orbit."

"Party foul, and on the first date too. I thought you didn't do dope any-more."

"I dabble in the manufacturing end of the spectrum. Frankly, all that metaphysical mumbo-jumbo about hallucinogens affecting perception in a meaningful way is wishful thinking. Poor Huxley." Fulcher stepped back, surveyed his handiwork while rolling a cigarette. The yellow flare of his lighter painted his face, made him a devil. "Oh, except for you. You're special. You've seen *Alpha* and *Beta*. As my pappy would say, you've got the taint, boy." He blurred around the edges. With each inhalation the cherry of his cigarette brightened, became Jupiter's red sore.

I noticed the walls were metallic—whorls whorled, pits and pocks formed. Condensation trickled. Smoke made arabesques and demons. The walls were a tapestry from a palace in Hell.

The panpipe started wheedling again and Thornton entered the room on cue. He pushed a rickety hospital tray with a domed cover. The cover was scalloped, silver finish flaking. A maroon handprint smeared its curve.

"This is a bad sign," I said.

Thornton was efficient. He produced an electric razor and shaved a portion of my head to stubble, dug a thumb under my carotid artery and traced veins in my skull with a felt-tip pen. He tweaked my nose in a fatherly manner, stripped off his coat and rolled his sleeves to the elbows. His skin gleamed like coral, cast faint reflections upon the walls and ceiling. Shoals of phantom fish scattered above, regrouped and swam into an abyss; a superhighway and its endless traffic looped beneath my feet; it rippled and collapsed into a trench of unimaginable depths.

I watched him remove a headpiece from the tray—a clumsy framework of clamps and screws; a dunce cap with a collar. Parts had never been cleaned. I wanted to scream when he fitted it over my head and neck, locked it in place with a screwdriver. I sighed.

Fulcher stubbed his cigarette, produced a palm-sized digital camera and aimed it at me. He gave Thornton a thumbs-up.

Thornton selected a scalpel from the instruments on the tray, weighed it in his hand. "Teddy was a friend—I would never use him as provender, but neither could I set him on the path to Olympus. There's limited room in the boat, you see. Weak, genetically flawed, but a jolly nice fellow. A gentleman. Imagine my disappointment when he showed up on my doorstep last fall. Not only had the old goat bought *Parallax Alpha*, he'd viewed *Beta* as well. He demanded to see *Imago*. As if I could simply snap my fingers and show him. Wouldn't listen to reason, wouldn't go home and fall to pieces quietly like a good boy. So I enlightened him. It was out of my hands after that. Now, we come to you." He sliced my forehead, peeled back a flap of skin. Fulcher taped it down.

"What?" I said. "What?"

Thornton raised a circular saw with a greasy wooden handle. He attached it to a socket in my headpiece. "Trephination. An ancient method to open the so-called Third Eye. Fairly crude; Ammon taught me how and a Polynesian tribe showed him—he wasn't a surgeon either. He performed his own in a Bangkok opium den with a serrated knife and a corkscrew while a stoned whore held a mirror. Fortunately, medical expertise is not a requisite in this procedure."

The dent in Fulcher's brow drew my gaze. I sighed again, saddened by wisdom acquired too late in the day.

Thornton patted me kindly. His touch lingered as a caress. "Don't fret, it's not a lobotomy. You wished to behold *Imago*, this is the way. What an extraordinary specimen you are, Marvin, my boy. Your transformation will be a most satisfying conquest as I have not savored in years. I am sure to delay your reintegration for the span of many delightful hours. I will have compensation for your temerity."

"Mr. Thornton," I gasped; trembled with the effort of rolling my eye to meet his. "Mrs. Chin said the glacier is coming. I dream it every night; flies buzzing in my brain. It's killing me. That's why I came."

Thornton nodded. "Of course. I've seen it a thousand times. Everyone who has crawled into my lair wanted to satisfy one desire or another. What will satisfy you, O juicy morsel? To hear, to know?" He yawned. "Would you be happy to learn there is but one God and that all things come from Him? Existence is infinitely simple, Marvin—cells within cells, dreams within dreams, from the molten Fingertip of God Almighty, to the antenna of a roach, on this frequency and each of a billion after. Thus it goes until the circuit completes its ambit of the core, a protean-reality where dwells an intellect of surpassing might, yet impotent, bound as it is in the well of its own gravity. Cognition does not flourish in that limitless quagmire, the cosmic repository of information. The lightning of Heaven is reduced to torpid impulses that spiral outward, seeking gratification by osmosis. And by proxy. We are bags of nerves and electrolytes, fragile and weak and we decompose so quickly. Which is the purpose, the very cunning design. Our experiences are readily digested to serve the biological imperative of a blind, vast sponge. Does it please you? Do you require more?"

A spike glinted within the ring of saw-teeth. Thornton casually pressed this spike into my skull, seated it with a few taps of a rubber mallet. He put his lips next to my ear. His breath reeked copper. "The prophets proclaim the end is near. I'll whisper to you something they don't know—the world ended this morning as you were sleeping, half-frozen on the mountainside. It ended aeons before your father squirted his genetic material into your mother. It will end tomorrow as it ends every day, same time, same station." He started cranking.

Listening to the rhythmic burr of metal on bone I was thankful the mescaline had soldered my nerve endings. Thornton divided and divided again until he crowded the room. Pith helmets, top hats, arctic coats, khakis, corporate suits, each double dressed for a singular occasion, each one animated by separate experience, but all of them smiling with tremendous pleasure as they turned the handle, turned the handle, turned the handle. Their faces sloughed, dough swelling and splitting. Beneath was something raw, and moist, and dark.

I glimpsed the face of the future and failed to comprehend its shape. Blood poured into my eyes. The panpipe went mad.

8.

The world ends every day.

Picture me walking in a rock garden under the dipping branches of cherry blossom trees. I love stones and there are heavy examples scattered across the garden; olive-bearded, embedded in the tough sod. God's voice echoes as through a gigantic gramophone horn, but softly from the lead plate of sky, and not God, it's Thornton guiding the progression, driving an auger into my skull while the music plays. Push it aside, keep moving toward a mound in the distance....

No Thornton, auger, no music; only God, the garden, and I. Where is God? Everywhere, but especially in the earth, the dark, warm earth that opens as a cave mouth in the side of a hill. God calls from the hill, in voices of grinding rock and gurgling water.

I walk toward the cave. Sleet falls, captured betwixt burning and freezing precisely as I am caught. Nor is the sleet truly sleet. A swirl of images falling, million-million shards fractured from a vast hoary mirror. There am I, and I and I a million-million times, broken, melting....

I walk through God's rock garden, trampling incarnations of myself....

Watery images flickered on the wall. A home movie with the volume lowered. Choppy because the cameraman kept adjusting to peer over the shoulder of a tall figure who attended a third person in the awful chair—my chair. The victim was not I; it was a mirror casting a false reflection. And it wasn't a movie in the strictest sense; I detected no camera, nor aperture to project the film. More hallucinations then. More something.

Teddy's face, trapped in the conical helm; his feet scuffed and rattled the shackles. Thornton blocked the view, elbow pumping with the practiced ease of a farmer's wife churning butter. Muffled laughter, walnuts being cracked. The image went dark, but the dim sounds persisted.

Claustrophobia gagged me. I was still strapped in the chair, the helm fixed to my head. There was a hole in my head. My right eye was crusted and blind. I was shuddering with chills. How much time had passed? Where had Fulcher and Thornton gone? Had they shown me *Imago* as promised? My memories balked.

As my faculties reengaged, my fear swelled. They had shredded my clothes, confiscated my belongings, tortured me. They would kill me. That was scarcely my fear. I dreaded what else would happen first.

The wall brightened with new images. *Sperm wriggled, hungry and fast. A wasp made love to a tarantula, thrusting, thrusting with its stinger. Mastiffs flung themselves upon a threshing stag, dangled from its antlers like ornaments. Fire ants swarmed over a gourd half-buried in desert earth—*

Fulcher drifted through the door, Clint at his heel. I remained limp when Fulcher scrutinized me briefly; he flashed a penlight in my good eye, checked my pulse. He murmured to his partner, and began unbuckling my straps. Clint hung back, perhaps to guard against a revival of my aggressive philosophy. Even so, he appeared bored, distracted.

I did not stir until Fulcher freed my arms. It occurred to me that the mescaline cocktail must've worn off because I wasn't feeling docile anymore. Nothing was premeditated; my mind was well below a rational state. I pawed his face—weakly, a drunken gesture, which he brushed aside. I became more insistent, got a fistful of his beard on the next half-hearted swipe, my left hand slithered behind his neck. Fulcher pried at my wrist, twisted his head. Frantic, he braced his boot against the chair and tried to push off. His back bowed and contorted.

A ghostly spider mounted a beetle; they clinched.

Growing stronger, more purposeful, I yanked him into my lap, and his beard ripped, but that was fine. I squeezed his throat and vertebrate popped the way it happens when you lift a heavy salmon by the tail. Stuff separates.

Clint tried to pull Fulcher, exactly as a man will pull a comrade from quicksand. Failing, he snatched up a screwdriver and stabbed me in the ribs. No harm, my ribs were covered with a nice slab of gristle and suet. Punch a side a beef hanging from a hook and see what you get.

A truck careened across a strange field riddled with holes. The vehicle juked and jived and nose-dived into the biggest hole of them all—

I dropped Fulcher and staggered from the chair. Clint stabbed me in the shoulder. I laughed; it felt good. I palmed his face, clamped down with full strength. He bit me, began a thick, red stream down my arm. He choked and gargled. Bubbles foamed between my finger webs. I waltzed him on tiptoes and banged his head against a support beam. *Bonk, bonk, bonk,* just like the cartoons. Just like Jackson Pollack. I stopped when his facial bones sort of collapsed and sank into the general confusion of his skull.

I fumbled with the screws of my helm, gave it up as a hopeless cause. I left the cell and wandered along the hall, trailing one hand against the rough surfaces. People met me, passed me without recognition, without interest. These people were versions of myself. I saw *a younger me dressed in a tropical shirt and a girl on my arm; me in a funeral suit and a sawed-off shotgun in my hand; another me pale and bruised, a doughnut brace on my neck, hunched on crutches; still another me, gray-haired, dead drunk, wild glare fixed upon the middle distance.*

And others, too many others coming faster until it hurt my eyes. They flowed around me, collided, disappeared into the deep, lightless throat of the hall until all possibilities were lost.

Weight shifted within the bowels of Thornton's Pleasure Dome. A ponderous door was flung wide and a chorus of damned cries echoed up the corridors. The muscles between my shoulder blades tightened. I picked up the pace.

The main area was deserted but for a woman sweeping ashes from the barrel stove and a sturdy man in too-loose long johns eating dinner at a table. The woman was an automaton; she regarded me without emotion, resumed her mechanical duties. The man put aside his spoon, considering whether to challenge me. He remained undecided as I stumbled outside, bloody and birth-naked. The icy breeze plucked at my scalp, caused my wound to throb with the threat of a migraine. I was in a place far removed from such concerns.

A better man would've set a match to the drums of diesel, blown the place to smithereens Hollywood style. No action star, I headed for the vehicles.

Twilight cocooned the valley. The sky was smooth as opal. A crimson band pulsed at the horizon—the sun elongated to its breaking point. Clouds scudded from invisible distances, flew by at unnatural velocity.

"Don't go," Thornton said. A whisper, a shout.

I glanced back.

He filled the doorway of the Quonset hut, which was tiny, was receding. His many selves had merged, yet flickered beneath his skin, ready to burst forth. His voice had relinquished its command, now waned fragile, as it traveled across the gulf to find me. "You're opening doors without any idea of where they lead. It's a waste. Sweet God, what a waste!"

I kept walking, limping.

"Marvin!" A hot lash of hatred and appetite throbbed from his dwindling voice. "Say hello to Teddy!" He shrank to a speck, was lost.

A fleet of canvas-top trucks shimmered upon an island in a sea of velvet. They warped and ran with the fluidity of quicksilver, a kaleidoscope revolving around the original. I picked the closest truck and dragged myself inside. Keys dangled from the ignition. The helm was too tall for the cab; I was forced to drive with my head on my shoulder. Fresh blood seeped from the wound and obscured my vision.

The truck bucked and crow-hopped as I clanged gears, stomped the accelerator and sent it hurtling across the rugged valley. One road multiplied, became three roads, now six. Now, I was off the road, or the road had melted. Bizarre changes were altering the scenery, toying with my feeble perception. The mountains doubled and redoubled and underwent the transformations of millennia—a range exploding forward, rounding and shortening, another backward, rearing into a toothy crown—in the span of heartbeats. It was a rough ride.

I found the knob for the headlights in time to illuminate the sinkhole a few dozen yards ahead. A rapidly widening maw. I slammed the brakes. The cab exploded with dust and smoking rubber. There was a tin-can-under-a-boot crunch and the truck yawed, paused at the rim and toppled in, nose-first. I performed a lazy belly flop through the windshield.

I didn't lose consciousness, unfortunately. I bounced and bones cracked along old fault lines. Eventually I stopped with a terrific jolt; a feather mattress dropped on a cavern floor. At least the truck didn't come down on top of me—it had lodged in a bottleneck. Its engine shrieked momentarily, sputtered and died. I stared up at the rapidly dulling headlights, as bits of sensation returned to my extremities. Ages passed. When I finally managed to gain my knees, the world was in darkness. What was broken? Ribs, definitely. A sprained knee that swelled as I breathed. Possibly a bone in my back had snapped; insufficient to immobilize me, yet neither could I straighten fully. Cuts on my face and hands. The pain was minor, and that worried me. Why not worse? I had landed in deep, spongy moss, was nearly buried from the impact. It sucked at me as I clambered to solid footing.

The darkness wasn't complete. Aqueous light leaked from slimy surfaces, the low ceiling of sweating rock. As my vision adjusted I saw moss claimed everything. Stinking moss filled crevices and fissures, was habitat of beetles and other things. Sloppy from the eternal drip of water, it squelched between my toes, sucked my ankles. This was a relatively small cave, with a single chimney jammed by the crashed truck. This wasn't a mine shaft; my animal self was positive about that. Nor did it require much heavy thinking to conclude that climbing out of there was impossible. I couldn't raise my left arm above waist level. A single note from the panpipe came faintly. From below. A voice may have murmured my name—I was gasping too loudly and it did not repeat.

A fissure split the rear of the cave, a cramped tunnel descended. Mastering my instincts, I followed it down. The cool air warmed, was soon moist as a panting mouth. Pungent odors clogged my nostrils, watered my eyes. Gradually, the passage widened, opening into a larger area, a cavern of great dimensions. The light strengthened, or my eyes got better, because pieces of the cavern joined as Mrs. Chin's photos had joined. And I beheld *Imago*.

Here was the threshold of the Beginning and End.

The roof was invisible but for the tips of gargantuan stalactites, all else shrouded. Moss, more moss, a garden, a forest of moss. But was it moss? I doubted that. Moss didn't quiver where it met flesh, didn't contract as a muscle contracts.

The walls glistened; they glowed not unlike the glow which seeped from Thornton's skin. Shadows of the world dwelt in the walls. Those most familiar to me rose from the depths like champagne bubbles. I passed Teddy's yacht near the surface, its lines quite clean despite being encased. Further along, a seaplane was suspended on high, partially obscured by gloom. It hung, fossilized, an inverted crucifix. There were faces, a frieze of ghastly spectators massed in the tiers of an amphitheater. I averted my gaze, afraid of who I might see pithed in the bell jar. Deeper, inside folds of rock that was not rock, were glimpses of Things to Come. Houses, onion domes and turrets, utopian skylines, the graceful arcs of bridges, rainforests and jagged mountains. And deeper, deeper yet, solar systems of pregnant globes of smothered dirt and vine, and charred stars in endless procession.

I caught myself humming The Doors' "This Is the End." I stood upon a shattered slope, weeping and laughing, and humming the song of death. Thinking probably the same thoughts any lesser primate does when confronted with apocalyptic forces. To these I added, *Damn you, anyway, Jacob! You can shove this favor in your big, flabby ass!* And, *I wonder if Carol is feeding the fish?*

Before me lay the cavern's boundary; another translucent wall. This area was subtly different, it bulged with murky reefs of dubious matter—I conjured the image of coiled organs, the calcified ganglia of some Biblical colossus. Dead roots snaked from an abyss to end abysses—a primordial sea from which all life had been egurgitated. My ears popped with a sudden pressure change. I detected movement.

I tried to run, but my legs were unresponsive, as if they had fallen asleep, and the moss shifted beneath my nerveless feet, dumped me on my backside. I flailed down the slope, which I realized was a funnel, or a trough. This occurred with excruciating slowness, but it was impossible to halt my weight once it got moving. Wherever my skin made contact with the moss I lost sensation. This was because the moss that was not moss stung with tiny barbs, stung me as a jellyfish stings. My legs, my back, right hand, then left, until everything from the neck down was anesthetized.

At the bottom, by some trick of geometry, I pitched forward to lie spread eagle against the curve of the wall. The rock softened, was vaguely gelatinous. I began to sink. Despite my numbed state, it was cold compared to the rank jungle of a cavern. Frigid.

As I sank, I thought, *Not a wall, a membrane.* Engulfed in amber jelly, tremendous pressure built upon my body, flattened my features. Wrenching my head to free it from imminent suffocation, to scream as an animal screams, dying alone in the wilderness, I saw a blossom of fire in the near distance. An abrupt blue-white flare that seemed to expand forever, then shrink into itself. I opened my mouth, opened my mouth—

The second flash was far smaller, far more remote. It faded swiftly.

I don't know if there was a third.

HOUR OF THE CYCLOPS

I quickly opened the door scriven with a ghastly orange symbol, and stepped through. Everyone in the cell was frozen at my unwelcome appearance. I shot the man to the left of the Ancient Apothecary. I shot the man to the right of the Ancient Apothecary. The Ancient Apothecary motioned with his unclean hand—a motion suspiciously akin to the loathsome symbol splattered against the door. I fell. A curtain settled over my eyes.

Well, next time I'd shoot the Ancient Apothecary first.

They made me talk.

"Here to rescue the virgin, hmm?" The Ancient Apothecary petted his sinister imperial.

"Or deflower her trying." I saw they had confiscated my array of devices lethal and malign. A wild-looking man was playing with them. He hunched, raptorlike, snickering. I dangled from rusty chains wrapped around the meaty portion of my forearms. It was cold, and water gurgled against rough stone. No virgins anywhere in sight.

The Ancient Apothecary was neither withered nor desiccated. Thick and supple as a bull, his eyes gleamed friendly spite. "Mr. Whatley?" He certainly did not speak like any heathen cultist I knew—more through the nose like a snobby English professor.

"Sure." I kind of shrugged. The chains creaked.

The Ancient Apothecary—whom I was amply warned to beware—smiled an evil smile. My identification—actually not mine, but that's complicated— shined betwixt his spicate fingernails. "So, Mr. Whatley, what is the deal with your blood?" He was a scientist, and any scientist in the world would have been smitten with that particular riddle.

I laughed. Our doctors were sensitive to the manifold hazards of this little assignment. Among other precautions, they siphoned the blood from my body, replacing the tired stuff with Yellow Ichor No. Five. It was experimental, but that didn't bother me. Doctors Chimera and Sprague had done all the usual tests on primates and captured operatives. I was the first agent to use it in the field, and so far so good.

The Ancient Apothecary laughed also. He ceased laughing and spoke rapidly in a language offensive to my ears. A pair of spindly surgeons emerged from the shadows; ivory cloaks shuttering—death-white carapaces of hunting beetles. They reeked of charnel; their nails were crusty. One stabbed my neck; the second stabbed the vein in my groin. Their horse syringes soon brimmed with ocher gel. The vile surgeons scuttled whence they came. I gasped and panted, at a loss for proper curses.

The Ancient Apothecary petted the oily crescent of his mustache. He trundled a circuit around my hanging body. "Whatever the secret of your wonderful elixir, my minions shall soon know it. Ho! And what is this scar progressing in a cruel groove to vanish under thy cranial canopy?"

"Hair replacement."

"Most suspicious, most alarming."

"Indeed. But enough about me. Don't you have a virgin to sacrifice?"

"Heh, heh!" The Ancient Apothecary bobbed his anvil head. He had been sneaking glances at his watch. "True, my dear succulent child, very true. Are you a believer then?"

"No. I just do what I'm told."

"Ah. What *are* your instructions?"

"Rescue the girl. Kill you."

"So sorry to thwart your plans. Much as I sympathize with your predicament, I cannot relinquish the Virgin Offering. When the stars fall into their proper design I shall render the Virgin, and Lord Cyclops will rear above the gelid sheets of His living tomb. We who revere the Lord of Shadow shall caper upon the squirming mound of our enemies; we shall light the great fires to welcome the Father of Decay as He lumbers forth to bellow cataclysm and ravish the earth!"

"Super," I replied.

"But I must appease the worms of curiosity—did the Church send you? Officious cata-mites! They meddle in my affairs with egregious determination."

"If you must know, then you must know; however, also know that I will happily die rather than divulge that information."

"Well, there will be nothing *happy* about it, Mr. Whatley! I will give you pain and suffer-ing of legendary measure!"

Again I laughed. "Pain means nothing to me. Do your worst."

"So be it." The Ancient Apothecary clapped twice like an imperious rajah in a bad old film.

"Mr. Spot! Please visit our guest with the best torments your febrile brain can devise!" Which is exactly what Mr. Spot did.

As I expected, the Ancient Apothecary grew bored and left to check on his project. I thanked the stars, all of them, good and bad—it was unlikely that my trick would affect him. After he had gone, I stopped screaming and regarded the one called Mr. Spot. Yes, I remembered him from the file picture. Not very charming in the flesh, either. "Mr. Spot," I said. "Mr. Spot, would you look at me for a moment.

The ugly man paused in his ministrations. "You've stopped screaming."

"Because I need to tell you something. Listen." I began the vocalization of a particularly nasty and profane string of syllables. This triggered Dr. Sprague's autohypnotic suggestion; my head lolled, my bowels heaved and expelled concomitant with glottal constriction. A membranous capsule came into contact with my teeth, I chewed heartily; I spat a virulent stream of venom into his eyes. Fat sizzled and popped. His face dissolved into a crater of green smoke.

Again with the curtain....

Mr. Spot was pretty much dead by the time I shuddered awake. I half expected the horrible little surgeons to appear. They didn't. It only required a few seconds to be free of the chains and when I was, I dropped heavily to the floor. There was a price to pay for this good fortune. The poison had affected me to a lesser, although ultimately no less fatal, degree. The skin of my arms was already whitening; dark purple welts encircled them like rings in deadwood. Thank goodness I could not see my face bloating, which it surely was.

Not my face, not my life, thank the stars. The distinction might be a trifle confusing. The body was already very comfortable; like an old boot. It should have been—it belonged to the very famous George Whatley, world-class hammer thrower. He was in phenomenal shape, unlike what I had grown accustomed to walking around in my ordinary skin.

Dr. Chimera guessed the Yellow Ichor No. Five transfusion would not be sufficient for the task at hand. This was the Ancient Apothecary, after all! Brain transplants are not so risky as the Ichor infusion, believe it or don't. Hell, the government had been doing them with chimpanzees for decades. It wasn't like we were that valuable. Best part was, due to the Yellow Ichor I had a superior degree of control over my anatomical functions. Breathing, pulse, I could slow them to a crawl. Pain? There was only the pain I could not help but imagine. Everything else was subject to interpretation.

Luckily for me, despite popular opinion, the brain is the last thing to go. There was a chance I could still find the girl and get back to Central before the creeping ague reached my precious gray matter. It was sort of a shame. This body had belonged to an Olympic athlete in the prime of his life—a hammer thrower. I really wasn't enthused about looking down and seeing the old potbelly again. Of course, unless I did something to stop the insane machinations of the Ancient Apothecary, it was a moot point. My superiors would be so displeased if I allowed him to succeed!

I found my clothes and my toys, and appropriated some of Mr. Spot's unorthodox medical tools. I got out of there.

Alaska is a vast frontier; the majority of that epic vastness is most charitably classified as wasteland. What better place to trifle with things Not Meant for the Eyes of Man? The Ancient Apothecary had chosen his lair fortuitously—an abandoned radar site near White Mountain, a tiny, native village eighty miles southeast of Nome. Too bad for the world at large that the radar site had been a little more sinister than advertised; deep shafts scored the permafrost into a complex of bunkers and vaults where certain, shall we say arcane, experiments were pursued during the Second World War. Things ended badly for the researchers; the site was boarded up and strung with now rust-twisted barbwire. Somebody important buried it in paperwork. Probably no one even knew about it anymore—the frigid Alaskan tundra is liberally pocked with the skeletons of abandoned military stations.

Ah, but the Ancient Apothecary knew, and what he knew, we knew, or close enough. The people I work for were unhappy about this development in the travels of our old nemesis. So long as the Ancient Apothecary confined himself to Asia, they didn't mind. There is nothing happening worth mentioning in Asia these days. Then the unthinkable—he appeared in Western Europe last year, moving on to Cairo where certain artifacts went missing from the home of an extremely private collector. Next, Brazil, where he visited several unmapped temples; and in Brazil three of our agents followed him into the rain forest. The Ancient Apothecary emerged without them and continued on to North America, swallowed up by the Alaskan wilderness. Along about here occurred the mysterious disappearance of a world famous-celebrity; couple that disappearance with an inauspicious alignment of constellations, and chaos tugged at the leash in H.Q. It seemed perfectly clear something had to be done about the Ancient Apothecary. Central took off the gloves; they sent me in to rectify the situation.

Time was increasingly of the essence. For reasons unavoidable and too convoluted to suffer explanation, we had cut this operation close to the quick. Some might question why Central didn't just bomb the place, or at the very least send in a team to safely extinguish the threat. Ever try bombing an anthill? As for the latter, well, the sad truth was that if I couldn't slip in and terminate the Ancient Apothecary, more troops were academic.

Honestly, his operation was dreary. Everything was gray metal or smooth, dark rock and dripping water. The lighting was bad; shadows pooled in wavery patterns. I moved along quickly, not overly worried about running afoul of guards. I had already killed the best ones and the Ancient Apothecary could scarcely support a private army after squandering his resources on arcana over the past few years. Nonetheless, I kept an eye peeled; there were other things to worry about when one dealt with opposition like this. Lets just say I watched where I stepped and made sure shadows were shadows before I moved into them.

Given the circumstances, a wiser, more pragmatic man than the Ancient Apothecary would have disabled the elevator. Then again, a pragmatic man would not have risked his advantage to torture me at all. He would have put a bullet in the soft part of my brain, had a nice chuckle and gotten on with his nefarious schemes. Yet there the elevator was; rickety mesh and exposed gears and all that sort of thing. I knew where it went. To accomplish what the Ancient Apothecary intended, he would need a deep dark cavern and the infinite seep of subterranean water.

The elevator was ancient as my enemy. It clattered all the way down.

At the bottom was a low chamber and a sturdy metal door. The door was locked and barred from the opposite side. Not a problem thanks to the white coats back at Central. Among the lethal appliances in my possession was a knife compartment oozing with a gelatinous compound and an electronic timing switch. I went into the elevator, crouched behind the frame and covered my ears.

A big hole materialized where the door had stood; the lights went dead in the room. Smoke formed acrid columns, not that it bothered me. Beyond the wreckage was a platform overlooking a narrow tunnel sloping down into utter blackness. I climbed down a ladder, touched on a penlight and examined the rails. There weren't any carts. Damn. I started walking; shambling, actually. My knee joints were stiff as dried leather; a distinct numbness emanated from both hands, forcing me to consciously squeeze the penlight. Oh, I truly hoped it wasn't far.

I distracted myself by thinking about the victim in this affair. Call her Ms. Smyth. I wasn't exaggerating when I referred to her as a celebrity. The Ancient Apothecary was up to big things; no ordinary woman would do. I had to hand it to him; Ms. Smyth was everything an insane cultist mastermind dreamed of in a ritual sacrifice. Her parents were some kind of genetic scientists; they grew her in a tube, and when she was a toddler they subjected her to a battery of tests—turns out the kid was a genius. They sent the genius to private schools—she graduated college with a double Ph.D. in astrophysics and theology by the tender age of seventeen. Still not good enough for the Ancient Apothecary. The girl decided to take up a sport, full-contact karate, no less. She tried out for the Olympic team, went to Melbourne, took the gold. Not good enough. She traveled around a bit, visited some mosques, gawked at the Pyramids and so forth. Then she wrote a paper speculating about the true nature of the universe. They decided to nominate her for a Nobel. While she was waiting to see how that turned out, just for amusement because one of her myriad close friends was an international recording artist, she took up the cello and discovered that playing it was about as difficult as holding her breath underwater. She became an overnight sensation and accepted a lucrative recording contract.

Good enough for the Ancient Apothecary? Not quite, not quite. Consider one final thing—Ms. Smyth was thirty-one years of age, brilliant, beautiful and fabulously rich. Also, she was an avowed virgin.

Yes, she dated a handsome Olympic hammer thrower, but the flower of her womanhood would not be plucked save on the marriage bed. Now the Ancient Apothecary was happy.

I could only wish to be so pleased. This was like slogging in wet sand. I began to concentrate on thoughts of better days—which meant I had to really work at it. Fortunately, my meditation classes with Dr. Sprague came in handy; I began to drift along on a sublime tide of nostalgia which sprang up quite unexpectedly. A trick of the mind in perilous times; it seizes upon a pleasant juncture and capsizes there....

A soliloquy:

How do you arrive at such a crossroads? No answer for that here, my friends. I had a life once; way back before school and what came after. There was a girl—not so spectacular as the amazing Ms. Smyth, but a nice girl and a pretty girl for all that. She had loved me despite my shortcomings, which unbeknownst to her, were incalculable.

Shambling along that darksome tunnel bored through prehistoric rock, I spilled with the recollection of a beach, an autumn beach, crescent curved and floating on the rim of God's Drinking Horn—red, gold, amber; the trees, the beach, the water. Lovers walked along the beach, not quite touching, there was no need, they already knew everything the press of flesh can spoil with its indelicacy. A tall, serious boy, pallid as chalk. His eyes mirrored the changeable sea and were not unkind. Beside him walked a girl of ivory and jet who smiled at things unspoken and looked at him often. A big dog trailed after, barrel chest dragging the sugar sand, foam bearded upon its laughing snout. The girl hurled shells for the dog, some she kept for herself, and one she handed to the tall, serious boy. The boy took the shell and put it in his coat and the sky grew dark, darker, darkest. The boy and the girl disappeared into the drifting haze, then the dog, then they were gone. The postcard blackened at the edges, burst into flame....

That was long, long ago. The tall, serious boy didn't exist anymore—if he ever had. Doors opened, he stepped through and discovered they wouldn't work from the other side. Some of those doors were peculiar; they removed him from the ordinary world. He got fat and homely and not a little mean-spirited. His back bent under unwholesome strains and he didn't seem quite so tall anymore, just stooped. His morals flexed a little and he was no longer considered serious, but jaded.

The girl was gone; something about a crash with no survivors, all hands lost. What did *lost* mean? Did she think of him in those final moments? She was pretty to the end, at least.

Where was that shell now? It fell out of my pocket one day; I don't remember where exactly. What was her name, the dog's name? Guess that's lost too. I reached the end of the beach. When they turned to go back—she and the dog—I kept on walking....

After a while the penlight went dim and fizzled into extinction. I shuffled along, groping with my arms, worried about the possibility of an unannounced shaft, or worse. I realized I could see my hands. God, they were getting hideous, floating before my eyes, glowing like noctilucent moths. Ahead there was a fuzzy light source. A dank odor came into my nose, plastered my hair into a mold. I was weaving drunkenly; my face felt too tight, pulling my mouth into an involuntary grin. Ha, ha. I focused on the gathering illumination and tried to stay in a proper line.

The tunnel let into a weird grotto; thick stalactites oozed above a broad shelf of polished rock; to the left of the rock was a lagoon. It was impossible to discern the scope of the lagoon as it extended into absolute pitch. Big, was my feeling.

Tall posts flanked the rock shelf; these supported floodlights. A mess of coaxial cable and dangling wire; a generator *whupped* in the background, but I didn't see it for the glare. A mechanized rail cart awaited its busy occupants. Two men guarded the entrance, though how one is supposed to guard anything with one's back turned is beyond me. I got my hands on them and dragged their bodies into the shadows before they could raise an alarm.

The Ancient Apothecary had started already. An altar was erected near the water's edge; obsidian plinths bracketed a raised bench of malachite and serpentine, the whole of it scriven with elaborate glyphs and runes. Blood grooves funneled down into the water. Ms. Smyth made a striking contrast draped naked and pale across the stone. So too the Ancient Apothecary swathed in crimson robes and wearing the unspeakable horned mask he had stolen from Brazil. His transformation was nothing short of diabolical. He chanted a dirge in his vile tongue; a piece of sharp metal flared in his hand when he gesticulated.

I was right on time.

It occurred to me that I resembled something out of a cut-rate horror show as I lurched into the light and came for him. Indeed, the Ancient Apothecary seemed completely surprised by my rematerialization. That didn't stop him from trying to stab me with his wicked dagger. Rigor encumbered or not, the hammer thrower's body had excellent reflexes. I caught the Ancient Apothecary's wrist and twisted hard. He dropped the knife and tried to form a symbol with his left hand. No real chance with that tactic, a sheen of sweat glimmered through the openings in his mask—rituals were grinding, thankless work and he was doubtless worn out. Besides, the advantage was all mine in that I wore the hammer thrower's body like a suit. Most pain signals stalled out before they penetrated my dying flesh; I was maneuvering the hulk by memory.

The Ancient Apothecary was very strong. He twisted, he struggled, he gnashed his teeth and kicked at my shins. I switched off the circuits governing bodily safety tolerances, callous to my tearing muscles and flexing tendons and bent the Ancient Apothecary into a horseshoe. He began to scream and his screams reverberated from the pitiless walls.

Those horrible cries were answered.

Distant at first, then rapidly drawing closer was an ominous splashing sound. Invisible to the eye, but not my prickling skin, a presence entered the lagoon. Sinuous coils of mist undulated across the water, mounted in stages and caressed the altar. Bubbles foamed and frothed at the edge of the abruptly chattering lights. I sensed great displeasure aimed in my direction.

So I hurled the Ancient Apothecary into the chilly lagoon. A tremendous roiling commenced to chop the water; waves came at the shelf with some violence and splashed around me. Ms. Smyth lent her own screams to the general cacophony.

"George!" She cried. "Oh my god! What is that?" Her eyes bulged to regard something happening in the lagoon. I knew far better than to look.

"Come, my dear. Best that we depart at once." I grabbed her and bundled her into the trolley, pushed the lever until it refused to budge. The poor little cart was doubtless whisking along at top speed. It still felt like we were creeping into the tunnel.

Back in the cavern, all the lights went out.

If the ride in the trolley was frightful, the elevator trip was like riding an updraft out of hell. Ms. Smyth clung to me, sobbing, as the lift jerked and jolted. The light bulb rattled in its dish and flickered crazily. Grinding noises started somewhere beneath our feet. We made it to the bunker where all was quiet—for the moment at least. I found Ms. Smyth a jumpsuit and a parka and got her to put them on.

She babbled, gripped by an understandable level of hysteria. "Oh, George, what did they do to your face? Are you sick? What the hell is going on? Who is the Cyclops?"

"Really, dear, I'm in something of a hurry." My tongue was cold and I had to speak slowly so she could understand. The floor vibrated now and again, heightening my anxiety. "Everything... is going to be fine. Please... on with your shoes, okay?"

"How did you find me, sweetheart? Look at your face! Stupid me, you can't very well do that can you? Did that crazy awful man beat you? He was in my hotel room when I came back from the lecture. I was going to call you, but he was there with this other horrible man that looked like a crow and they grabbed me and put a rag over my mouth—"

"Put on your coat, honey." The floor was trembling. Could a disembodied brain shriek with terror? Could you tell? It was an effort to lift my hands. My eyelids were not unlike cast-iron shutters ready to drop. I cinched her hood and pushed her toward the stairs.

"—Chloroform, I think. I woke up in a room with no windows, but I don't know where I am. Where am I, George?"

"Safe now," I said. We were on the stairs, climbing. I led the way at first, holding onto the handrail and dragging my dead weight forward one step at a time. I had a nightmare like that once—the kind where you run and run, but your legs won't move and the monster is right there, right behind you—

Ms. Smyth snapped free of her unhinged state with remarkable alacrity. Prompted, no doubt, by her affection for this George fellow. She took my arm and pulled me along as best she could. We stumbled, fell against one another, rose and pressed onward. The noises grew louder below and behind. I tried not to think about them. Better to ponder climbing these interminable stairs, to contemplate the mystical act of swinging one leg after the other, again, again, again—

We got away.

It was cold; October in Northern Alaska can't be described as anything else. Stars drilled bright holes in the sky. Dawn was a fingernail streak against the rim of the eastern horizon. To the west, downsloping drumlin hills merged with a bank of crystalline fog and the rough hide of the Bering Sea. The ground was patched with diamond-edged snow, tufts of grass and rocks. I saw tracks; it seemed the friendly surgeons had escaped when they heard trouble. I wasn't worried—the tracks led off and suggested rapid steps.

I felt better in the open air; an illusion perhaps. It gave me the strength to steer her through a cluster of crumbling Quonset huts and jagged sections of tangled wire. Wind whistled through the spokes of the signal tower, sucked the breath from our mouths. We were out, yes. However, the radar site was too close for comfort and the sun was on its way and time was of the essence.

It wasn't far. I took her around the swell of a hill to the shelter of a jumble of shale and larger stones; a place where we could watch the sunrise. I sat her down in the lee of the rocks and moved to regard the heavens in their dispassionate glory. I tracked the constellations, as the Ancient Apothecary must have done. There, there and there. Oh, indeed the angles were unmistakable, yet the Ancient Apothecary had drawn the wrong conclusion from their spectral dance. I could no longer feel any part of my body, but I thrilled with pleasure to witness feral Aldebaran shimmer in the lower firmament.

How could the Ancient Apothecary have been so careless? So deluded? Any fool could tell that it was not the Hour of the Cyclops. Rather it was the time of my master, He Who Is Not to Be Named, to flow down from the crevices between the stars in icy space and lay claim to this wretched ball of dirt.

"Who are you?" Ms. Smyth asked.

Slowly, I turned, extending my deathly smile in comfort and reassurance. "G-George… George." Speech was all but impossible now.

Ms. Smyth was neither comforted nor reassured. Her eyes were very bright. Madness or hysteria or both. "I don't think so." She cast about, a wild animal scenting for unseen preda-tors. It is possible she recognized the bare bones of my humble altar to the Slitherer of the Stars, animal intuition piqued by invisible lines of power throbbing from the misshapen rocks with a scaly caress promising the cruel delights to soon visit every shivering sack of nerves and blood on the planet.

Maybe it was a lucky guess.

The Ancient Apothecary's god might have been satisfied with a single virgin offering. Not so, my master! For Him, nothing short of a double sacrifice was acceptable. I thought of the hammer thrower's brain—his virgin brain— nestled in its briny tank and my fellows in their gallant costumes, ritual knives at hand, awaiting the exact instant when the stars would fall right….

I pulled a curved and scalloped knife from the folds of my parka, held it pressed against my side as I staggered toward the cowering Ms. Smyth. "It's all right…dear. Let me…warm you…"

I don't know how many times Ms. Smyth shot me. Spurts of flame jumped from her coat pocket and into my chest. I think I heard the cracking report…or that might have been the ice floes rubbing together. Might have been my teeth clacking. I really couldn't say how she got her hands on the revolver. When we fumbled on the stairs? A lightweight model made of aluminum; so light I hadn't noticed its absence in the confusion…

No matter. She sobbed and cursed and threw the gun aside. There was no hesitation in her, she didn't waste a moment questioning this violence against the beloved, albeit grotesque, form twisting at her feet.

She ran away down the hill and out of sight; head down, knees pumping high against her chest like a track star I had to admit the girl was fast. Nothing I could do about it. Yellow Ichor No. Five was a miracle. Sadly, most of it was leaking into the snow. My arms were dead, my legs twitched and stilled. If a brain could scream, mine was surely doing that. Nobody was listening.

The sun bubbled up over the rim of the world. I couldn't even close my eyes to make it stop.

ALSO AVAILABLE

The Croning

By Laird Barron

Strange things exist on the periphery of our existence, haunting us from the darkness looming beyond our firelight. Black magic, weird cults and worse things loom in the shadows. The Children of Old Leech have been with us from time immemorial. And they love us . . .

Donald Miller, geologist and academic, has walked along the edge of a chasm for most of his nearly eighty years, leading a charmed life between endearing absent-mindedness and sanity-shattering realization. Now, all things must converge. Donald will discover the dark secrets along the edges, unearthing savage truths about his wife Michelle, their adult twins, and all he knows and trusts. For Donald is about to stumble on the secret... ...OF THE CRONING.

"Bottom line: *The Croning* is one of the very best horror novels that I've read in decades—and Laird Barron is the next coming of H.P. Lovecraft. Mark my words."
—Paul Goat Allen, BarnesandNoble.com

US $14.99 paperback ISBN: 978-1-59780-231-4

Occultation and Other Stories

By Laird Barron

Laird Barron has emerged as one of the strongest voices in modern horror and dark fantasy fiction, building on the eldritch tradition pioneered by writers such as H. P. Lovecraft, Peter Straub, and Thomas Ligotti. His stories have garnered critical acclaim and have been reprinted in numerous year's best anthologies and nominated for multiple awards, including the Crawford, International Horror Guild, Shirley Jackson, Theodore Sturgeon, and World Fantasy awards. His debut collection, *The Imago Sequence and Other Stories*, was the inaugural winner of the Shirley Jackson Award.

He returns with his second collection, *Occultation*. Pitting ordinary men and women against a carnivorous, chaotic cosmos, *Occulation*'s nine tales of terror (two published here for the first time) were nominated for just as many Shirley Jackson awards, winning for the novella "Mysterium Tremendum" and the collection as a whole. Featuring an introduction by Michael Shea, *Occultation* brings more of the spine-chillingly sublime cosmic horror Laird Barron's fans have come to expect.

"Heartbreaking, hilarious, sophisticated, and gory, these stories will thrill, trouble, and haunt Barron's fans and have newcomers scrambling to search for his other work." —*Publishers Weekly*, starred review

US $15.99 paperback ISBN: 978-1-59780-514-8

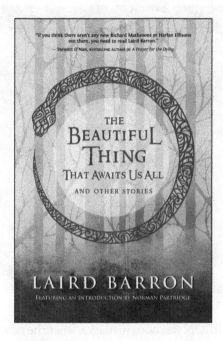

The Beautiful Thing That Awaits Us All
Stories
By Laird Barron

Over the course of two award-winning collections and a critically acclaimed novel, The Croning, Laird Barron has arisen as one of the strongest and most original literary voices in modern horror and the dark fantastic. Melding supernatural horror with hard-boiled noir, espionage, and a scientific backbone, Barron's stories have garnered critical acclaim and have been reprinted in numerous year's best anthologies. His work has been nominated for multiple awards, including the Crawford, International Horror Guild, Shirley Jackson, Theodore Sturgeon, and World Fantasy awards.

Barron returns with his third collection, *The Beautiful Thing That Awaits Us All*. Collecting interlinking tales of sublime cosmic horror, including "Blackwood's Baby," "The Carrion Gods in Their Heaven," and the World Fantasy Award–nominated "Hand of Glory," *The Beautiful Thing That Awaits Us All* delivers enough spine-chilling horror to satisfy even the most jaded reader.

"Relentlessly readable, highly atmospheric, sharply and often arrestingly written—Barron's prose style resembles, by turns, a high-flown Jim Thompson mixed with a pulp Barry Hannah." —*Slate*

US $15.99 paperback ISBN: 978-1-59780-553-7

LAIRD BARRON was born in Alaska, where he raised and trained huskies for many years. He moved to the Pacific Northwest in the mid '90s and began to concentrate on writing poetry and fiction.

His award-nominated work has appeared in *Sci Fiction* and *The Magazine of Fantasy & Science Fiction*, and has been reprinted in *The Year's Best Fantasy and Horror*, *Year's Best Fantasy 6*, and *Best New Fantasy: 2005*.

Mr. Barron currently resides in Olympia, Washington, and is hard at work on many projects, including a novel.

Find Laird Barron online at
www.lairdbarron.com